T O T A L
CHAOS

T O T A L
CHAOS

❖ 🐺

A Novel of the Breedline Series

With Breedline Love,

Shana Congrove

SHANA CONGROVE

Library of Congress Control Number: 2016916244
ISBN: Hardcover   978-1-5245-4734-9
                   Softcover   978-1-5245-4733-2
                   eBook   978-1-5245-4732-5

Print information available on the last page.

Rev. date: 11/14/2016

To order additional copies of this book, contact:
Xlibris
1-888-795-4274
www.Xlibris.com
Orders@Xlibris.com
739611

To Pat. Your compassionate heart and vibrant soul will be missed.

Praise for the novels of the Breedline

If you're looking for a good read, don't pass up Sweet Chaos, of the Breedline Series. You won't be disappointed with this sexy page turner. Who needs Christian Grey when you can have Jem and Jace. The author takes you on a journey through life, love, revenge and fantasy. Shana is an extremely talented writer who keeps you on the edge of your seat through every turn of the page.

—Angela Moore

AWESOME from start to finish! As a fan following Shana Congrove's story, Total Chaos/A novel of the Breedline series in FanStory, I was drawn into the story and literally could not stop reading until the last chapter. It is enticing, enchanting and full of excitement with each turn of the page. I recommend this book to all readers even if this is not your genre.

—CDEaves

I have been reading Shana's book(s) for some time now, her previous book in the breedline series, and this current book. "Total Chaos". This talented writer has captured both my interest and my amazement at her unique and expansive talent. She is a most exciting and imaginative writer.

This book about the struggle between light and dark forces, is both new in concept and combines old fables and legends into a modern cohesive setting. The book is thoroughly absorbing and action packed with fascinating characters, both dark and dangerous antagonists and bright and upright protagonists. I can fully recommend these books both for young adult readers and up to my age (74).

—Roy Owen, 2015 Fanstory poet of the year

Novels in the Breedline Series by Shana Congrove

Sweet Chaos

Total Chaos

Coming soon: Unleashed Chaos

Available wherever books are sold or at Xlibris.com

Author's Acknowledgments

WITH IMMENSE GRATITUDE TO:

God's loving grace. Thank you for giving me the "precious gifts" to motivate and encourage me with everything I do.

All the readers! Thank you for stepping into my fantasy world of the Breedline. I appreciate all your support and feedback!

Thank you so very much: All my family, friends and coworkers. Your constant encouragement and positive words kept me going! ☺

To my son, Nathan: Thanks for all your support and for letting me use you as a character. I'm so proud of everything you do. Love you! ☺

None of this would be possible without my beloved Carl (**a.k.a. Drakon Hexus**)—you're my soulmate, best friend, and adviser. I've never felt truly loved until I met you. I love you, honey! ☺

Special thanks and shout-out to my talented friends on Fanstory: R. Williams, Alexis Leech, Roy Owen, JLC Emerald River, and to everyone else that has dedicated their time... thank you for your patience and expert advice. You're greatly appreciated! ☺

Always... with love to my little companions, Sissy and Baby—every day you're there to greet me at the door with lots of doggy kisses and unconditional love. XOXO, Mommy ☺

❧ Glossary

BREEDLINE - A species of humans that have the ability to change from human form into wolf. They are not like the old legend of the Lycanthropy myth. Breedline species can shift into their wolf at will. The moon has no power over them. They do not pass their ability to other humans with a bite or scratch like the Lycanthropy myth. The Breedline gene is passed down to offspring that are born identical twins. Most Breedlines can live among the human race, but their species must be kept a secret. In wolf form, they have super strength, speed, and heightened senses. Their lifespan is the same as a normal human, but they are immune to illness and disease. Only a silver bullet to the brain will kill them. All males change into their wolf at the age of eighteen. Females do not go through the change until they are mated by their true Breedline mate.

BREEDLINE TWINS - Identical twins that are born from either one or both parents of the Breedline species. They have a strong unbreakable bond from birth, are born with telepathic abilities, and have the power to sense the other's emotions or injuries. In some cases, the bond between twins is so strong that if one dies, the other twin may pass on, especially if they don't have a mate.

BREEDLINE BONDING - The male Breedline spends his life in search of his true mate. When the male comes in contact with her, he instantly feels a simultaneous, desirable attraction and she becomes the most important thing in his life. He is there to love, protect, and cherish her until death. Once they are mated, they are bonded for life. It is possible for them to have more than one mate in their lifespan.

BELOVED - A word used by a Breedline to express the bond to their mate.

DOUBLE BONDED – In some cases, male Breedline twins bond with the same female, but one will carry a stronger bond. Usually one of them must sacrifice for the other twin.

BREEDLINE COVENANT - The Breedline species must live within the boundaries of a Covenant, which is only formed with their species. The Covenant is governed and ruled by a head council. The council keeps their laws in order and oversees the species population.

THE BREEDLINE QUEEN - Over centuries, the Breedline Covenant is ruled by a true queen. If there is no queen living, the Covenants are ruled by an appointed head council until another queen is born. A Breedline queen is born once every one hundred years. Once a female Breedline is mated and turned into her wolf, the queen status is quickly known by her massive stature, black fur, and red eyes. Her alpha wolf has twice the strength, speed, and size of any Breedline. The queen is expected to rule over all the Breedline Covenants where she will be respected and obeyed by all Breedline. This is their absolute true law.

THE QUEEN'S RING - This ring has been passed down to all Breedline queens for generations. When the new queen places the ring on, it instantly shifts in size to fit her finger.

TRUE LAW - All Breedline Covenants have an ancient book of laws that must be obeyed. If any of these laws are disobeyed by either sex, they can be shunned or no longer protected by their Covenant. If a Breedline takes another life out of revenge, or evil—other than protecting their life, and the life of another—they will never have the ability to shift back to human, and are then cast out as a rogue wolf.

ROGUE WOLF – A Breedline species that has been shunned by their Covenant for taking another life out of revenge or evil and forced to live as a wolf until death without the ability to change human again. Some rogue wolves form into packs, which can be dangerous for other Breedline species.

RED (BLOOD) MOON - When the full moon passes through the amber shadow of earth, producing a midnight eclipse visible across North America. So begins a lunar eclipse tetrad—a series of four consecutive total eclipses occurring at approximately six-month intervals. This incredible light beams into the heart of earth's shadow, filling it with a coppery glow and transforming the moon into a great red orb. During this time, all Breedline species that are mated have a strong desire to create offspring. This is also a time when Breedline females are more fertile for the conception of twins.

CHIANG-SHIH DEMON (Kiang shi, a.k.a. Ramael Arminius) - An ancient demon that inhabits the body of a Breedline fetus before it's born, or during a Breedline's death. It continues to take the soul over the natural lifespan of the child, or the deceased Breedline. When the demon possesses a fetus, it breaks the bonding and telepathic abilities of their twin when they are born. If the demon possesses a deceased Breedline's body, it must do so before the soul passes on. If the soul is not intact, the body will soon die.In most cases, the Chiang-shih demon will take the life of the other twin, even before their birth. The twin that is born with the demon will bring only evil to whomever they encounter. Their sole purpose is to gain full control of another soul, and seek world domination.Only two ways the demon can be cast out of the soul it possesses: by its firstborn son, and the Angel of Mercy, Zadkiel. The Beast is the only one who can kill a Chiang-shih demon.

THE BEAST – The second-born son of the Chiang-shih demon. When he is provoked into a rage, he will shift into his Beast instead of his Breedline wolf. The Beast is an enormous, dangerous two-footed creature that has wolf-like features. One bite has enough venom to kill the Chiang-shih demon, and leave the soul of the person the demon possessed unharmed.

SHADOW WALKER (a.k.a. Shadow Figure, or Black Mass) - The perception of a patch of shadow as a living, humanoid figure, particularly interpreted by the Breedline as the presence of a malevolent entity. When a Breedline species dies and does not pass on to the other side, they are left to roam the earth as a shadow of themselves—a ghost. They will not pass on until they have settled unfinished business before their death.

ZADKIEL (Tzadqiel, a.k.a. "Righteousness of God") - The archangel of freedom, benevolence, and mercy, and the patron angel of all who forgive. Breedline species tradition considers him to be the Angel of Mercy.

SUCCUBUS (a.k.a. CREEPERS) - Creatures that search for, and feed off, the blood of the Breedline species. Creepers are skilled at extreme sexual pleasure, and the ecstasy they create is exceedingly intense and highly addictive. They cast off a scent that hypnotizes Breedlines into overwhelming sexual urges. They use their human-like bodies and beautiful features to control and influence their thoughts.They have the ability to reach into the Breedline's mind during sleep, casting a spell of dreams about sexual contact or intercourse. And one much less obvious manifestation of Creepers is nightmares—realistic, graphic, terrifying nightmares that rob the Breedline of sleep. Over a long period, it can lead to severe fatigue and depression, leaving them emotionally and spiritually drained. Death can occur if they completely take over the Breedline's body.

HALF-BREED - This species is born with the genes from both Breedline and succubus. They can bond with either a full-blood Breedline or another half-breed. They do not have the ability to change into the Breedline wolf, but they do need blood from them to survive. With the power to hypnotize, most Breedlines have minimal respect and credence toward the half-breed species.

WICCA (or Wise One) – According to the Breedline species, a Wicca is the goddess of magic, witchcraft, the night, moon, ghosts, and necromancy. A Wicca is also considered to be a demonic spirit. It is unclear to the Breedline if they act under the orders of the devil, or they are simply not understood and treated as outcasts. They have the ability to do white magic (good) or dark (evil).

KATAKO (a.k.a. Lucas, or Dark Shadow) – The Chiang-shih demon's offspring that is born both Breedline and Wiccan. After one year, the Katako develops into an adult with mind of a child, without reaching full maturity. It has the power to appear translucent, or become completely invisible. Being born half Breedline, it can shift into a wolf and transform, or mimic another creature with the power to instantly travel from one place to another. Their true purpose of creation is to bring forth the souls stuck in purgatory by using one drop of its blood. The Breedline Queen's bite is the only way to destroy it.

GOLEMS (a.k.a. The Death Army) – Creatures that are created by dark Wiccans with the power of necromancy. By releasing the souls of demons stuck in purgatory, the Wicca can give them the ability to shape into a creature that is made from earth. These creatures have various qualities, such as mass strength, enormous stature, and the power to consume their victims by saturating them with mud.

GUARDIANS (a.k.a. Spirits of the Forest) - They originated during the Middle Ages with the purpose of protecting all creatures, especially the Breedline, from the destruction of any creation made by a dark Wicca. They have the ability to stay invisible with the power to move through any barrier and over any distance instantly.

🐾 The story so far...

Four-year-old identical twins, Jace and Jem—born of the Breedline species, a race of humans that have special powers and the gift to change into wolf form—were tragically present when their mother, Katlyn Gray, was murdered, and their uncle Jackson brutally beaten and left in a coma. Without any other relatives, the twins are placed with a loving family. Three months later, their uncle survives his injuries and reunites with his nephews. Approving of their foster family, he lets the couple adopt them only if they promise to let him stay close by the boys and build a relationship as they grow up. As the only link to their secret world, Jackson introduces them into the Breedline Covenant and what they will become as they reach the age of eighteen. The shocking new life they discover has other unknown species and mystical creatures, which must be kept hidden from humans and their new family.

Growing up, Jace's life continues to spin out of control when the identity of his mother's murderer is uncovered. Seeking revenge against his real father, Alexander Crest—who is possessed by a Chiang-shih demon—Jace unexpectedly meets Tessa Fairchild, his Breedline bonded mate. Fighting her own demons, Tessa has been haunted by mysterious dreams about a black wolf since childhood. As Jace tries to win her over and earn her trust, he finds out Tessa has no knowledge of being born an identical twin, or a Breedline.

Plotting world domination, Alexander uses his demon blood to force rogue wolves into joining his army. With the help of his illegitimate son, Sebastian Crow, and his loyal council members—formed by Breedline traitors—Alexander searches for his chosen son to unlock the key to unlimited power, and the destruction of humans and half-breeds.

As Jace wins Tessa's affections, she discovers his secret and she was born of the same species. During the first change into her Breedline wolf, she becomes the next Breedline queen, bringing great responsibility she was not ready for. But when she decides to take on the duty, she's unprepared for Jace's curse. Being born with the gene of his father's demon, he must learn to control his rage as the Beast within him is unleashed.

The battle between the Chiang-shih demon and the Breedline finally comes to an end when Zadkiel, the Angel of Mercy, casts the demon out of Alexander. After years of roaming the earth as a shadow walker, Katlyn Gray—Jace and Jem's biological mother—soul is finally freed to cross to the other side.

When Zadkiel healed Jem from his lethal injury that was inflicted by the demon, his binding spell was lifted, bringing back his lost memories. Alexander was forgiven by the Breedline and not blamed for the demon's sinister crimes. All the rogue wolf army that was created by the demon were also pardoned for their past crimes and offered a safe haven, or the choice to rejoin with their families.

Before Jem takes them all back through the portal to the California Covenant, he proposes to his bonded mate, Mia Blackwood. As Drakon Hexus and Tim Ross stay behind with the grim task of burying Sebastian's body that is still upstairs after Jace took him out with a silver bullet, they soon discover their plans have changed.

🐾 *Chapter One*

The Chiang-shih demon was cast out of Alexander's body, and reborn in Sebastian's cold corpse as Eve—Sebastian's bonded mate—is desperate to bring him back to life with her blood.

With evil corruption, the demon returned to the world as he had come into it many years before: possessing another soul, only this time his body was that of a full-grown man, not an infant.

When the demon took over Sebastian's body, a quick moment of conscious awareness passed fast. His body was in agony, his veins filled with acid, and every inch of him felt as if he was burning from the inside out. Gasping in pain, he curled into a fetal position and threw up Eve's blood.

In the midst of blurred vision and the uncontrollable crippling heaves, Eve reached out to him. As her hand smoothed up and down his arm, the rhythm of her soothing touch calmed his head and eased his stomach. Managing to roll onto his back, the demon tried to regain his vision while staring out of Sebastian's eyes.

When his vision finally cleared, a female came into focus. Her face was delicate and pale. Looking at her closely, he noticed her beautiful, long black hair flowed past her breasts.

"Your eyes—" She winced, looking into his cold stare. "Why are your eyes black?"

Avoiding her question, he began to choke again. Unaware of the demon inside her beloved's body, she reached out and gently touched his face. He calmed with her gentle caress.

"It's going to be okay," she murmured. "All that matters is... you're alive."

With visions roaring through his head, his memory flashed back. He saw images of Jem throwing a dagger, and the Angel Zadkiel casting his soul out of Alexander's body. He could even feel himself rising from

Alexander, and floating into the night sky. And now he was in control of another body, trapped inside his own son.

The demon shook his head slowly. "No... no..."

As he grappled with the implications of his new body, a deep hunger swirled in his belly. On impulse, fangs protruded into his mouth and a low hiss escaped through his thirsty lips.

Smiling, Eve looked into his eyes. When their connection was made, scenes were shown to him, like pages flipping inside a picture book. The story that unfolded made him both cringe and aroused. Since she was Sebastian's bonded mate—and they were both half-breeds—the mere thought of needing her blood to survive disgusted him.

The demon extended his hand, beckoning Eve closer. Inhaling her fragrance, he caught the sweet scent of her blood. Curling back his lips, he exposed his fangs.

As she offered her wrist, Eve's crimson eyes flashed wide. "Please, Sebastian, take my vein."

Without permission, he reached up and grabbed the back of her head. Pulling her close, he bit hard. Sucking deep, he tasted the sweetness of her blood as it rushed down his throat.

It was like the finest wine, quenching his thirst and giving him strength. As he nursed her vein, she purred, softly at first, then louder, until it turned into a moan.

When he got his fill, he breathed in deep. God, she smelled good... and for some reason her scent seemed familiar to him. With flashbacks of Sebastian's memories, he recognized the fragrance of jasmine.

Instantly, his body became aroused when her hair fell over her shoulder, brushing the side of his neck. Tilting his hips, he felt the agony of his arousal. In a flash, another one of Sebastian's memories jolted in his head. It was Eve at his throat, and under his body.

Placing her hand on his shoulder, she appeared concerned. "Sebastian, are you okay?"

Hearing her voice created an unfamiliar emotion deep inside his chest. Using his fingertips, he gently brushed over her cheek. Confused, he clenched his brows. "I... remember you."

Smoothing her hand over his, she whispered, "I love you, Sebastian."

In the blink of an eye, he snapped back to reality. Narrowing his eyes in anger, he gripped her hips with both hands, pulling her close. "You belong to me," he growled.

* * * *

Meanwhile...

Drakon and Tim explained to all the rogue wolves they were welcome to stay in the castle for a safe haven, or free to leave to return to their family. But if they chose to stay, they would be responsible to help repair the damage to the roof after Zadkiel, the Angel of Mercy, blasted through the ceiling, making his grand entrance.

Now all Tim had left to do was help Drakon bury Sebastian's body. Digging a hole and tossing him in it wasn't a pleasant thought, but he was relieved to finally say good riddance to the bastard. Just as he was about to follow Drakon up the staircase to retrieve Sebastian's corpse, his phone went off. Reaching in his back pocket, he pulled it out.

"Hello—"

"Tim?" Cassie's voice on the other end sounded anxious. "I'm calling about Angel and the baby."

Tim abruptly stopped on the staircase, not caring about his task ahead. "Is everything all right?"

After Cassie confirmed Angel and the baby was doing fine, he handed the phone to Drakon. Cassie had called because she wanted to let him know everyone returned back to the Covenant safe, and touch base with Tim's bonded mate and their newborn baby girl. She also wanted to check on her beloved, Drakon.

God, Tim thought, his beloved Angel was now the mother of his child. The two of them had always had a deep bond, and shared a dominant and submissive relationship. But now that they had a daughter to care for, he wasn't sure if that part of their relationship would stay the same. Man, this parenting stuff was stressful, he thought, releasing a long sigh.

After Drakon ended the call, he handed the phone to Tim, refocusing his mind back to the present.

Leaning against the stair railing, Drakon smiled. "She was just worried."

Placing his hand on Drakon's shoulder, Tim glanced toward the top of the stairs. "Come on," he said, releasing a deep breath. "Let's get this over with."

* * * *

As Eve focused on the words Sebastian had said, she smiled with satisfaction. "And you belong to me as well."

With his eyes flared wide, he grabbed her arm with a tight grip. "I belong to no one." He flushed red, and anger bristled visibly from him.

She tried to pull free and made a show of getting huffy. "You're hurting me!"

He paused when he heard noises coming from outside the door. He loosened his grip, and gave her a look that told her without words to shut up. "Someone's coming," he said in a low voice. "We're getting out of here."

Jerking free of his hold, she shot to her feet and placed her hands over her hips. "I'm not going anywhere with you until you apologize."

With his sight on whiteout and his muscles energized by mania, he was all action as he rose onto shaky feet, trying to balance his new body. "Fine," he snapped back. "Stay here if that's what you want. I'm sure the Breedline would love to find you here."

Eve shifted her eyes toward the door as cold fear replaced the heated fury that boiled in her veins. With a quick attitude adjustment, she agreed without haste. "Okay." She reached for his hand. "I'll go with you."

Using his free hand, he reached forward as a surge of electricity shot out of his palm. It flickered and danced like waves rippling through water. After waiting for it to open wide enough, he stepped through the light with Eve at his side. Vanishing through the portal, they left no trace behind except the bloodstain on the floor.

* * * *

Swallowing hard, Tim followed Drakon up the stairs. As they reached the top, Drakon pulled out his pistol and positioned his back against the wall. "I'm not taking any chances."

Standing on the opposite side of the door, Tim silently counted to three. In one swift movement, he cranked the knob and swung it open. Rushing inside with their weapons pointed, they scanned over the room.

Finding it empty, Tim cursed in frustration. Starring beyond the open door, he noticed the room was decorated with feminine taste. There were hanging light fixtures that resembled diamond earrings and silk floral drapes over the windows. When he looked at the white marble floor, he noticed a pool of fresh blood.

Tim linked his hands in front of himself. As he stood in silence, the whole thing struck him as surreal. He could not possibly fathom how Sebastian could have survived a silver bullet to the head. In a fit of rage, he pounded his fist through the wall.

Drakon cleared his throat once and then twice. "It was Eve," he muttered. "I don't know how she did it, but somehow she managed to bring that smug prick back to life."

Tim ground his teeth together. He shouldn't have been surprised over what Drakon just said, but shit, hearing the words was kind of shocking. He would have never guessed Eve had the power to bring Sebastian back from the dead.

"Well?" Drakon shrugged his shoulders, waiting for Tim's next move. "What do we do now?"

Rubbing his throbbing knuckles, Tim took a minute to gather his thoughts. "We go after him."

🐾 Chapter Two

Placing his gun back into his holster, Tim looked down the staircase. Closing his eyes, he sent his instincts outward, and after a moment, he realized their next step was notifying the council members to arrange a meeting. Lifting his lids, he quickly moved down the steps with Drakon close behind.

As they reached the bottom of the staircase, Tim reached for his phone. "I've got to call Tessa," he said, his voice strained with exhaustion. Ordinarily, his first move would have been to handle this on his own. But since Tessa was their queen, he had to let her know Sebastian was missing. After what Sebastian had done to her, he regretted revealing the dreadful news.

"She'll need to notify the council members," he tacked on. "And send Jem through the portal as soon as possible. We'll need his help getting back to the Covenant."

Drakon honed in on his mood with pinpoint accuracy, and nodded without saying a word.

When Tessa answered, he told her the grave news. She was silent for a long time, as if grappling with her thoughts. Then she told him she would send Jem their way, and contact the council.

When Tim ended the call, he made a sound of exasperation. "Let's go through the rest of the place."

After checking every inch of the castle, they came up with absolutely nothing. All the bedrooms were in order with their toile drapes, antiques, and luxurious duvets. They searched the second floor, and all was clear. On the lower level, it held all the housing for the rogue wolves, a training center, as well as fighting gear and computer equipment. When they asked the demon's former rogue army if they'd seen Sebastian or Eve, they were completely lost with words, their expressions of utter shock.

Malachi O'Conner—Alexander's former rogue—instantly stepped forward, appearing perplexed. "Why are you asking if we've seen Sebastian? I thought he was dead."

"His body is missing," Drakon reluctantly answered. "We think Eve somehow brought him back to life with her blood. We're not exactly sure what happened. Just make sure you let us know if you see anything out of the ordinary."

Alarm prickled up Malachi's spine. He blinked and stared up at Drakon, not at all sure what to say. Finally, he managed to speak out loud and said, "I don't feel safe staying here."

Drakon nodded. "I understand. If anyone else wants to leave, it's your choice. But I don't think you're in danger. If Sebastian is alive, he won't risk coming back here."

Without a place to go, most of them decided to stay. Only a handful of the others immediately began to pack their things, especially Malachi and his two younger brothers Seth and Kaleb.

"Thank you for all your help." Malachi extended his hand toward Drakon. "My brothers and I have decided to leave."

"You're welcome, Malachi." Drakon shook his hand. "If you change your mind, you're welcome to stay. Just let us know where you want to go, and we'll make sure you get there."

* * * *

Later, Drakon ran a check on the security system's master board out by the training facility. When he finished, he went back to report to Tim. "I hacked into the alarms. Nothing was triggered or bypassed either through a code or a security card," he explained. "Sebastian must have escaped through a portal."

Drakon was a computer geek, and while others would look at him and immediately think he was just a hulking Neanderthal, he was an intelligent man.

Suddenly a voice echoed through the foyer. "Where are you?"

"In here!" Tim called out.

When Jem and Jace stormed into the room, the shock in Jace's voice was evident. "Shit, how the hell did Sebastian survive a silver bullet?"

"Christ..." Jem sighed, curling his fingers into tight fists, tension bristling in tangible waves.

"Our guess is Eve," Tim suggested.

"How could she have the power to bring him back from silver?" Jem asked, glancing at Tim as he talked. "Her blood alone cannot heal him from that. I know he was born with the demon's blood, but the ability to travel through the portal was all the power he had."

Tim nodded. "That's a good question."

Jace fidgeted with impatience, shifting his weight back and forth. "Do you know how Sebastian got out of here?"

"He must have used the portal," Tim said in a serious tone. "It's not like he walked down here past us and went through the front door."

"You don't think Alexander's demon—," Jace paused, letting out a strangled breath, tension and anxiety swamping him.

Jem's eyes widened and he took a hasty step back as if Jace had thoroughly stunned him. He damn near swallowed his tongue as he stumbled with his words. "A-are you suggesting the demon went into Sebastian's body?"

"That's not possible," Drakon interrupted before Jace could reply.

With a confused expression, Jem muttered, "I thought after Zadkiel cast him out of Alexander, he banished him back to hell."

Tim's gut tightened. He didn't want to think of worst-case scenarios. "Let's not get carried away," he said, snapping everyone's attention back to him. "There must be a good explanation for all this."

Everyone nodded in agreement, their expressions grim.

In utter disbelief, the four of them walked back into the foyer. As Tim glanced around the place, his brain churned, desperately searching for answers. "All right, let's head back to the Covenant."

* * * *

Stumbling through the portal, Sebastian tried to gain his balance holding onto Eve's arm. Conjuring the portal and traveling to her apartment sucked all the energy he had left. When his knees gave out, he tripped over his own feet and fell to the floor.

Eve reached out to him, and grasped his hand. "Are you hurt?"

On limp and shaky feet, he forced his body to stand. "I'll be fine." He jerked his hand away, and stood on his own.

"You need to rest," she insisted, reaching out to him again.

Quickly, he shoved her out of the way. Bending over, he gasped in pain. As the dry heaves hit him, black liquid poured out of his mouth. When it was over, he wiped his lips and glanced at his hand. It was his blood... his demon blood.

Eve stepped back. "Ew... what the hell is that?"

"It's nothing." He coughed. "I'm still healing from the silver bullet." He lied, trying to shut her up.

"Come, darling," she muttered in a soothing tone, putting a hand on his shoulder. "You need to rest."

When he nodded, she added, "You can use my shower to wash up. I still have some of your clothes here."

Before he knew it, he was under Eve's shower, washing the remnants of his dead son's blood from his long, black hair. Looking down, he watched as the red funnel ran down the drain at his feet. After he washed off, he stepped out and reached for a towel. Standing outside the shower, he saw his reflection in the mirror and stared at his new body. He had a tall, lean muscular stature now. Not Alexander's huge, warrior physique he had before.

Sebastian's body resembled elegance with a regal appearance. Yes, he was in a younger body, he thought, staring at himself. But he was also weaker.

When he came out of the bathroom with a towel wrapped around his waist, Eve was waiting for him. Her bright crimson eyes widened when she saw him.

"Come with me." She offered her hand. "I'll help you to bed."

Staring at her through Sebastian's eyes, thoughts flashed into his head. He'd intended to leave her behind and travel to his old condo after he'd healed. The problem was, he had to keep her around. His new body required her blood to survive, leaving him no choice but to keep her close. After his body healed, he would find a safer location far away from the Breedline.

As she helped him to the bedroom, he moved like an old man.

Letting the towel drop to the floor, he sat down on the edge of the bed. "After I rest, we're getting the hell out of here," he said hoarsely, easing back on the mattress.

With gentle hands, she placed a blanket over him. "Where do you want to go?"

"Back to my—," he hesitated before he almost slipped up, and revealed his secret. "My father's condo," he confirmed, trying to convince her. "I need to pick up some things before we find another place to stay."

She smiled. "I'll start packing my things while you rest."

Whatever, he thought. At this point, he didn't care what she did. With his eyes barely open, he felt like an invalid. "Wake me up in a few hours," he said in a weak voice.

Before she left, she turned off the light. A few minutes later, he shut his eyes and drifted off into a deep sleep.

🐾 *Chapter Three*

One after the other, they came back to the Breedline Covenant through the portal. When it vanished, they saw Tessa, Mia, and Cassie, anxiously waiting for their arrival.

"Thank God," Tessa said relieved. "We were so worried about you."

Hearing her voice, Jace snapped his head in her direction. His expression was of total admiration as he grinned ear to ear.

Jace moved closer with his hand extended and—

Suddenly, a white light took the place of his vision, wiping out everything he saw. It felt like he was caught in an electric flash. As he desperately tried to focus, his body started to spin like a fast carousel, spinning round and round.

Swaying side to side, he heard voices coming at him from a distance. As he gasped for air, his heart pounded in his chest. Feeling like his head was about to split in half, he dropped to his knees.

He felt his mouth stretch wide, working as if he were trying to scream, but then spasms overtook him, jerking through his entire body, knocking him backward and sending him flat on his back.

* * * *

Even though Eve made no sound, the demon knew she was in the room. When she sauntered over toward him, she turned on the lamp beside the bed. Inhaling through his nostrils, he caught the scent of her arousal.

As she lowered her hand to feel his skin, he quickly grabbed it.

"What are you doing?" he said gruffly.

She gasped at his quick response, and smiled at him. As his eyes roamed over her naked body, he saw a citrine stone necklace at her throat glowing against her paper white skin. Her long black hair was pushed over her shoulders, revealing her small, tight breasts. Her lips matched the color of her hypnotic, crimson eyes.

A soft moan escaped her lips when he released her cold hand. Cautiously, she pulled back the blanket and marveled at his bare skin. There was so much she wanted to see of him that her eyes didn't know where to begin. Tracing down his thighs, they lingered lower.

"Can I touch you?" Her question ended with a soft purr.

The demon felt Sebastian's body come alive with a needy sensation. He steeled himself when her hand slowly closed around his arousal. With only a moment of contact, he pulled back sharp as he slipped out of her grip.

"I've missed you terribly," she purred. "Don't you want me, darling?"

Hearing her question registered hatred in his eyes. "No," he said bluntly.

This time she grabbed him, and dug her nails into his shaft. "You will beg for me," she demanded.

Sucking in a quick, painful breath, he grabbed her arm with a tight grip.

"Let me go!" She cried out, trying to break free of his grasp. "You're hurting me!"

He was tempted to break it, but his sex was on fire at this point, raging with heat, pulsing with the need to take her body, and drink her blood. The thrill of her fighting back made him even more aroused. At the same time, he took pleasure and loathed her all the same. Both struggled to maintain the power position, and needing each other to survive.

Without effort, he tossed her across the bed like she weighed nothing. He used Sebastian's body to fill his need as he forced himself inside of her, knocking her forward until her head banged into the headboard. When her legs shook in a series of waves, he hated giving her the satisfaction she came for.

After Eve's climax came to a hilt, her lips drew back with a hiss, revealing sharp fangs. In the blink of an eye, her head shot forward and pierced his neck. When she sucked in his blood, she gagged when it went down her throat.

"What the hell is wrong with your blood?" She choked. "It tastes awful!" She wiped her mouth in disgust, feeling like she was going to be ill.

Leaning down, the demon dragged his fangs across her shoulder. Lifting his head, he grabbed her throat with one hand. "I will be the only one drinking tonight," he growled.

"But...," she tried to speak against his grip, and gasped for air. When he eased up to let her breathe, she uttered, "But what about me?"

He put his brain on lockdown, and focused on her question. Surviving on her blood, he needed to keep her strong. With his eyes locked on hers, he murmured, "I'll make sure you get what you need."

As she stared into his dark eyes, her body stiffened. "I want only pure blood," she said in a pouty tone. "I want blood from a pure Breedline."

* * * *

With Jem and Tessa by his side, Jace regained consciousness.

His mind scrambled to think. *What just happened?* In a rush Jace tried to sit up, but heavy hands held him down.

"Just stay put, Jace," Tim urged.

When Jace craned his neck around, he saw Alexander looking anxious by the door. The moment he saw him, he opened his mouth to speak as every neuron in his brain started to fire, and the white light came back. When another wave hit, it sent Jace's body into violent spasms.

"Oh God!" Tessa clapped her hand over her mouth and stepped back. "He's doing it again!"

With both hands, Tim held Jace's shoulders down trying to control his erratic movement.

Feeling his own body being sucked under, Jace stretched his hand out, straining toward Alexander.

"What's wrong, Jace?" Tim's voice above him faded in and out. "Can you tell me what's wrong?"

Jace turned away from Alexander, and focused his eyes on Tessa.

Kneeling down next to him, she grasped his hand. The instant their palms touched, Jace blacked out again.

When he came to, he faintly heard Tim say, "Jem, call Dr. Carrington."

It took considerable effort to speak as exhaustion ringed Jace's eyes. "W-what... h-happened?"

With her hand entwined with his, Tessa gently squeezed. "You passed out, honey."

Moments later, Tim helped Jace to his feet, worry etched into every groove of his face.

"Let's get you down to Helen's exam room." Tim held him steady. "She's on her way."

"Is there anything I can do to help?" Alexander asked, his tone expressing concern.

"Thanks." Tim shook his head. "I got this."

Jace gave Alexander a puzzled look before he finally found his voice again. "We may need your help," he said, an edge of steel lacing his tone. "Sebastian's body is missing, and there's no way he could have survived the silver. It could be possible the demon may have possessed him."

Alexander was so overcome with grief and guilt that he could barely maintain his composure. *God,* he thought. *How was he going to help them?* All his memories of the demon had vanished. It was like he had a snapshot case of amnesia.

Alexander nodded in agreement, but his expression stayed grim. "I'll do whatever I can to help."

Jace almost smiled, but nodded instead.

"Come on." Tim tugged at him. "Let's get you down to the exam room."

Jace turned regretfully to Tessa, and included Jem in his gaze. "Wait here," he said quietly. "I'll update you after Helen's done examining me."

Tessa's face bloomed with worry. "Are you sure?"

"I'll be fine, baby." His lips formed a half-smile. "I'll meet you upstairs when I get done."

Before they left the room, Tim turned toward Alexander. "We're having a council meeting tonight. I want you to attend. We'll need to know the names of the council members that helped the demon. You're the only one that can give us that information," Tim explained, waiting for a reply.

"I'll be there."

"Oh, I almost forgot." Tim shifted his eyes in Drakon's direction. "Did you make sure Malachi and his brothers got a flight out of Paris?"

"It's taken care of," Drakon quickly replied.

"Thanks, Drakon," Tim said, and looked at Jace. "Ready?"

Jace nodded, and reluctantly allowed Tim to help him out of the room.

🐾 Chapter Four

It wasn't long after Jace made it to the exam room when Dr. Helen Carrington walked in. Being born Breedline, she was a physician at the Bates Medical Center. On occasion, she made house calls to the Covenant to avoid the prying eyes of humans.

Closing the door behind her, Helen moved next to Jace. "What seems to be the problem?"

"I'm not exactly sure how to explain it," he said in a hoarse voice. "I saw a bright light and felt dizzy. The next thing I remember is blacking out."

Holding onto a notepad, she wrote as he explained. "I see," she muttered, looking at him through a pair of thick framed glasses. "Well, let's start with some routine exams, and then I'll need to take a blood sample."

With an ophthalmoscope in her hand, she held it close to his eye. "Hmm..." She squinted, examining his eye with the instrument.

"What is it?" Jace queried, his eyes widening with worry.

"Well—"

She was stunned for words. His irises held a colorless splendor of sparkles reflecting off the light in her instrument. It shined so bright, reminding her of a full moon on a cloudless night.

"Your eyes seem to have changed," she muttered, amazed by her discovery.

"What do you mean... changed?"

"It's hard to explain," she said puzzled. "There's some kind of lights reflecting in your irises."

"What does that mean?" he asked bluntly.

Standing up straight, she removed the ophthalmoscope. "I've never seen anything like this before. Let's move on to another test."

"What's wrong with me?" Jace blurted, no longer able to contain himself.

"Hang in there, Jace," Tim said calmly, placing his palm on his shoulder. "We'll figure this out."

As soon as she was done checking his temperature, pulse, ears, and blood pressure, and listened to his heart, she took a sample of his blood. "Everything else seems to be normal," she confirmed. "We'll just wait for the blood results to get back after I drop them off at my lab. If you have any other symptoms, or if this happens again, give me a call."

Jace nodded. "Thanks, Doc." He scooted off the exam table. "What about my eyes?"

"Don't worry, Jace. Your vision seems to be normal," she reassured. "I'll be back after I get your blood results to check them again."

She didn't want to alarm him, but she'd seen a report on this before. When she'd found this documentation, the hospital hadn't made the move to computerized records. Everything had been saved in files. This record had clearly been transcribed by data processors and put away marked as confidential. The file reported of a similar case with the same light in a patient's irises. A German physician named Dr. Hans Autenburg reported, after taking several blood tests, his discovery of cellular regeneration.

The study, dated back in the seventies, reported some kind of supernatural rapid regeneration in a human, he called SPECIMEN ONE. The patient had the ability of tissue regeneration. He stated in the medical reports the patient's body levitated at periods of time, and was translucent during what he called "The Repairing Stages." This ability didn't just speed up healing, the patient never got sick, and completely stopped aging at thirty.

The research ended when the patient disappeared a year later, and Dr. Autenburg was found murdered. She couldn't find anything on reports of his assailant being captured. The files were locked up as confidential and never looked at again, until she found them. This was her life mission. To find a patient that carried the same cells, especially a Breedline species. She was searching for a cure for the Breedline natural aging process.

Before Helen left, she turned toward Tim. "By the way, I've got some good news. Angel and the baby will be getting discharged in the morning. You can come by the hospital after eight and pick them up."

"That's wonderful news." Tim's expression lit up. "I was just going to give her a call. Thank you, Helen."

"No problem." She smiled, holding the door open. "Just make sure you bring a car seat for the baby." Shifting her focus on Jace, she said, "I'll call you as soon as I get your results back."

"Thanks," he said, waving as she walked out.

As they stepped out of the exam room, Tim looked at Jace. He appeared worn out, but then anyone would. Going through what he just experienced, and getting poked and prodded at was exhausting. He was even a little wiped himself. "You want something to eat, my man?"

"Nah," Jace replied. "I think I'll go lie down for a while before the council meeting this evening. Plus, I need to spend some time with Tessa. She's been through a lot, and now she's all stressed out since Sebastian's body came up missing."

"Get some rest," Tim said. "I'll see you later."

Leaving the exam room, Tim jogged up the staircase looking very much like a nervous father. As he prepared to call Angel, his thoughts went to what Helen had told him. He needed to have a car seat in order to take Natalie home. *When would he find time to do that?* he thought.

At least there was some good news. Jace's doctor visit had been all good, for the most part. Other than a weird thing going on with his eyes, he was healthy, and the results on his blood tests would be back soon. With luck, they would find out what caused him to go into some kind of seizure. Hopefully it was nothing serious.

When he reached for his bedroom door, he stopped in his tracks when he heard screams coming from downstairs. Wheeling around, he hit the stairs as the piercing cries sent chills down his spine.

❧ Chapter Five

Bolting down the stairs, Tim followed the screams into the recreation room. Pushing through the double doors, he stepped inside as Jace ran past him, almost knocking him down. A bright light spilled into the room, and the scene was instantly carved into his memory: Mia was in hysterics as Jem floated in midair. Levitated, his body was completely surrounded by beams of light.

Looking down, Jem expected Jace to make some kind of light comment. Instead he froze with a deer-in-the-headlights look. He wasn't even blinking as he stared up at him.

Shifting his eyes, Tim was staring at him from the doorway with an expression of shock. And so was Mia. She had her hands clamped over her mouth with tears falling down her cheeks.

Snapping out of whatever trance he'd been in, Jem muttered, "What's happening to me?"

Jace's jaw dropped. "What the hell—"

Taking a deep breath, Mia dropped her hands and moved closer. "Oh my God, Jem." She looked at him in horror.

"Don't worry, honey," Jem said drifting back down. His body was almost translucent, appearing like a glowing ghost. "I'm okay." He took her hand and gave it a gentle squeeze.

Tim's stare grew uneasy. "Jem, what happened?"

Shrugging his shoulders, Jem shook his head. "I don't know. We were just about to relax and fix a drink, when I felt this warm sensation rush through my body. The next thing I knew, I started glowing and floated toward the ceiling."

Mia's mouth opened slightly. "I thought you were... on fire."

Leaning down, Jem kissed the top of her head, and squeezed her to him. "I'm so sorry, honey."

Mia's crimson eyes traveled down his translucent body, tracing over the foreign light. She turned into his chest and hugged him fiercely, and thought to herself, what if this had something to do with the demon? The panic-stricken part of her was desperate to know. *Oh God.* Just thinking about it made her shake.

In a flat, firm voice, Jace said, "What if you stay this way?"

Reaching for his phone, Tim said, "I'm going to call Helen. I'm sure she won't mind making the trip back once she sees what's going on here."

Jem hid his frustration and decided if he had to be put through an examination, he couldn't think of a more qualified physician. Not long ago, Helen had saved his life.

Jem's gaze flared brightly as he looked down at Mia. But then just like that, it was gone and a quick emotion passed over his face. *Was it fear,* she thought. She couldn't tell, because he closed them when he leaned down to kiss her.

Opening his eyes, he gave her a look so filled with love that she could scarcely breathe.

"Mia, I'm going to be just fine," he murmured automatically.

Her heart throbbed at the fearlessness of his voice. Her lips parted hesitantly, as if she grappled with what to say. Reaching up, she cupped his face with her hand and whispered, "I love you."

He wrapped his arm around her waist and anchored her firmly against him. "I love you too."

* * * *

As midnight neared, Eve put on a pair of tight leather pants, and a black lace top to match. In the bathroom, she reached up to open the medicine cabinet to retrieve her makeup, and winced when she saw herself in the mirror. The reflection staring back was horrible. Dark shadows circled under her eyes, and her cheeks were thin and bony. Panic kicked in as she looked at her grim appearance.

Lifting the edge of her blouse, she peeked at her stomach. The skin was sunken and revealed each detail of her ribs. She was desperate for Breedline blood, and needed it soon. Without nourishment, her frail body wouldn't last much longer.

"You ready?" Sebastian's voice echoed behind her.

Looking away from her own reflection, she saw him looming behind her, dressed in black Versace jeans, and a J. Crew leather jacket. His coal eyes were pegged on her skin she exposed.

"I need to feed, soon." Her brows clenched tight. "I won't last another twelve hours."

He narrowed his stare, and nodded. "Let's go."

With desperation in her eyes, she turned around. "I'll need pure blood from a Breedline."

Handing her a jacket, he muttered, "Don't worry. You'll get what you need."

Shrugging into the thing, she looked up at him. "How?"

"Let me worry about that," he said firmly. "Give me your hand."

With trembling fingers, she slowly reached out. She had never feared him before, and somehow that changed. Swallowing hard, she hoped the contact would lead to an embrace. But he wasn't interested in hugging. Instead, he put a small gun in her hand without even brushing her skin.

She recoiled in distaste. "Where did you find this?"

"It was on the top shelf of your closet. Where are the bullets?"

She shook her head, feeling ugly, and ignored his question.

"Eve... look at me." When she did, he glared at her. "I asked you a question."

"In the top desk drawer by the bed," she quickly responded. "They're silver bullets."

Snatching the gun out of her hand, he turned away. As he walked out, she noticed he had a knife at the small of his back, and wondered how many other weapons he had hidden.

After Eve gathered a small bag, she took a deep breath, and reached out for Sebastian. With his free hand, he created a portal. As they stepped through, they ended up in his old condo.

The place smelled like a combination of lemon floor wax and some kind of spice fragrance. When she heard the security alarm get turned off, she glanced back and saw Sebastian right on her heels. Glancing around the room, she could barely see her hand out in front of her face. Without any lights on, she only saw shadows and shapes, more the pattern of the furniture and the walls than anything else.

"What are we doing at Alexander's condo?"

"Wait here." He swiftly guided her to a nearby chair. "I've got some things I need to get. It won't take long."

When she reached out to turn a lamp on, he stopped her. "No lights."

As she nodded, she was aware of Sebastian pointedly taking interest in the other room.

Down the hall, he went into his old office, and found everything in order. He opened the desk drawer with a combination lock that held his bank card, cell phone, and other information he would need to secure a new location.

Before he went back to the room where Eve was waiting, he unlocked his phone and made a call. Waiting for Samuel Mercier to answer, he grew impatient.

"Master?" Samuel said confused.

"Yes, this is your master speaking."

"Y-your voice..." Samuel stammered. "It sounds like Sebastian's."

"Sebastian was killed. I'm taking over his body," the demon said with bared teeth. "Zadkiel cast me out of Alexander's body, and now I need all of my loyal council member's support."

"Oh?" He muttered, sounding surprised. "What can I do to help?"

"I will need you to locate another place for me and my companion. Call me on this number when you're successful."

"Of course, Master."

After he ended the call, he shut his office door, wondering if he would ever live here again. He had a feeling he wouldn't.

Locking his office, he moved back into the room with Eve. "I need to make one more stop—"

Abruptly, a loud howl came from outside the door. The amplified sound crawled up Eve's spine like a cold chill. Sebastian grabbed her and hauled her back against his body. "Stay quiet," he whispered in her ear.

Another howl came from the other end of the condo. The next one sounded near. They heard a seething growl rumble from the hallway, getting closer and closer.

Just as Sebastian stretched his arm out to create the portal, the front door behind them smashed open, sending the wood frame splintering, and the glass shattering into shards.

Eve screamed as Sebastian yanked her out of the way. The only place to go was behind a sofa, and he shoved her in that direction, shielding her with his body. With only moments to spare, he reached inside his jacket and retrieved his weapon.

At the sounds of claws clicking across the wood floor, he leveled his gun and pulled the trigger.

☙ Chapter Six

An hour later, Helen arrived at the hospital to test Jace's blood samples in the lab. She was excited to continue her research on cellular regeneration, and hopefully she'd find what she'd been searching for all these years.

Heading to the hospital entrance, she heard her phone buzz. Reaching into her bag, she grabbed it and saw a message from Tim Ross. After listening to it, she hurried to her car, and drove back to the Covenant. From Tim's description of what happened to Jem, he might be as helpful to her research as his twin brother Jace.

With a junkie's rush, she was anxious to get back. Helen Carrington, a practical, single woman in her forties, was a great physician. As she had no ties to a husband or children, all her spare time was spent on research. She'd been born with the IQ of a genius and her ability to handle a crisis was astounding.

When she finally arrived, she reached toward the passenger seat to grab her bag and instantly felt an exhilarated rush, but also exhaustion was beginning to set in. Massaging her temples, she felt like she had a vise clamped onto her forehead. She didn't usually get headaches, but it had been a hectic day, and she'd had a lot of caffeine and not much food.

Getting out of her car, she walked to the Covenant's front entrance where Tim was waiting. When he led her into the recreation area, she gasped in shock. Resembling Patrick Swayze's character in the movie *Ghost*, Jem's body was entirely engulfed with some kind of glowing energy.

"So?" Jem shrugged. "What do you think this is?"

With her mouth wide open, Helen blinked, trying to get words to register in her brain. "I'm... not sure." Reaching toward his translucent form, she wondered if her hand would go through him.

When she touched his arm, he felt solid with an unusual warm energy. Pulling her hand back, she glanced over her shoulder at Tim. "I'll need to use the exam room to run some tests."

He nodded. "Of course."

As they entered the room, Helen heard the paper crinkle as Jem hopped on top of the padded table. In spite of his translucent body, he was still a solid form. Reaching into her bag, she pulled out the ophthalmoscope and explained to him what it was for. Looking through the instrument, she saw the same thing she did with Jace. His irises reflected numerous sparkles of light.

"Would you let me get a blood sample?"

"Yeah, sure," his voice sounded nervous. "Do you have any idea what's causing this?"

Mia interrupted. "How long is he going to stay like this?"

Removing her glasses, she folded them up and placed them in the breast pocket of her coat. "Your body should go back to normal in a few hours. I won't know anything until I get your blood tests back," she explained. "But if I'm right, your blood is creating a cellular regeneration."

At the exact same time, Jem and Jace blurted, "What?"

"Are you talking about the ability to regenerate the body's cells?" Tim interrupted before Helen could answer.

She nodded. "That's exactly what I'm talking about."

Confused, Mia shook her head in disbelief. "Are you saying he's going to stop aging?"

"I'm not certain, but it's a possibility." Helen sat down next to Jem. "Listen... I wasn't going to say anything until I got Jace's blood results back, and knew for sure. But I've been researching an old file I came across dated back in the seventies. A German physician discovered a patient with the ability to regenerate cells. His reports showed superhuman healing, and the ability to basically stop aging when he reached thirty. The patient's tests also revealed the same lights in his irises as yours, and he would periodically levitate with a mass of energy that surrounded his body. The file also reported that his body would go into a translucent state once every ninety days, which only lasted a few hours."

After she finished explaining what she had discovered, there was a period of silence in the room. Speechless, everyone kept their eyes on Helen.

Tim sighed, thinking the worst. "Have you told anyone else about this?"

"No," she stated firmly. "No one knows I even have the file. I'll also make sure Jace and Jem's test results are kept confidential."

Trying to comfort Jem, Helen stood and placed her hand on his shoulder. "Make sure you don't let anyone in the Covenant see you this way. If this gets out, we could cause a panic."

"What about Tessa?" Jace sank down in a chair, feeling overwhelmed. "I don't keep secrets from my mate."

"I don't see any reason why not," she replied. "She is the queen. I'm sure she will keep this information confidential as well."

After Helen left, Jace shook his head. "I can't believe there's a possibility we could live forever. What about our family. Does this mean we'll outlive everyone we know?"

"Let's not get too worked up over this, and blow it all out of proportion," Tim said, running his hand over his short trimmed hair. "After Helen reviews your blood work, we'll discuss the issue then."

Jem scooted closer to the edge of the table. "I guess I'll stay here until this wears off."

"I'll stay here with him," Mia said without hesitation.

Holding the door half open, Tim turned and looked over his shoulder. "I've got to make a quick phone call. I'm picking up Angel and the baby in the morning. Let's try to keep the chaos down to a minimum."

* * * *

When a loud pop echoed through the condo, Eve covered her mouth and screamed into her hand. After Sebastian fired his weapon, a screeching high-pitched howl was the last thing they heard.

With his index finger held over his lips, Sebastian gestured Eve to be quiet. "Stay here," he whispered, and darted for the back door.

From out of nowhere, he was hit from behind and knocked to the floor.

"No!" Eve screamed.

Lying flat on his stomach, Sebastian felt like he'd been hit by a train. Gasping for air, he rolled over on his back. When he looked up, he saw a huge set of canines coming toward his face. With a quick movement, he clamped his hands around its thick neck. Using all his strength, he twisted and squeezed until the wolf's torso contorted into a deformed arch. With little effort, he tore its head off completely like a piece of overripe fruit. Dropping the head, he shoved the torso to the floor as it crumpled into a heap.

When Sebastian got to his feet, another wolf hit him. Knocking him to the floor again, the wolf lunged toward his throat. Thinking fast, he grabbed its neck and squeezed it into a bone-cracking angle.

Roaring in pain, it thrashed in his grip. When it finally went limp, Sebastian paused to catch his breath. Pushing it off, he realized the rogue army that took him years to build was now hunting him down.

Wiping the blood from his face, he got to his feet and walked toward the sofa. "You can come out, Eve."

Crawling out of her hiding place, Eve looked up and saw Sebastian standing above her. As he glared at her, his dark eyes were terrifying. She'd never seen him like this before.

Sebastian grabbed her hand. "I told you not to make a sound!" As he yanked Eve to her feet, she lost her balance and nearly tripped. "You will learn to obey me!"

With a tight grip on her arm, he conjured another portal. Quickly stepping inside, they vanished into thin air just as fast. When the room was left in silence, a dark figure came lurking out of the shadows. Sebastian had killed the two rogue wolves, not knowing he'd left behind a third.

🐾 Chapter Seven

When Drakon received a frantic call from Malachi, he could barely understand him over the phone. After he finally managed to calm him down, he told Drakon he saw Sebastian at Alexander's old condominium and the grave news about his brothers.

Ending the call, Drakon immediately got in contact with Tim and Jace. After explaining the situation, they met Jem in the exam room. Waiting for his body to stop glowing, Jem told them he would be there as soon as he returned back to normal.

Arriving at the location where Malachi was waiting, all three of them stepped out of their vehicle and lurked in the shadows of a large oak at the end of a long drive. Not far stood a two-story condominium that was previously owned by Alexander Crest.

Looking at the place gave Jace a serious case of the creeps. Even though the condo resembled an old Victorian style, the front windows reminded him of the house from the 1970s *Amityville Horror* film.

Drakon strode ahead of them in the darkness, and disappeared around the back. A few minutes later, he reappeared and signaled them over.

Heading in his direction, they saw a bright light coming from inside, followed by a deafening scream.

Tim motioned for them to follow. "Come on, let's go!"

When they came around the corner, they noticed the front door was busted into pieces. As they entered, Jace instantly placed his hand over his mouth and gagged. "Jesus..." He choked. "What the hell is that smell?"

Glancing at the floor, Tim saw a trail of blood leading down a hallway. Following it, they came into the main dining area.

Drakon shook his head. "Good God."

Inside, it looked like a scene right out of a slasher movie. The bodies of two Breedline wolves were twisted and partly torn apart.

Jace swallowed down the bile in his throat. "Is that Malachi's brothers?"

Abruptly, they heard a voice carry from another room. "Please... please don't hurt me!"

Following the sound, it led them into the kitchen. When they rushed in, they saw Malachi cowering in a corner completely naked with Jem standing above him. He was speaking to Malachi in a gentle voice. "I promise, Malachi. I'm not going to hurt you."

Jace was relieved to see Jem, not to mention the fact that he'd stopped glowing. "When did you get here?"

Looking away from Malachi, Jem turned toward Jace. "About ten seconds ago."

Jace pointed at Malachi. "What's wrong with him?"

"I think he's in shock after he saw me come through the portal."

Drakon moved next to Malachi, and extended his hand. "Jem is not going to hurt you."

"But..." Malachi mumbled. "He's the son of the demon."

As Drakon helped Malachi stand, he took off his jacket and handed it to him. "Listen, Malachi, we're all here to help you."

He slipped into Drakon's jacket, which was five times his size. Looking down at his bare feet, he remembered how Drakon had always kept his word. Lifting his chin, he let out a deep breath. "Okay. I trust you, Drakon."

Towering over him, Drakon placed his huge palm on Malachi's shoulder. "Explain to us what happened here."

"It was... Sebastian," he muttered in a shaky voice. "He killed my brothers."

"Are you sure Sebastian was here?"

Covering his face, Malachi sobbed into his hands.

With his palm still on Malachi's shoulder, Drakon said in a soothing voice, "It's okay, Malachi. Take a deep breath."

Lowering his hands, he sucked in a deep breath. His body shook so badly his words came out in waves. "Yes... and he had... a woman with him."

"Was it Eve?"

"I think so." He lowered his head. "I couldn't tell for sure."

Drakon clapped him on the back. "You're going to be all right, Malachi. We're here to help you."

Tim looked taken back. "Malachi, what were you and your brothers doing here?"

"After you told us about Sebastian's disappearance, we went through Alexander's room back at the castle in Paris and found the address to this place." He took another deep breath. "We just wanted to see if he might be here. I didn't think he would be strong enough to overpower all three of us."

"I don't believe Sebastian is strong enough to do that to Seth and Kaleb," Tim said as his jaw hardened. "I think we're dealing with someone else."

Jace's reaction was instantaneous. "What do you mean by that?"

Tim's entire body was tense. He knew it was difficult for them to hear, but he didn't hold anything back. "I think you were right, Jace."

Bewildered, Jace crossed his arms. "Right about what?"

Tim let out a long sigh, swallowing the knot in his throat. "About what you said earlier," he muttered with a voice full of raw emotion. "I think it's a possibility Sebastian's possessed by Alexander's demon."

Jem narrowed his eyes, and made a sound of disgust. "Sorry, what did you just say?"

"Easy, Jem." Tim held up his hand. "I'm just trying to piece all this together. We don't know anything for sure yet."

"Wait a minute." Drakon spoke out. "We haven't even thought about checking Sebastian's apartment. That could be his next stop."

Without hesitation, Jem extended his hand and created a portal. "Well, what the hell are we waiting for?"

"We'll come back to get you," Drakon told Malachi. "And don't worry, buddy. We'll make sure your brothers get a proper burial."

Malachi nodded, his eyes gleamed with relief. "Thank you, Drakon."

Turning toward Jem, Drakon asked, "Do you remember how to get to Sebastian's place?"

He nodded and held up his other hand, motioning Drakon over. "Yeah, let's go."

* * * *

When Sebastian and Eve traveled through the portal across town, they found themselves inside a place Eve had visited frequently in the past. It was Sebastian's apartment.

With a confused expression, she asked, "Don't you think we're taking a risk being here?"

"I won't be long," he told her. "Wait here." He strode down the hallway over to the bedroom and opened the door. Feeling sick to his stomach, he willed his weak body across the room and flopped down on the edge of the bed. With his arms wrapped around his stomach, he felt helpless in this new body. Closing his eyes, he couldn't wait to get over his weakness and regain his—

Abruptly, his eyes flipped open when he heard a crackling noise close by. Standing up, his body seized as he stared at the door. Other than Eve, there was someone else in the apartment. His first instinct was to escape through the portal... but he couldn't survive without Eve.

🐾 *Chapter Eight*

As Jem stepped through the portal with Jace, Tim, and Drakon, he scanned the surroundings and recognized Sebastian's apartment.

In a low voice, Tim said, "Let's split up. Drakon and I will check the back rooms. You two go down the hall and check the bedrooms. Yell if you see Sebastian. Is everyone clear?"

Nodding in unison, they split up in opposite directions.

Startled, Sebastian froze when the bedroom door opened. "They're here," Eve whispered, locking it behind her.

Sebastian's expression hardened. He grabbed her arm, gripping it forcefully and pulled her close. Just as he was about to conjure the portal, a loud bang caught his attention. Dropping his hand, he turned around and saw Jace standing in the open doorway.

While Jace's brain tried to process what was reality and what couldn't possibly be real, he noticed the dark depths in Sebastian's eyes. It was the same evil glare he'd seen before in Alexander. Every one of his gut instincts told him this was all wrong. He stumbled back and his hand flew to the door frame to regain his balance.

Jace's face went from confused to complete rage in two seconds flat. "Son of a bitch!" he swore.

At that moment, Sebastian stood stock-still. He seemed as shocked as Jace was at first, but then his lips formed into a smug grin.

The smug look on his face made Jace want to hit him. He shot him a murderous glare that said, *I'm going to kill you.*

From across the room, Sebastian's voice amplified around the room, seeming to come from a distance greater than the one between them. It was familiar and unrecognizable at the same time, echoing in a strange way. "Did you miss me?" His words drifted into a conceited laughter.

Throwing Jace into a mass of anger, his hands formed into fists. And all the memories of what Sebastian had done to Tessa came crashing down in full force. He was going to kick his damn ass for what he'd done, and torture Sebastian endlessly.

Reaching behind his back, Sebastian snatched his weapon and shifted into firing position. Without warning, he aimed the gun at Jace, and pulled the trigger.

Searching a room down the hall, Jem heard an awful popping sound. He didn't think twice. Hearing the noise, he rushed out of the room. In the near distance, he saw Jace hit the floor, flat on his back.

"Jace!" Jem shouted as he ran in his direction. From out of nowhere, there was a brilliant flash of light, like a bomb had gone off. Stunned by the brightness, Jem dropped to his knees and clapped his hands over his face shielding his eyes.

As the illumination receded, a mighty roar echoed through the apartment, and Jem slowly uncovered his eyes.

At the end of the hallway, he saw Jace's Beast. Standing at least seven feet tall, it was in a rage, with teeth like a saber-tooth tiger and a slashing pair of claws the size of daggers.

When the Beast let loose another howl, Eve stiffened in shock and screamed. Its head whipped in her direction with a savage glare. Its white coated fur was full and thick with its lips curled back into a snarl. Positioning itself in an attack stance, it snapped its jaws.

Before Sebastian escaped through the portal, he lifted an eyebrow and quirked the corner of his mouth up in a sneer. "Give the queen my regards."

Just as the Beast lunged forward, Sebastian vanished, taking Eve with him like shadows as they passed through the portal.

With another deafening roar, the Beast wheeled around as if looking for something to rip into pieces. Noticing Jem, its eyes locked in his direction. Then it charged at him, running on two legs as the pounding of its stride shook the hardwood floors.

Coming from behind, Jem heard Drakon's voice. "Jem, get out of there!"

Looking over his shoulder, Jem and Drakon exchanged a look. Jem held up his hand and signaled Drakon to stay back.

As he turned back around, it all seemed to move in slow motion. Jem stepped closer to the Beast as it prepared to lunge at him, and Drakon moved inches closer to Jem as all three of them looked at each other for a split second. Refocusing on one another, they went right back to the collision course they'd started on.

Preparing to be torn into shreds, Jem felt himself beginning to hyperventilate. Thinking fast, he stood his ground and tried to telepathically communicate with Jace.

"Please, Jace... remember. It's me. I'm your brother, Jem."

The Beast stopped right in front of Jem and fell into a crouch. It was so close Jem could feel the hot breath on his face. With his palm trembling, Jem extended it inches from the Beast.

Cocking its head, the Beast's yellow eyes blinked. Leaning closer to Jem's hand, it inhaled through his nostrils.

In one more attempt, Jem tried to get into its head. He knew Jace was in there... somewhere.

"That's it, brother. You can do it. Don't you remember me?" he asked, holding his breath until he was lightheaded.

Abruptly, it heaved a deep breath, and then the massive Beast started to shake. Lifting its head, it let out a high, piercing howl.

Jem stepped back and watched as the Beast dropped to his knees. There was another flash of light, and Jace's form resurfaced, lying naked on the floor.

Kneeling beside him, Jem shrugged out of his jacket, and draped it over Jace.

Curled into a ball, Jace's body shook. With his eyes squeezed shut, his shoulder was bleeding from Sebastian's bullet, and his mouth moving slowly. "I'm... sorry."

Drakon wouldn't have believed it if he hadn't seen the whole thing for himself. Jem had calmed the raging Beast once again.

Tim rushed over and knelt down on the other side of Jace. Noticing the wound on his shoulder, he said, "Damn, Jace. That was a close call."

Slowly sitting up, Jace looked up at Tim. "I'll... live."

Tim nodded. "Let's get you back. We'll have Helen take a look at that shoulder."

Reaching out, Tim wrapped his arm around his waist, and Drakon held onto his shoulders to keep him steady.

When they managed to keep Jace on his feet, Jem conjured the portal.

* * * *

When Sebastian and Eve returned to her apartment, she jerked her hand out of his. "What the hell was that?"

Sebastian pictured the Beast, recalling every aspect of the thing from his yellow eyes to the massive set of teeth in its jaws. He wanted to tell Eve the Beast was his son. A deadly creature he'd created, but he couldn't let her know he wasn't who she thought he was. Instead, he shrugged his shoulders. "Don't worry, we're safe here."

"I'm sick and tired of traveling to all these different places just to suit your needs." She glared at him with her hands on her hips. "What about my needs? I need blood!" She said in a bitter tone. "I don't have much time left!"

In a split second, he lunged forward and grabbed her by the throat. He moved so quick she couldn't even register his movement. As he slammed her against the wall, she clawed at his hand, gasping for air.

With a tight grip, he lowered his voice into a growl. "You will... obey me."

When he released her, she dropped to the floor in a heap. Curling into a ball, she rubbed her throat. Looking up, she cringed at the dark depths of his soulless eyes. Now, she'd become fully aware of his true identity. He wasn't the Sebastian she once loved.

"You'll get what you need," he said roughly. "Wait here until I return. Do you understand?"

With an expression of terror, she quickly nodded. All she could think about was getting away from him, but she was too weak. Desperate for blood, she had no other choice.

❧ 🐾 Chapter Nine

Returning to the Breedline Covenant, they helped Jace's exhausted body down to the exam room, and muscled him on top of a padded table.

"Stay put, and rest," Tim urged. "I'll let Tessa know what's going on."

Jace's shoulders sagged. "Thanks," he groaned.

Moving toward the door, Tim opened it halfway and looked over his shoulder at Jem and Drakon. "We need to talk."

When they stepped out, he checked his watch. Noticing the time, he let out a long sigh. In just four hours, they were meeting with the council members. And to make matters worse, he still hadn't called Angel. He shook his head and wondered how he was going to survive the next few hours. *Christ,* he thought. *He hadn't even picked up a car seat for the baby yet.*

With his mind back in focus, he cleared his throat. "We've got a meeting with the council in four hours, but we need to get back to Malachi and help him first. Do you guys think you can handle this without me?"

"Don't worry." Jem nodded. "We'll take care of it."

Tim paused before he asked, "What if Sebastian shows up again? Do you have enough weapons?"

"I got it covered." Drakon took out his gun and checked it. "But I could use another clip. Can I borrow one of yours?"

Reaching into his gun holster, he pulled out his extra clip. Before he handed it to Drakon, he warned, "It's loaded with silver."

"Good," Drakon responded, grinding his teeth. "It may come in handy."

"Call if you need backup, and let Malachi know he's welcome to stay in the Covenant."

"Will do," Drakon agreed, tucking the clip inside his jacket.

* * * *

33

Traveling through the portal, they returned to Alexander's condo. Moving across the lawn at a jog, Drakon's body was primed and pumped. He covered the distance in no time at all, barely breaking a sweat.

Jem's mind was sharp as the night air, churning over what had happened with Jace. His biggest concern was whether he would have the ability to calm Jace down the next time he lost control.

As they approached the front of the condo, they caught a flash of movement inside. On instinct, Drakon flattened against the wall next to the open door. With his weapon ready, Jem followed his movement. Coming from inside, they heard a sound of crunching glass, like popcorn popping. Someone or something was moving in their direction.

With their weapons pointed, they rushed inside and saw Malachi, in wolf form, lurking in the doorway.

"Christ, Malachi!" Drakon withdrew his aim, swinging the muzzle toward the ceiling.

Ducking his head in submission, Malachi let out a low whimper.

Jem grumbled, and shook his head. "We could have shot you." Lowering his weapon, he tucked it inside his jacket. "You'll have to change back, Malachi. We're going to need your help."

* * * *

An hour later, Jace's wound had almost completely healed. As Tessa helped him back to their bedroom, he sat on the edge of the bed and grimaced. Rubbing his temples, he felt like his head was wedged in a vice.

Flipping off the bathroom light, Tessa came out with a glass of water in her hand. Moving close to the bed, she held it out to him. "Here, take this." With her other hand, she handed him a small capsule. "You look like you're in pain."

After he took it, he eased back against the pillows with his brows furrowed. "Tessa, I'm worried I might hurt someone."

"Shhh..." She soothed.

"But...?"

"No buts," she said in a firm tone. "Get some sleep. We'll talk later."

Jace looked at her like he wanted to argue. There was an obvious conflict in his eyes as he weighed the matter and decided whether he wanted to protest. Instead, he just nodded.

Wearing next to nothing, she slid in bed beside him. The moment she was between the sheets, he curled himself around her.

"Tessa?"

She opened her eyes. "Yeah?"

He reached for her hand and gently squeezed. "I love you."

She smiled, and snuggled her back against his chest. "I love you too."

When sleep eventually took them over, Jace drifted into a dream as his eyes moved under his lids. As the hours passed, Jace came awake in the middle of the night screaming. "Run, Tessa!"

The first thing Tessa did was reach out blindly for him. "Jace, it's okay." She caressed his face. "I'm right here."

When he sat up, he turned his head. Letting out a deep breath, he finally realized she was right beside him. "I'm... sorry." He went back to rubbing his temples. "I was having a—"

She reached out and took his hand. "You're fine, honey. It was just a dream."

Staring into her emerald eyes, he thought about the stress his body had been going through lately. He was worried about not being able to control the Beast, and hurting Tessa. And the fact that Sebastian was still alive and possibly possessed by the demon. He was going to need a drink... and soon.

"How am I going to get rid of—," he paused briefly, and made sound of weariness, "—this thing?"

She could see the concern in those blue eyes a mile away. "It's part of you, Jace," she said, pressing a kiss to his cheek. "I'll always love you with or without it."

He pulled her body against his. "I love you, Tessa." She was wearing only a T-shirt, and he slid his hands underneath, spanning her lower back.

"Do you think it's something the demon passed on to you?"

Before he answered her question, he braced himself for something bad to happen. Nothing like that came. All he felt was a warm sensation in his chest. Love unbridled with the chaos of his curse.

Smoothing her hair back, he muttered, "I can't think of any other explanation."

Pulling from their embrace, he laughed a little. "I guess we're like beauty and the beast. Of course I'm beauty," he said mischievously.

"You're full of yourself, aren't you?" She rolled her eyes. "I'm glad you can find the humor in all this."

He smiled at her, but his eyes appeared worried. "I love you, my beauty."

"And I love you," she said with a light giggle, "my beast."

"Come here." He pulled her close, and gently nibbled at her neck.

After Jace made love to Tessa in an unhurried, tender way, he held her in his arms, and couldn't stop worrying about the Beast. And neither could she.

* * * *

Depleted of all her energy, Eve sat in bed with her legs curled against her chest, waiting for Sebastian to return with the blood she needed to survive.

Abruptly, she heard screams coming from outside the room. When the door swung open, Sebastian pushed a young girl inside. Falling onto the floor, she scrambled back to her feet and tried to escape. Grabbing onto her arm, Sebastian tossed her back to the floor.

Sobbing, the girl screamed, "Why? Why are you doing this to me?"

Eve was on her feet, her fists down at her sides clenched into balls. "She's a child! Why did you bring a child to me?"

Chapter Ten

Eve was furious with Sebastian. Sure, she'd done her share of evil in the world, but there was no way she was going to harm a child.

"It's not the time to get picky!" Sebastian barked. "I brought what you asked for. A pure Breedline! You'll take what I bring you, or you'll starve!" Storming out, he slammed the door and locked it from the outside.

In desperation, the girl scurried to the door, and pounded her fists. "Please, someone help me!" Realizing no one was going to help her, she sunk to her knees and sobbed.

When Eve inhaled the girls scent, her fangs elongated with a hiss. Her hunger rose like an animal's instinct to hunt its prey. Dying of thirst, Eve slowly crept closer.

Cringing in fear, the girl covered her mouth and screamed into her hand.

Nearly overcome by the urge to feed, Eve forced herself away from the girl. Moving back to the bed, she sat with her back against the headboard. Wrapping her arms around herself, she lowered her head and wept.

Witnessing Eve's breakdown, the girl found courage to speak. "Are you... a succubus?"

Eve nodded without looking at her.

She searched Eve for some sign of what she was thinking. Finally she gave up and voiced her question aloud, "Are you going to kill me?"

Releasing a deep breath, Eve lifted her chin and stared at her. "No. I'm not going to kill you." Wiping the tears from her eyes, Eve asked, "What's your name?"

With caution, the girl approached Eve and stared into her crimson eyes. "My name is Kara." She drew in a deep breath and blew it out. "Kara Saintclare."

Moving slowly, she sat down beside Eve. "Is that man... your husband?"

Lowering her head in shame, she collapsed her face into her hands and sobbed. Kara reminded her of the past, bringing back her childhood memories. Abandoned at birth, she was tossed in and out of foster homes. Treated like a captive prisoner, she was tortured for years. When she finally escaped at the young age of fifteen, she was homeless on the streets until she met Sebastian. Just like her, he was an unwanted and an unloved child, creating unstable and mentally ill adults.

Loving her unconditionally, he became her bonded mate. Two months later, her foster father found her and forced her back home. Before Sebastian got to her, she'd been beaten and raped. In a savage rage, Sebastian brutally murdered him. After that, she never had to worry about living in fear... *until now.*

Feeling helpless, Kara scooted closer to Eve. "I'm sorry. Did I say something wrong?" With courage, she reached out and peeled Eve's hand away from her face. "If you promise to help me, I'll give you some of my blood."

Eve looked up and stared at her a long moment, obviously studying her with avid curiosity. And then her eyes widened as she focused on Kara's wrist. Though her fangs unsheathed, and she was starved, Eve could not drink from a child.

As the door swung open, Kara screamed when she saw Sebastian. His anger stirred when he saw the girl was still alive. Glaring at Eve, his hands formed into fists. "Why haven't you fed?"

Because she was still suffering from hunger, Eve's cheeks were hollowed, and her body looked grim and desolate. With a hateful stare, she shook her head, refusing his offer.

"Think you're too good for the gift I brought you?" Sebastian said through gritted teeth. As he stalked toward the bed, Kara screamed and cowered next to Eve.

"Please, Sebastian," Eve begged. "Don't hurt her."

When he grabbed Kara, she kicked and screamed, trying to escape his firm grip.

In her weak state, Eve passed out and slid into oblivion.

Eve finally awoke with Sebastian standing over her, enraged. Trying to focus, she saw something in his hand. "Drink this," he said roughly, tossing a plastic bag on the bed.

Inhaling the rich scent of blood, Eve's hunger instantly rose. Struggling to sit up, she noticed one of her hands was bound to the bed.

"What's this?" She tugged at the rope. "Why is my arm bound like this?"

Sebastian leaned over her, and narrowed his black eyes. "I'm going to teach you a lesson."

With her free hand, she reached for the bag. As she brought it to her lips, her body trembled as she poured the blood down her dry throat. Immediately, she felt a surge of euphoria rush through her veins.

"Damien!" Sebastian shouted, looking over his shoulder. "Bring her in!"

When footsteps aroused Eve's attention, she glanced at the doorway and saw a man with Kara's limp body in his arms. As he dropped her to the floor, she fell like a rag doll.

Fury rose within Eve that it choked her throat and made her shake. She growled through bared fangs, "What have you done?"

When there was no reply, Eve searched the bed and wished to hell there was something to throw—but there was nothing. Unleashing her anger, she opened her mouth and screamed. The pitch rebounded off the bedroom walls, magnifying to an earsplitting thunder. She strained against her bound wrist until it sliced into her skin. As she pulled with all her strength, the bed post cracked and splintered.

Watching Eve's reaction, Sebastian was unsure of the rage he'd let loose. Turning in Damien's direction, he dropped his voice. "Leave us."

When the door clicked shut, Sebastian pointed at Kara. "Your disobedience caused this."

Eve hollered at the top of her lungs, tugging at her restraint. "Release me, damn you!"

Sebastian sprang forward and grabbed her throat. With a tight grip, he snarled in her ear, "You will obey me."

In the blink of an eye, she whipped her head forward, nailing him in the face, and his grip loosened for a split second. Looking up, she saw something black on his face. Releasing his hand from her throat, he stumbled back and wiped it away.

She half expected to be slain on the spot, and prayed it would be over quick. Whatever consequence came upon her head was better than a tortured existence with him. Pegging him with a hard stare, she said, "I would rather wither away, before I obey you."

Before anything more could be said, Sebastian reached behind his back. When he brought it around, he held a whip in his hand.

With her eyes squeezed shut, her body stiffened as she braced herself for the first strike. As it slashed across her flesh, she opened her eyes and screamed.

He gave her everything he had and more. One after the other, he struck her until his head fell in exhaustion and he couldn't lift his arm anymore.

Chapter Eleven

Drakon and Jem stood outside the gates of a private mausoleum, waiting for Malachi. After cremating what was left of his brothers, they'd helped Malachi prepare Seth and Kaleb for their final resting place.

From the north, a woman and a man approached, both of them slender and tall. They were dressed in black and their skin seemed oddly pale.

They watched as the couple moved closer with their hands entwined with each other's. Drakon heard a rustle across the ground. Glancing over his shoulder, he saw Malachi.

He was coming through the gate, his arms were tucked into a black parka that was too big for him, and he was shuffling his feet through the sea of dead leaves. Lifting his chin, the expression on his face changed when he saw the man and woman walk up.

With his arms extended, he darted toward them. "You came!"

Obviously recognizing Malachi, they wrapped their arms around him in an embrace. After a brief hug, Malachi turned in Jem and Drakon's direction. "I want to introduce you to my friends." He wiped his eyes, and said, "This is Chrissy and Brandon. She was Seth's finance, and Brandon is her brother." He turned toward the couple, and smiled. "This is Drakon and Jem. They helped with the burial."

As their eyes met Drakon's, they stood stock-still. He had a leather holster strapped around him, and their eyes widened when they saw the size of his weapon. He was dressed like a hitman, his cropped Mohawk and the hard stare fitting the image perfectly.

Chrissy found herself staring into his eyes for the longest moment. Noticing her crimson eyes, Drakon instinctively knew she must have been a half-breed. When he nodded in their direction, they offered each other their hands at exactly the same time.

"Thank you," her voice was level, and calm. "I appreciate everything you've done to help with the arrangements."

Looking into the couple's eyes, Jem realized what they were. Just like him, Seth had bonded with a half-breed. "You're welcome, and we're sorry for your loss," he said.

After expressing condolences to Malachi, and paying their final respects inside the mausoleum, they walked away in silence.

Drakon softened at Malachi's obvious grief. "You okay, Malachi?"

He nodded. "Thanks for all your help."

Jem reached out and clapped Malachi on the back. "We need to get back to the Covenant. The council meeting will be starting soon."

Drakon placed his palm on Malachi's shoulder, and squeezed. "You're going with us. Tim asked for you to attend the meeting. You're a witness to the council. You need to report what happened."

"Okay," Malachi mumbled, lowering his head. "I'll go."

Using the portal, Jem took them back to the Covenant. As they approached the door, Malachi felt his heart pound in his chest.

When Drakon opened the door, Malachi found himself taking a deep breath. As they moved inside, everyone in the meeting grew quiet and stared in their direction. As he glanced across the room, his eyes came to a halt when he saw the queen. Tessa turned toward him, and her emerald eyes softened. And for some reason, that made him want to tear up—not that he would have admitted it to anybody, especially Drakon.

Thinking of everything he had been through, he heard her say. "Please, have a seat."

On instinct, he bowed his head and took another deep breath.

As they sat down at the table, she rose from her chair and looked in Alexander's direction. "Alexander, we need all the names of everyone that conspired against the Covenant to help the demon."

Anxiety wrapped around his throat, as he squeezed his airway tight. "I'm sorry, Tessa." His voice was so faint Tessa could barely hear him. "I know I should have told you sooner." He raised his voice, the tone expressing remorse. "When I first arrived to the Covenant all my memories of before vanished. I know everyone here finds very little credence in me, but I solemnly swear I am telling the truth."

Jace shot out of his chair, and pointed his finger at Alexander. "You're a damn liar!"

"Sit down, Jace," Tim said firmly.

Jace reluctantly snapped his lips shut and then retook his seat, but he continued to stare belligerently at Alexander.

All Jem could do was shake his head and break the eye contact with Alexander by looking down. It was either that, or spout something he might regret later.

Drakon rubbed his jaw. "What about the Breedline truth serum? We could use it to see if he's speaking the truth?"

Tim shook his head. "The test can only be performed by a Wiccan. In case anyone else here knows how to locate one, I'm not even sure if they still exist."

Leaning forward, Jem inhaled through his nostrils. Even though Alexander's warrior frame was tense and stressed, he couldn't sense fear. This was good, he thought. Usually fear meant you had something to hide.

In the brief silence, Tim looked at Alexander and studied his face. God, he couldn't believe he actually trusted this man. After all they'd been through, he understood why Jace felt nothing but anger toward Alexander. Even though he was possessed by a demon at the time, he'd still murdered his mother. He shifted his stare toward Jace. His lips tightened further, and he could positively see the hatred in his eyes. Tim knew he was never, ever going to forgive Alexander.

He refocused back on Alexander. "Are you going to be able to help us destroy Sebastian even though he is technically your son?"

Alexander's brows clenched. "If it comes to that, I'll do the right thing."

Drakon leaned back in his chair and crossed his arms. "Why would you help us? We're not forcing you."

"Everyone in the Covenant has been good to me, even after all the horrible things—" He paused and swallowed hard. "I owe you my life. If it wasn't for you, I'd still be possessed by the demon."

Feeling the need to seal the pact between them, even though he knew it was going to piss off Jace, Tim rose from his chair and extended his hand.

Reaching out, Alexander shook his hand.

"There's one more thing," Tim added. "We're almost positive the real Sebastian Crow is dead, and we have evidence of the Chiang-shih demon possessing his body.

The silence in the room seemed to stretch endlessly. And then it broke out with a low chatter as the council members raised their voices.

Colin Tate, a council member from the Arizona Covenant, shot to his feet. "What? I thought the Angel of Mercy cast him back to hell?"

A voice cursed across the table from Colin, and then muttered, "Is there nothing we can do?"

Another council member representing the Tennessee Covenant spoke up. "How did we not see this coming?"

All at once, everyone started raising their voices, pointing out their own opinions. With all the noise, it was difficult for Tim to understand a word they were saying.

Tessa cleared her throat. "Everyone, please." Her voice sounded annoyed. "Please, calm down."

Rising from her chair at the head of the thirty-foot-long table, she waited for everyone to quiet down. She drummed her fingers on the table, her brain overwhelmed by all the voices. Moments later, she'd had enough. Tessa quieted the chaos by raising her voice. "I said calm down!"

As she got their attention, the room silenced and focused in her direction. Her gaze swept the room, and she halted at the far end of the table when she noticed someone was still standing. With her hands on her hips, Tessa narrowed her eyes and said, "You too, Mr. Tate."

There was the soft sound of a chair getting pushed back on the rug, and then Colin bowed his head, and sat down.

"We must remain calm," she muttered, her voice clear and in charge. "If we panic now, the demon will gain control." Her eyes shifted toward the left. Pointing at the collection of books, she said, "Maybe if we do some research, we can find out what will destroy it."

The council members were quiet as their expressions shifted into something she'd hoped to see. They all stared back at her, unwavering support reflected in their eyes.

"She's right," Drakon agreed without haste. "We might find some information on Jem's powers he inherited from the demon. They could be useful."

When Tim nodded in Drakon's direction, he stood up, his chair creaking quietly. "At this point, I don't think we have any other options. The question is, where do we start?"

* * * *

Tim awoke the next morning anxious to get to the hospital to pick up Angel and their newborn baby. Thanks to Cassie and Mia, he was prepared with a car seat.

Before he stepped in the shower, he glanced in the mirror. As he stared at himself, he realized his reflection looked exhausted, which made sense. He'd stayed up late with everyone searching through endless books. Feeling defeated, they called it quits at two o'clock this morning.

After a shower, he drove to the hospital, and worried about bringing Angel and the baby back to the Covenant. With the demon still alive, no one was safe.

When he saw Helen standing outside Angel's room, he waved in her direction. With a chart in her hand, she motioned him over.

"Angel and the baby are doing great," she reassured, placing her palm on his shoulder. "All her release papers are filled out. She's all yours."

Tim liked Helen. Hell, he owed her. When Angel went into delivery, Helen had saved her life.

"Thanks, Helen." He hugged her. "This wouldn't be possible without you."

"You're welcome." She pulled from their embrace. "Angel's recovered beautifully, and Natalie's thriving. Since she's a half-breed, she's progressing so much faster than a pure-blood Breedline baby."

He sighed in relief. "That's great."

"So?" Helen raised her brows. "How are you doing with the whole father thing?"

He shook his head. "I'm not sure. I don't think I've had time to process the whole thing yet."

"I completely understand." She smiled. "Would it be okay if I stopped by the Covenant later? I've got Jace and Jem's test results back."

"Of course, I'll let them know."

After he said good-bye to Helen, he slowly reached for the door to Angel's room. When he opened it, Angel was cradling Natalie in her arms.

"Hello, honey," Tim whispered. "How's my girls?"

Looking up, Angel's eyes widened with excitement. "Everything's perfect. Come in, honey." She gestured him over. "Someone wants to see you."

For some reason, the expression on his face brought back memories of the first time they'd met. Ten years ago, she'd met him at a popular nightclub. Watching him sit alone at the bar, she instantly knew he was the one. When their eyes connected, they bonded for life. After acknowledging his dominant side, she enjoyed becoming his submissive partner. Even though she wasn't a pure Breedline, he still loved her all the same.

When he stood beside them, Natalie looked in his direction. Her unfocused eyes pleaded as her little arms reached for him.

"Come here, precious." He picked her up and hugged her close to his heart.

Staring into his daughter's crimson eyes, he wondered if he was cut out to be a good father. He never thought about having children. Yes, he wanted Natalie to have a good father, and that was the primary concern. The pregnancy had happened so quickly they hadn't had time to plan anything. If it weren't for Cassie and Mia, he wouldn't even have a car seat. He couldn't imagine life without Angel, but he was worried if he could be the parent Natalie deserved.

Natalie grasped his thumb, and held it with such strength.

His eyes widened. "She's so strong," he said, amazed.

Tugging at his thumb, she managed to get it to her mouth.

With tears streaming down his face, his chest swelled with renewed purpose. They were both his family—his and his alone. One was his heart, and the other a piece of himself. Both completed him.

Getting out of the hospital bed, Angel buried her face in his chest as he held their young. And then, in midst of their loving embrace, Natalie made the most adorable coo.

❦ *Chapter Twelve*

Safely arriving back to the Covenant, Tim helped Angel to their room and watched for the first time as his daughter was fed. Natalie stirred and made a little noise when Tim leaned down and kissed her forehead.

"She needs a crib," Angel whispered.

"Make a list, honey. I'll make sure she has everything. We'll make the guest room next to ours into a nursery."

Before he closed the door, he said quietly, "Get some rest, honey. I've got a meeting with Helen. I'll be back later to check on you."

She smiled. "I love you."

"Love you too."

Standing outside the room, he glanced over his shoulder at the bedroom door and felt a glow of contentment rush through him. His family was safe and sound, and that was his new mission in life.

* * * *

Helen had just arrived, and was waiting in the foyer. Reaching into her duffle bag for her files, she heard a door open and close. When she glanced up, her mouth dropped open.

Standing merely inches away, Alexander stared in her direction. His eyes were the color of a clear blue sky. His physique resembled a Viking warrior, with his tall stature. Oddly, he looked a lot like Jace and Jem.

Clearing his throat, he said politely, "Is there anything I can help you with?"

"I... I'm Dr. Helen Carrington," she stammered. "I'm here to see Tim Ross."

"Ah, yes," he replied. "I've heard your name mentioned. I'm sorry..." He extended his hand. "I'm Alexander Crest."

Surprised, she said, "Oh, you're the Alexander Crest. I mean, you're Jace and Jem's biological father. I thought you looked familiar."

With a puzzled expression, he responded, "Uh, yes. I'm their... father. Please..." He waited for her to accept his hand. "Please, don't worry. The demon is gone."

"I'm so sorry," she said regretfully. "That was rude of me. I didn't mean to imply anything." She shook his hand. "It's nice to meet you, Alexander."

When their hands made contact, she felt an odd sensation. Almost as if her body had static electricity running through each of her nerves. And then she felt something else. Her body stiffened as her thighs tingled. *Oh my*, she thought.

A deep voice came from behind them. "I'm sorry to keep you waiting, Helen."

Startled, Helen jumped at the sound of Tim's voice, and let go of Alexander's hand.

There was a long moment before she could speak. Her heart was beating so hard, she felt like she was going to start panting. "No problem. I was just going over some of my files." Her voice sounded nervous.

Tim frowned. "Are you all right, Helen?"

Forcing a smile, she put both hands up in ward-off mode. "Oh, I'm perfectly fine. Just excited about what I've discovered on the test results."

"I see you met Alexander?" Tim asked.

"Oh, yes," she said out of breath. "It was a pleasure to meet you, Alexander."

He bowed his head. "It was all my pleasure, Ms. Carrington."

Alexander's mouth twitched into a half-smile as he watched Tim escort Helen out of the foyer. As he felt the room closing around him, all his instincts fired up. He took the wheel and grabbed control. The instant their hands touched, all those possessive male impulses that had been dormant for years came out. As he thought of her body, he felt himself harden, and the word *beloved* rolled around in his brain.

As Tim held the door open to the exam room, he said, "Sorry to keep you waiting, Helen. I'll go see what's keeping Jace and Jem."

"Take your time. I'm in no hurry."

Alone in the room, she thought about Alexander's eyes. They were unlike any she'd seen before, the beautiful unique color, like looking out into the ocean blue. Her heart beat faster the more she thought about him, and suddenly she felt ridiculous.

When the door opened, she jumped and wheeled around.

"Sorry, Helen." Jace's raspy voice caught her attention. "We didn't mean to startle you."

"Oh, you're fine. My mind was just miles away."

"So?" Jem shrugged his shoulders. "What did you find out with the test results?"

"Oh, yes." Focusing on the files, she opened them up. "Please, have a seat." She gestured them over to the chairs nearby, including Tim.

There was no small talk. No chatty, how's-the-weather, or the-holidays-are-coming-up-fast kind of stuff. Helen knew the guys wanted answers now.

Before she was in her chair, she said, "Both of you carry the gene for cellular regeneration."

"So what exactly does that mean?" Jem queried.

Removing her glasses, she took a deep breath. "It basically means you'll stop aging when you reach thirty."

Jace frowned. "You mean we're never going to die?"

She held up her hand, motioning for them to wait. "The answer is no, and yes. You can still die from silver, or a fatal injury. But your body will continue to regenerate cells. Once you reach the age of thirty, you will live on forever without aging."

Holy crap, Jem thought as he tried to process Helen's words. He'd wondered what this meant for him and Mia. There were things in life you could undo, and this was not one of them. "Is there a way to stop it?"

"I'm not sure," she implied. "But I've been searching for years, trying to find someone that carries this gene. Do you know what this could mean for the Breedline species?"

There was a long pause, and Tim crossed his arms. "You're trying to find a cure for the Breedline aging process, aren't you?"

Coming up with a reply, she glanced down at the medical records, the pens, the binder clips, and the phone on the desk. And then she finally said, "Yes, I am. But please, look at the possibilities it could have for our species. Someday we'll be considered a dying breed. Our bloodline is getting less and less each year. Please," she pleaded. "You must agree to let me do the research. You two are the key to unlocking the secret."

"Well, I'll agree to do whatever you need for your research," Jace blurted. "I don't want to live to see everyone around me get old and die while I live on forever."

Jem nodded. "Count me in too. I agree with Helen. This could be mean a lot to our species."

Waiting for Tim's response, he just shrugged his shoulders. "Don't look at me. It's not my body she's going to be poking and prodding on." He chuckled. "Besides, I agree with all of you. This could be a miracle to the Breedline. All I ask is one promise from everyone in this room. This stays between the four of us until we find out where this goes. Do we agree?"

Everyone agreed except Jace. "What about Tessa? She's our queen, and my mate. She needs to know."

"I agree," Jem spoke up. "I don't want to keep this from Mia either."

"That's fine." Tim nodded in their direction. "I'll need to keep Drakon updated as well. But no one else, and that's final."

"I'll need to do my research here," Helen insisted. "I don't trust keeping the files and medical reports anywhere else."

Tim nodded. "I agree. Let me know what you'll need for your research, and we'll make it happen."

Before they left, Tim remembered there was something else he needed to ask Helen about. Realizing she was a book collector, she might have one about the Chiang-shih demon. "Helen, I need to ask you a question. You may be able to help me with something important."

"Sure. What can I help you with?"

"We've been searching for information on destroying the Chiang-shih demon that possessed Alexander. I know you have a huge collection of books on ancient creatures. Do you think you have anything on this particular one?"

"No, I'm sorry, I don't. But I do know a Wicca that does."

Surprised, Jace popped a brow. "You know a Wicca? I thought they were just a myth."

"Indeed, they exist. In fact, she's my niece."

"Do you think she could help us?" Tim asked.

"Of course, I'll call her this afternoon. I can arrange for you to meet her."

Tim let out a sigh of relief. "Thank you, Helen. I'd appreciate that."

Her curiosity got the best of her, with Alexander on her mind. "If you don't mind me asking, why do you need this book? I thought the demon was destroyed."

"Ah... so did we." Tim cocked a brow. "There are circumstances that have led us to believe it may have possessed Sebastian Crow."

In shock, she placed her hand over her mouth. "What..." As she looked at the three of them, she realized the magnitude of their desperation. "I'm so sorry. Hopefully my niece can help you."

Tim forced a smile. "Thank you, Helen."

With the door half-open, Tim was just about to step out behind Jace and Jem when Helen said, "Tim, may I speak with you in private?"

As Tim's head lifted and angled her way, he said, "Sure."

Stepping back into the room, he sat down next to Helen. "What did you want to talk to me about?"

"I would like to ask you some questions about Alexander."

Looking at her suspiciously, he said, "Okay."

"Would it be possible for me to get a blood sample from him?"

"Where are you going with this, Helen?"

"Well, he's Jace and Jem's biological father, right?"

"Yes, he is."

"It could be a possibility that he carries the same gene."

"Yes, you might be right. But I don't want him to know about this."

"I could make something up. I could just tell him I'm doing a physical for everyone in the Covenant."

"You mean lie?"

Her brows lifted. "It's all for the good of science."

"All right, just make sure he doesn't find out about the research."

She smiled. "Of course."

Chapter Thirteen

When Drakon heard the shower running, he walked over to the open door and saw Cassie inside. Taking a deep breath, he watched her back arch as she washed her hair. With every move she made, his breathing became heavier, and his heart began to flutter. Closing his eyes, he thought about joining her. Instead, he opened them and turned away.

As Cassie rinsed the shampoo from her hair, thoughts of Drakon came to mind. The second she finished drying off, she was going to march into the bedroom and seduce him. She wanted him, and she was going to have him.

With nothing but a towel wrapped around her body, she padded into the bedroom and eased onto the bed next to Drakon. With one hand, she removed the towel and reached for his hand with the other.

"Cassie—"

Releasing his hand, she tackled him so fast Drakon never saw it coming. One second he was staring at her breasts, the next, he was pressed flat on his back with Cassie staring down at him.

As he felt the warmth between her thighs, his body screamed to be inside her. Just as she started to move, he reached up and placed his palms on her shoulders. Even though his arousal screamed in protest, he held her still.

"Cassie, wait."

"I want you, Drakon," she pleaded. "Please, make love to me."

Letting out a deep breath, he tried to think of the right words to say. Before he could mutter a word, she'd unbuttoned his pants and was about to work his zipper.

Grabbing her hand, he kept it from going further. "Cassie, no."

Her brows furrowed. "Please don't say that."

Lifting her off his body, he said, "I love you, Cassie... but?"

"Then make love to me," she insisted.

He shook his head. "It's too soon."

As she stared at him confused, her lips began to quiver.

"Cassie, please don't be upset."

Covering her face, she sobbed. "I need you, Drakon."

"Come here." He pulled her closer. "Let me hold you."

Rubbing her eyes, she laughed in a devastating little burst. "I am destined to go to my grave a virgin, aren't I?"

"Oh, Cassie." He held her tight. "I didn't say I wouldn't be with you."

Pulling out of their embrace, she looked at him with tears glimmering on her lashes.

He smoothed his fingers through her wet curls. "I want it to be special."

"It will be special now," she groaned.

"Sweetheart, let's just hold each other tonight." He dried her tears with his thumb. "If we end up doing nothing but holding each other all night, at least we'll be together. I just want to feel right about taking what's so precious from you. Okay?"

She nodded as more tears fell down her cheeks. "You're right," she whispered. "We should take our time."

"It isn't because I don't want you." He kissed her on the shoulder, and made her smile. He didn't want to rush into anything, but he knew that their lovemaking was inevitable. Anticipation would make it all the sweeter when they did finally come together. He'd spend hours lavishing attention on her, learning everything that pleased her. Her needs would always come before his own.

Reaching around the back of her neck, she said, "Wait, I almost forgot." She unclasped the gold cross necklace he'd let her wear before he left to Alexander's castle in Paris. Opening her palm, she held it out. "This belongs to you."

"It looks better on you," he remarked.

"No, it was your father's. It belongs with you."

"I will take it back under one condition." When he reached across the bed, she heard the nightstand drawer open. As he brought his hand back, he looked at her and smiled. Her eyes widened in surprise when he opened his hand. Inside was a beautiful gold cross necklace with black diamonds in the center. "This belonged to my mother, and I want you to have it."

"Oh, Drakon, it's beautiful."

After he placed it around her neck, he pressed a soft kiss between her shoulder blades. "I love you, Cassie."

"I love you too," she replied, smoothing her hand over the diamond cross positioned below her throat. With his gold chain in her grasp, she reached up and placed it around his thick, muscular neck.

Removing his shirt, he kicked off his shoes and eased under the covers next to her. With her head tucked against his bare chest, they feel asleep in each other's arms.

Later in the night, he awoke and glanced down at Cassie. Sound asleep, she was beautiful with her lips slightly parted. Staring at her, he wondered if the time was right. Moving closer, he kissed her neck while his hand drifted over her thigh.

Feeling his warm hand move across her skin, she opened her eyes.

Moving his body next to hers, she felt his arousal brush against her skin. Lowering his head, he pressed a light kiss on her lips.

"Are you going to make love to me?"

"Yes, Cassie."

Taking it slowly, he unbuttoned his pants and slid them down his strong legs. Reaching to his elastic band of his boxers, she tugged them down until his erection sprung free.

Oh God, she thought, scanning over his body. He was like looking at a perfectly sculpted piece of art.

With his hand, he lifted her chin to meet his face. Looking into his eyes, she saw an erotic anticipation.

She winked. "You are so very naked."

Sliding on top of her, he glanced down her body and murmured, "So are you."

With a soft touch, she ran her hands down his back, and slipped lower. As she smoothed over to his hips, his arousal pulsed with the desperate need to be touched. Capturing her hand, he halted her movement. "Cassie, I want you to do something for me."

Her eyes widened with excitement, wondering what he wanted.

"Let me help you through this, okay? Let's make this night all about you."

Before she could protest, he covered her mouth with his. He treated her with tenderness. Every touch was soft and gentle, and every kiss was slow and unhurried.

When he parted her thighs, she didn't flinch or hesitate. Focusing on the gold chain that hung around his neck, she was ready to take him inside. Her body shuddered when she felt his warmth settle between her soft folds.

Bracing himself above her, he stared down into her eyes. Letting out a deep breath, she ran her hands over his muscular hips again, and felt them tighten as he lightly rocked against her.

"You're so beautiful, Cassie," he whispered. "Are you okay?"

"Yes."

With gentle movements, he eased in and pulled back, each time a little deeper. Closing her eyes, she felt a pinch as he stretched her more. Arching her back, she moved her hips with his rhythm as their tempo fell into sync.

Abruptly, she stiffened when she felt him enter all the way. Squeezing her eyes tight, she let out a deep breath.

When he noticed her pain, he halted his movement. "Cassie, look at me."

As she opened her eyes, tears spilled out.

"Are you okay?"

In silence, she shook her head as more tears fell.

"I'm sorry, sweetheart." Furrowing his brows, he started to pull away. "I don't want to hurt you."

"No," she pleaded, trying to keep him from slipping free. "Don't stop."

Pressing a soft kiss on her lips, he pulled away and whispered, "I have a better idea."

Moving lower, he peppered light kisses that trailed down her chest and to her belly. Closing her eyes, she shivered in excitement when she felt his warm tongue slid between her folds. With every movement, a tingling gathered inside her. She felt a warm pleasure stir around her, and it rose higher and higher. In a blissful release, she suddenly felt her body shudder with an unfamiliar sensation. As her body felt light and limp, she opened her eyes in a daze. When they focused, she saw him staring at her in total awe.

Waiting for her approval, he said, "Was that okay?"

"Amazing," she purred.

He smiled at her response.

She frowned. "I'm sorry I couldn't continue. I won't change into my wolf... will I? You must think I'm a terrible lover."

"I'm in no hurry, sweetheart. You felt wonderful." He kissed the tip of her nose. "Thank you."

"But... I didn't even give you pleasure."

"That's not important." He shook his head. "You gave me something more precious. Your trust. That means the world to me. I love you, Cassie."

Wrapping her arms and legs around his body, she squeezed him tight. "I love you too."

Chapter Fourteen

Early the following morning, Eve awoke in a wave of panic. Trying to calm her breathing, she didn't recognize her surroundings. With her hand bound to a chain, everything was dark and unfamiliar. Stuck in a dense, cold blackness, she was robbed of sight no matter how hard her eyes strained. She could have been in a dungeon, or in a cave.

Memories of feeling helpless shot through her head from years back. During her childhood, she'd been tossed into a life of torture, waking up each day in darkness wondering what was going to be done to her and by whom. Now, that feeling was back.

Each day she'd been treated like a piece of property. The abuse was inevitable whether she was being beaten or mentally tortured. Used up until her foster father was satisfied, and then discarded, left to lie, degraded and locked away, alone in the darkness.

Losing her mind, she wondered who her owner was now. Was it the monster from her past, or the one that was possessing Sebastian. Both seemed to be spawn from the same evil creature.

Trying to free herself, she frantically pulled at the chain attached to her wrist. Exhausted, she felt trapped in the damp darkness of her captor's prison, taking the very breath from her silent screams. Soon, he would come for her.

Gasping in pain, she clawed at her throat from the thirst for blood. Desperate to be freed, she yelled, "Please... someone help me!"

Echoing loudly as they drew near, she listened to the footsteps approaching from outside the room. With the instinct of a caged animal, she grabbed and pulled against her restraints, fighting to get loose.

The sounds of creaking metal ripped through the room as the door swung open. When the light poured into the dark room, she winced at the brightness, closing her eyes. When he moved closer, she slowly opened them and recognized his face.

* * * *

Feeling a warm hand on her shoulder, Cassie opened her eyes. Lying on her side, Drakon was tucked in tight against her back. When he felt her stir, he whispered from behind, "Good morning, sweetheart."

"Good morning."

As she stretched her legs, she could feel the soreness between her thighs. Remembering last night, she wished she could give him the same pleasure he'd given her.

"Cassie... I want to—"

"What?" She twisted a little so she could see him.

His eyes had that hard, tense gleam, but there was something else in them. There was a glowing need that had nothing to do with their bodies.

"What were you going to say?"

"Cassie..." His voice was a dark driving demand in her ear. He gently rolled her onto her back, and gathered her against his chest. As she listened to the fast pace of his heart, her thighs ached and began to tingle.

"Drakon, what's wrong?"

He cleared his throat. "Cassie, will you marry me?"

She lifted her chin, and stared into his deep blue eyes. "Yes..."

Grinning ear to ear, he said, "You've made me the happiest man alive, and I promise to do this properly with your father's permission... and a ring."

She smiled. "I love you, Drakon."

"I love you, my beloved."

When the alarm clock buzzed, he reached over and slapped it into silence.

She yawned. "I guess we should get up."

As she started to get out of bed, he quickly pulled her back down and slipped his hand between her legs.

"Drakon—"

Leaning closer, he pressed his lips against hers, and glided his fingers lower. "Let me please you again, Cassie."

She felt the same warm tingling pressure build up, and then burst free in an inferno of heated sensations. With loving attention, he helped her ride out the climax as she moaned in elated bliss.

Nothing else could give him this much satisfaction than to watch her during this moment. If he died tomorrow, he knew he would die a completed man.

* * * *

Sebastian's long, black hair fell forward, shielding his face as he looked down at Eve. "Have you learned your lesson yet?"

Trembling in fear, her eyes shifted to his. "Yes," she said in a hoarse voice, holding up her wrist. "Will you please free me?"

He narrowed his callous stare, and stood in silence.

Rattling the chain, she pleaded, "I beg you, Sebastian. Release me of this confinement."

With a twisted grin, he shook his head. "You cannot be trusted, Eve." His tone was hard-bitten. "You'll stay confined to this room, and freed only when I need you."

She started to struggle, and the harder she fought, the more satisfaction overtook his face.

"Where have you taken me?"

He smiled a wicked grin. "My trusted council has seen that I have a proper estate, which barely suits my acquired tastes. Something I could never rely on you to do."

"Please, Sebastian. Don't leave me in here."

"Don't worry. I'll make sure you're fed." He faked a smile. "I'll need you strong enough to keep me thriving. And you'll get the blood of a pure Breedline. But if you resist the blood again, I will see that you're beaten into submission."

"You're not the real Sebastian, are you?" Her voice trembled. "He would never treat me this way. My beloved worshiped me."

His breath stopped, as if she'd choked him with her very hand. Formed into fists, his hands shook with anger. Kneeling down, he stared at her with eyes of rage and slapped her so hard it hurt his own palm. As she spat out blood, she wondered if one of her teeth wasn't missing.

While his eyes bored into hers, she thought for sure he was going to kill her, and a sudden calmness came over her. At least the suffering would be over with. Death would be glorious at this moment.

Sebastian shook his head as if he knew her thoughts. "No, you will not get the satisfaction of death."

Turning her head, she cursed under her breath. "I hate you."

"Look at me!" When she refused, he tried to force her face around. "You will learn to worship me."

Jerking free, she wiped her mouth. Noticing the blood on her hand, she felt weak and defenseless. When he left, and locked her in alone, she found a corner in the room. Sitting with her back against the cold, damp wall, she curled her knees against her chest and wrapped her arms around herself. As she rocked herself back and forth, she prayed for either freedom, or death.

Chapter Fifteen

After Cassie came down from her wonderful climax, Drakon glanced down her body. Moving lower, he was enchanted by the sight of her. "Christ, Cassie."

Her knees snapped together. "What's wrong?"

"Not a thing." He pressed his lips to the top of her thigh and stroked her legs, trying to part them gently. "I've never seen anything so beautiful."

Moving toward her mouth, he inhaled through his nostrils. "Your scent drives me wild." He kissed her forehead, and the tip of her nose. Then he pressed a hard, passionate kiss to her lips.

"Mmmm," he murmured. "I'm so lucky."

She shrugged her shoulders. "Why?"

"Because..." He breathed in the scent of her hair, and blew gently into her ear. "You complete me."

She laughed a little as his breath tickled her ear.

"You captivate me, you know that?" He kissed her again. "You really do."

Hearing his soothing words, she rolled on top of him and leisurely peppered kisses that lingered a little longer, and went a little lower each time. His eyes rolled back as he moaned.

Glancing down his body, she saw he was aroused. Placing her palm on his stomach, she drifted lower.

He quickly reached for her hand. "Cassie—"

"I want to touch you there."

Shifting his hips, he said, "Do you know what will happen if you do?"

"Yes. Teach me." She begged him with her eyes.

"Are you sure?"

"Yes. Please, show me."

His eyes shut for a moment, and his hard sculpted chest expanded. Lifting his lids, he slowly eased his hand down his chest and to his tight stomach. Moving one of his legs out to the side, he captured himself in his palm. With a slow, smooth movement, he stroked his arousal.

With a quick glance, he saw her smooth her tongue over her lips. "Cassie," he moaned. "I could get lost just looking into your eyes."

She moved his hand away. "Please, let me try."

When she took hold of him, his head tilted back with a moan. She was hesitant at first, but she followed his example, running her grip up and down, amazed at how his satin skin slid over the hard core of him.

When he groaned, she stopped. "Am I doing it right?"

"Yes," he hissed. "More."

As she moved into a faster rhythm, his mouth fell open, moaning in ecstasy. His chest rose higher with each breath, creating a glisten of sweat that covered his body.

"Cassie," he gasped. With a curse, he knotted the sheets up in fists until his grip was tight. She felt his body jerk and shudder. A second later, something warm and thick came out of him in pulses, covering her hand.

When his eyes finally opened, they were hazy with a satiated gaze. "Thank you, Cassie."

She smiled and kissed him. "Was that okay?"

"Yes... it was wonderful."

After falling back asleep from all their extra morning exertion, Cassie awoke an hour later. Feeling elated, she checked the red glow of the alarm clock. Looking over her shoulder, she saw Drakon lying on his back with his hand on his muscular chest. His face displayed a peaceful expression as he slept.

She felt a chill on her bare skin as she slipped from under the sheets. Moving quietly, she gathered her clothes and felt something wet on her thigh. Glancing down, she saw blood.

"Cassie," he whispered. "Come here, sweetheart."

Startled, she nearly dropped her clothes. "I—ah," she stammered, trying to hide the blood. "I didn't mean to wake you."

When he held out his hand, she went to him. He snaked his arm behind her leg, and pulled her onto the bed as her weight rested on one knee. Looking at her inner thigh, he wiped away the remnants of her virginity with one gentle stroke.

Noticing the stain on the sheets, she shook her head. "I'm sorry I ruined the sheets."

"Don't worry about it, sweetheart. I can buy new ones."

Dropping her head, she felt as if she'd made a mess of everything. She wondered if her inexperience would drive a wedge between them.

He grasped her hand, and pressed a kiss over her soft skin. "It's okay, Cassie."

She nodded, and smiled. "I'm going to get something to eat. Would you like anything?"

"I'm going to hop in the shower first. I'll meet you down in the kitchen later."

Before she left, she looked over her shoulder and watched him. The image of him naked was going to be on her mind all day. His muscular back, tight hips, and those long, strong legs of his made her want to join him in the shower. But before she attempted to make love with him again, she wanted to learn more without him having to teach her everything. She decided to visit Tessa before she went to the kitchen for breakfast.

* * * *

Just as Cassie was about to knock on Tessa's door, it swung open.

"Hi, Cassie," Tessa said surprised. "I was going downstairs for breakfast. Would you like to join me?"

"I... I think I might need someone to talk to."

Tessa motioned her inside. "Of course, come in."

Cassie opened her mouth to speak, but she couldn't find the right words.

"It's just you and me in this room," Tessa said. "You can talk to me, Cassie."

"Okay," she sighed. "I can't believe I have to ask about this. Being a nurse practitioner, I should know all about the human anatomy."

"Oh?" After a long pause, Tessa added, "And?"

"I-I was a virgin until last night." Cassie stumbled with her words. "And it—"

"Hurt?" Tessa interjected. "It hurt my first time too."

Cassie shrugged. "Really?"

"Yes." Tessa raised her brows. "It was very painful, and I wasn't sure what to do."

"You didn't know what to do your first time, either?"

When Tessa nodded, Cassie was relieved. "It wasn't all painful. I mean, Drakon was gentle and he made me feel... amazing. He makes me... he's just so... the way he touches me, I get... Oh, sorry. I can't believe I'm telling you this."

Tessa chuckled. "That's all right. I know what you mean."

Cassie smiled, and went back to talking. "I was just so overwhelmed, and I'm worried there's something wrong with me."

"There's nothing wrong with you, Cassie." She tried to reassure her. "Oh, did you turn? I mean, did you turn into your Breedline wolf?"

"No... we didn't finish. He stopped when he knew I was in pain."

Tessa reached for her hand. "Don't worry. You'll know when the time is right."

"Did it hurt when you first turned?"

"No." Tessa shook her head. "I actually didn't feel anything. It happened so fast."

"How did you get through it with Jace when you—" Cassie paused and shrugged. "—you know?"

"My first time wasn't with him."

"Oh." Cassie blushed. "I didn't mean—"

"Don't worry about it." Tessa patted her hand. "Remember, I'm ten years older than him. I actually didn't care for sex until I met Jace. Being in love with the person you're with makes a big difference." Tessa grinned. "Anyway, sex is an invasion for the woman. It takes a little getting used to. Don't worry. I'm sure Drakon will be patient with you."

"He asked me to marry him."

Tessa's eyes widened with surprise. "What did you say?"

"I said yes."

"That's wonderful, Cassie! Congratulations!"

"Do you think you'll marry my brother?"

"I hope so." Tessa's tone enlivened more. "We've been talking about it."

Cassie stared into Tessa's emerald eyes and smiled. She realized that in her whole life, no one had ever made her feel comfortable enough to talk so openly with.

"Thank you, Tessa. I can see why my brother loves you so much."

Tessa leaned in and hugged her. "You're like my family now. I'm always here when you need someone to talk to."

"I feel much better after talking to you."

"Come on." Tessa stood, and held out her hand. "Let's go eat breakfast with our men."

❧ *Chapter Sixteen*

$\mathbf{B}$efore Helen left the exam room, she stood up stiffly, stretched her arms over her head, and arched until her back popped. Moving toward the door, she reached out to open it at the same time someone pushed it from the outside. When it opened, Alexander stood in the doorway.

Startled, she jumped.

"I'm sorry, Ms. Carrington," he said with concern. "I didn't mean to startle you."

With her hand on her chest, she let out a sigh. "That's okay, and you can call me Helen."

"Okay... Helen."

"It's odd that you're here," she remarked. "I was just on my way to find you."

"Oh?"

"Um, y-yes," she stammered. "Tim asked me to do a routine physical for everyone in the Covenant. So, when do you have free time?"

"I'm not busy now."

"Okay, good." She stepped back, and motioned him inside. "Please, come in."

When he walked past her, his silky blond hair breezed back. She breathed in deep, and caught an unusual scent coming from him. It was like the smell of the woods after a thunderstorm. Sex was the first thing that came to her mind. *God*, she thought. *If only she could bottle this up.*

Focusing back, she walked over to the file cabinet. As she nervously opened the drawer, she fumbled with a new chart.

Preparing his file, Alexander stared at her from across the room. Her looks were not so much beautiful as mesmerizing. Her face was square, her features almost masculine without pouty lips, and no thick lashes. And there were no big breasts pushing against the white physician's coat she had on, no curves in her hips as far as he could see. But he wanted her like she was the last woman on earth. Meeting her yesterday for the first time, he'd felt the Breedline bond when their hands touched. And from her reaction, he knew she'd felt it too.

"This will just be a routine check-up," she explained as she wrote something down in his file. When she looked up, her glasses slid down her nose. Pushing them back up, she asked, "Are you taking any medications?"

With his hands over his thighs, he shook his head.

In the silence she tried her best to run a clinical eye over him. "I'm going to check your eyes," she told him with a medical instrument in her hand. When she leaned closer, she held it to his eyes. "You'll see a bright light, but try to keep from blinking."

Alexander's eyes slid down and roamed over her body. When she shined a small light in front of his face, his icy blue eyes quickly lifted back up.

Staring into the instrument, she studied his irises and let out a disappointed sigh.

"Is anything wrong?" He asked.

"No," her voice sounded dispirited. "Everything is normal."

He frowned. "That's a good thing, right?"

"Oh, yes," she quickly replied, changing her discouraged tone. "Would it be all right if I take a blood sample?"

"Yes."

Snapping on a pair of latex gloves, she opened up a new syringe and wiped his arm with an alcohol pad. "You'll feel a little sting."

After collecting a few vials of blood, she placed a Band-Aid over his skin. "There, all done."

In the brief silence, he stared into her eyes. "Thank you, Helen."

Meeting his brilliant stare, she knew for sure he was her bonded mate. "You're welcome," she finally said. "I'll let you know when your blood results come in."

Slowly, he placed his hand over hers. "What exactly are you checking my blood for?"

Looking down at his hand, it had been a long time since she'd felt a man's touch. Her skin began to tingle when the sensation traveled up her arm and over to her chest.

"Uh... just routine tests," she mumbled, glancing up. "I'll check your glucose range, and cholesterol levels."

"Helen, will you give me the pleasure of joining me for dinner tomorrow night?"

Surprised, her eyes widened. "Yes, I would love to."

His eyebrows popped. "Wonderful. Where shall I pick you up?"

"I can just meet you here. How about six o'clock?"

Alexander blinked. *I'm in love*, he thought. "Six o'clock sounds perfect."

* * * *

Jace couldn't stop thinking of the results from the blood tests Helen gave him and Jem. *Christ*, he thought. *After he reached thirty, he would actually stop aging.* As he glanced at Tessa, his mind reeled at the evolutionary possibilities, but he also considered more practical matters. He wondered how she would react when he told her the news.

"Come sit down, baby." He patted the side of the mattress next to him. "There's something I've got to tell you."

With a concerned expression, Tessa sat down next to him.

He cleared his throat. "My test results came back."

She shrugged. "And?"

"She tested Jem too."

"Why did she need a blood sample from Jem?"

"Right after Helen finished examining me, we all heard screams coming from the recreation room. When Tim and I rushed in there, Mia was screaming. Jem's body was levitated off the floor, and he was glowing like a huge disco ball."

She gasped. "Was he all right?"

"Yeah, he's fine." He brushed it off like it was nothing. "It went away in a few hours."

"So what did Helen find out?"

"Let me try to explain." He took a deep breath. "Helen told us about a medical report she found a couple of years ago. The files were about a human patient studied by a German physician dated back in the seventies. Evidently, his patient had some form of cellular regeneration."

"What does that have to do with you?"

"There's more," he sighed. "The patient experienced unexplainable sparks of light in his irises, and levitation abilities. The physician also discovered his patient would stop aging when he reached thirty."

"What does all this mean?"

"Tessa—" He hesitated for a moment. "We carry the same gene."

She shook her head. "What? Are you saying you will stop aging when you turn thirty?"

He slid his arm around her. "Helen is doing some research using our blood, and she believes she can find a cure to stop the aging process in our species."

"Are you serious?"

He nodded. "Yes."

With his arm wrapped around her, she leaned her head on his shoulder. The rational side of her rejected the thought out of hand, but at her core she was logic driven. With a shake of the head, she looked up at him. "But what if she doesn't find a cure? I'm already ten years older than you as it is. I will continue to age, while you stay young forever. What will happen then?"

His face softened at her obvious concern. "Baby, let's not worry about it." He kissed her forehead. "Let's focus on right now."

She forced a smile. "Okay."

In an awkward moment, words hovered in the air between them, things that they kept to themselves.

❧ Chapter Seventeen

Before Tim headed upstairs to check on Angel and the baby, he put all his problems in the back of his mind. The last thing he wanted was to appear stressed.

He'd almost made it to the top of the staircase when he heard banging at the front door. Turning around, he cursed under his breath. Hurrying back down, the banging grew louder.

"Hold on!" His voice carried. "I'm coming!"

When he opened the door, he saw Dimitri Saintclare standing outside with a grim expression on his face. It had been two years since he'd last seen him. His father, Amaud Saintclare, brought him to the Covenant before his eighteenth birthday for a safe environment while he experienced his first change into his Breedline wolf.

Noticing his desperation, Tim asked, "What's wrong, Dimitri?"

Without saying a word, he rushed inside and broke down into tears. "It's my sister, Kara," his voice trembled. "She's missing."

Tim gestured him to a nearby chair. "Sit down, and tell me what happened."

Held in the highest esteem, the Saintclares were admired and well-respected within the Breedline community. Ten years ago, Amaud built a clinic for disabled children in honor of his late wife. His daughter, Kara, was like a fine jewel to the family. In her spare time, she always volunteered at the clinic. After graduation, she was planning to join a Catholic monastery, vowing to a religious life. Having always kept a close eye on his sister, Dimitri knew she didn't just disappear out of their home. Someone must have taken Kara against her will.

"When she didn't come down for breakfast this morning, I went up to her room and she was gone. No one has heard from her since, and her phone is shut off." He dropped his head. "It's not like her to leave without telling someone, and she never turns her phone off."

"Does your father know?"

Lifting his head, Dimitri nodded. "He's so distressed, he had me come. Please, tell me you'll help us."

Placing his palm on Dimitri's shoulder, he said, "Of course. We'll do our best to find her."

With a sigh of relief, he muttered, "Thank you, Tim."

"Call your father and tell him I'm on my way. I'm going to bring someone with me. His name is Drakon Hexus. He's a trusted friend."

At the same time Dimitri called his father, Tim got ahold of Drakon. After explaining the situation, they headed over to the Saintclares' estate.

When they were escorted into the Saintclares' formal study, Amaud rose from his chair and steadied his weight on a cane. With a relieved expression, he extended his hand. "Thank you for coming, Tim."

Tim shook his hand, and introduced Drakon. "This is my good friend, Drakon Hexus. He's agreed to help me search for your daughter."

Amaud eyes widened as he looked at Drakon's massive stature. With his hand trembling, he reached out to Drakon. "Thank you, Mr. Hexus. I don't know what I'll do if I don't find my little girl."

With a compassionate tone, Drakon said, "I promise, we'll do everything we can to find her. Can you give us a list of Kara's friends and their contact numbers? We'll also need all the places she normally goes to."

"Of course," Amaud's voice cracked. "Dimitri will get that information for you. Please, have a seat." He pointed to the chairs across from his. "Would either of you care for a drink?"

Sitting down, Tim shook his head. "No, thank you."

"I'm fine, thanks." Drakon nodded, sitting up straight. "Mr. Saintclaire, can you tell us about your daughter, or anything that you can recall that was out of the ordinary the night before she was found missing?"

"Yes, yes, of course. My daughter... my beautiful Kara," he praised, reaching into his front pocket. Pulling out a handkerchief, he wiped his eyes. "She's the most caring person you will ever come across."

When Drakon checked his watch, he acknowledged the fact that a lot of time had passed since the girl went missing. "And that night, sir," Drakon said politely, "did anything happen out of the ordinary in this house?"

While Drakon waited for him to recollect the previous events, Amaud cleared his throat. "She awoke in the middle of the night and came downstairs. When I heard her get up, I checked to see if she was all right. She told me she was just getting something to drink. Afterward, I watched her go back upstairs. That was the last time I saw her." He wiped his eyes again. "Kara's bedroom is upstairs if you would like to take a look."

Drakon quickly got to his feet. "Yes, I think that's a good idea."

Using his cane, Amaudi slowly eased out of his chair. "Dimitri will escort you to her room. I will... wait here."

With a slight nod, Tim rose from his chair. "Of course."

Just as Tim turned to leave, Amaud reached forward and snagged his hand. "May I have a word with you?" He whispered. "Please, just between us?"

While Tim stayed behind, Dimitri led Drakon upstairs to Kara's room.

"Truly, my daughter is still of innocence... of purity," Amaud muttered, collapsing back into his chair. "She is untouched by—"

In the pause that stretched out, Tim knew what he was concerned with. If they didn't get her back in her virginal condition, she wouldn't be accepted in the Catholic monastery.

"I cannot say this in front of my son," Amaud continued. "But my daughter... if she has been defiled..." He paused as tears filled his bloodshot eyes.

"We'll do the best we can to get your daughter back." Tim leaned forward, placing his palm on Amaud's shoulder. "That's all I can say."

After Tim left Amaud, he hurried upstairs to Kara's room while Dimitri waited for him outside the door. "This is Kara's bedroom." Dimitri moved aside gesturing him through the doorway.

Tim helped Drakon scan the reinforced windows. There was steel everywhere, separating the panes of glass and fortifying the sturdy wood panels. To get in without someone on the inside helping wouldn't be easy.

Tim wandered around, looking at the silk drapes and the matching pink walls. The first thing he noticed was everything seemed to be in its place. Shelves against the back wall were stacked neatly with books. A dressing table had a hairbrush on it with various perfumes and nail polish. All of which were arranged in neat rows. Tim pulled open a drawer and found a small notepad. But when he looked through it, nothing was written down.

Drakon looked out the window into the back yard. Through the spindly arms of the leafless branches, another estate across the property was visible. He inspected all the windows, the door, all the handles, hinges, and locks. There had been no sign of a break-in, and nothing suggested any kind of a struggle, which meant she had either left on her own, or let whoever had taken her inside. He thought it highly unlikely the abductor would have dragged her out through the house. Kara would have woken everyone kicking and screaming. No, he thought. She went quietly.

"Nothing is disturbed, inside or out." Tim crossed his arms. "No scratches on the floors, or marks on the wall, which may mean..."

"She may have let them in, or known them," Drakon interjected.

Thinking to himself, Tim thought of all the possibilities. The question was, what caused Kara to leave the house in the middle of the night, leaving nothing out of place, and taking nothing with her? One answer came to mind: a male. Fathers didn't always know all of their daughters' lives, and what they did. Staring out the window, he traced the grounds and the trees... and then the estate next door.

Standing beside him, Drakon asked, "What do you suggest?"

Tim kept his eyes trained in the far distance. "We're going to make a visit to the neighbors."

Chapter Eighteen

After a quick shower, Helen threw on a black skirt and a teal silk blouse. In the full-length mirror on her dresser, she looked over her outfit. She wondered if she should wear her hair up in a bun like she always did, or let it down tonight. The thought froze her in place. She drew her hands through her long auburn hair, letting it slip through her fingers and fall to her shoulders. A long sigh escaped her lips as she looked at her reflection in the mirror. "No," she said out loud. She'd made her mind up as she gathered the lengths together. Twisting it into a knot, she clipped it up in a bun.

A few minutes later, she was out her front door and walking to her car. When the breeze blew through her thin silk blouse, she realized she'd forgotten to put on a jacket. Going back inside, she grabbed a thin linen jacket, losing her keys in the process.

Where did I put the car keys? she thought, searching all through the house, her purse, and her jacket. Letting out a deep breath, she reached into her purse and took out her cell phone. Before she made the call, she freed the clip from her hair and finger-combed it as best as she could. She'd changed her mind, and decided to wear her hair down.

When she finally made the call, Tim Ross answered, "Hello, this is Tim."

"Tim, this is Helen. I'm sorry to bother you, but could you please give a message to Alexander?"

"Uh, sure," he sounded puzzled.

"I was supposed to meet him at the Covenant, but I've seemed to have misplaced my car keys. Could you please let him know I will need a ride?"

"Y-yes, of course," he stumbled with his reply. "I can come pick you up if you would prefer."

"Oh, no," she said politely. "We're actually going out for dinner, and it would be easier if he just picked me up. He'll also need directions to my house, if you don't mind."

"Okay, I'll make sure he gets the message. Would you like me to give him your number?"

"Yes, thank you. I'd appreciate that."

"You're welcome, Helen. You can always call if you need anything."

"Oh, wait. I almost forgot," she said. "I have good news. As it turns out, my niece Celina happens to have the book you're looking for. She's interested in meeting with you."

"That's great," his voice sounded relieved. "Please, give her my cell number. I'd like to meet with her as soon as possible. And thank you, Helen."

When the call ended, she waited outside. The evening was so quiet, and this is why she loved living outside of the city. She had no neighbors close by, and the nearest house was at least two miles away.

About a half an hour later, a full-size Cadillac turned into her road, and accelerated with the sound of a purr. As the sleek black car pulled into her drive, she could barely see Alexander through the tinted windows.

She watched him step out of the car, and stroll toward her. He was in a sharp black suit with a black open-collared shirt underneath. His long hair was pulled back from his face, falling in thick, blond waves past his shoulders. He looked sexy, powerful, and sophisticated.

He smiled as he came up to her. "You wore your hair down. You look beautiful."

"Thank you." She felt her face blush. "You look great too."

He lifted his hand as if to touch her, but hesitated. He knew if their hands touched, he would instantly get aroused. "Are you ready to go?"

"Oh, yes," she eagerly replied. "I'm sorry you had to pick me up in such a short notice. Somehow I've misplaced my car keys."

"It's no problem. I preferred picking you up anyway."

Opening her door, he said, "I made reservations at Chez Panisse. I hope that's okay with you."

"That sounds wonderful. I've never been there before, but I've heard great reviews."

When she slid into the passenger seat, she glanced at the new interior to avoid staring at him. "This is a nice car," she praised. "Is it new?"

"Thank you." He turned facing her. "I just got it a couple of days ago."

When Alexander pulled into the restaurant's parking lot, he drove to the front entrance. As he stepped out, he handed the keys to the car attendant. Moving to the passenger side, he opened her door and held out his hand to her. Placing her palm in his, he watched her step out, feeling a sudden warmth rush through his body.

As they were escorted to their table, he pulled out a chair for Helen. Sitting down across from her, she quickly looked down and opened the menu. With his eyes steadied on her, he noticed her skin was smooth and flawless. Her thick, beautiful auburn waves fell past her shoulders. He liked the fact that she only wore a small amount of makeup. She wasn't anything like the women he usually was attracted to, but she held his attention like no other had before.

"The smoked duck breast is fabulous here," he suggested. "The rocket salad and house-made red sauerkraut that comes with it is delicious."

When she looked up at him, her hazel eyes took his breath away.

"That sounds like heaven." She smiled. "I think that's what I'll have."

As the waitress came over, she slowly put down a glass of water in front of Alexander. He could tell the woman's eyes were lingering on him. "Hi, I'm Missy," she said in a sultry voice. "Would you like to try one of our red wines?"

"Yes, I'll have the Vinos de Madrid. Helen, what would you like?"

"I'll have the same."

The waitress stepped closer to him. "Would you like to hear about our chef's choice tonight?"

"No, thank you," he replied. "We've already decided what we want."

Ignoring Helen's presence, the waitress kept her eyes on Alexander as she listened to his every word. "I'll be right back with your drinks." She smiled at him and left.

Clearing his throat, he asked, "What do you enjoy doing in your spare time?"

"Well... I spend most of all my time at the hospital, and when I'm not there, I do a lot of research in my free time."

"Oh," he said curiously. "What kind of research are you working on?"

Remembering Tim didn't want her mentioning anything about cellular research, she dismissed the topic. "Oh, it would just bore you to tears. Tell me what you do."

Alexander frowned as the waitress leaned in front of him with her ridiculous, oversized breasts and presented his glass of wine. The waitress looked a little awkward when she set Helen's glass down. "Can

I get you and your sister anything else?" As if family obligation was the only reason a man like him would be out with a woman like her.

"No, we're fine," he said annoyed. "And she's my date, not my sister."

"Uh, I'm sorry," she uttered in disappointment. "I'll be back shortly with your food."

Helen had to give him credit for being a gentleman. As they sat across the table from each other, he didn't seem to notice any other woman in the restaurant. And there were plenty of beautiful women here, especially Missy, the flirty waitress.

She lifted her glass and took a sip of her wine. "So, tell me what you do?"

"Well, since my life had been taken over by the demon almost since I was born, I—"

"I'm so sorry." She interrupted before he could finish. "I completely forgot about that. Please, forgive me."

"No, it's all right. Actually, I was thinking of supporting a good charity."

In surprise, her voice lit up. "Really?"

"Yes." He nodded. "I think I could help out a lot of others, especially since I've inherited my family's fortune."

Oh my, she thought. He wasn't just gorgeous, he was giving too. Talk about the total package. The sincerity in his voice made her want him even more.

When the waitress arrived with a heavy tray, she placed their plates down and lingered until Alexander thanked her pointedly.

Helen noticed he ate like a total gentleman, with refined manners.

Abruptly, he lifted his chin and stared at her. "You keep staring at me. Do I have something on my face?"

She shook her head embarrassed. "I'm sorry."

"I'm not." He leaned back in his chair. "I like your beautiful eyes on me."

Glancing down at her plate, her body immediately flushed as she wondered what else he was good at. God, she could just imagine the kind of lover he must be. That muscular body, those long strong legs, his soft lips...

His brow arched. "So... what are you looking at?"

Nervously grabbing her glass, she took another sip.

Fortunately, the waitress arrived to pick up the plates and broke the moment. "Was everything okay?"

As Alexander looked over, you could tell the woman was practically in heat. He nodded in her direction. "Fine, thank you. I'd like to order your famous dessert to share with my date." His eyes shifted toward Helen with a wink. By the time he ordered the bittersweet chocolate custard, and some coffee, Helen was relieved the conversation had been changed.

"Good choice." The waitress smiled and slipped something on the table next to Alexander. Looking down, he saw a napkin with a number and a name on it. Winking at him, Missy sauntered off.

Helen looked over at Alexander, and cracked up. When he saw she was laughing over the uncomfortable situation, he began to laugh too.

"This was wonderful, Helen. Thank you for having dinner with me. I would love to see you again."

She smiled, and blushed again. "I would like that."

Chapter Nineteen

Before they left the Saintclares' estate, Drakon suggested they ask the hired help if they saw anything unusual the night Kara went missing.

In an estate this size, there usually was a house and groundskeeper. They already knew Amaud had his own driver who also served as a personal butler. Hopefully if they noticed anything out of the ordinary, pity and compassion for Kara would keep them from withholding any information or secrets. Sometimes the back of the house knew things the front did not.

"Excellent idea." Tim raised a brow. "We'll talk with each one, privately."

Heading down the long staircase, they finally encountered a long hallway leading into the kitchen. As they stepped in, the housekeeper was sitting at the table drinking a cup of coffee. When she noticed them standing across the room, she put down her cup, and shot to her feet. "May I help you?"

"Sorry to bother you," Tim said, urging her with his hands to sit back down. "My name is Tim Ross, and this is Drakon Hexus. We were sent by Mr. Saintclare to investigate the disappearance of his daughter. May we ask you a couple of questions about that night?"

"O-of course," she stammered. "May I get you some coffee?"

Drakon refused as he smiled at her. He noticed she was pale and shaky, as if she were in trouble.

"Oh, no, thank you, ma'am," Tim said politely.

Drakon sat across from her. "May I ask your name?"

"Uh, yes," she said nervously. "My name is Korrine. Korrine Staples."

"And how long have you worked here?"

"I've been employed with the Saintclare family for two years. I was hired right after Mr. Saintclare's wife passed away."

Tim sat next to Drakon. "Did you know Kara well?"

"Not really," she replied. "She mostly kept to herself, but I know she was a joy to her father."

"What about her brother, Dimitri? Did they get along well?"

Tim watched her blink nervously. "They seemed to get along all right I suppose."

"And you were not aware of anything... that would lead to Kara suddenly leaving this house without notifying anyone?"

Korrine's left eyebrow twitched, followed by a long silence.

Tim leaned forward, and lowered his voice to a whisper. "If you're worried about losing your job if you say anything, you have our word that neither of us will reveal what you say."

Korrine cleared her throat. "There was one thing I did see," she said cautiously. "But—"

"I promise nothing you say will leave this room," Tim assured.

"There was a man," she whispered. "He was in her room late that night."

"Did you speak to him?"

"N-no." She quickly shook her head. "I was in the kitchen cleaning the oven late that night when I heard someone come in. It was Kara. She was just getting a glass of water. She said she had a headache. After she went back upstairs, I thought she might want something for the pain. As I went upstairs, I noticed a bright light coming from the inside of her room. When I peeked through the cracked door way, I saw a man with long black hair standing in her room. Then—"

"Go on, Ms. Staples," Drakon encouraged. "What happened next?"

"I'm sorry, but I don't remember." She began to sob. "All I can remember is his black eyes. They had the coldest look in them. And then I must have blacked out because I woke up later that night lying on the floor outside her bedroom door."

"Did you check her room when you woke up?"

"Y-yes." She nodded. "But Kara, and that man... was gone."

Tim frowned. "Why didn't you tell anyone what you saw?"

"I'm so sorry." She wiped her eyes. "I was afraid."

Tim looked at Drakon with a raised brow. "Do you think it could have been—?"

Before he could finish his sentence, the kitchen door swung open. Amaud's butler came into the room with a disapproving expression on his face.

"We were just talking with Ms. Staples about the night Kara disappeared," Tim explained. "It seems she doesn't have any information that will help us. Can we ask you some questions... Mr.—?"

The butler straightened his jacket. "My name is Herbert Stanley, thank you," he said in an English accent. "Yes, of course. I am at your service, gentlemen."

After Korrine quietly excused herself, Tim and Drakon asked Herbert a few questions. He told them he retired early that night, and made sure the house was secure and locked up properly. He stated that no one could have gotten in from the outside without setting off the security system. And it wasn't until the next morning that he was aware of Kara's disappearance.

"What about the groundskeeper?" Drakon asked. "Surely you have someone to maintain the estate's grounds on a regular basis."

"Yes." Herbert nodded. "Mr. Zackery Cribs. He's been employed with the Saintclares for fifteen years. We also have part-time hired help. It takes more than one person to maintain the Saintclares' grounds."

Drakon stood. "Would you take us to him on our way out? We'd like to ask him some questions."

"Of course, sir." He pointed to the back door. "Right this way."

Tim got to his feet. "Is Mr. Saintclare still available?"

"No, sir." Herbert shook his head. "He has retired for the day, and that's why I came to see you. He has bidden you farewell as he has taken suddenly ill. He wanted me to give you this." He handed Tim a folded piece of paper. "I believe this is the list of names and phone numbers you required."

"Yes, thank you." Tim reached out and took it.

"If you'll follow me, gentlemen, I will escort you to Mr. Cribs."

Outside, the air was thick with humidity. Indeed, it was summer as they trudged through the grounds. With purpose, Herbert walked around the back of the estate to the part of the gardens that were overlooked by Kara's bedroom.

When he stopped right under Kara's window, he didn't look up. He looked outward across the flower beds and the well-kept hedges. He pointed toward a small, dark-skinned man wearing a wide-brimmed hat.

"Mr. Cribs!" Herbert called out. "Excuse me, Mr. Cribs!"

The man was crouched on his knees pulling weeds. When he finally heard his name being called, he stopped what he was doing and stood. He waved at them in acknowledgement, and began to walk in their direction.

"Yes, sir," Mr. Cribs promptly stated. "What can I do for you?"

Herbert introduced him to Tim and Drakon, and politely excused himself.

Tim held out his hand. "We'd like to ask you some questions about the night Mr. Saintclare's daughter went missing."

Mr. Cribs shook Tim's hand, and nodded.

"What time did you retire that evening?"

"It was around eight o'clock. I was tending the garden late that night."

Tim crossed his arms over his chest. "Did you notice anything that night that was out of the ordinary?"

Without haste, he uttered, "This is none of my business. I pay no attention to the Saintclares' personal affairs."

"It is your business if it helps us find Mr. Saintclare's daughter," Drakon snapped back.

"This will get me fired! Mr. Saintclare will not believe me."

"Please," Tim said in a calm tone. "Mr. Cribs, if you know anything that can help us find Kara, you must tell us what you saw."

"All right." He let out a deep breath. "I was putting away my garden tools when I saw a bright light come from her window."

"Did you see anyone?"

"I saw a tall, dark figure." He pointed at Kara's window. "It looked like a man."

"What else did you see?" Drakon queried.

"Just another bright light, and then the figure disappeared."

"Are you sure?"

"Yes, I swear. That's all I saw."

Tim turned toward Drakon, and narrowed his stare. With a nod, they said the same thing at the same time. "Sebastian—"

"Thank you, Mr. Cribs." Tim extended his hand. "You have helped us out a great deal."

Shaking his hand, he pleaded, "Please, just find her. Ms. Saintclare was always kind to me. She always loved the garden. Please... bring her home."

Tim focused on the estate next door. "We'll do our best."

Getting behind the wheel, Drakon said, "Before we visit the estate next door, I think it's a good idea to bring Jem along just in case we get ourselves in a pinch."

Tim nodded. "That's a good idea. It could be unpredictable and potentially dangerous if indeed Sebastian is living there. We may need the portal as a fast escape plan."

Chapter Twenty

Turning her head toward the window, Eve immediately covered her face with her free hand to block the morning sun. She wondered what time it was, and how many hours she'd been locked up here.

With her eyes closed, she could barely breathe as exhaustion took over. Lying flat on her back with one hand chained to the wall, she'd been in this position since Sebastian last visited her.

The air around her was warm, and the room was musky. She wanted to die at this moment as her wrist burned from the steel cuff, and her back ached from the hard, damp floor.

Opening her eyes, she wondered if this was her new prison, trapped here forever. As she starved for blood, her throat ached from the ghastly dryness.

Gathering her will, she took a deep breath, and another... and finally forced her upper body off the floor. Her head swam wildly, the ceiling, the floor and the walls spinning, trading places, until she wasn't sure whether she was on the ceiling, or not.

The vertigo got worse as she shifted her legs off the floor. When she stood, her balance gave out. Falling toward the wall, she slammed into it and had to hold herself up by clinging to the chain bolted into the wall.

With all her strength, she shouted, "Sebastian!"

"Shhh—"

Scanning left, and right, Eve turned her head toward the door. "Who's there?"

There was a short stretch of silence, and then she heard, "Please be quiet."

She cried out, "Who's there? What do you want?"

Moving closer to her, Damien eased himself down on one knee. "It's me... Damien." He reached his arm out with his wrist close to her face. "Please, take it," he whispered. "Take what you need."

She looked at his wrist, and licked her dry lips. "Why do you offer this to me? Does Sebastian know you're here?"

"Yes," he replied. "He asked me to bring another girl for you, but I offered myself at my own will."

"W-why would you do that?"

He inhaled a deep breath as the darkness in him shifted, and he exhaled heavy. "Because... I don't want to see you suffer anymore."

"Then please, let me go," she sobbed.

"I will do what I can to help you, but it will take time."

"He's not really Sebastian, is he?"

He shook his head. "No, the demon took over Sebastian's body when he died."

"What happened to Alexander?"

"He's living in the Covenant, but he doesn't remember anything after the Angel of Mercy cast the demon out of his body."

"Why did you betray your Covenant in the first place?"

He frowned. "I don't like to live by their rules, and I detest humans. They're weak and worthless. The only thing they're good at is destroying one another."

Removing his coat, he spread it over the hard floor and motioned her on it. "Come sit here."

When she cautiously eased down, he sat down beside her and reached out to her. "You're starving, aren't you?"

"Yes," her voice trembled, obviously uncomfortable with him. Damien was very attractive and looked as if he was in his twenties, close to her age. His eyes were dark brown, matching his shoulder-length hair that curled around his collar.

"Lie on me." He patted his thigh. "Lay your head on my lap."

She moved on him slowly, crawling into his lap, as her mouth parted and her fangs unsheathed.

For a split second the evil in him growled, and he suddenly called on his rational side to chain his Breedline instincts, halting the sexual need to dominate her.

Abruptly, her eyes fixated on his wrist and dilated.

Her hunger was so strong, he could clearly sense it. "Go ahead, Eve. Take it."

With a hiss, she bit him. He moaned as soon as the sweet pain struck his body. In the glow from the window, her long black hair was like a shawl of silk.

Pressing his body against hers, he shut his eyes. It had been so long since he'd held anyone, and though he couldn't afford to let in much emotion, he found Eve breathtaking.

When she had enough, she pulled back and licked her lips. "Thank you, Damien."

Reaching out, he moved his hand over hers. When he lifted her hand to his lips, he pressed a soft kiss over her skin. "I swear, I'll be back for you," he said with promising eyes.

* * * *

As Sebastian sat down in front of a computer screen, the persistent buzzing noise echoed through the room. Looking at the security camera, he saw images of three men standing outside the entrance. Enhancing the zoom until he saw their faces clearly, he froze when he realized who they were. Silently cursing, he pulled out his cell phone and waited impatiently for Damien to answer.

The feeding with Eve had put Damien into a peaceful state of mind. First time he'd closed his eyes and rested in forever. Before he completely slipped into sleep, he felt his cell phone go off. Reaching into his front pocket, he glanced at the caller ID and saw it was Sebastian.

He answered, "Yes, Master."

Sebastian cursed, "Get your ass downstairs! The Breedline head council is at our front door, and he's brought company."

"I'll be right down."

Before ending the call, he said, "Make sure you get rid of them!"

Sebastian wasn't surprised they'd found the estate. Kara's disappearance had been news within the Breedline species, and her family must have hired the Covenant to find her. Even though this estate was half a mile away, he should have known they would come to the house next door. He wasn't thinking clearly when he kidnapped that girl for Eve. The damn housekeeper must have remembered seeing him. Given the time, he would have completely scrubbed her memory.

Right now the estate was sealed up tight with security, so there was no way they could get in without being seen. The previous owner was a paranoid war veteran that suffered from a severe case of schizophrenia. The shutters covering the windows and doors were bullet- and fireproof. And the house was made of stone walls that were three feet thick. To top it off, Taliah had placed a temporary binding spell on the estate, keeping Jem from entering through the portal.

❧ *Chapter Twenty-One*

Early that morning, Helen arrived at the Breedline Covenant with boxes of files loaded in the back seat of her car. She was going to do most of her research in the room the Covenant provided her, so she needed to relocate all her files.

With her arms full, she wobbled to the front entrance when she heard a familiar voice. "Let me give you a hand."

When she looked around the two boxes stacked in her arms, she saw Alexander reach out and grab one.

"Oh, thank you," she said relieved. Even though she kept herself in shape running three miles a day, her age was beginning to catch up with her. She just turned forty-two a couple of months ago and she wasn't as strong as she used to be.

"What are all these?" His frown made him look like true warrior material, taking him far away from the sexy male pinup stuff.

Her brain flickered trying to come up with an answer as she reached out for the door. "Just some files I'll be keeping here."

"Here, let me get that for you." He quickly moved in front of her and opened the door.

"Thank you." She looked away from his perfect face and stepped inside.

"Are all these files going to your exam room?"

"Yes." She made a beeline down the hall, and glanced over her shoulder. He was right behind her, even though she'd left him standing in the doorway. With her heart pounding like she'd just finished running a race, she set the box down and wheeled around.

After he set down the box he was carrying, he hurried back to her car.

"Alexander, I can get those," her voice carried as she tried to catch up with him.

When she caught up to him, he said, "Please, let me help you."

As she stepped back, he came forward until she bumped against the car. Looking up, she stared into his blue eyes. Shying away, she reached for the car door as his hand shot out and clamped on the seam between the window and the roof.

"Helen?" He whispered close to her ear.

Startled, she jumped feeling his raw seduction. Her inner thighs tingled as she imagined his body pressed up against hers. With a treachery shift, her mind changed into something needy instead of being bottled up tight.

"I need to get these boxes in—"

"Not yet." His breath caught in her ear sending shivers down her body.

She heard him take a deep breath as if he were inhaling her scent. Her body loosened with a flood of heat that built up between her legs. God, she wanted this man.

"Helen."

"Yes?" She lingered the word in a whisper. She had to open her mouth to get enough air into her lungs.

His hands fell onto her shoulders and pulled her body against his. "May I kiss you, Helen?" He slid his hand up her throat, and on the side of her face. "Just *once?*"

Feeling weightless in his arms, she swayed from side to side. Tilting her head back, she said, "Yes."

His lips hovered over hers as his hands trembled. It had been so long since she'd been kissed, and never by a man like him.

As he pressed his lips against hers, the contact was soft, gentle, and unexpected given his size. Alexander couldn't exactly explain the sensation inside his skin. It felt like some kind of electric tingle all through his muscles. And it had kicked off hard the moment his mouth had touched hers.

Just as his lips lifted from hers, a buzzing noise came from her jacket. Reaching in her pocket, she glanced at it. "I better get this." She smiled nervously. "It's my niece."

He stepped back to give her space. "Of course."

"Hello... Celina?"

"Hi, Aunt Helen. Did you get in contact with the head council?"

"Yes. I just talked to Tim yesterday. He was supposed to call you."

"Well, I'm on my way right now. I hope that's okay?"

"Yes, of course, honey. Tim's not here right now, but I'm sure he'll be back later," Helen told her. "As a matter of fact, I just got here myself. I stopped by to drop off some of my files. By the way, I heard your sister is in town. You don't think she's going to start problems again, do you?"

There was a stretch of silence. "Yeah, I heard that too." Celina gritted her teeth. "Taliah always creates trouble wherever she goes." She meant to stop there, but suddenly the words were coming out and she couldn't shut up. "That's one of the reasons why I'm here to help the Covenant. Using our Breedline bond, I read Taliah's thoughts. She has been summoned by an ancient demon, and I think it's the same one in the book they're looking for."

"Oh my G—"

"Yeah, ah..." Celina paused. "Look, Aunt Helen, I gotta go. I'll see you later."

"No, wait, Celina—"

Celina pulled the car over to the side of the road, and turned off her phone. Staring out the window, she thought of Taliah. Resting her head on the steering wheel, she hated the thought of how dangerous her own twin sister was. She knew Taliah was going to be bad news for the Breedline.

Helen stuffed her phone back inside her jacket and sighed. "This is terrible news." She shook her head.

"Is something wrong, Helen?"

She staggered on her feet. "I need to sit down."

Quickly grabbing her waist, Alexander held her steady and helped her inside. When she plopped down in a nearby chair, he sat in the one beside her. "What's wrong, Helen?"

"It's my niece, Celina. Her twin sister's in town and—"

He shrugged his shoulders. "That's good news, right?"

"No, that's terrible news. Both my nieces are Wiccas, but one is good and the other is—"

"I take it she doesn't practice white magic?"

Helen shook her head. "No, she's evil. It's as if one came from heaven, and the other was spawned from Satan himself. Taliah killed her own parents when she was just a child."

"I'm so sorry, Helen. That's awful. Do you think she means to do harm to the Covenant?"

Helen nodded. "Celina said her sister was summoned by a demon. She thinks it could be the same one that possessed you."

"What?"

She reached out, and grasped his hand. "I'm sorry, Alexander. Celina is heading this way with an ancient book on this particular demon. It could have information on how to destroy it."

He gently squeezed her hand. "I want to help."

"Thank you, Alexander. We're going to need all the help we can get."

Chapter Twenty-Two

Enraged, Sebastian stalked around the room listening to the irritating sound coming from the front door. He had lost it at one point, screaming at Damien on the phone as he let loose all kinds of obscenities. Without a choice, Damien had taken the whipping like a pussy, getting quiet and cowering down. Damien's submission drove Sebastian insane. He'd always hated it when his men didn't fight back.

Hearing Damien scramble down the stairs, Sebastian cursed under his breath as he kept a close eye on the surveillance cameras. Damien was a total failure as a second in command. He hadn't been able to do anything right. It was Samuel that found this place, when it should have been Damien. Sebastian didn't give a shit about the dead girl, but what he'd worried about was the body. He'd left that task up to Damien. The last thing he needed was the Breedline Covenant getting involved. So he had to get his hands dirty, making sure they got rid of the frickin' corpse so no one would find it.

He knew Damien was better off with a silver bullet to the head, but he was short-handed as it was. He'd thought Damien was intelligent at first, but in reality the little bastard was weak, and he was sick of it. For the meantime he would keep him around until Taliah created his new death army. She was a young Wicca with the ability of necromancy. Although she was born a Breedline, she hated her own kind. With her malevolent powers, he could finally vanquish all humans and half-breeds, and any Breedline that stood in their way.

As Damien rushed down the stairs, he was prepared for another hell of a tongue-lashing after he got rid of the nosey Breedline. His master had been ripping pissed about the three Breedline standing at their front door, as if it were his fault. And the thing was, Sebastian would go on and on with his punishment until he was bored.

Jem waited outside as thoughts of fresh anger stirred in him. Desperate to get his hands around Sebastian's throat, he would fight to his death to protect his species. Losing his patience, he pounded on the door the second time.

With the sound of an eerie creak, the door finally opened.

"Damien Spence?" Tim was shocked to see him. "What are you doing here?"

Calmly, Damien pushed his hair back and slid one hand in his front pocket. His expensive suit fell open, revealing his broad chest. "Greetings." He grinned with a raised brow. "Please, do come in." He stepped aside, and motioned them in.

The moment they walked in, Jem knew Damien was hiding something. Instinct had Drakon easing one hand behind his back, close to the weapon he always carried on his belt.

Tim narrowed his stare. "Do you live here?"

"Oh, no." He chuckled. "I'm just visiting. Samuel Mercier owns this place." His lips lifted into a sly grin. "In fact, he just purchased it not too long ago."

What a lie that was, Tim thought as he stared at him. "Why would Samuel purchase a house here? He has a house in France."

Damien stopped smiling. "I guess he's decided to move." His mouth pulled up at the corners again, but his eyes held a cold stare.

Jem stayed silent, wondering where in the hell this was going.

Tim appeared surprised. "I didn't know you two knew each other well."

"Oh, yes." He rubbed the whiskers on his chin with his long fingers. "We're distant cousins. He asked me to stay and look after the place while he's gone."

Drakon stepped closer. The French chandelier's light over him picked out his high cheekbones, his hard jaw, and his heavy shoulders. His Mohawk had been trimmed, the black stripe no more than two inches off his skull. "We need to ask you some questions about the Saintclares' estate that's about a half a mile from here."

Damien cocked a brow. "Of course. Is there any particular reason why?"

"Yeah." Drakon nodded. "Amaud Saintclare's daughter is missing."

"Missing?" A flicker of unease tightened in Damien's chest.

"You haven't heard?" Tim asked while he watched for his reaction.

"No, I haven't. This is terrible news." His voice sounded fake. "When did this happen?"

"Two days ago. Her name is Kara. Did you know her?"

From out of nowhere, Damien felt an overwhelming wave of guilt, like someone had poured feelings into him. "Sorry to hear that. No, I didn't know her."

Jem took a step forward with his hands clenched tight. "Could we take a look around the house?"

Damien's instincts fired up. "I-I wouldn't feel comfortable giving you permission. I'm sure Samuel wouldn't mind, but I'd rather wait until he returns."

Jem smirked. "How 'bout you call him."

Damien rubbed his eyes, thinking of something to say. "Sure, I'll go give him a call."

Before he turned around to leave, a hand grabbed onto his arm. Jem's face was hard as stone, and so was his grip. "Make the call here."

"Let go of me." Damien gritted, trying to pull his arm free. "If you don't mind, my phone is upstairs."

Tim nodded in Jem's direction, motioning him to let Damien go. The hard grip dissolved as Jem nodded back.

Damien walked over to the curving staircase and hurried up to his room. The sheets on the bed were thrown back, all a mess as he searched for his phone. With a feeling of dread, he dialed Samuel's number. When he answered, Damien explained the sticky situation he was in. He didn't want the Breedline to search the house and find Eve locked up. She might very well sing like a canary. Samuel told Damien he would call Tim's cell, and make up an excuse that would give him some time to hide Eve. Just as Samuel ended the call with Damien, Tim's phone went off.

Reaching into his jacket, Tim pulled out his phone noticing the unfamiliar number. "Hello, this is Tim."

As Samuel rambled on the phone about absolutely nothing of importance, Tim tried to ask him about the estate.

"Wait a minute?" Jem looked at the top of the staircase. "Where's Damien?"

"Chances are, he's hiding something upstairs," Drakon said. "Why else would he keep us from going through the house?"

When Tim finally ended the call, they faced the long staircase. Without saying a word, all three of them took off at a silent jog, moving quietly up each step.

Damien tore out of his room and hurried to where Sebastian kept Eve locked up. He had no choice but to get her out before they found her. Frantically, he dug into his pocket for a key to unlock her door. When he managed to get it unlocked, he swung the door open.

"Eve," he whispered. "I'm going to get you out of here."

Over in the dark shadows, he heard the sound of chains rattling. "Damien, is that you?"

"Yes, it's me." He rushed over to her and freed the cuff from her wrist. "Let's get you out of here." Grasping ahold of her hand, he guided her toward the door. As Damien swung it open, Sebastian stood in the doorway with a snarl on his face.

"Where the hell do you think you're going?"

Eve panicked, and fell to her knees. "No!"

Sebastian grabbed her arm, and jerked her to her feet. With his other hand, he reached out with his palm and summoned the portal. Just as fast as it appeared, they disappeared, leaving Damien standing in the room alone.

At the top of the staircase, Drakon put his palm on his weapon when they heard a woman scream.

Chapter Twenty-Three

After parking her Volkswagen Beetle, Celina looked out the window at the majestic Breedline estate. It reminded her of a castle in the fairy tales her mother used to read to her as a child. Getting out of her car, she was amazed by the beautiful architecture. Standing outside an enormous set of double doors, she reached for the doorbell. As she pressed it, the chime amplified from the inside. When the door opened, she was immediately welcomed by Tessa, the Breedline's new queen.

"You must be Celina... Helen's niece."

Celina bowed her head. "Yes, ma'am. It's a pleasure to meet you."

Tessa smiled, and motioned her inside. "You can call me Tessa, and it's a pleasure to meet you too."

As Tessa escorted her inside the foyer, Helen greeted her with extended arms. "I'm so happy to see you, honey."

Celina wore blue jeans and a black parka, her beautiful red hair pulled into a ponytail. Her intelligence was way beyond her years, at the age of twenty-three. Recently graduated from college, she was excited to start her new job here in Berkeley as an editor at a prominent publishing house.

Helen expected her to race over with an excited embrace, but she just stared at her with an exhausted expression. Celina was beautiful, but stress showed on her face, or maybe she was just so numb after all she'd been through. She had very little reactions left to show after her twin sister had gotten away with murder as a child. After the death of her parents, Celina had never been the same. Now, Taliah was back... summoned by the Chiang-shih demon.

Finally, Celina smiled and hugged her back. "It's good to see you, Aunt Helen." She dropped her arms, but didn't move away, just stayed close. Then she reached out and hugged her again.

Pulling from their embrace, Celina reached into her handbag. When she brought her hand out, she was holding onto an old, leather-bound book. "I brought the book Tim asked for."

"Oh, thank you," Tessa's voice sounded relieved as Celina handed it to her. "I appreciate you helping us out."

"You're welcome, and I hope it's—"

Abruptly, their attention turned toward the doorway when Alexander walked in.

Helen blushed and clasped onto Celina's hand. "I'd like to introduce you to a friend of mine," she whispered.

Celina smiled at Helen, noticing how she looked at him, and how he looked at Helen.

"Alexander, this is my niece, Celina Baldolf."

Alexander extended his hand. "It's a pleasure to meet you, Celina." He was anxious to meet her. Actually, he was nervous. He'd never met a Wicca before.

Excitement lit up on her face when she took his hand. "I've heard all about you. You're the Alexander Crest, right?"

"Yes." He shook her hand.

"I would love to pick your brain," she boasted. "May I speak with you later?"

Alexander lowered his chin and stared at her from underneath his lids, wondering what she wanted to talk about. Most likely she wanted to ask him about the demon. Lifting his head back to level, he muttered, "Uh, sure."

Startled, Helen jumped when she heard her cell phone inside her jacket. Recognizing the ringtone, she sighed. "Oh, it's the hospital. Excuse me just a moment. I have to take this call."

A few minutes later, Helen rushed back in and grabbed her purse.

"Aunt Helen, is something wrong?"

"I'm sorry, dear, but I've got to go. There's an emergency at the hospital." She checked her watch. "I'll call you later, okay?"

Celina nodded. "Okay."

"Celina's welcome to stay here as long as she wants," Tessa offered. "I think considering what's been going on, she would be safer here."

"Thank you, Tessa." Helen smiled, and looked at Celina. "What do you think, honey?"

"Sure." Celina nodded. "But only if it's not too much trouble."

"We'd love to have you here," Tessa insisted. "Helen tells me you love books, and that you have quite the collection."

"Yeah, I guess you could say I'm a bit of a nerd. All I do in my spare time is mostly read."

Tessa pointed down the hall. "We recently added a new section of mythology in our library. Would you like to see it?"

"That would be awesome."

As Helen said her goodbyes, Alexander walked her to her car, and Tessa escorted Celina to the library.

"Here we are." Tessa motioned her inside. "Let me know if you need anything. I'm going upstairs to check on Angel and the baby."

"Thank you, Tessa."

* * * *

Pacing inside the library, Kyle felt caged by all the bookcases full of leather-bound classics. They reminded him of all he hadn't read, all the literary stuff he'd never been a part of, all the higher education he hadn't had.

Street smarts were his deal, and he'd always thought that was enough. Except now he wished he would have applied himself more. After his parents died twenty years ago, his uncle Tim never gave up on him. He always encouraged him to better himself, and make the most out of his life as he grew up here in the Breedline Covenant.

With a curse, he forced himself to check out the new books on mythology. Looking through the titles, he fiddled with the hole in his front pocket. Not sure which book to pick, he straightened his worn-out jeans and stretched his toes. He loved to hang out in comfortable clothes and bare feet.

When his attention was drawn by the one titled *Bulfinch's Mythology*, he reached up and pulled it out. Opening the inside, he read out loud, "Stories about Gods and Heroes." And suddenly, the smell of an ocean breeze drifted into the room. Closing his eyes, he inhaled the fragrance and let out a sigh. Slowly, he opened his lids and turned his head.

Oh my God, he thought, bracing himself with one hand against the book shelf. *She's beautiful.*

Celina appeared in the doorway like a princess, and his mind completely seized up, seeing her not as real, but as a figment of his imagination. Her deep red hair and light green eyes captured his soul. As she stared at him from across the room, his racing heart transformed her into a vision right out of the books on mythology: Greek goddess Afirdi, the goddess of love and beauty. And he was her unworthy servant.

Noticing Kyle, she held up her hand and waved in his direction. "Hi," she said with a shy grin.

"H-hi," he stammered. She was everything he'd ever dreamed of and nothing he'd dared ask for. She was too good for him on his very best day.

Moving closer, he ditched his bad attitude and smiled from ear to ear.

She moved slowly, as if she couldn't feel her own legs. Jesus, she felt weak in his presence. Her heart began to beat faster, and her breathing picked up. She swore he could have been a twin to one of her favorite musicians from an eighties metal rock band.

There was a long stretch of silence as their stares warred. Then his scent—that masculine, clean fragrance—intensified until it flooded the room. Her body began to shake, and her mouth parted with a sigh.

When he heard the soft sigh come from her lips, he was instantly aroused. With wide eyes, his words came out as soft as a whisper. "My name is Kyle. Kyle Jones."

She inhaled his scent and smiled a little, aware of a blast of heat flaring in her body. "I'm Celina."

A curious expression crossed his face. "Do you need any help?"

This time, she moved closer. "I'm Helen Carrington's niece. Tessa brought me here while I wait for my aunt. She had an emergency at the hospital."

His body jerked at the sound of her voice. "Oh, yeah. I know Doc Carrington. She's a nice lady."

She pointed to the book in his hand. "So what are you reading?"

Glancing at the book, he appeared confused. He shrugged his shoulders. "Oh this? It's nothing. Well, it's one of the new books we just got in. It's about all that mythology stuff. Do you like to read?"

She giggled. "Yeah, I love to read, and I love anything about mythology. Looks like you do too."

He looked down, ashamed because he never read anything in here. The only thing he read was the articles in *Playboy*.

She reached for the book. "May I?"

"Oh, sure." He offered it to her. As their hands made contact, the word *beloved* slammed into his head. His lips parted with a low growl, and all his nerve endings popped like she'd zapped him with the heaviest dose of static electricity.

Instantly, she jumped and snapped her hand back when she felt a surge run up the base of her spine. She gasped, "Did you feel that?"

"Are you kidding me?" His body quivered. "I would have to be a paralytic not to have felt that."

Chapter Twenty-Four

As the night fell, Sebastian looked out Eve's apartment window with gritted teeth. They barely escaped with Eve through the portal. Damien's stupidity almost got them caught.

Following today's incident, it was time to shift focus elsewhere. Between emails and his cell phone, he'd tracked down the rest of his council members. At the same time he scheduled a general-assembly meeting for tomorrow night, he prepared them for an update, and an introduction to Taliah Baldolf.

After some thought, he'd decided to move the rest of his council members close by in his new estate. He needed the reinforcement until Taliah created his new death army.

Eve was covered in bruises and stripped of her clothes, her wrists were bound to the bed. Her face was swollen where Sebastian had slapped her. With her hair a mess, she looked completely worn out and angry. As tears flowed down her cheeks, she cried out, "You're not the real Sebastian, are you?"

With a hateful glare, he pulled out a knife from behind his back and stalked in her direction. "Did you figure that out on your own, or did that worthless piece of shit Damien rat me out?"

Pulling at her restraints, she struggled to get free. When he extended the blade, she screamed in terror. With her legs tucked against her chest, she squeezed her eyes shut and held her breath. As she prepared to feel the burn of the blade, her arms suddenly became free when Sebastian cut the rope.

When she opened her eyes in shock, he was staring at her with disgust. "You're filthy, and you're beginning to smell. Come." He reached out to her. "I'll bathe you."

Waiting for her to obey, he stared into her pink-eyed, blotchy-cheeked, broken-down face. With a sigh, he gently gathered her into his arms and carried her to the bathroom. Slowly, he lowered her down on the edge of the tub and turned on the water. As it filled the bath, she covered her face and began to sob.

"Please, Eve," he said in an exhausted tone. "Don't cry."

Lowering her hands, she stared into his black eyes. "What have I done to deserve such cruel punishment?"

"I must have full control." He used his thumb to wipe her tears. "I will not tolerate your continuous defiance."

After he tested the water's temperature, his dark eyes softened. "Your bath is ready." He offered her his hand. "Let me bathe you."

Easing into the warm water, her body shuddered. Treating her as if she was a child, he tenderly shampooed her long hair as each finger softly massaged her scalp. He scooped her into his arms after he finished rinsing her hair, and wrapped her in a towel.

Lowering her down, he placed her in his lap. With her head rested against him, she wept into his neck. Gently stroking her wet hair, he moved his hand lower and rubbed her back.

"I'm sorry, Eve," he whispered. With her in his arms, he carried her to the bedroom and laid her on the bed.

Within a few seconds, he turned off the lights and curled next to her as she drifted off into a dark and troubled sleep.

* * * *

As Tim, Drakon, and Jem hustled toward the room where the screaming came from, Damien suddenly stepped out.

With his weapon pointed, Drakon shouted, "Don't move!"

Damien's eyes were wide, shimmering with panic. "What's all this about?"

Jem rushed over. "We heard a woman scream." Narrowing his eyes, Jem pushed Damien aside. "We're going to search this room."

Damien glared with his finger pointed toward the staircase. "I demand that you leave this house at once!"

He flinched when a huge hand abruptly appeared in his face. Jem had him around the neck, lifting him off the floor until his feet dangled. Jem's voice was deadly cold. "If you don't stay out of our way, I'm going to rip out your eyes and feed them to you. We clear?"

In response, Damien's mouth worked like a one-way valve. Air went in, but nothing came out while he lost control of his bladder.

Letting him drop to the floor, Jem grinned. "I'll take that as a yes."

Damien scooted against the wall in fear. As he looked up at Jem, his face was pale with a red streak around his throat.

Jem leaned over with his finger in Damien's face. "Stay put!"

With eyes wide with terror, Damien quickly nodded.

While Jem disappeared into the room with Tim following behind, Drakon stayed out in the hall with his weapon close by. As Drakon waited, he saw lights flash from inside the room. A minute later, they were back out.

"The room is empty." Jem focused his stare on Damien. "It looks like someone was held captive in there. Explain why there are steel cuffs attached to chains bolted to the wall?"

"Don't look at me." Damien shrugged his shoulders. "They were already there when Samuel purchased the estate. The previous owner was a paranoid schizophrenic. Samuel said he was a war veteran that had it designed in case of a catastrophic disaster."

With one brow lifted, Jem glared at him. "Is that so? Maybe we should search the rest of the house."

Tim crossed his hands over his chest. "I spoke to Samuel over the phone before we came upstairs, and he gave us permission."

Drakon looked back and forth between the two of them. "You two go ahead while I keep an eye on this one," he suggested, narrowing his eyes at Damien. "Holler if you need me."

There was a short silence, and then Tim said, "All right, let's get this over with."

Thirty minutes later, they came back upstairs. "Damien was right," Tim declared. "This place is built like Fort Knox. But that's about all we found. No one else is in the estate."

Drakon shook his head. "It doesn't make any sense. Why would a guy like Samuel Mercier want an estate this size, and not keep it staffed?"

Interrupting the conversation, Tim's cell buzzed. Reaching into his back pocket, he glanced at the caller ID and said, "It's Tessa."

"Hello, this is Tim."

"I hope I'm not interrupting anything."

"It's fine. What's going on?"

"Helen's niece, Celina Baldolf, is here, and she brought the book you asked for."

"That's great news," his voice sounded relieved. "Tell her not to leave. We're on our way back."

"I asked her to stay at the Covenant," Tessa said on the other end. "I hope that's okay."

"Of course she can stay. We'll see you in a few."

Chapter Twenty-Five

After Kyle and Celina's hands accidently touched, there was an awkward pause. In a semi-state shock, Kyle opened his mouth and stuttered, "D-did we?"

Moving fast, Kyle reached out and grasped Celina's arm as she stumbled back. "Are you okay?"

When she nodded, he placed his arm around her. "Do you need to sit down?"

"Yes, please." Her body swayed. "I don't know what came over me."

Helping her to a nearby couch, he noticed she was still unsteady. As she leaned against him, he helped her sit down.

"Do you want me to go get help?"

When she didn't speak right away, he pushed further. "Celina, did you hear me?"

"I-I'm okay," she stammered. "Did we just bond?"

Whoa— he thought. Far as he knew, when they touched, he did feel something. And the word *beloved* came to his mind. Not to mention the erection he had since she first walked into the room. "Yeah, I think we did."

When her dizziness eased, she asked, "So what do we do now?"

"I guess—," he shrugged, "—we should get to know each other."

Suddenly, she started to giggle.

He chuckled. "What's so funny?"

"I never expected this to happen to me. I've never even—"

"Me neither." He shook his head. "I mean... I never thought I would bond with anyone either."

"I do have a question," she queried.

"Ask me anything."

"Do you have family here?"

"Uh..." He hesitated, thinking about her question. "My family died when I was young. I was raised here by my uncle Tim after their death."

"Oh..." She tensed, not sure what to say. "I'm sorry about your family."

He sighed. "Yeah, me too."

"So, your uncle is the head council here?"

"Yep." He nodded. "Why?"

"I'm actually here to see him. I've brought a book he's been searching for."

"Really? What's the book about?"

"It's about the Chiang-shih demon," she replied. "Tim's been searching for a Wicca to help your Covenant destroy this particular demon, and—"

In the awkward silence that followed, he said, "And?"

"Well..." She hesitated. "I'm a Wicca."

"You're a real Wicca?"

Searching for an approval on his face, she uttered, "Yes."

"So can you actually do magic? I mean, can you do spells and stuff?"

Surprised by his reaction, she wasn't sure how he thought of her now. Most Breedline didn't have much to do with Wiccas. And while she worried, she fiddled with the loose threads on her jeans.

When she didn't look him in the eye, he sensed her anxiety. "Did I say something wrong?"

"You're not upset that I'm a Wicca, are you?"

Reaching for her hand, he squeezed a little. "Heck no! I think that's sooo cool."

Lifting her chin, she looked at him. "You do?"

"Hell yah!"

Staring at each other, he had a screaming thought flash through his pea brain: This was his Breedline mate. He was going to fall in love with this woman. And he wanted her to know it.

Releasing the tension in her shoulders, she let out a deep breath. "That's a relief."

He stroked her hand with his thumb and decided it was a crying shame he didn't have the gift of words. He wanted to say something smart and tender, except he just came up dry. With his typical lack of finesse, he blurted, "I want to kiss you."

Her eyes widened.

Oh, crap! He thought. Too much, too soon—

She laughed softly. "I would like that."

Clearing his throat, he mumbled, "You would?"

She blinked a couple of times, and nodded.

Leaning into her, he put his mouth on hers and brushed her lips. Good lord, they were the softest he'd ever felt. The way her warmth felt against his set off a five-alarm fire in his body, reminding him how desperate a man could be when he kissed a beautiful woman.

"Excuse me." Tessa cleared her throat. "I don't mean to intrude, but Tim's back. He's ready to see you, Celina."

Kyle lowered his head, and blushed. *Oh, man, this was so wrong,* he thought. He had no business kissing Celina in front of the queen. Hell, he hoped she didn't catch a glimpse of his massive erection.

Celina squeezed Kyle's hand. "Can Kyle come too?"

"Sure, why not."

Before Tessa left, she looked over her shoulder and winked. "Whenever you two are ready, we'll be down in the dining area."

Celina giggled, and turned toward Kyle. "You ready?"

"Yeah." He grinned ear to ear. "Thanks for including me."

"Thank you...," she smiled, "for the kiss."

He blushed again. "It was all my pleasure."

Chapter Twenty-Six

Lying in bed next to Eve, Sebastian had a frustrating sense—even with her exhausting disobedience—he still had compassion locked away in his memories for her. At times, she disgusted him, and all he wanted to do was kill her. Other times, he felt a craving for her, needing to keep her alive. Hell, he didn't know what he wanted to do with her.

Staring at her while she slept, he noticed the uneasy expression on her face. Wondering about their past, he couldn't imagine what they had in common other than the need for one another's blood. Part of him wanted to get rid of her, but his logical side knew he had to keep her alive for blood—at least that's what he wanted to believe, or did that part of his brain from the past love her?

He utterly defied the word *love*. He sure as hell never expressed it after he'd accidentally killed his beloved Katlyn in a heated rage. He was a straight-up empty vessel when it came to loving something other than power. For the past how many years, the Breedline species had been crossbreeding with humans, and half-breeds. He, however, wanted to change all that. The way to eliminate humans was to break the collective will of their society, and the first step was destabilization.

With the help of Taliah, he would form a new army and create war. After everything was attacked and decimated, what was left of the world would have no choice but bow down to his leadership. After the Breedline were finally forced into nothing but total shambles, he would go in and broom up what was left.

The only better alternative he could think of was the human plague. His plan was working so far; with Taliah on his side there would be no stopping him this time around. He'd been pissed that Damien hadn't done his job of getting rid of the Breedline when they showed up looking for the missing girl. Sebastian reveled in the thought of killing the bastard, but he learned something interesting: Damien had a soft spot for Eve. He would enjoy the torture. Keeping them apart was going to be a fun game.

As the thought made him smile, his stomach growled. His thirst for blood burned in his throat.

* * * *

Following behind Celina, Kyle watched the movement in her small hips, and suddenly, her voice popped into his head. After she'd confirmed her Breedline bond for him, those words would never leave his thoughts. He quickly moved his eyes toward her back. Oh man, he had no business staring at her in a disrespectful way. Hell, the mere thought of her gave him another erection. The idea of making love to her almost drove him mad. He pictured her naked, sprawled under his body, as he—

The word *STOP*, with red flashing lights, screamed inside his head. He had to clear his mind from all those images before they went into the dining room to meet with his uncle, Tim.

Next, the word *BELOVED* shot through his brain like a lightning rod. Quickly, he discreetly slid his hand down to his groin and shifted himself in a more comfortable position before they walked into the room.

As they entered through the doors, Tim was standing at the head of the table with a book in his hand. Glancing around the room, Kyle noticed Tessa, Jace, Jem, and Drakon seated and anxiously waiting.

"Celina, please come in." Tim cocked a brow when he saw Kyle walk in behind her. "I see you brought a guest with you."

"I hope that's not a problem?" She asked, turning toward Kyle.

"Of course not." He smiled. "Kyle is welcome too." He motioned them inside. "Come, have a seat."

"Thank you." Celina sat down next to Tessa, and Kyle took a seat next to her.

Tim extended his hand. "It's a pleasure to meet you, Celina." He introduced everyone else at the table. "And of course you've met Tessa, our queen."

She took his hand, and nodded. "It's a pleasure to meet everyone. And thank you for inviting me to stay here."

"You're welcome, Celina." Sitting down, Tim cleared his throat and slid the book in her direction. "Your aunt Helen tells us you're familiar with the Chiang-shih demon, and you may have the ability to help us destroy it."

Celina looked down at the old, leather-bound book. "I'm sorry I haven't had time to read over this. When Helen called, I grabbed the book and quickly headed this way."

"So you don't know for sure if the book says anything about destroying the demon?" Jem asked from across the table.

She shook her head. "I can't say positively since I haven't read through it, but I do know it's the only book written on this particular demon."

Jace rubbed his palms together, impatience simmering in his eyes. "So let's open it up, and get cracking."

"Well, unless you can read Hebrew"—Celina pointed out—"you're not going to be able to decipher what it says."

Jace shrugged his shoulders. "Hebrew?"

"You do know how to read Hebrew, right?" Drakon asked with anticipation.

Celina quickly nodded. "Oh, of course."

Jace threw up his hands in relief. "Thank the gods!"

"I can read through it tonight," she offered. "It will take me time to get through it, but I'll get back to you as soon as I find something helpful."

Tim stood back up, and offered his hand to her again. "Thank you, Celina."

With her eyes locked with Tim's, she shook his hand. "You're welcome. I'm glad to help."

Before they all got up to leave, Celina held up her hand. "Wait. There's one more thing. And it's about my sister, Taliah."

Tim eased back into his chair with his jaw tensed. "She's here, isn't she?"

"Unfortunately, yes."

Jace crossed his arms. "Why am I sensing bad news?"

"My sister causes widespread destruction wherever she goes. Since she's recently severed our Breedline bond, I haven't been able to hear her thoughts. But—"

Tessa reached out, and gently grasped her hand. "We know you're not anything like your sister."

"Somehow I was able to hear...," Celina hesitated, and looked down in shame. Lifting her chin back up, she said, "I heard one of Taliah's thoughts the other day. She's been summoned here by a demon. I think it might be the same one you're talking about."

Jace muttered something obnoxious under his breath while Tim spoke over him. "What do you think the demon wants with your sister?"

"Taliah has the power of necromancy."

Jace shook his head. "What the hell is necromancy?"

"It's the ability to use black magic for a method of communicating with the dead."

"Great," Jace sighed. "What's the demon going to have her do? Make an army of zombies?"

Everyone quickly turned in his direction, and frowned.

"What?" His brows popped. "I wasn't serious."

Abruptly, Jem asked, "Celina, can your sister do that? Can she bring back the dead?"

In the brief silence following his question, she felt the tension building in the room. Nodding slowly, she said, "Yes."

Chapter Twenty-Seven

With Eve curled against him, Sebastian awoke with her scent almost driving him into a blood frenzy. Glancing at the clock, he realized it was time to get up and head back to the estate.

"Eve." He nudged her with his hand. "Wake up."

She let out something close to a purr, and stretched. Her body arched into his, turning his morning erection into a raw need. As she came awake, memories of how she'd ended up in this bed suddenly startled her. Immediately, she went rigid when she sensed Sebastian beside her.

Pushing her long hair back, he smoothed his hand down her shoulder and nestled into the crevice of her neck. As he inhaled her scent, the fragrance stirred hunger deep in his gut, and woke his appetite from its slumber with a roar.

Eve's anger toward him had been pent up while she'd been chained and abused. Only mere thoughts of unleashing it kept her thriving to stay alive. She had a choice at this moment: Let him take what he wanted, and stick around, or deny him and die. Turning her body toward him, she shifted her eyes to his. He looked like the same Sebastian she always remembered. His face was the kind of thing females dreamed of except for his cold, black eyes. Lifting her palm, she reached up to him.

Surprise flared in his eyes as he flinched at her approach. Her hand suddenly came to a halt, waiting for his approval while her fingers trembled. Letting out a deep breath, he reached up and took her hand. Pulling it toward his lips, he gently pressed a kiss on her soft skin.

Nervously licking her dry lips, she offered him her wrist. With a fast move, he bared his fangs and punctured her vein. As he took the first taste, her blood was so pure it blazed in his mouth and down his throat. The fire it ignited in his stomach strengthened his body, and satisfied his thirst.

When he finally had taken his fill, he released her wrist and licked the wound closed. Parting her lips, she breathed through her mouth and wondered if she had enough energy left to please him. Even though he was compassionate at the moment, the demon still made her skin crawl. Rolling onto her back, she squeezed her eyes shut, feeling every sore muscle in her body. All the flashbacks of Sebastian's punishment threatened to send her on a screaming terror. Opening her lids, she stared up at the ceiling, praying for the courage to keep from bolting.

"Eve," he whispered.

Tracing back over the last couple of days, she barely heard a word he said.

Reaching out, he gently pulled her close. When he looked into her crimson eyes, he saw fear. Her gaunt face expressed panic and dismay.

"I'm not going to hurt you," he murmured. "Not anymore."

Glancing toward the door, she thought about running.

"Look at me, Eve," he pleaded. "I'm sorry."

Moving her eyes back on him, she asked, "Why didn't you tell me you took over Sebastian's body?"

"Because I was afraid you would leave me if you knew the truth."

"Did you kill him?" Her voice cracked. "Is his soul trapped somewhere?"

He shook his head. "Jace killed him, and his soul is in purgatory."

She froze for a split second. "How did you get into his body?"

"When the Angel of Mercy banished me from Alexander's body, I saw you trying to bring Sebastian back to life. That's when I took possession of his body."

As she started to shiver, he wrapped his arm around her, keeping her flush against his body and willing his warmth to go into her.

"Did Sebastian even have a chance to live before you took over?"

"No. He wouldn't have survived the silver bullet."

After a moment, she laid her head against his chest, and her trembling eased off.

"I'm sorry for everything, Eve," he whispered close to her ear. "For treating you like I did. You didn't deserve that. Please forgive me."

In the silence, he held her with care because that was all he had to offer. And he wasn't mistaking this exchange for what it wasn't. An apology wasn't a declaration of love. Yet the truth helped her, somehow. It was still a far distance from the way she'd hoped things would have ended up, but it was better than not having her beloved Sebastian at all.

* * * *

When Tim, Drakon, and Jem finally left Samuel's estate, the confrontation disturbed Damien. He would later reflect that you never knew who you're going to cross tracks with. You just never knew how a simple decision would change things. Sometimes the choices didn't matter. Others... took you into unexpected situations.

At the current moment, however, he had yet to come to that realization. All he could think about was Eve.

After gathering his composure, he went into his bedroom and stripped out of his pants. Staring at his soiled undergarments, his anger raged. Never in his life had he ever lost control of his bladder out of fear. He paced around—going out of his bedroom, and then into the bathroom—back and forth, until he finally ended up in the shower.

As soon as he finished toweling off, he sat down on the bed, and put his hands on his knees to calm himself. When his heartbeat was slow and steady, he took a deep breath. Silently plotting his revenge, he was startled by the loud ringtone coming from his phone. Stretching out his arm, he snatched it from the nightstand.

His brows furrowed as he answered, "Damien speaking."

Samuel Mercier's irritating French accent was loud on the other end. "Did you get rid of the Breedline?"

The sound of his voice drilled into Damien's head, making him want to put a bullet through his brain. "Yeah." Damien gritted his teeth. "But there was a slight altercation."

"An altercation?" Samuel bit out. "What are you talking about?"

"They insisted on checking the estate with or without your permission. I tried to stall them, and get Eve out before they found her."

In irritation, Samuel's voice dropped. "Well, go on!"

"Sebastian, or should I say, our master," Damien said with sarcasm, "took off with Eve through the portal before they found her."

"Did they search the house?"

"Don't worry," he reassured him. "They didn't find anything. But they still suspect something's up."

"I'll contact Sebastian and let him know what's going on. Don't go anywhere until I get back with you," Samuel insisted. "We're supposed to have a meeting with all the council members. Sebastian's bringing someone important, so don't do anything stupid. Do you understand, Damien?"

"Yeah." He rolled his eyes. "I hear you."

Chapter Twenty-Eight

Tim agreed to meet first thing tomorrow with Celina to discuss what she'd discovered in the book. Since it was written in Hebrew, she was the only one who could read it. With luck, she'd find what the Breedline was looking for—a way to destroy the Chiang-shih demon.

After finding out Celina's twin sister had the power of necromancy, not to mention the possibility that she might be conspiring with the demon, everyone in the meeting was ready to call it a night.

Before Kyle and Celina left the room, Tim said, "Kyle, I need to talk to you."

Turning toward Celina, Kyle muttered, "I'll meet you downstairs in the kitchen. If you're hungry, I'll fix you something to eat."

Leaning against the doorway, she smiled. "That sounds great." Her ponytail moved with her body as she turned around and walked out the door.

Grinning ear to ear, Kyle watched her walk away. Drawing his attention, Tim cleared his throat. "Kyle—"

Kyle wheeled around. He looked at Tim, his role model, the man he put all his trust in and said, "Oh, sorry."

Tim had his hands crossed over his chest with an eyebrow cocked. "You've bonded with her, haven't you?"

When the question drifted over to him, Kyle's eyes widened. "Y-yeah," he stammered. "I think I have."

"Have you two talked about this?"

Kyle looked into the eyes of the man who had been his savior, his mentor, and the closest thing to a father he'd ever known. As their stares locked, Kyle registered all the stuff they'd been through over the years while he'd lived with his uncle.

He nodded, and swallowed hard. "Yeah, we did. She feels the same too."

Tim's serious expression suddenly changed. His brows softened, and his tight lips turned into a grin. "That's great news." He patted him on the shoulder. "I'm glad you found your bonded mate."

Kyle relaxed, and let out a sigh of relief. "Thanks."

With that said, Tim ducked out of the room, leaving Kyle alone in the wake of a kindness and respect he could only hope to live up to someday. When the door closed, a thought came to mind. He wanted to be like his uncle. Heading down to the kitchen, it felt good to feel that way. Ever since his parents died, and his uncle took him in, he'd always appreciated and respected him.

* * * *

Later that night, Cassie awoke feeling disorientated. She had no idea how long she'd been asleep waiting for Drakon to return from his meeting. After pulling a double shift at the hospital, Cassie was so exhausted she didn't bother eating dinner before she fell asleep. When she lifted her head, Drakon was across the bed, lying on his side. Without a pillow, his head rested in the crock of his arm. Glancing around, she noticed all the pillows where gathered around her body, instantly making her feel terrible. Christ, she'd become a pillow hog. Letting out a deep breath, she watched him sleep. He looked tired even as he slept. His brows were furrowed, and his mouth appeared tense.

The comfort she took seeing him in bed was a relief. But still, she worried about him. She hated the thought of him helping Tim search for Sebastian.

"Drakon?"

The instant she whispered his name, he opened his eyes. When he saw her, the tension left his face and his lips curled into a smile.

She patted the empty space between them. "Come here."

He waited a moment, cocking his head as if he heard a sound. It was her stomach, growling under the covers. "Are you hungry?" He scooted next to her. "I can get you something to eat."

"No, thanks." Her eyes shifted toward the bathroom. "I really don't feel like eating anything."

"Would you like to take a shower?"

"Yes." She nodded. "I fell asleep before I could take one. A hot shower would feel wonderful."

It made him feel good to have someone to take care of. He quickly sprang out of bed and headed toward the bathroom. Before he turned on the shower, he set out two towels and a washcloth.

Without saying a word, he reached down and scooped her into his arms. When he lifted her from the bed, the sheets fell away from her body. His eyes widened when he saw she was naked.

Carrying her into the bathroom, she looked up at him. "Will you take a shower with me?"

Talk about long silences. But then, as he looked into her pleading eyes, he nodded.

After he removed his sweat pants, he opened the shower door. As he followed behind her, his body brushed up against her back when he shut the glass door.

The shower stall was a generous size for one person, but it was close quarters for two, especially his size. Reaching for the bottle of shampoo, he watched her ease under the falling water. Pouring a small amount in his palm, he offered to wash her hair. As he began to shampoo, she tilted her head up, and brushed her wet hair against his chest. Before she turned around to rinse the suds, her balance shifted, and she fell back against him. His body instantly reacted, twitching and hardening in all the right places.

There was a pause... and then he reached for the soap. Moving slowly, he traded places with her. After he washed his body, he knelt down, working up a good lather in his hands, and smoothed his hands over her foot. When he motioned for her to lift it, he massaged over her sole and up onto her heel, worshiping each foot without expecting anything in return.

Moving higher up onto her thigh, he pressed a tender kiss to the outside. When he got to her hip, he stopped. Standing up, he gave her the soap so she could wash whatever else she needed.

Standing on her tiptoes, she reached up and cupped his face. Pulling him closer, she pressed her mouth against his.

"Come to bed with me," she murmured, opening the shower door.

Shutting off the water, he followed her. Accepting the towel she handed him, they dried off together, staring into each other's eyes. She was wrapped from her chest down while he covered only his hips.

Sliding into bed, he clicked off the light. With Cassie cuddled against him, he closed his eyes, not expecting to sleep. Instantly, his thoughts transported into a different plane of existence, bringing him back to when he was younger. Memories of the past haunted him. After the death of his first bonded mate, he hated the thought of ever having to go through that again. He would never be able to overcome that with Cassie. All he cared about now was they were together while the rest of the world drifted away into a fog. He never thought it would be possible to fall in love with someone again.

Chapter Twenty-Nine

Rubbing her temples, Taliah lounged in an oversized couch in the penthouse Sebastian rented out. She had a tension headache that ran from the base of her skull all the way into her frontal lobe. Digging into her purse, she pulled out lighter and a small Ziploc baggie. There were advantages to being a pothead, she thought. She flicked her lighter a couple of times, and it finally held a flame as she lit the end of a joint.

After just two puffs, Fredrick Mercier rushed into the room with a panicked expression on his face. He was Samuel's identical twin, except Fredrick was skinny. Samuel, on the other hand, needed to lose a few pounds. But they both spoke in an irritating French accent that got on her nerves.

"No!" Fredrick squawked, waving his arms around. "Please, Miss Baldolf! You can't smoke that in here."

Taking one more hit, she leaned forward and stubbed it out. "Oh, chill, Freddy," she said in a raspy voice, exhaling at the same time. "It's not like the cops are waiting outside the door."

Shaking his head, he gritted his teeth. As he stood in place, with his nostrils flaring, the antique grandfather clock abruptly chimed, causing him to jump. Moving toward the window, he pulled back the drapes and looked out. Man, he'd feel better about this whole thing if he'd just came up with an excuse when Samuel called him in to babysit her.

To hell with this, he thought. He wasn't going to be responsible for what she did, not for one more minute. Turning his head, he stared at her with a scowl on his face. If only he'd been briefed about the vile things she'd done in her childhood, he'd never agreed to this in the first place. To top it off, she had the most appalling wardrobe... hippie combined with Goth.

With a hateful glare, his upper lip curled, crinkling his nose. "I'm going downstairs to find something to calm my nerves. I won't be long."

Offering him the bag of marijuana, she muttered, "This works wonders for that."

Rolling his eyes, he shook his head. "I'll have Azzo come sit with you until I get back."

"I don't need a nanny," she spat. "Especially a creepy dude named Azzo." She shivered in disgust. "Who names their kid that anyway?"

Crossing his arms over his chest, he let out heavy sigh. "His name happens to be Corbin Azzo, and he's perfectly capable of doing his job. I'm sure he's just as excited to be here as you are. Besides, I'm not leaving you here alone."

"But I'm not alone." She looked at a shadow across the room. "He never leaves my sight." She arched a brow, pointing her finger at the dark figure.

When Fredrick followed the direction she was pointing at, he quickly flattened against the door. With wide eyes, he slapped his hand over his mouth, trying to muffle his screams.

"What—" He gasped, trying to figure out what exactly it was.

Standing in the far corner of the room was a shadowed outline that appeared to be some kind of creature with red, glowing eyes.

"Oh, I'm sorry." She smirked. "I forget to introduce you."

"I-I—" He stuttered in fright, dropping to his knees.

Her lips curled into a devious smile. "Fredrick, you're not scared... are you?"

"Please!" He pleaded. "Keep it away!"

"Come on, Freddy." She chuckled. "Grow a pair."

"W-what the hell is it?"

"Now you're just being rude." She pointed toward the door, motioning him to leave. "Go! Get out!"

Scrambling to his feet, he managed to get them to move as he bolted out the door. Watching him shrink in terror gave her a feeling of pleasure and satisfaction. When the door slammed, she heard screams coming from behind it.

With a high-pitched giggle, she shrugged her shoulders. "Was it something I said?" Her eyes returned to the shadow in the corner. "Come, darling." She patted the empty spot on the couch beside her. "Come sit by Mommy."

* * * *

Down on the second floor of the Breedline estate, Kyle carried two mugs over to the kitchen table, praying he didn't dump hot cocoa down his leg. He'd filled them with a special recipe he'd made himself, so God only knew what it tasted like.

"You need help?" Celina offered, sitting at the table.

"Nope, I got it." With his hands full, he moved in slow motion. "I hope you like hot cocoa. I kinda have my own recipe," he said, setting the mugs down.

Celina looked in hers. "You even added little marshmallows."

"If you don't like it, you don't have to drink it." He shook his head. "It won't hurt my feelings."

She lifted the mug and took a sip. The yum that followed was more than he could have hoped for.

"Mmmm," she said with her eyes closed. "This is really good."

Scooting his chair closer to the table, he sat right next to her. As he took a drink from his own mug, he thought he'd done a pretty damn good job. "So, would you like something to eat?"

Celina glanced up over the rim of her mug. "Sure. What did you have in mind?"

He leaned back against his chair, and couldn't help staring into her beautiful green eyes. "I make a mean sub sandwich. How does that sound?"

She took another sip. "That sounds great." She smiled at him so widely, dimples showing on both sides of her cheeks. And what do you know... he liked them. They gave her pretty face some character.

At the same time Kyle stood up, someone in the doorway cleared their throat. "Mind if I join you two?"

Turning toward the kitchen door, they saw Helen with her hands on her hips, and a big grin on her face.

"Hey, Doc," Kyle called out from the open refrigerator. "I was about to make us a sandwich. Would you like one?"

"Thanks, Kyle." Helen walked over to the table, and plopped down next to Celina. "Hold the mayo."

Smiling at Kyle, Celina curled a strand of her hair around her finger.

"He's cute," Helen whispered in her ear.

"And he's smart too," Celina whispered back.

It seemed like Cupid had been working overtime around her lately, Helen thought. Then again, stranger things had brought people together. All that really mattered was the right pair ended up together. Yeah, life was good. She knew that look in Celina's eyes. It was the same look she got when she first saw Alexander. It was the look of a bonded Breedline female.

As Celina sighed, Helen said in a low voice, "I think someone's in love."

"How can you tell?"

Helen placed her palm on Celina's forearm. "I know that look." She smiled. "I'm happy for you, honey."

"Thanks, Aunt Helen."

"How did the meeting with Tim go? Did you find anything helpful in your book?"

"I'm going to go over it tonight." Celina let out a deep breath. "It's written in Hebrew."

"Would you like some help?"

"You can read Hebrew?"

"Of course." Helen nodded. "I have a few hidden talents."

"I would love the help." Celina placed the book on the table. "It's pretty thick."

When Kyle returned with a platter of sandwiches, they all dove in and ate. After all, they had a long night ahead of them, and they needed fuel to get through it.

Staring at the leather-bound book, Celina felt her heart beat faster. Feeling pressured, she hoped she'd find what they were all looking for. The breath she hadn't been aware of holding slowly released out of her lungs, a reaction from thinking about the demon and her twin sister. Deep down, she knew her sister was helping Sebastian. Taliah wouldn't stop at anything until she found a way to destroy everything in her path.

"Celina, is something wrong?" Kyle asked, noticing her worried expression.

With a fake smile, she shook her head. "Don't worry, it's nothing." *Yeah, what a lie that was*, she thought.

❧ Chapter Thirty

When Sebastian and Eve returned back to his estate, he led her upstairs and told her she would be staying in his room from now on. Entering the hallway that led to his bedroom, she took a deep breath and walked with him on loose legs. When he opened the door, a scent of fresh-cut flowers invaded her nose, the sweetness swelling, taking over, and replacing the air. Her throat seemed to close up as if she was suffocating. Clamping her hand over her mouth, she was definitely going to throw up.

With shaky hands, and legs like Jell-O, she pushed past Sebastian into the bathroom, locking herself inside. Falling to her knees, she bent over the porcelain bowl. Her throat worked through the dry heaves, sending nothing up but air.

"Eve," Sebastian called out from behind the bathroom door. "Are you okay?"

Breaking out into a sweat, her head began to spin. She struggled for breath as death entered her mind. She wasn't afraid of dying, but just the opposite. She feared she would live in misery for an eternity.

"Yes," her voice trembled. "Please, could I have some privacy?" Taking a deep breath, she tried to calm herself when she heard a phone ring on the other side of the door.

"All right," he agreed. "I'll be back shortly to check on you."

There was a long pause, and she finally heard the door close. After a while, she watched as her tears fell down into the stool, creating ripples on the water's surface. With all her strength, she got to her feet and turned around. She looked into the mirror: her face was marked with red blotches, and her hair was a ragged mess.

When Sebastian glanced at his phone, he noticed it was Fredrick Mercier. He'd ordered Samuel Mercier to send his brother Fredrick and Corbin Azzo to watch over and escort Taliah to the estate later that evening.

Before Sebastian answered, he let out a long sigh. "Fredrick, I told you not to call this number unless it was urgent."

"M-master, please," Fredrick pleaded. "There's a—"

"Stop stumbling around!" Sebastian barked. "Tell me what's wrong!"

"It's Taliah." Fredrick gasped, trying to catch his breath. "She has something horrible in her room!"

"You're not making any sense. What's in Taliah's room?"

"It's... it's some kind of creature," he ranted. "I think it's a ghost."

"Listen to me," Sebastian ordered through gritted teeth. "I don't know what you're talking about, but if you leave her unattended and something happens to her, I swear you'll be less worried about a ghost after I get done with you."

"But—"

"Get her packed and bring her here! Do you understand?"

"Y-yes, Master."

Sebastian cursed as he ended the call.

Just as Eve reached up to fix her hair, she heard the bedroom door open and slam shut. She shook herself into focus, and grabbed a washcloth.

Sebastian jiggled the door knob. "Eve, unlock the door."

Wetting a small, square cloth, she wiped under her eyes. Tossing it aside, she tried to fix her hair.

"Eve, open this door."

Cursing under her breath, she quickly opened the door. "I'm sorry," she murmured with her head lowered. "I'm just not feeling well."

"You need to feed." He reached out for her hand. "I'll have Damien come in and serve your needs."

She lifted her head with a confused expression. "But I thought—"

He interrupted her by holding up his hand. "He's only here to give you the pure Breedline blood your body needs, and nothing more. He is aware if he steps out of line again, I will kill him," he said without haste. "Go and lie down. I'll send for him."

When Sebastian left the room, he headed downstairs at the same time Damien was coming up. He stopped and looked into Sebastian's dark, empty eyes.

"I was just going up to my room. Is Eve here?"

"She's upstairs in my room," Sebastian replied firmly. "She needs to feed. I'm counting on you to do something right for once. Do not disappoint me."

"I-I—" Damien stuttered his words.

Sebastian pointed upstairs. "Go!"

With a nod, Damien muttered, "Yes, Master."

Outside of Eve's bedroom door, Damien took a deep breath and softly knocked. When there was no answer, he called out, "Eve, it's Damien. May I come in?"

When she heard Damien's voice, she pulled the blanket higher and straightened her back against the headboard. "Please, come in."

When the door slowly opened, he stood in silence, staring at her from across the room. "Are you okay?"

With a half-smile, she glossed over the situation, telling him only that she didn't feel good because she was weak.

Closing the door, he moved toward the bed and sat down. "I promise I will find a way to get you out of here."

She shook her head. "It's too complicated, and I won't let you risk your life. Sebastian—"

He reached out to her. "You don't worry about him." His voice smoothed out into a purr. "I will take care of you."

"Thank you, Damien, but I can't let you do that. Sebastian promised he wouldn't punish me anymore. I'll be just fine."

He clasped her hand. "He's lying to you, Eve. The demon gets off on hurting you. Can't you see that?"

"Don't worry about me. I'll be fine." She faked a smile. "Damien, I... I need your blood again." She squeezed his hand. God, she hated using him. But who else could she go to? She didn't want Sebastian kidnapping another person just to supply her blood, and then kill them later. She would never forget what he did to Kara. That would stay engraved in her mind forever.

"Do you want my wrist, or would you rather drink from my neck?"

She gripped the blanket that was pulled up to her waist. "Your wrist will be fine."

When he scooted next to her, she stretched her legs out and sighed with utter exhaustion. Her body became relaxed as he reached out, offering his wrist.

"Take me," he urged. "You need to feed."

"No, Damien." She turned away. "I can't do it."

At the same time she tried to get up, he lunged at her, taking her by the shoulders, and held her down. Moving between her legs, he pressed his body against hers. While she pushed at him, he kept her close, nuzzling her neck, and breathing against her skin. Before long, she stopped fighting.

"Eve, please. Take me," he groaned.

The instant she latched onto his neck, her name shot out of his mouth as he felt a burning blaze of aroused pain. After Sebastian had taken her away, all Damien could do was think of her. He listened to her satisfied sounds as she drank his blood, transforming his heart into an icon from his childhood. She was the Madonna of salvation and love... and he was her unworthy servant.

When Eve finished, she stretched out beside Damien, resting her head on his chest. With his arms wrapped around her, she felt safe and closed her eyes, drifting into a deep sleep.

Hours later, she awoke in total darkness as panic started to set in. She'd lost all track of time, wondering how long she'd been asleep. As she rose up, her head whipped side to side, and she saw someone lying next to her. Leaning closer, she focused and immediately recognized the person sleeping beside her.

Slowly easing back down, she tried to calm her heavy breathing and jumped when she felt a cold hand grasp her arm.

"It's just me, Eve," Sebastian whispered. Pulling her closer, he scooted his body against hers. She felt a warm breath on her neck as he whispered, "I want you, Eve."

Chapter Thirty-One

At midnight, Kyle was exhausted after staying up with Celina. They'd searched for hours, trying to find something, anything, in the book that would help them destroy the Chiang-shih demon. Her aunt Helen was called to the hospital and couldn't stay to help them decipher the book. With no luck, and feeling utterly helpless, Celina didn't find a thing. When her eyes couldn't focus anymore, they decided to get up early and go through it one more time. Maybe if she was lucky, she'd find something her tired eyes just overlooked.

Later that night, after calling it quits, Kyle stared at the ceiling above his bed, and let out a long sigh. As he glanced around the room, his eyes stopped at the bass guitar that hung on the wall. It was a signature series SB Black 'n' Gold from Clifford Lee Burton, best known as the late bass guitarist for the American thrash metal band, Metallica. He sweated blood and tears over the last six years to save up for it. It was glossy black with a touch of gold dusted around the edges.

For some strange reason he always said a prayer in front of this particular guitar right before he played in a gig Jace scrapped up for their band. He didn't know jack about art, but he felt like he had a masterpiece on his wall.

An hour later, he was still wide awake staring at the wall. Only once he'd got up to use the bathroom, and then he was back between the sheets again. He'd been lying in bed trying to take his mind off Celina. From out of nowhere the picture of her beautiful red hair and green eyes came to him. In a stunning moment of boldness, he imagined the two of them together. She had her soft lips pressed against his, with her arms tightly wrapped around him. *Jesus... God in heaven,* he thought. His mind filled with thoughts of being inside of her. And suddenly he hardened, followed by a raw pain gnawing at his stomach.

Okay, this could start to get irritating, he thought as he looked down. Especially if he woke up in the morning this way and... yeah, she noticed it. He felt guilty about what he'd pictured in his mind. He would die if she ever found out—

A light buzzing caught his attention, and brought him back to reality. Reaching toward the night stand, he grabbed his phone. It was a text from Celina. She thanked him for staying up late with her and mentioned she looked forward to seeing him in the morning.

As he texted her back, a smile grew on his face the size of Texas. Yeah, everything was working out great so far between them, he thought. He couldn't wait to see her again.

* * * *

Fredrick's nerves were on pins and needles when the thought of going back into Taliah's room entered his mind. Desperate for a drink, he checked his watch. He had two hours before the hotel bar closed.

With grim resolve he pulled up a seat at the bar and ordered a gin and tonic. He hoped like hell it would give him liquid courage to face the ghostly creature if it reappeared again.

The first cocktail was good, but the second one was even better. After ordering a third, he glanced around the room, and noticed two men flirting with the same female. He could tell she wasn't interested in either one. She was a tiny thing, no more than five-four even with her high heels, but her hair was huge. Dressed in a tight silver mini-dress, she looked like a stripper.

When she caught his stare, she smiled back with a wink. Rudely walking away from the two men, she sauntered in his direction. He quickly turned around when he saw her coming over.

"Well, aren't you cute." Her eyes roamed up and down his body. "Are you lookin' for some fun tonight, honey?"

Nervously shifting in the seat, he took a deep breath. For God's sake, he thought. Maybe sex would calm his nerves. "W-what's your name?" he stammered, staring into her crimson eyes.

"Susy," she replied with the S lingering. "What's your name, sweetheart?"

"Fredrick."

"I love your accent." She licked her lips. "You're not from around here, are you?"

"No," he stated nervously. "I'm originally from France."

"Well, Fredrick from France." She held out her hand. "What do you say we ditch this place and go back to my room?"

With a nod, he reached out and took her hand. Following her lead, he had a feeling this was probably a bad idea. He'd never paid for sex in his life, but unfortunately, he didn't seem to care at the moment.

When she stopped at suite 111, she took out her key card and swiped it a couple of times to unlock the door. Pushing it open, she pulled him into a huge room. Her penthouse was even nicer than the one Sebastian had for Taliah. It was decorated in an old Victorian style with a chandelier that hung from a vaulted ceiling. Being raised in France, he recognized the type of antique furniture inside. He noticed the French influence and realized it was obviously dated back during the Civil War.

"This is a nice room," he muttered, taking out his wallet, waiting for her to name the price.

"Two hundred," she purred, holding up two fingers.

Reaching into his wallet, he anxiously dug through it. As he pulled out the bills, his hands shook when he offered it to her.

With a raised brow, she quickly snatched it out of his hand. "Is this your first time with someone like me?"

There was a long pause, and then he finally nodded.

When she reached for his belt, he stumbled back and banged into the door. "Sorry," his voice cracked.

"I'm going to take good care of you, Fredrick." She stepped in close with her oversized breasts, and pressed them against him. "Look into my eyes," she commanded.

Staring into her hypnotic eyes, he instantly fell into an induced altered state. Tucking one hand into his waistband, she tugged him forward. Willingly, he obeyed her order, unable to control his mind.

Leaning closer, she took a deep breath, inhaling his scent. In response, his body stiffened.

"Relax, lover," she murmured, guiding him to a bed.

When he sat down, she eased him flat on his back. Feeling helpless, he kept his eyes on hers. The second her stare moved to his throat, she let out a hiss and bared two large fangs. As she struck hard, he instantly felt a burn spread from his neck to the tips of his toes. Sunk deep into his vein, she drank him down as he slowly drifted into nothing but darkness.

Hours later, he finally opened his eyes and slowly peeled his face off the cold tile floor. Feeling groggy, he struggled to set up. When he managed on two feet, he lost his balance, swaying side to side. Steadying himself against the wall, he glanced around the room. Unfamiliar with his surroundings, he tried to remember his previous events, but his mind was a total blank. Nothing came to his memory after he went to the bar last night. *God, where the hell was he?*

Stumbling to the door, he reached out with one hand and braced himself. Glancing at his watch, he noticed the time. "Bloody hell," he cursed. It was eight o'clock in the morning. Rushing out the door, he immediately felt gravity taking over when his legs wobbled like a puppet on strings. Before he crashed to the floor, he caught himself and steadied his feet, free falling into a state of panic. His attention snapped back when his phone rang. With shaky hands, he fumbled inside his jacket and pulled it out.

"Hello," he answered out of breath.

"Where the hell have you been?" Corbin barked. "I've been calling you all night!"

"I'm sorry," Fredrick mumbled. "I don't remember."

"What do you mean you don't remember? Have you been drinking?"

There was a short pause as Fredrick tried to recall the night before again. "The last thing I remember is having two... three drinks in the bar last night. The rest is a blank."

"Just get back here," Corbin bit out. "Sebastian was expecting us to bring Taliah to the estate last night."

"Just give me five minutes," Fredrick pleaded. "I'll be right there."

"Hurry, we're waiting on you!"

"Wait," Fredrick blurted in desperation. "Did you notice anything unusual in Taliah's room?"

"What?" Corbin's voice sounded irritated. "I don't know what you're talking about."

"Uh... never mind." Fredrick took a deep breath. "I'll be there in a minute."

Chapter Thirty-Two

By nine o'clock Taliah was packed and in the back of a black Mercedes on her way to Sebastian's estate. Up front, on the other side of the partition, Corbin Azzo sat stiff as he drove in silence. Next to him Fredrick had his head turned, gazing out the window. Both were dressed in black with a mood grim as death.

The car's windows were darkened to such a degree she couldn't tell if it was daylight or dark. Rolling down her window, she stuck her head out into the morning air. From the angle of the road, she knew they were coming off a mountain, even though it was covered by a dark haze.

The fabric of her jacket made a crinkling sound when she reached into the inside pocket. Pulling out a joint, she held it up to her nose and sniffed. When the flick of her lighter ignited the end, the faint smell of marijuana drifted around the back seat.

She saw Corbin looking at her from the rear-view mirror as she placed the cigarette to her lips and inhaled the drug. With a glare, his handsome face displayed annoyance. The tattoo on the side of his neck was beautifully done, and she wondered why he'd picked the design of a dragon. The instant he let down the partition, his brows furrowed. "Please, Miss Baldolf... would you mind putting that out?"

Shaking her head, Taliah rolled her eyes. "Stop being so uptight," she groaned. "You guys need to learn to relax a little." Opening the ashtray, she let out an irritated sigh and dabbed the blunt out.

Clearing her throat, she rolled up the window. "So... tell me why you're enemies with your own kind?"

Without haste, Corbin replied, "They mix with humans and half-breeds, and we don't agree with their laws."

She looked toward the passenger seat. "What about you, Freddy?" She mocked with a smug grin. "Why do you hate them so much?"

In the silence that stretched out, Fredrick felt woozy, especially thinking about the creature. *God,* he thought. *Was that thing in the car with them?*

"Hello!" She impatiently snapped her fingers. "I asked you a question."

"Sorry, but the Master doesn't like us talking about this." He reached over and pressed the button to close the partition, leaving her in complete absence of sound.

"Yeah, whatever." She smirked, flipping them both off. Leaning back into her seat, she closed her eyes as the sedan drove through the fog.

Almost an hour later, she awoke when her head bumped against the window. She straightened to see where they were and leaned forward. "Are we getting closer?" she asked in a raised voice, knocking on the glass divider.

Lowering the partition, Corbin's voice came clear. "Yes, we're almost there."

A few minutes later, Corbin stopped the Mercedes in front of a sturdy metal gate with a sign that read PRIVATE in bold letters. As the gate opened, they drove up a concrete ramp, leading them down a long driveway. When they arrived to their destination, Taliah rolled down her window and stared at the massive estate. The place looked like Fort Knox with all the bars over the outside windows.

Corbin cut a glance over his shoulder in her direction. "Stay in the car."

Reaching for her purse, she waited in the back seat and watched him scan the area after he stepped out of the car.

Opening her door, he held out his hand to her. "We'll have your suitcases brought up to your room later."

"I can manage on my own," she insisted, gesturing his hand away.

"Suit yourself." He lowered his hand. "Follow me."

Getting out of the car, she followed him to a set of metal doors. The whole time he stayed close, she felt like he was her own personal bodyguard with Fredrick not far behind. After Corbin pressed a series of numbers on a panel, an alarm beeped twice, and the doors opened.

Once they were inside, he quickly led her down a corridor to a small elevator. Before entering, he turned toward the left and to the right, checking to make sure it was clear.

"Do you live here?" she questioned, even though she knew it was self-evident.

"Yes," Corbin replied. "We have rooms on the top floor."

When the elevator swayed, Fredrick caught Taliah's upper arm in a swift motion before she lost her balance.

She flashed a fake smile. "Thanks, Freddy."

With an abrupt halt, the elevator doors opened to a long hallway. Stepping out, she lifted her head and glanced around. The elegant lighting from the crystal chandelier spread throughout the royal marble floors.

"Nice place," she expressed.

Fredrick motioned her forward. "Please, keep moving."

Following behind, they took her to the end of a narrow hallway. Neither Fredrick nor Corbin noticed the shadow moving with them along the wall.

Stopping outside a door, Fredrick reached into his pocket and took out a gold key. "This will be your room." Unlocking the door, he turned in Taliah's direction and inhaled sharply. "Oh... God!" He gasped, pulling the door closed.

"Fredrick, what's wrong?" Corbin queried.

In a state of shock, Fredrick's eyes stretched wide. "O-over t-there," he mumbled, pointing toward the wall by Taliah.

When Corbin saw the shadowed creature, his mouth dropped. "What the hell—"

"His name is Lucas," she said annoyed, walking over to the shadow. "He's my guardian, and he never leaves my sight. I demand you treat him with respect." Her eyes narrowed. "Do you understand?"

When they didn't respond, she whispered something to the shadow. As she faced them again, her upper lip curled into a snarl, and her green eyes changed into the color of golden amber.

Vanishing before their eyes, Taliah disappeared across the space, taking form behind Corbin with a knife to his throat. Fredrick stumbled back against the wall and reached for his weapon. Pointing it in her direction, his hand trembled as Corbin's jugular was on the verge of being slit.

"I'm sick of everyone disrespecting my son," she hissed in Corbin's ear. "And I'm tired of playing by your rules."

A few drops of blood dripped down his neck as she dug the knife deeper into his flesh. "Now apologize to him!"

Corbin dragged in a breath. "I-I'm sorry."

"That's better." She loosened her grip. "I'm waiting, Fredrick."

"I'm sorry." He lowered the gun. "Please, Taliah," he begged. "We don't mean any disrespect."

Smiling in satisfaction, she removed the blade and pushed Corbin. He fell to the floor struggling for air.

"Just remember, no one tells me what to do," she threatened. "Now give me the damn key!"

In a panic, Fredrick scurried over, and handed it to her. Walking backward, he tripped and crashed into the wall.

Before she went into her room, she looked over her shoulder. "Go tell your master I want to speak with him."

"Y-yes, ma'am," Fredrick stammered, scrambling to his feet.

She pointed toward the hall, motioning them to leave. "Go!"

Fredrick reached down and clasped onto Corbin's hand. Pulling him up, they scurried away in retreat.

With the key in her hand, she unlocked the door and pushed it open. Before she stepped inside, she waited for Lucas. "Come, sweetheart," she muttered in a tender voice.

Drifting over, the monstrous creature whimpered as it floated inside.

❧ *Chapter Thirty-Three*

"I want you, Eve," Sebastian repeated his words in a soft whisper.

From the opposite side of the bed, Eve made no reply to the words the demon spoke. When he whispered his desires, she was under no illusions of what he was going to do to her. And as her fear kicked in, she shied away from thoughts of her bonded mate. Closing her eyes, she couldn't grasp the thought of sharing her body with someone who portrayed her departed beloved.

As she lay defenseless, her hands trembled while his eyes roamed over the thin sheet that covered her body. When he reached for it, she flinched with a tight grip.

"Eve, you belong with me," he purred.

The mattress dipped as he scooted closer. As she felt his warm breath brush against her neck, her body shivered in fear. His voice deepened, "Did you hear me?"

When he leaned in to kiss her, she panicked. Taking a deep breath, she inhaled a blend of expensive spiced cologne. The scent was the hook that snagged her, pulling her through the keyhole of her past, and bridging the horrid span of her childhood. When his lips finally touched her skin, she recoiled and turned away.

"Please, Eve." He shifted above her. "Let me love you."

With her eyes squeezed tight, she stiffened, bracing herself to be punished.

"Open your eyes." He caressed her face with his fingertips.

Slowly lifting her lids, she blinked in surprise. When she focused on his face, she saw the evil in his dark stare.

"I'm not going to hurt you," he said in a tender voice.

Praying it wasn't a trick, she took a series of big breaths and prepared for the worst. With every ounce of strength she had left, she refused to relent to him or anyone else. She would die fighting.

"Eve... don't you want me?"

In the silence that followed, he didn't press further. Instead, he leaned forward and placed a light kiss on her forehead. "Get some sleep," he muttered, rolling over.

Even after all these weeks of confinement, she was looking for an escape... and she would be that way until she drew her last breath. Having led a violent life, it was entirely unsurprising if she was going to meet a brutal end. The urge to run drove her to think of her beloved... the real Sebastian. She thought of when they'd been together—not the last time when she watched him die—but when he was alive, worshiping every inch of her. God, she missed him. And yet his body was lying next to her, but his soul was replaced.

Turning toward him, she glanced over his broad shoulders and down his sculpted arms, wishing Sebastian back.

"Sebastian," her voice quivered, not knowing what else to call him.

The instant she said his name, he turned to her. He waited for a moment, cocking his head as if listening for sounds. "What's wrong, Eve?"

"May I ask you something?"

Moving on his side, he rested his head on the inside of his arm. "Yes." His eyes seemed to soften.

The comfort she took seeing his kind expression was a relief. Building up the courage, she paused before she asked what she desperately wanted to know.

"What's your real name?"

When he didn't immediately respond, she took it he didn't want to tell her.

"My name is Ramael," he bluntly stated. "You must swear to never speak of it again."

She nodded in his direction as tears trickled down her face. The weeping that came out of her was utterly uncontrollable, welling up so fast it all but exploded from her soul.

"Please don't cry." He reached out, and placed his palm on her cheek to wipe the tears away.

Awkward as the situation was, his touch felt comforting, and brought back memories. As she wept, he tried to decide whether he should hold her. Taking a risk, he moved closer with his hips pushing into hers. And although she tensed up, expecting something sexual, he wasn't aroused.

For some reason the closeness eased her mind. She relaxed when his warm, bare chest pressed against hers. With his hand on her neck, he gently drifted down the small of her back. Together, they held on to each other, and she felt that commonality between them... their shared half-succubus sides latching onto one another.

Between one heartbeat and the next, she was consumed by an inner energy that stilled the ache in her heart. Pulling from their embrace, she reached up and cupped his face. On impulse, she leaned forward, placing her lips against his.

It happened so fast, he couldn't believe it. Later, he would play and replay everything over and over, stretching out this moment endlessly. Her lips were incredibly soft, and very warm.

When the sheets fell away from her, she shuddered in his arms. The contact released all her fears, transforming them into the past.

"Take my vein," she moaned.

In the midst of the passion, he sucked on her throat and growled. "Are you sure that's what you want?"

"Yes," she urged. "Please, take it now."

Moving on top of her, he dragged one fang across her throat. There was a pause, and then his bite sliced into her soft skin.

* * * *

The next morning Eve came out of a fuzzy haze like a cork surfacing on still water. Bobbing along, things came and went out of focus. But the second her brain flipped back on, she screamed, "Sebastian—!"

Rolling onto his side, he reached for her. "I'm right here."

As he said those three words, it was like he'd unplugged the sound to the whole world. Realizing he wasn't her true beloved, a cold rush hit her, and the familiar dread she'd felt drifted back.

Burrowing deep into her thoughts, he read her mind. Staring into her eyes, he sensed regret as she eased off the bed.

"I'm going to take a shower," she told him, glancing over her shoulder.

In the bathroom, she paused at the mirror and sighed. Her image brought back memories of her beloved and the bond they'd shared. She'd memorized every part of him, and now he was a different person in the same body. And who knows? She thought, looking at herself. Maybe she could she learn to love Ramael.

As if he'd been summoned by her thoughts, he came up behind her. His height towered over her, dwarfing her reflection. Looking in the mirror, she stared at his shadowy face, tracing over his handsome features, and then she saw his eyes. The pupils were dark black, not gold like Sebastian's used to be.

Without permission, he ran his fingers through her long, silky hair. The instant he did, she relaxed and felt like reality was merging into something entirely different.

Slipping his hand down her hip... and lower... he gently pulled her against his sudden arousal. "I want to shower with you," he murmured.

Abruptly, the grandfather clock from downstairs started to chime, followed by persistent knocks pounding on the bedroom door. Eve noticed the irritation on his face. His brows clenched, and his lips formed into a tight line.

"I'll be right back." After a quick kiss, he withdrew his arms. Reaching for a towel, he wrapped it around his waist.

For a moment, it felt like the good old days, back in the arms of her lover. "Is everything okay?" she queried.

"It will be as soon as I get you in that shower," he said, heading toward the door.

When he turned around, Eve winced with her hand over her mouth.

Across his upper back was...

❧ Chapter Thirty-Four

When he heard Eve gasp, he looked over his shoulder. Her eyes were wide, and she had her hand covering her mouth like she'd just seen a ghost.

"Oh my God," she mumbled, pointing at his back.

Turning his head, he flinched when he saw his backside in the mirror. With his brows clenched, he cursed at his reflection.

A large portion of flesh over his shoulder blade revealed a repulsive dark patch. Reaching around his back, he touched it with his finger. Instantly, he drew his hand away, cringing in disgust when black liquid oozed out.

"What is it?" Eve stepped back.

Abruptly, the knocks at the bedroom door became more persistent.

Frowning, he shook his head. "Get me a towel."

When she handed him a small washcloth, he carefully wiped the black substance that resembled ink and realized what it was. His demon blood was rejecting the body he'd possessed, and he was running out of time. When Sebastian died, his soul passed onto purgatory before he'd entered his body. Without the original soul, this body would soon perish.

"I'll get a bandage." Eve rummaged through the bathroom cabinet. Finding a first-aid kit, she came up with a large bandage and gauze tape.

When the loud knocking continued, he barked, "Hang on!"

"Should I clean it before I put this on?" Eve asked with the bandages in her hand.

"No." He took a deep breath. "The bandage will be fine."

After she placed it over the wound, he carefully got dressed.

"Ramael... is something wrong—"

"Don't call me that," he grumbled. "I told you to never speak of my name again. You will address me as Sebastian."

With a confused expression, she nodded. "Is something wrong with you?"

"It's nothing. I'll be fine."

Before he went to the door, he kissed her cheek. "Thank you, Eve."

As he approached the door, he cracked it open. "Who's there?"

"I'm sorry to disturb you, Master. It's Fredrick... and Corbin," his voice sounded stressed. "May we speak to you in private?"

Aggravated, he yanked open the door and stepped out.

"What do you want?"

"M-master," Fredrick stuttered. "We brought Taliah to the estate like you asked, and she—"

"Well, go on!" He snapped.

"S-she's brought some kind of creature with her," his voice trembled. "It looks like a ghost, and she called it her son."

Narrowing his eyes, he turned toward Corbin. "Did you see it?"

"Yes, Master," Corbin replied. "She threatened to cut my throat."

"Why would she do that?" He glanced back at Fredrick. "You must have done, or said something to provoke her."

"We didn't do anything." Fredrick shrugged.

Crossing his arms over his chest, he let out an exhausted breath. "Stay away from her," he demanded. "Do you hear me?"

When they didn't respond, he shouted, "Answer me!"

"Y-yes, Master," Fredrick stammered.

Corbin bowed his head. "Yes, Master."

"From now on, I'll deal with Taliah myself. In the meantime, you keep your distance with her. Are we clear?"

When they agreed, he stumbled against the door. The wound on his shoulder blade surged in pain like he'd been set on fire.

Corbin reached out to help him. "Master, are you all right?"

Composing himself, he waved Corbin away. "It's nothing. I'm fine."

When Corbin lowered his hand, Sebastian reached for the door. "Make sure you prepare for the meeting. All the council members will arrive this evening."

Fredrick nodded. "Yes, of course, Master."

As he opened the bedroom door, an odd shiver in his body bubbled up. Stepping inside, he moved without the power and grace he was used to. Slowly, he went into the bathroom and removed his shirt. As he looked into the mirror, Eve came up behind him and saw the bandage soaked with the same vile, black substance. As he removed it, the patch on his back was larger and the flesh underneath smelled rotten.

Eve panicked. "What's happening to you?"

"Taliah can fix this," he stated firmly.

"Who's Taliah?"

Moving toward the shower, he cranked on the water. "She's a powerful Wicca that's going to help me change this human-infested world."

Avoiding his statement, she changed the subject. "Do you want me to help you bathe?"

"No." He removed his pants and stepped under the water.

Before he shut the glass door, she said, "I'll be in the bedroom when you finish. You'll need help with a fresh dressing."

After showering, he staggered back into the bedroom with a towel around his waist. Without the energy to get dressed, he sat down on the edge of the bed. When Eve bandaged his wound, he eased back and closed his eyes. Feeling nauseous, he placed his hand over his stomach.

Eve sat down beside him. "When will I meet her?"

With his eyes barely cracked, he looked at her. "Soon," he replied in a frail voice.

Feeling uneasy, she worried about his condition. "You don't look so well. Do you want me to get her?"

"No," he said without haste. "I just need to rest."

She smoothed her palm over his leg. "Let me know if you need anything."

When she left the room, he closed his eyes. His brain waves blended into a whirl, but his body was too weak to sustain consciousness. Drifting into a deep sleep, he had a vision. Floating above his own body, it was like he was actually looking down at himself. Moving through the darkness, he was surrounded by thick fog as he entered an old cemetery. Coming to a large mausoleum, he saw a light flicker from the inside. Opening an iron gate, he stood between rows of coffins on each side. Kneeling down, he smoothed his hand over the one marked with a cross... only to see his arm was not his own. His flesh turned into a black, transparent shadow. Panicked, he thrashed around the bed trying to wake himself, but he'd sunk too deep to get free of the dream.

Chapter Thirty-Five

When Kyle's cell phone buzzed, he woke up and rolled over. Grabbing it off the nightstand, he saw a text message from Celina: Meet me in the kitchen. BTW, there's a fresh pot of coffee.

Feeling excited, he slid his legs out from under the covers and got out of bed. Not bothering with a shower, he darted for the closet and grabbed a pair of jeans and a T-shirt. Before he zipped up, he padded into the bathroom, used the facilities, and brushed his teeth.

Before entering the kitchen, he inhaled the strong aroma of fresh brewed coffee coming from inside. Reaching for the door, he glanced down at his bare feet and cursed. Now that he'd bonded with Celina, he was going to have to step it up a notch and work on his bad habits.

After pouring himself a cup of java, he heard someone come in. When he turned around, Celina was standing in the kitchen doorway. Her hair was pulled back into a messy ponytail and her eyes were puffy. Even though she looked like she'd been up all night, she was still gorgeous.

With the mug close to his mouth, he immediately lowered it and offered it to her.

"No thanks." She smiled. "I've already had four cups."

Lifting the porcelain rim to his lips, he paused and asked, "Have you had breakfast?"

"No, have you?"

Shaking his head, he took a sip of his coffee. "Come sit down." He motioned her toward the table. "I'll whip us something up."

Finally deciding on bacon, eggs, and cherry Danish rolls, she watched him prepare the food. "You like to cook, don't you?"

He nodded holding a spatula in his hand. "Yeah, I suppose I do."

After the combination of the salty bacon and sweet glaze, she leaned back in her chair. "I'm stuffed." She let out a long exhale, rubbing her stomach. "Thank you, Kyle. Everything was delicious."

"You're welcome." Reaching for the last Danish, he offered it to her. "There's one more left."

"No, thanks." She shook her head. "I couldn't eat another bite."

Watching him lick the frosting off his fingertips, she caught sight of his tongue and felt a stirring in her body. Taking a deep breath, she glanced down his body and noticed his bare feet. Smiling, she giggled.

When he realized what she was laughing at, his face turned three shades of red. "Sorry, I forgot to put on shoes."

"No, don't apologize." She lifted one foot, revealing her flip-flop. "I like being comfortable too."

At the sound of a baby crying, they stopped laughing and turned around. Without a shirt, and barefoot, Tim walked into the kitchen with one hand holding onto Natalie, and the other rubbing his eyes.

He yawned so hard, they heard his jaw pop. "Sorry, she's been up all night." Groaning under his breath, Tim mumbled, "I smell coffee."

Kyle pointed at the coffee pot and asked, "Would you like some?"

As he shifted Natalie on his hip, his voice perked up. "That sounds great."

When Kyle handed him a cup, Natalie whined and reached for it. "No, sweetheart." He kissed her forehead. "That's not for you."

"She looks a lot like you," Celina commented.

"Yeah, she does, except her eyes," Kyle added. "She has Angel's eyes. But she's got your chin and eyebrows."

Glancing down, he looked at Natalie and cocked a brow. "Hmmm... that's what Angel says."

Crinkling her little face, she started to fuss. "Shhh," he whispered softly, and put down his coffee. "Daddy's got you." He cuddled her close, and gave her a bottle.

Taking to it immediately, she cooed and squeaked the way babies do when they're content.

"Thanks for the caffeine." He reached for his coffee, and took the last sip. "I better get her upstairs to bed."

Before he left, he turned toward Celina. "Did you find anything helpful in the book?"

She shook her head, feeling defeated. "Unfortunately, no," her voice sounded bone-tired. "I've been up since four o'clock going through it again. So far I haven't found anything."

"I appreciate all your help, Celina." He smiled. "Let me know if you find anything."

* * * *

When Angel woke, she stretched her arms across the bed, feeling well rested. Tim had taken care of Natalie all night, giving her a much-needed break.

Going by the clock on the bedside table, she'd slept all through the night. Since she'd given birth, this was the first time she'd gotten a full night of rest without having to get up.

Thinking about that moment brought back memories of how Natalie changed both her and Tim's lives. She'd been in her full trimester without the slightest acknowledgement of the pregnancy. *God, what a nightmare that had been,* she thought. On that morning, she'd looked down at the wetness on the sheets, wondering for a moment whether she'd lost control of her bladder. Then she felt an excruciating pain in her lower abdomen followed by a lot of blood. Ten minutes later she'd been flat on an exam table with Dr. Helen Carrington stating she was getting ready to deliver a baby. Like a lot of dramatic things, the birth was a surprise, but when Natalie arrived, it was a glorious moment.

Coming back to the present, she eased out of bed and headed for the door just as Tim came in.

"She's finally sleeping." He yawned.

Everything had changed when Natalie was born. The rhythm of their nights and days were off—not to mention sleep—and it had been a while since they had time alone.

She reached up and cupped his face. "Thank you, honey." When she kissed him, it ended up being long and slow.

"I missed you last night," he whispered.

"I missed..."

His tongue in her mouth silenced her, as did his hands, which ended up on her hips.

When he picked her up, she wrapped her arms around his neck. Placing her cheek to his ear, she felt the soft brush of his morning stubble against her skin.

Before he managed to get her to the bed, cries came from the baby monitor that quickly escalated into a full-blown wail.

She raised her brows. "I'm so sorry."

He kissed her cheek, and lowered her onto the bed. "I'll go, honey."

There absolutely was no expression of disappointment in his eyes, or his tone. He'd never been resentful of Natalie; if anything, he'd been too self-sacrificing.

"No, sweetheart." Her eyes softened. "You've been up all night." She stood up. "I'll go."

He winked. "We'll continue this later."

As Angel hurried down the hall, she could hear Natalie crying at the top of her lungs. Opening the nursery door, she rushed over to the crib. "Shhh," she soothed. "Mommy's here."

Natalie reached her little arms out and calmed some—especially as she was picked up. After a fast diaper change, she eased down into a rocking chair with Natalie in her arms. As the baby finally settled, Angel let her head fall back against the rocker in a state of satisfaction. She loved being a mother.

Gently placing Natalie back into her crib, she quietly left the room. Hurrying back to the bedroom, she prayed Tim was still awake and in the mood.

Opening the door, she looked toward the bed and noticed he managed to remove all his clothes. His heavy breathing signified he was sound asleep, with his brows relaxed, and his lips partially open.

Removing her robe, she slipped under the blanket. The warmth radiated from his body when she curled next to him, feeling sensual against her bare skin. She felt him stir as he put his mouth to her ear and whispered, "I love you."

"I love you too."

Rolling on top of her, he murmured, "I want you."

Smoothing her hands up his heavy arms, she trailed over the pads of his tight chest and down to his stomach.

When he nestled his way in between her legs, she felt his arousal against her thighs.

She shivered as he blew a light breath over her nipple. He was so careful with her, caressing them with his hands and kissing them softly. "I've missed this," he purred.

He moved lower, and she arched her back in anticipation. When he looked up, she saw the intense expression in his stare. He was once again the dominant lover he'd always been.

"I want to go slow." His warm breath prickled her skin.

That wasn't going to be a problem, she thought. For him, she would do anything.

They made love three times... once on the bed, on the floor halfway to the bathroom, and again in the shower.

Afterward, they wrapped themselves in thick towels and climbed back in bed. She curled back around his warm body as they drifted off to sleep.

❧ *Chapter Thirty-Six*

Early in the morning, Jace headed downstairs to the estate's gym. When he'd finished with the weights, he hopped on the treadmill. To keep a fast pace, he lost himself in the music blaring through his earbuds. The heavy metal on his phone was loud enough to drown out the pounding of his feet. The first three miles flew by fast. At the fifth mile, he'd built up a sweat. When mile seven arrived, he reached for the speed control and dialed it down. His butt had been royally kicked, leaving his lungs screaming, and his thighs burning.

Grabbing the towel he'd draped over the console, he brought it to his face and wiped the sweat out of his eyes. As he reached out to put it back, Jem stepped in front of the machine.

Pressing the stop button, Jace pulled out his earbuds. "What's up?"

"She's gone," Jem uttered in a miserable tone. "Mia's gone."

"What do you mean she's gone?"

"She got upset with me last night and left."

"Why?" Jace shrugged. "What happened?"

"She told me she didn't want to wait a year." Jem exhaled. "She wants to get married within six months. She's already picked out her dress."

"And... you're not ready?"

Jem sighed. "Yes... No... I don't know!"

"I thought you were ready to get hitched?"

"I am. It just... hit me all of a sudden. After everything that's happened with Alexander, and finding out Sebastian's missing, I would rather wait until things quiet down."

Placing his palm on Jem's shoulder, he chuckled. "Brother, it's never going to quiet down around here. If you love her, you should just do it now. I've actually been thinking of asking Tessa."

Jem's brows popped. "Really?"

"Yeah." Jace smiled. "Why wait when we know they're the one?"

"You're right. I'm such an ass."

Jace patted his shoulder. "Nah, you're just nervous."

Checking his watch, Jem noticed the time. "I'm worried about her." He shook his head. "I drove to her apartment last night, but she wasn't there. Every time I call her, it just goes to her voice mail."

Leaping off the machine, Jace grabbed his phone. "Come on. Let's go find your woman."

* * * *

Mia unlocked the door to her apartment she'd kept even after moving in with Jem, and stepped in. As she glanced around, the place brought back memories that made her think of him. After their argument last night, she'd stormed out of the Covenant and drove around most of the night crying. She worried he was getting cold feet about the wedding. Hopefully, she prayed, it was just his nerves. Later this morning, she decided to come here and get some rest. As she entered the kitchen, she rummaged through the cabinets looking for something to eat. Thinking of food made her think of Jem again. She remembered the first time she made him dinner in this kitchen.

As she got lost in her thoughts, her stomach growled. She debated whether to have plain oatmeal or go all out and make pancakes. Searching through the pantry for the pancake mix, she heard a loud crash coming from down the hall.

Reaching into the silverware drawer, she pulled out a butcher knife. When she got closer to the bedroom, she called out, "Who's there?"

With the knife in her hand, she tiptoed toward the bedroom and flattened against the wall. Slowly peeking around the corner, she looked inside.

Abruptly, she jumped and almost dropped the knife when a black cat darted out. "Christ!" She gripped it tight and blew out a deep breath. "You scared me to death!"

Padding over to her with its tail straight up, it weaved in between her legs purring.

Bending down, she sat the knife on the floor and swept the cat into her arms. "How in the world did you get in here?"

The cat meowed and rubbed its head against her neck.

Curious, she went inside and noticed the window cracked with a broken vase on the floor. "How did that get open?"

Startled, she wheeled around when she heard a knock coming from the front door. "Jesus—"

Hurrying down the hall with cat in tow, she looked out the peephole. She smiled when she saw Jem and Jace anxiously waiting outside the door.

When she opened it, Jem's brows relaxed with relief. "Thank God you're all right." He reached out for her. "I've been worried about you all night, honey."

The cat jumped out of her arms, and ran toward Jace.

Weaving around his leg, he bent down and picked it up. "Well, who do we have here?"

With the door wide open, Jem left Jace outside with the cat, and wrapped his arms around Mia.

"I love you, honey." He cradled her face in his palms and brought his mouth to hers. Even though they were only apart for one night, it felt like forever. Shaking his head, he muttered, "I'm sorry, Mia. Will you still marry me?"

"Of course." She caressed his face. "I love you."

He pulled her in tight again, and held onto his mate. "I love you too."

Standing in the doorway, Jace whispered to the cat, "I guess we should give these two love birds their privacy."

"Go ahead and take the car." Jem motioned for him to leave. "I'll ride back with Mia."

"Wait," Mia called out. "Jace, will you take the cat with you?"

"Who does he belong too?"

She shrugged. "I found him in the bedroom. The window was left half-open, and he must have gotten in through there."

He nodded. "What's his name?"

She shook her head. "I haven't a clue. You can name him... or her."

Lifting the cat's tail, Jace confirmed, "It's a boy!"

"Congratulations." Mia snickered. "He's all yours."

Rubbing the feline's head, Jace chuckled. "Come on, Buddy. Let's get out of here."

Chapter Thirty-Seven

Eve opened her eyes, and glanced at the clock. In a panic, she shot upright, thinking the time couldn't be right. She'd been asleep on the couch for two hours since she left Sebastian—how had she lost track so badly?

It took her no time at all to make it up the stairs and to his room. Knocking on the door, she called out, "Sebastian." She waited for a response. When there was none, she reached for the knob and put her ear to the door. Hearing nothing, she barged in, finding him still in bed.

Wings of panic fanned as she caught sight of him. For a split second, she thought about escaping, but instead she rushed to him. "Sebastian!" She shook his shoulders.

After numerous attempts to wake him, she placed the side of her face over his and sensed a faint breath coming from his parted lips. With all her strength she shook him one last time and screamed, "Ramael!"

Like a strike of dual matches, his eyes flashed wide. She gasped when she saw his pupils. It was the oddest thing: one moment they were black and the next they were completely white.

In a semi-state of shock, she glanced around the room trying to figure out what to do. Her first thought was to call an ambulance... except that was ridiculous. A human hospital couldn't help with his condition. Instantly, Taliah came to mind. She'd remembered Sebastian telling her Taliah could fix this.

Without hesitation, she dashed out the door, and ran smack into Damien.

Grasping her arms, he steadied her. "What's wrong, Eve?"

"Where's Taliah's room? I need her help!"

He motioned for her to follow. "Come with me."

Outside her room, Eve pounded on the door. "Please!" She pleaded. "Taliah, open the door!"

When it swung open, Taliah cursed, "What the hell—"

Eve ranted hysterically, "Something's wrong with Sebastian!"

With her voice calm and in control, Taliah said, "Take me to him."

Following them inside Sebastian's room, Taliah inhaled the strong scent and knew exactly what was wrong. "His body is dying," she confirmed.

"Can you help him?"

Narrowing her eyes, she glared at Eve. "I will need a blood sacrifice."

"What the hell does that mean?" Damien barked.

"If you want him to live, one of you must offer your blood," she explained. "I give my word." Her lips curled up like a bow. "You'll live through the ritual."

"I'll do it," Eve quickly offered.

With his adrenaline running, Damien's rage made him shake. "No!" He yelled with his hands wound into tight fists. "Please, Eve," he begged. "We don't even know if she's telling the truth."

"Sorry, Damien," her voice trembled. "I have to do this."

"Follow me." Taliah stared at Damien. "Bring his body to my room."

There was no way he was going to let Eve do this. As Damien lunged at Taliah, all hell broke loose. Suddenly, he felt something grab around his throat and lift his body off the floor. In a swift motion, he was tossed across the room like a rag doll. When he hit the wall, the forceful impact whipped his head back. Falling to the floor, Damien gasped for air.

Eve screamed, and rushed to him. "Damien, are you all right?"

Taliah stood in the doorway with a smug grin on her face. "Had enough?"

Slowly sitting up, he coughed with his hand over his throat. Feeling helpless, he kept his mouth shut and nodded.

Regaining his composure, Damien muscled Sebastian off the bed and carried him to Taliah's room with Eve close behind.

Taliah pointed toward a raised platform. "Put him there."

She wrapped herself with a black robe, and pulled the hood over her head. From underneath the draping fabric, light spilled out as she floated above the floor. Reaching down toward Sebastian, she took his face into her palms, and lifted his head. Lowering her face to his, she began to chant.

As the chanting continued, Eve and Damien settled back against the wall and watched.

Abruptly, she stopped and snapped her fingers. "Come here." She motioned Eve over.

When Eve stood next to her, Taliah opened a wooden box full of daggers. "You must choose one."

With shaky hands, Eve placed her finger on top of one. "Ah," Taliah expressed with a cocked brow. "You chose the blood dagger."

Grabbing Eve's hand, she held the blade above it. Eve's mouth flew open with a sharp wince as she sliced it across her skin. With a tight grip, Taliah held Eve's wrist over Sebastian's lips, letting the blood run down his throat.

Instantly, Sebastian arched off the platform and gasped for air. With his eyes wide, his voice croaked like he was holding back a scream.

"Sebastian!" Eve called out.

At the sound of her voice, he lifted his arm and held out his hand, moving his mouth soundlessly.

Taliah wrapped a cloth around Eve's wound and said, "He needs to rest." She glanced at Damien. "Take him back to his room."

Without haste, Damien scrambled over and obeyed her command.

When he laid Sebastian on the bed, Eve smoothed his long hair out of his face. "Are you in pain?"

"No," he said in a hoarse whisper.

Sitting on the edge of the bed, she reached for his hand and pressed her lips to his knuckles.

As his brows clenched, his eyes pleaded. "Please, stay with me."

Eve turned around when she heard Damien clearing his throat. "Master, do you want me to reschedule the council meeting?"

"Postpone it." He paused, and took a deep breath. "Tell them to be here tomorrow evening."

"Yes, Master," he agreed, and left them alone. As he walked out of the room, he closed his eyes and tried to erase the images of Eve in his head. Sooner or later, Damien thought, the demon was going to hurt her again. Next time, he was going to be there to stop him. Every dragging night without her... was a forever hell.

Gently, Eve stroked her fingers over Sebastian's face. When he flinched, she pulled her hand away. "Is there anything I can do for you?"

He nodded. "Will you... read to me?"

Before she got to her feet, she memorized his face, realizing it might be the last time if Taliah's ritual didn't work. For all her life, her heart had not been prone to breaking. She'd long suspected it was a result from her childhood. The kind of abuse she suffered had hardened her heart over the years.

Getting up, she paused and looked over her shoulder. Just then, his handsome face reminded her of the man she once loved. It was then she knew what she'd been fighting all along, and for once, she felt no desire to hide her feelings.

Across the room, Eve searched through several books on a shelf. Reaching out, she selected *The King Must Die* by Mary Renault. With the book in her hand, she slipped in bed beside him and read until he fell asleep. Closing the book, she glanced down at him and saw the pain on his face. His brows were furrowed, and his lips were formed into a tight line. Pulling up the blanket, she tucked her body against his and closed her eyes.

Chapter Thirty-Eight

After the subtle hint of wanting to be alone, Jace took the cat and left the apartment, giving Jem and Mia their privacy. Watching him leave, Jem pushed the door shut with Mia still pressed against his body. She was wearing a pair of tight jeans and a loose T-shirt. He slid his hands underneath, feeling the warm skin of her lower back.

"I missed you last night."

She sagged against him. "I missed you too."

Pulling back, he frowned when he noticed tears spilling from her eyes. Reaching up, he brushed both her cheeks with his thumbs.

"I was making breakfast." She smiled, trying to switch the mood. "Are you hungry for pancakes?"

Placing a kiss against her hair, he inhaled. "That sounds delicious." God, he loved the way she smelled. Her scent reminded him of sweet jasmine, and more glorious than any perfume.

Leading him into the kitchen, she motioned him toward a chair. "Have a seat."

The image of her preparing food for him suddenly warmed his heart. Moving behind her, he latched onto her waist, and pulled her against his chest. With a shudder, he dropped his head down into her fragrant, silky hair and gathered her up, molding her softness to the contours of his body.

"Let's eat," she giggled, tugging him back to the table.

When he parked it, she asked, holding the plate of pancakes, "How many?"

"Two, please."

After she placed them in his plate, she reached out and smoothed her hand through his shoulder-length waves. "Eat. Then I'm taking you to bed."

He cocked a brow. "Mmmm... that sounds better than pancakes."

She prepared them exactly the way he liked: loaded with butter and syrup. He ate both of them, and though they should have perked him up, the exhaustion of being up all night had a death grip on his body.

She took his hand. "Come on, let's go to bed."

He rose to his feet, tucked her against him, and together they walked down the hallway leading to the bedroom.

Outside the room, she tightened her arms around his waist and cuddled against his chest. Inhaling, she closed her eyes and breathed in his scent.

"How does September twenty-six sound?" He whispered close to her ear.

In surprise, she looked up. "That's the same day we first met. Are you sure?"

"Yes, honey," he said, staring into her eyes. Her long eyelashes accentuated the color of her irises. "It'll be perfect."

"I love you, Jem."

He grinned. "I love you, more."

Reaching down, he swept her into his arms and carried her into the bedroom. Staring at him with bright crimson eyes, she waited for his touch. Sitting her on the bed, he gathered her T-shirt and pulled it over her head. Glancing down, he noticed her breasts were tight at the tips already.

When she slid her jeans down her long legs, he glanced over her smooth skin, and to her perfect hips. And the place below her navel... that was his heaven.

Quickly slipping out of his clothes, he sank down beside her and eased back. "Come here," he whispered with his hand held out.

As their hands joined, he pulled her on top. Shifting his body, he rolled her on her back. She smiled from underneath his body, and ran her hands up his smooth back, feeling his thick muscles as he held himself above her.

Moving beside her, he reached toward the column of her neck and swept his hand down, stopping over her heart. Feeling the fast rhythm, he placed his lips to the center of her chest and peppered soft kisses.

"I love you," he murmured against her skin. "I am so in love with you, Mia."

* * * *

When Jace arrived back at the Covenant, he carried the cat inside. Upstairs in his room, he placed Buddy in a chair. "Wait here." He smoothed his hand over the cat's fur, and went into the bathroom to take a shower.

His body was stiff and ached after the seven miles he'd run this morning. Cranking on the water, he stepped under the warm spray. After a quick shower, he dried off, threw on some clothes and padded over to the bed and collapsed. With his head laid back, he heard a muffled meow coming from across the room.

Lifting his head, he looked at the chair he'd put the cat in, and saw two glowing eyes underneath. Getting up, he walked over and knelt down. When he wiggled his fingers, a paw appeared.

"It's all right, Buddy," he said in a soft tone. "You'll get used to this place."

Slowly crawling out, it rubbed against his hand and purred.

Abruptly, he lifted his head when his phone rang. Recognizing the ringtone, he knew it was Casey Barton.

Heading over toward the bed, he grabbed his phone off the nightstand and answered, "Hey, what's up?"

"We're playing at Big Star tonight."

Jace closed his eyes, and let out a heavy sigh.

After a stretch of silence, Casey asked, "Hey, you there?"

"Yeah, I'm here." He pushed his wet hair out of his face, and cleared his throat. "I can't tonight."

"Seriously?" Casey laughed. "When do you ever turn down a chance to play at Big Star?"

"Tonight's not a good time."

"You got better plans?"

As much as he hated the idea of turning down a chance to play at his favorite place, he'd rather take the night off and make love to Tessa.

"All right," Jace finally agreed. "What time is the gig?"

"Ten," he replied. "We're going on right after the cover band. Don't forget to tell your brother. I've already told Kyle."

"We're the headliner?"

"Yeah," Casey's voice spiked with excitement. "Cool, huh?"

"That's awesome, bro!"

When Jace ended the call, he picked up the cat and stroked behind its ears. "Let's get you a can of tuna."

With the cat in tow, he stood at the top of the staircase and glanced out the colorful stained glass window as the morning sun glistened in. Just as he took a step, a loud crash came from downstairs. Startled, the cat jumped out of his arms and darted toward the sound.

Chapter Thirty-Nine

Hours after Sebastian and Eve drifted into a deep sleep, she awoke with a whisper in her ear. "You really loved him, didn't you?"

Startled, she flinched and her eyes snapped to his. Clearing her throat, she muttered, "Yes."

"When you look at me, do you think of him?"

She paused before she answered. "Yes."

Staring at her with his soulless black eyes, he took a deep breath. "Is that why you helped save my life?"

She nodded in silence.

"Do you think you could learn to love me?"

Logically she knew the demon had possessed the Sebastian she once loved, but he was still in the body of the man she couldn't stop loving. At first, he was cruel and ruthless. And now he seemed to have changed somehow. He was kinder, more compassionate with her. In her heart, she wanted to pretend he was Sebastian, though she knew he was never coming back.

Tears clouded her eyes, but she didn't allow them to fall. "I don't know."

Gently grasping her hand, he pressed a tender kiss on her soft skin.

She forced a smile. "How do you feel?"

"Better now," he stared at her with compassion, "thanks to you."

"Would you like me to replace your bandage?"

When he nodded, she went to the bathroom to retrieve a washcloth and new bandages. Opening the medicine cabinet, she was amazed by the supplies he kept on hand. Inside, she found bandages of all kinds, including gauze tape and surgical kits. Grabbing what she needed, she went into the bedroom and sat next to him. Helping him turn on his side, she carefully peeled the tape from his skin and removed the gauze. Stunned, she gasped when she saw what was underneath.

Stretching his neck, he tried to look. "What is it?"

Astounded, she said, "Your wound... it's already healing."

Inhaling a deep breath, he exhaled in relief. "Good."

Working the washcloth around the edges, he flinched when she moved to the center.

"I'm sorry." She pulled her hand away. "Does it hurt?"

"No." He smiled a little. "It's fine."

After she placed a clean dressing over his wound, he frowned at the sound of a sharp knock coming from the bedroom door.

"You stay put, I'll go," she offered.

When she opened the door, a tall, thin man stood on the other side with a silver tray in his hands.

He nervously cleared his throat. "I'm Fredrick Mercier," he said in a heavily accented voice. "Is he awake?"

Abruptly, Sebastian called out, "Come in, Fredrick."

He nodded at Eve, and moved past her. After placing the tray on the bedside dresser, he bowed his head. "How are you feeling, Master?"

"I'll be fine."

"I thought you might be hungry."

Closing his eyes in exhaustion, he muttered, "Thank you, Fredrick."

With his lips drawn thin, he stared down at Sebastian. "I'll come back later, Master. Is there anything else I can get you?"

"No. That'll be all."

As Fredrick turned around, he froze when he met Eve's eyes. Noticing the odd color, he cringed in fear.

Narrowing her stare, she shrugged. "Is there something wrong?"

"No." He quickly looked down, and hurried past her. "Excuse me, please."

When the door closed, she heard Sebastian wince. "I feel a little lightheaded," he groaned. "I need to get out of—"

When he struggled to get up, she rushed over and placed her hands on his shoulders halting his movement. "No, Sebastian. You shouldn't move." With one hand on his shoulder, she reached up with the other and smoothed through his silky black waves. "I'll feed you."

Closing his eyes, he craned his neck, and tilted his head closer so she could reach more of his hair.

As she ran her hand through his long strands, it reminded her of the past. Letting out a sigh, she pulled away and reached for the tray of food. With a plate in her hand, she forked a piece of steak. Holding it in front of his lips, he opened his mouth and took a bite. As he ate, his eyes were steady on hers. The black depths somehow appeared softened, and less frightening.

After he finished off most of it, she put the plate away and cuddled next to him until he drifted off to sleep. Just as Eve's eyelids started to close, she heard a soft knock at the door.

Quietly, she eased out of bed and padded toward the door. When she opened it, Taliah glared at her. As the overhead light cast down on her blazing red hair, it brought out the light green in her eyes.

"Please, come in." Eve moved aside, motioning her in.

Without a word, Taliah walked in with a smug expression on her face. When she sauntered past Eve, something drifted behind her. Sensing an odd presence, Eve felt a cold chill run down her spine. Shivering, she instantly crossed her arms. Out of the corner of her eye, she caught a glimpse of a shadowed figure with glowing eyes. When she turned her head, it disappeared.

When Taliah plopped down beside Sebastian, he opened his eyes. Turning around, she scowled at Eve defiantly. "If you don't mind, I would like to speak with him in private."

Eve shifted her eyes toward Sebastian as if waiting for his response.

He nodded in her direction. "It's okay."

When she didn't leave, Taliah pointed at the door. "Go!" She ordered. "Leave us."

🐾 *Chapter Forty*

As Jace rushed down the staircase, he heard the loud noise coming from inside the kitchen. Opening the door, he stood in shock. "What the—"

With pots and pans scattered all over the floor, he noticed little bare feet sticking out of the bottom pantry. In disbelief, he moved closer and knelt down.

"Natalie?"

Out of the corner of his eye, he caught a glimpse of a black ball of fur dart past him in a flash. Sticking out of the pantry next to the little feet, he saw the cat's tail wiggling back and forth. Next, he heard a meow echo from inside followed by little sounds of a child giggling.

Startled, Jace lost his balance and fell backward when he saw Natalie crawling out with the cat. In his amazement, she'd made a miraculous growth spurt. Only yesterday, she could barely hold her head up on her own. Now, she'd grown the size of a toddler that could obviously manage to climb out of a crib and down stairs.

Mumbling gibberish, she looked at Jace pointing at the cat.

"Kitty," he told her.

"K-Ki... ddee," she mumbled, trying to mimic his words.

Jace shook his head. "How in the world did you get so big?"

Bobbing her head up and down, she let go of the cat and pointed at her belly. "B-Beeg!"

"Come here, sweetheart." He patted his lap, motioning her over.

When she easily crawled to him, he stood up with her in his arms. "Your Mommy and Daddy are going have a coronary when they see you."

* * * *

Reaching into his closet, Alexander pulled out a Louis Vuitton blazer. Sliding it on, it felt tight over his broad shoulders. Even if the thing was custom-tailored, he would still feel stuffed into it with his Viking warrior size.

Glancing into the full-length mirror, he paused and stared at himself. *Good lord*, he thought. The tight blazer made him look ridiculous. Instantly, he stripped it off and hung it back up. With impatient hands, he pulled his hair back and tied the long length with a strap of leather.

Pumped to see Helen, all he could think about was burying his face in her hair and inhaling her arousing scent.

Staring into the mirror again, he practiced a smile. As he widened it, his cheeks felt like they were going to crack. Rubbing his jaw, he thought of Helen and the strong bond he felt for her.

"Look at you." The sound of Drakon's baritone voice boomed through the open doorway.

Alexander wheeled around. "I'm surprising Helen with breakfast." He straightened his collar. "Is this too much?"

"No." Drakon chuckled.

Alexander shrugged. "Are you sure?"

Drakon nodded. "You look just fine."

"Thanks."

"Tim wants us all to meet in the library later this evening," Drakon said, leaning against the archway. "He wants you there too."

Alexander felt uneasy. "Is this about that book... Celina brought?"

Drakon nodded again, crossing his arms over his chest. "Yeah, and hopefully it has the information we're looking for."

"What time?"

"Five o'clock," Drakon confirmed.

Just as Drakon turned away to leave, he stopped and said, "Hey, Alexander?"

Catching his attention, Alexander looked in his direction. "Yeah?"

"I think Helen's an intelligent, beautiful woman. She'll make a good mate." He grinned. "I just thought you'd want to know."

"Thanks, Drakon."

"And I think she's really interested in you too," he tacked on.

Alexander cocked his head to the side. "Really?"

"Yeah, I've seen the way she looks at you."

With a smile, he waved as Drakon left. "See you at five."

* * * *

As Helen paced back and forth, her flat heels clicked over the tiled floor. After two trips around the room, she came to rest in front of her workstation. Reaching into the pocket of her white coat, she retrieved her glasses. Placing them on, she looked into the microscope and sighed. Working long hours, she was exhausted, trying to find the cure for the Breedline aging process.

Rubbing her tired eyes, she decided to take a break. Getting up to use the bathroom, she turned on the light and caught her reflection in the mirror. Taking a closer look, she swore her hair was starting to turn gray. She hardly recognized herself from the dark circles under her eyes, and the pale color of her skin. Displeased at her appearance, she sighed as she took off her glasses and placed them back into her pocket.

With intentions of spending the rest of the morning without any interruptions, she frowned at the sound of a knock.

Moving to the door, she opened it with a surprised expression. "Alexander."

Mustering a smile, he held up a white bag. "I hope you like croissants."

"Oh, that sounds delicious. Thank you."

Motioning him inside, she guided him to her desk in the corner of the room. Placing the bag on top, he pulled out a chair for her. As she sat down, she watched him move to the chair across from her. He looked handsome dressed in a casual pair of jeans and a button-down, collared shirt. She felt a warm flush drift across her skin when she noticed his long waves were neatly pulled back.

The aroma of pastry and coffee spiked her appetite when he opened the bag. He pulled out a Styrofoam container, and two coffees. "How's your research coming along?"

"Oh, it's going just fine," she replied, reaching for a coffee. As she took a sip, she'd thought of what she'd just told him. It was a bit of an overstatement. Actually, she'd been putting in a ton of hours, but hadn't even got close to finding a breakthrough.

He placed his palms on the desk facing up, gesturing for her hands. "Well, I hope your research is very successful."

Placing her hands in his, he entwined his fingers with hers.

"Thank you, Alexander." Pulling out of his hands, she nervously reached for her coffee again. As she lifted it to her mouth, she spilled some on her lab coat.

"Oh, heavens," she muttered, trying to wipe it off. "I'm terribly clumsy, aren't I?"

She removed the coat, and placed it over the empty chair next to hers.

"No... not clumsy," he murmured. "I think you're absolutely beautiful." His eyes softened. Leaning forward, he pressed a tender kiss to her lips.

As their kiss lingered, she gripped the arm of her chair and inhaled the breathtaking scent of his cologne. When he slowly pulled back, he noticed she was blushing.

She smiled. "Thank you... for breakfast."

Staring into each other's eyes, Helen jumped when her phone rang. Pulling her eyes away, she glanced at the number. "Sorry, but I have to take this call."

He nodded, and reached for his coffee.

She answered in a professional and controlled voice, "Dr. Carrington speaking."

With her brows clenched tight, she listened carefully. "I'm actually here in the exam room," she said. "Bring her downstairs. I'll be waiting."

"Is everything all right?" Alexander asked.

"That was Tim. It's about his daughter, Natalie."

"Is she sick?"

"No, she's experienced a rapid growth rate, which of course is normal for a half-breed. They're bringing her here right now."

"Oh." His brows arched. "Was Tim and Angel not aware of that?"

"By the tone of his voice, I'm guessing not."

He nodded. "I'll give you some privacy." He rose from his chair, and moved to the door. "I'll be right outside if you need anything."

Chapter Forty-One

Without saying another word, Eve silently exited the room, giving Taliah and Sebastian privacy. Outside the door, she sagged against it and sighed. Closing her eyes, she withstood the dimness only a moment before panic popped her lids open. Stiffening her resolve, she forced herself to be strong, but it was a battle. Damn it... she hated being shut out. Then again, she wondered what Taliah had to say to Sebastian that was too private for her to hear.

* * * *

When the door clicked shut, Taliah leaned forward, placing her index finger to Sebastian's chest. "This body will not thrive much longer. I can only keep it alive for a short while. Sooner or later you will need to possess someone else. This time, the soul needs to be intact."

"Are you sure there's nothing you can do?"

Shaking her head, she smirked. "It's Eve you're worried about, isn't it? If you're no longer in this body, you think she'll leave, don't you?"

Sebastian instantly frowned, and lowered his head. When he lifted his chin back up, he glared at her. "There has to be another way."

With a cocked brow, she suggested, "What about Damien?"

"What does he have to do with this?"

She rolled her eyes. "Haven't you noticed the way they look at each other? They're practically in love."

"That's not true!"

"Whatever." She chuckled. "It doesn't matter what you think. You're going to need a healthy body, and Damien's would be perfect. And I'm sure Eve wouldn't mind."

He narrowed his stare. "If it comes to that, I don't want you saying a word of this to her. Do you understand?"

With a sarcastic gesture, she used her hand, motioning her lips zipped tight. "My lips are sealed."

Turning toward the shadow in the corner of the room, Sebastian kept his stare. "Lucas... you need to make sure you stay out of sight," he ordered. "You're scaring the hell out of my council members. I need them thinking with their heads on straight."

Taliah burst out laughing. "Your council members are weak!"

"Don't push me, Taliah," he said through gritted teeth.

Moving toward the door, she paused and looked over her shoulder. "If they boss me around one more time, I'll cut off what little they already have."

"Don't worry, I've already warned them."

Reaching for the door, she added, "You need to make a decision within a few weeks. If you don't want Damien's body, I'm sure we can find another suitable candidate."

* * * *

Not long after Helen ended the call with Tim, he rushed into the exam room with Natalie in his arms and Angel close behind. They were so panic stricken, they had Natalie upset and crying.

Reaching for Natalie, Helen whispered, "Shhh... you're okay, sweetheart."

As Tim handed her to Helen, he asked, "Is this normal for her to grow at this rate?"

Natalie cradled her head against Helen's shoulder, and rubbed her red, puffy eyes. Grabbing a tissue, Helen dabbed her tears away. Natalie took a couple of deep breaths, and exhaled with little hiccup noises.

"Yes, it's perfectly normal," Helen reassured. "Since she's half succubus, she'll continue to rapidly grow until she reaches the size of a two-year-old. From there, she'll stop and develop normally."

Angel leaned forward, and kissed Natalie on the cheek. "It's okay, honey. Mommy and Daddy loves you."

Moving closer, Tim smoothed his hand over Natalie's curls.

"You're going to see more changes each day, or two," Helen explained. "You need to prepare yourselves. Tomorrow she might be walking."

Angel shook her head. "Growing up in human foster care, I wasn't aware of this. Later, I found out a succubus child develops somewhat faster, but I had no idea it would be like this."

Placing a kiss on top of Natalie's head, Helen rocked her in her arms. "Everything's going to be just fine. You might want to think about getting her some new clothes." She chuckled glancing down at Natalie's stretched pajamas. "She's going to need a bigger size."

In frustration, Tim added, "We're definitely going to need a baby gate too."

Natalie whined with her arms straining toward Tim. As he reached out, she instantly went to him and cuddled her head into the crevice of his neck. When he caressed her back, she lifted her head and looked into his eyes. Pointing her finger, she mumbled, "Daa... daa."

With a feeling of joy, Tim grinned ear to ear.

Tears sprang into Angel's eyes. "I can't believe she said her first word."

Tim chuckled. "According to Jace, her first word was kitty."

"Ki... ddee!" Natalie clapped her hands.

Tim whispered in her ear, "You like that 'ol kitty cat, don't you?"

As she wiggled in his arms, her eyes lit up with excitement.

"Come on." Tim kissed her cheek. "Let's go find him."

Before they left, Angel hugged Helen. "Thank you, Helen. We're so lucky to have you here."

"You're welcome, and I'm glad to be here."

❧ Chapter Forty-Two

After no response to numerous calls and texts, Jace decided to drive back to Mia's apartment to find Jem. When he pulled up, her car was still in the driveway, which meant they were still here. Stepping up to the front door, he rang the doorbell and waited patiently. When no one answered, he knocked, and still got nothing.

Jem gathered Mia close and tucked her head into his neck. With his arm wrapped around her, he had no interest in whoever was pounding on the door. Unless someone was dying, he wasn't getting up.

Lying next to Jem, Mia stretched her legs and looked up at him. His brows were clenched and his lips were drawn into a tight line. "Jem, it could be important."

He sighed in frustration, and shut his eyes. "Shhh." He gently stroked the side of her face. "Just wait for a little while. Maybe they'll go away."

When the pounding became more persistent, he loosened his hold on her and lifted his head. Smoothing his hair back, he exhaled a deep breath. "I guess they're not going to give up," he groaned, shifting his legs out from under the blankets. "I'll be right back." He kissed Mia, and grabbed his pants.

After slipping into his jeans, he headed toward the door. Peering into the peephole, he cursed under his breath. When he swung the door open, he glared at Jace. "You'd better be bleeding."

"Sorry." Jace shrugged. "Was I interrupting something?"

Motioning Jace to stay put, he stepped inside and threw on a T-shirt. When Jem came back out, he closed the door. "What's so important?"

"We've got a gig at Big Star tonight."

Although Jem wasn't pleased with the interruption, he was excited about the news. "When did you get the gig?"

Jace propped his arm against the door. "Casey called me when I got back this morning. He's the one that got it for us."

"What time?"

"We go on at ten, right after the cover band."

Jem's eyes lit up. "We're the headliner?"

Jace nodded with his fist held out. "Don't leave me hanging, bro."

Rolling his eyes, Jem reached out and bumped knuckles with him. "Oh yeah, I almost forgot."

Jem shook his head. "Please don't tell me you've got bad news too."

"Nah, it's about Natalie. She's crawling now."

"What—"

"I'm serious." Jace arched a brow. "I was going downstairs to feed the cat, and I found her in the kitchen digging pots and pans from the pantry. She looks like she's almost a year old."

"How'd this happen?"

"According to Helen, all succubus babies grow at a faster rate," Jace explained. "After she gets the size of a two-year-old, she'll grow normal from then on. Anyway, you should have seen Tim and Angel when I took her back upstairs." He cracked up. "I thought they were going to have a heart attack."

"Wow." Jem shook his head. "I had no clue. I wonder if Mia knows about this."

Jace smirked. "If you guys plan on having kids someday, I think you should bring it up in case she doesn't know."

Jem reached up and rubbed his jaw. "Yeah, you're right."

"So why didn't you answer your phone this morning?" Jace frowned. "I've called you like a billion times."

Jem's lips curved into a coy smile. "Sorry."

"Okay, I get it." Jace batted his brows. "Make-up sex."

Without a word, Jem grinned ear to ear.

Moving toward his Jeep, Jace paused and looked over his shoulder. "Don't forget, we've got a meeting with Tim at five."

Jem waved. "Okay. I'll see you later."

* * * *

When Sebastian awoke later that afternoon, the first thing he did was reach for Eve. As she lay beside him, her eyes were closed. Watching her sleep, he noticed how her eyelashes fluttered and the soft sounds of her breathing. As his mind drifted, he thought about the conversation with Taliah. Before his current body was completely unusable, he had a few weeks to make a decision. And then Damien popped into his head.

His first instinct was to kill the bastard. Instead, he forced himself to be rational. If Eve really cared for Damien, maybe she would accept it if he possessed his body. Emotions filled his black heart, swelling it to the point of pain.

Wondering how his wound was healing, he reached around to his shoulder, and carefully removed the bandage. Stretching his neck, he looked at it out of the corner of his eye. It had already closed, and by tomorrow it would be nothing more than a scar. It didn't matter anyway, according to Taliah this body wouldn't last much longer.

"How are you feeling?" Eve's soft voice whispered next to him.

Her gentle voice snapped him back to reality. Suddenly, he felt an unbridled love and the chaos of his curse all at once. Without hesitating, he asked, "Do you have feelings for Damien?"

She froze. "What—"

"I won't be angry if you do."

"Yes," her voice trembled as tears built up in her eyes. "But I care for you too."

Feeling empty on the inside, he took a deep breath. Exhaling slowly, air eased out of his parted lips. "It's okay. I'm not mad."

"You're not?"

In silence, he shook his head.

Confused, she frowned. "What made you change? Why do you care for me now?"

Rolling over on his back, he ignored her questions and stared at the ceiling. "Eve, there's something I have to tell you."

Quietly listening, she could sense something in his tone was off. As he turned in her direction, his face expressed grief. "Soon I will have to take another body."

Her brows clenched together as if she was in pain. "But... why?"

Chapter Forty-Three

Exhausted, Celina sighed as she slumped in her chair and stared at the book feeling defeated. She'd searched through it the entire morning, and into the late afternoon. Sitting beside her, Kyle was stretched out in his chair with his bare feet propped up on the table.

"Nice feet." She chuckled.

"Thank you." He smiled, wiggling his toes.

Sitting up, she asked, "Hey... do you have a pocket knife on you?"

Confused, he reached into his pocket and dug it out. "What do you need it for?"

"Let's just say I have a sneaky suspicion about something."

As she reached for the blade, he frowned. "Be careful with that."

"Don't worry." She grinned. "I've handled one of these before."

In surprise, he arched a brow.

Opening the book to the back cover, she dug into it with the knife. Peeling back a page that was sealed, she found a small piece of paper hidden underneath.

He shrugged. "What's that?"

"I'm not sure?" She opened it, and smoothed it out. "Let's find out."

Quickly, he placed his feet on the floor and scooted his chair closer. "Well... what does it say?"

Her jaw dropped. "I don't believe it."

Puzzled, he shook his head. "What?"

"I found it!" She stood up and fist pumped into the air. "The demon can be destroyed!"

He rose from his chair. "How?"

With the book and piece of paper in her hand, she said, "It says a creature called the Beast can kill the Chiang-shih demon."

He grabbed his cell phone. "I'll call Tim and let him know you found something."

* * * *

When Tessa awoke, she was surrounded by a pile of pillows, and for a moment, she had no idea how long she'd been asleep. A quick glance at the clock told her it was already three o'clock in the afternoon.

Lying in bed, she rubbed her eyes and stretched her legs. Slowly sitting up, she noticed a bottle of water on the nightstand and a plate of fresh strawberries. She shook her head and found herself smiling. Jace must have come in sometime during her nap.

As she reached across the bed, her phone rang. Instead of grabbing the water, she picked up her phone and answered. "Hello."

"Hi, baby."

She grinned at the sound of Jace's voice.

"Hi." Closing her eyes for a moment, she could picture his gorgeous blue irises. "Thanks for the strawberries, sweetheart."

"You're welcome. Did you have a good nap?"

"Yes I did." She yawned. "I was just dreaming of you."

"Was it good?"

Easing back against the pillows, she crossed her legs at the ankles. "Of course."

"By the way, I've got a gig at ten tonight."

"That's great, honey." Her voice perked with enthusiasm. "Where are you playing?"

"We're going to be the headliner at Big Star."

In surprise, she sat up straight. "Really?"

"Yep," he replied.

"So, where are you now?"

A noise from outside the door caught her attention. When it opened, Jace stood in the doorway holding up his phone. "I'm right here."

With a coy smile, she wiggled her finger motioning him to the bed. "Come here, sexy."

Moving to the edge of the bed, he pulled his T-shirt over his head and worked at the button fly of his jeans. "Hold on, baby," he grunted, sliding them down his legs.

Underneath the comforter, she slipped out of her sweats and T-shirt. Tessa threw off the covers and slid her legs out from under. As she stood, she heard him take a hissing breath.

"Make love to me," she whispered.

"I thought you'd never ask." He winked, moving closer. When he pressed his body against hers, she felt his soft, long hair brush across her skin.

Slipping his arms around her waist, he spun her around and eased back onto the bed. "Mmmm," he purred, reaching for her hand. "I like the view better from down here."

Just as she grasped his hand, her phone started to go off. She turned and looked at the nightstand. On some level, she wanted to let whoever it was go to voice mail, but since the meeting with Tim was drawing near, she expected the call might be important.

On impulse, Jace stretched over to the bedside table and grabbed her phone. Looking at the number, he recognized it was Tim's.

After a steady inhale, he forced himself to his feet and handed it to her. "It's Tim."

When she answered, Jace sunk back down on the bed and stared at her as if he were trying to listen to what Tim was saying on the other end.

"What's going on?" He asked after she ended the call.

Plopping down beside him, she turned to face him with a worried look in her eyes. "Celina's found a way to destroy the demon."

In the silence that followed, he must have read her expression... or her emotions. "That's good news, right?"

Clearing her throat, she wondered exactly how to answer him. Dropping her eyes from his, her voice came out in a whisper. "It has something to do with a creature called the Beast."

He froze and arched a brow. "That could be me."

Placing her palm over his hand, she stared into his hard, closed face. "We're not sure. We'll know more at the meeting."

His brows drew tight and his arms crossed over his chest as if he was trying to figure out how to express himself. And then his emotional grid suddenly lit up with all kinds of dark things and she got the impression he was going to explode in anger. Instead, he lowered his head and relaxed his shoulders, exhaling in a long breath.

In the silence that droned on, all she could think of was... he was shutting her out. Her voice yanked his head up. "Let's take a shower together."

Turning in her direction, his lips formed a smile. "That sounds like heaven."

Placing her hands to his face, she leaned forward and pressed her mouth on his. "I love you."

Standing up, he reached for her hand. "I love you more."

Chapter Forty-Four

Later that evening, Jem and Mia headed back to the Covenant to attend the meeting. As he drove in silence, he reached over to the passenger seat and grasped her hand. "I love you, honey."

She smiled. "I love you too."

Pulling into the driveway, he parked the car and shut off the engine. "There's something I want to ask you."

Facing him, she looked concerned. "What is it?"

Completely baffled, he wasn't sure how to bring up the subject. Thinking of the past, he remembered what Mia shared with him a few months after they'd met. At birth, she'd been dumped into human foster care, leaving her clueless about her species. He wondered if she knew the differences between a human and a succubus baby. Clearing his throat, he asked, "Did anyone ever tell you about what happens to a succubus baby after they're born?"

Shrugging her shoulders, she appeared confused. "What are you talking about?"

Jem swallowed nervously. "I mean... did you know when a succubus baby is born, it grows at an unusual rate?"

Her eyes widened in surprise. "No. Who told you this?"

"When Jace came by earlier, he told me something happened to Natalie."

"Is she okay?"

"Don't worry, she's just fine. Jace told me he found her downstairs in the kitchen this morning all by herself. Apparently, she'd grown enough within a few hours to crawl out of her crib and climb down the stairs."

"Are you serious?"

He nodded. "I guess when Jace took her upstairs to Tim and Angel, they flipped out. Angel had no idea this could happen."

"I didn't know that either," she sighed. "So, what did they do?"

"Helen happened to be downstairs in the exam room when they found out. When they took her there, she explained it was normal for her species. She said Natalie would begin to grow at a normal rate after she reached the size of a two-year-old."

"That means if we have a baby, it will—"

Gently squeezing her hand, he muttered, "It doesn't matter, Mia. I would love to have a child with you."

Her eyes softened. "You would?"

"Yes, honey."

Wiping the tears from her eyes, she smiled. "I'm so lucky to have you."

Leaning closer, he gently pulled her into a hug. "No, honey. I'm the lucky one." Glancing at his watch, he noticed the time. "Come on. It's close to five. We better go."

* * * *

After sharing an extended shower, Jace and Tessa got ready for the meeting. Blow-drying her hair, Tessa raised her voice over the noise, "Go ahead, honey. I'll meet you there in ten minutes."

At the end of the hall, Cassie kissed Drakon before he headed to the meeting. As she watched him walk away, her attention was instantly alerted when she heard her brother's voice a few doors down. She'd recognize Jace's raspy voice anywhere.

Stepping into the hallway, his long hair was damp as if he'd just taken a shower. He was dressed in a pair of tight-fitted jeans, and a black T-shirt with his band logo on the front.

When Jace saw Cassie, she motioned him over.

"Hey, baby sister." He grinned, moving in her direction. "What's going on?"

"Where's Tessa?" she asked, looking behind him. "I thought she was supposed to go to the meeting."

"She's coming. Did Drakon already leave?"

"Yeah, he just left."

Sensing her anxiety, he frowned. "Cassie, is something wrong?"

As she slumped against the wall, her voice dropped, "There's something important I want to talk to you about. Can you stop by after the meeting?"

"Yeah, sure." With an arched brow, he looked at her suspiciously. "Are you and Drakon okay?"

She smiled. "Actually, we're perfect."

Leaning down, he kissed her cheek. "Good, I'll see you later. Love you."

"Love you too."

As Jace walked away, Cassie inhaled a deep breath and sighed in relief. Stepping back inside her room, she thought about Drakon's proposal and realized she hadn't thought about how Jace would react to the news. The mere thought of telling her overprotective brother that she was getting married made her anxiety come back in full force. Exhaling a shuddering breath, Cassie tried to ease her nerves. No matter what, she was looking forward to spending the rest of her life with Drakon after all this was over.

* * * *

When Tessa entered the room, everyone rose from the chair and bowed. With a slight nod, she motioned them to have a seat.

Waiting at the head of the table, Jace stood beside Tessa's chair. As she approached, he pulled it out for her. As soon as she sat down and settled her feet under the table, she flinched when she felt something brush against her leg. Glancing underneath, she saw a black cat.

With a raised brow, she leaned over and whispered in Jace's ear, "Whose cat?"

He chuckled quietly. "I'll tell you later."

At the sound of a door clicking shut, the noise caught everyone's attention when Kyle and Celina walked in.

Rising from his chair, Tim motioned for them to have a seat. "Thank you for coming, Celina."

She smiled and placed a book on the table. Searching the room, her eyes stopped at the head of the table. When she saw Tessa, she bowed her head and took a seat next to Kyle.

Tim started the meeting, his voice strong and calm, "Celina, will you explain to everyone what you found in the book?"

In silence, everyone anxiously waited for her to speak. Celina tried to stop her eyes from nervously bouncing around the room. With too many eyes focused on her, she felt caged. Across from her, she noticed Mia staring at her with deep crimson eyes. Quickly looking away, her eyes stopped and focused on the guy with a Mohawk they called Drakon. Unable to keep the eye contact going, she looked down and reached for the book.

With shaky hands, she grasped a folded piece of paper and carefully unfolded it. Clearing her throat in the thick silence, she finally looked up. "Basically, it says a creature called the Beast can destroy the Chiang-shih demon. With one bite, the venom will kill it instantly."

Hearing the news, everyone at the table immediately turned in Jace's direction.

Feeling completely clueless, Celina shrugged her shoulders. "Does anyone know what beast this is referring to?"

Chapter Forty-Five

In disbelief, Eve was speechless after the demon had finally confessed what was wrong with him. As Sebastian's body progressively continued to deteriorate, he would be forced to take possession of another person. No, she thought. She couldn't bear the thought of losing her beloved again.

"Eve," his eyes pleaded, "I don't have any choice."

"Who will you--," inhaling a deep breath, she focused on suppressing her emotions, "--possess?"

"After a great deal of thought, I've chosen someone you have affections for."

In response, she wanted to scream at the top of her lungs. "Please, don't say—"

Grasping her hand, he gently squeezed. "I'm going to take Damien's body."

As she lost control, tears spilled down her cheeks. "When?"

"Soon," he said firmly. "I only have a few weeks left."

Eve's body overrode her mind. Snatching her hand from his, she shook her head. "I won't let you do this," she said bluntly. "You'll be killing Damien."

His handsome face tightened in pain, and he rubbed the middle of his chest, as if she had fisted up his heart and squeezed it dead. "You will agree with this."

She narrowed her eyes. "And if I don't?"

Without hesitation, he forced his lips against hers. Before his tongue slipped inside and stole her ability to be logical, she quickly pulled free from his embrace.

"Sebastian, you know this isn't going to work. I can't..." she paused, looking at him with pain in her eyes, "I can't do this." And then she turned her head.

Furious, he rolled over. With his jaw clenched, the tension in his neck strained. "Leave me," he mumbled, facing away from her.

Easing out of bed, her body trembled in fear. "I'm sorry, but—"

Snapping his head around, his dark eyes glared in her direction. Motioning her to leave, he shouted, "I said go!"

Cringing at his aggressive tone, she lowered her head and walked away. On the way out, she wanted to slam the door in anger. Instead, she left it open.

Alone in the room, he felt empty without her. With his fate sealed, he was running out of options. He had no other choice but to take Damien's body with or without Eve's approval.

In frustration, he shot out of bed slipping on a small rug that covered the slick hardwood floor. Losing his balance, he smacked his head on the corner of the nightstand, sending a lamp crashing to the floor. As his mouth stretched wide, he screamed in agony. Lying motionless, he felt pain radiate from the base of his skull to his lower back.

Down the hall, Eve heard the noise coming from Sebastian's bedroom. Overcome with panic, she rushed back inside. The instant her eyes locked on him, she scrambled to his aid.

He was momentarily surprised when he felt hands on his shoulders. "Sebastian...," Eve sobbed, "are you okay?"

Before he passed out completely, he reached up and touched her cheek. "Eve," he gasped in pain.

Kneeling beside him, she gently grasped his hand. "I'm right here."

As his lids managed to flicker open, he looked at her, feeling utterly helpless. It was all he could do to breathe. With blurry vision, he kept his eyes on her face. "My legs," his voice strained. "I can't move them."

Eve's hand went to the cut on his forehead. Applying pressure, she muttered in a soothing voice, "Shhh... it's going to be okay." With her free hand, she reached for his phone.

As he closed his eyes, the last thing he heard was Eve talking to someone.

* * * *

It didn't take Jace long to realize why everyone in the room was staring at him in silence. Shifting nervously in his chair, he felt a warm sensation over his skin. "Is it hot in here?" he wiped the sweat off his forehead. "Or is it just me?"

When no one answered, he braced himself and then opened his mouth with a heavy sigh, "So?" his brows popped, "I bet I can guess what everyone is thinking. It's me, right? I'm the Beast the book is describing."

Scooting her chair closer to Jace, Tessa reached for his hand. "I knew there was a reason for it." She entwined her fingers with his. "Now we know its purpose."

With a puzzled expression, Celina looked at Jace. "I don't understand? You're the Beast?"

Dogged by a crushing disappointment, Jace forced himself to answer, "I guess so." It killed him to think he had the power to destroy the demon all this time. Absolutely killed him.

Jem's ribs seized up hard, compressing his lungs to the point of pain, until he could draw no more air down his throat. Exhaling a deep breath, he shot out of his chair. "I can't believe this! All this time... Jace had the ability to destroy the demon?"

His reaction caused Tim to look over. Completely baffled, he wondered why they hadn't figured this out earlier. Before anyone got out of line, Tim stood, motioning Jem to sit down. "All right, let's all try to calm down," he said firmly. "At least we know now. Our next step is locating Sebastian."

Sitting back down, Jem crossed his arms. "Even if we find him, how are we going to keep him from escaping through the portal?"

Across the table, Kyle glanced over at Jem. "Maybe we could find a way to distract him."

The answer occurred to Tim after he heard Kyle's suggestion. "That might be a good idea."

Surprised, Kyle arched a brow. "Really?"

Overcome with confusion, Jace muttered, "Will you please explain what you're talking about?"

"We could use Eve as the distraction," Tim explained. "Since she's Sebastian's bonded mate, we could use her as bait."

"But the real Sebastian is dead," Jace implied. "Why would the demon care about her?"

It was so obvious and yet it struck him with surprise. Tim couldn't believe the idea hadn't dawned on him sooner. "Since the demon is living in Sebastian's body, he'll need Eve's blood to survive."

"Aha!" Kyle expressed with triumph. "If we capture Eve... Sebastian will come crawling."

❀ Chapter Forty-Six

Lying in the floor in an unnatural position, Sebastian waited for help to arrive. Below his waist, he felt no pain, but only a slight tingle, as if his circulation was completely cut off. In concentration, he closed his eyes and tried to move again, but his legs wouldn't budge.

Inhaling a deep breath, he recognized a familiar scent and knew Eve was still there. Slowly, he opened his lids and glanced over at her. As she knelt beside his broken body, tears spilled down her cheeks. From the corner of his vision, he saw Taliah standing above him. With a black hooded robe draped around her body, she reached up and removed the hood, revealing her bright red hair.

The sound of someone close by clearing their throat alerted his attention. Angling his head to the side, he met the eyes of three council members: Damien, Fredrick, and Corbin. Focusing on Fredrick's shocked expression, he measured whether the guy was about to faint.

As frustration set in, Sebastian's throat tightened, making it difficult to get air into his lungs. All he could do was shake his head. "I can't feel my legs," he gasped, forcing the words.

In the brief silence that followed, Eve twisted around and looked up at Taliah. "Can you help him?"

"He's going to die—"

"No," the tension in Eve's voice was thick. "There must be something you can do."

Taliah's tone became cold, "There's nothing I can do."

With her eyes flared, Eve shot to her feet. "Do something!"

In the wake of Eve's outburst, consciousness ebbed and flowed through Sebastian as his sight blurred, and then regained focus. "Taliah," he dragged in a breath before losing consciousness, "I command you..."

Taliah's voice was barely louder than a breath, "I don't have enough power to save his body."

Shaking her head, Eve frowned. "I thought you were all powerful?" Her voice was a rough charge—the frantic nature of which was a bit surprising to Taliah. "Just fix him!"

There was silence, and then a glow appeared beneath Taliah's robe as the hood lifted of its own power. "Bring him to my room."

Upon the demand, Damien and Corbin scrambled toward Sebastian. As Taliah floated out of the room, they carefully lifted Sebastian off the floor and followed close behind.

Fredrick, on the other hand, was terrified to move. Frantically, he snapped his head side to side, searching the room. Afraid of coming in contact with Taliah's son, he darted to the door and stuck his head out. Finding nothing, he watchfully tiptoed out and flattened against the wall. In desperation, he ran down the hall toward his room. Reaching into his pocket, he fumbled around for the key. With unsteady hands, he tried to unlock the door. Out of the corner of his eye, he saw a dark shadow coming down the hall. Fright rose within him such that it choked his throat and made him lose control of his bladder. Petrified, he squeezed his eyes shut and held his breath.

"What the hell are you doing?"

The sound of a familiar voice snapped his eyes wide. As he whipped his head around, he saw Corbin's massive form standing beside him.

Fredrick lifted his arms in relief. "Thank God," he gasped.

With the sight of Fredrick's unfortunate accident, Corbin shook his head in disgust. "What's wrong with you?"

Out of breath, Fredrick bent over and placed his hands on his knees. "Sorry, I thought you were Lucas."

"Christ, Fredrick," Corbin muttered with his arms crossed. "Get changed and meet me outside Taliah's room."

When Corbin stormed away, Fredrick managed to open the door. Scurrying inside, he quickly locked himself in.

* * * *

"Please, Sebastian," Eve pleaded, gripping his hand. "Wake up."

There was a long silence, filled by the pounding of her heart. Swallowing hard, he lifted his lids, meeting her eyes steadily.

"Taliah is going to help you." When he didn't reply, she said, "Sebastian, did you hear me?"

Without a word, he nodded. Feeling a sharp stick into his arm, he was suddenly floating, rendered carefree by the agony in his body—and yet in spite of his curse, he was drifting into a strange peacefulness. His fingers twitched in hers, and then he faded away.

Holding a syringe, Talaih glared at Eve. "He needs to rest."

* * * *

Rubbing his jaw, Jem thought about Tim's idea. Using Eve as bait had made sense, but he knew it was near impossible to get to her. "My question is this," he asked. "How are we going to separate Eve from Sebastian? We don't even know how to find them."

"I do."

Everybody looked over in Celina's direction as she spoke up. As Kyle scooted his chair closer to her, she could sense his quiet strength resonating out to her—and she needed it. Even though she knew a way to help them, she had no idea how they were all going to react to what she was about to say.

Confused, Jem shrugged his shoulders. "How?"

"Taliah has cast a spell, breaking our telepathic bond, but I think I can break through it," Celina said nervously. "If I can locate her, there's no doubt we'll find Sebastian. And I'm sure he has Eve stashed nearby."

"How long will this take?" Tim asked, crossing his arms.

"Give me forty-eight hours. That should be enough time."

Tim dropped his hands and rose from his chair. "We'll meet back here when Celina is ready."

Glancing around the table, Celina watched as everyone got up to leave. Without conscious thought, she raised her hand. "Wait!"

At the sound of her voice, everyone turned around. With a bewildered expression, Tessa muttered, "Celina, is there something else you want to tell us?"

"Yes," she replied with a heavy sigh. "I have the power of teleportation."

Everyone glanced back and forth at one another—while Tim's brows lifted in shock.

Standing behind his chair, Jem shook his head. "What exactly does that mean?"

"It's something me and my sister were born with. With one thought, we can disappear from one place and instantly appear at another."

Drakon chimed in and asked, "Like a portal?"

"Yes." She nodded. "It's something similar."

Abruptly, the silence in the room pressed in on her. Sensing the stunned disbelief, she stiffened in her chair, waiting for their response.

There was a long period of quiet, during which Celina's anxiety doubled. And when she went to open her mouth to breathe more deeply, she found that even her jaw was hard to move.

All at once, there was a clattering, as everyone pulled out their chairs and sat back down.

Jace blurted, "Holy... shit. Are you serious?"

With a nod, Celina swallowed hard.

There was a long pause. Then Tessa said slowly, "Would you be willing to use this power to help us?"

She bowed her head. "Of course."

"Thanks for letting us know, Celina." Tim nodded in her direction. "This may work to our advantage."

Chapter Forty-Seven

As Sebastian's consciousness slowly came back, he forced his heavy lids open. Thick draperies were down over the windows, but the glow from a light in the bathroom was enough for him to see his surroundings. Across the room, he saw a massive fireplace with lit candles placed around the mantel. He was definitely not in his room. And then, he remembered everything.

Yes... he recognized where he was—and indeed, he was in Taliah's room.

In his condition, he couldn't have moved himself here; he hadn't the strength. There was but one explanation, he thought. His council members brought him here.

Lifting his head, he did a quick scan of his body. His upper body felt okay, fingers moved as he wiggled them. His head throbbed like it had been put through a concrete wall. And when he tried to move his legs, nothing happened. He looked down at his feet, tried to wiggle his toes, and got nothing again.

Taking a deep breath, he inhaled through his nostrils and caught the scent of a lovely fragrance. Turning his head, he saw Eve asleep in the chair next to him. Immediately, an odd peace overcame him, one that was either the calming shroud of death, or the realization that his time was up.

Reaching out, his arm felt like it weighed more than his entire body. Stretching across his body inch by inch, he struggled until he finally touched a lock of her hair. The soft feel of it eased the pounding in his head.

The instant Eve felt his touch, she opened her eyes. The first thing she saw was Sebastian's fingers wrapped around a long strand of her hair.

Surprised, she whispered, "Sebastian." Rising from her chair, she leaned closer. "You're awake."

When he opened his mouth to speak, nothing came out. With his brows clenched tight, his chest rose higher and his breathing jagged.

"Just relax." She grasped his hand. "You're going to be okay."

Fixated on their linked hands, he tried to calm down.

She put her other hand on his cheek, feeling the rough stubble of his facial hair. "It's all right, Sebastian. I'm not going to leave you. I promise."

As his breathing slowed, he opened his mouth again. In a raspy voice, he muttered, "I'm... sorry."

In a tender gesture, she kissed him. "Stay here. I'll tell Taliah you're awake."

Frustrated, he glanced down at his legs. "I'm not—," he struggled with his words, "—going anywhere."

"I'll be right back," she murmured.

When Eve stepped out, she heard someone snoring. Sitting in a chair next to the door, Damien was sound asleep with his head tilted back against the wall.

"Damien."

Startled by her voice, he shot to his feet with his eyes wide. "Sorry." He yawned. "I must have drifted off. So, how's he doing?"

"He just woke up."

Clearing his throat, he shook his head. "Taliah told me he'll never walk again." His eyes softened as if he was glad from the news.

"Yes, I know."

"Did you tell him?"

"No," she sighed. "Not yet."

Reaching out, he placed his palm on her shoulder. "I'm sorry... about all this."

With the feeling of being sucked downward, she was totally losing it. Dropping to her knees, she buried her face in her hands, emotion overcoming her.

He was at her side in a flash, kneeling beside her. "Eve, you don't have to stay here anymore. Now is your chance to leave and finally be free of him."

"I know," her voice was thick with tears. "But I can't help the way I feel about him."

Damien captured her mouth in a quick, hard kiss then said, "Listen to me, Eve. That body in there is Sebastian's, but his soul is gone."

In the silence that followed, she stood up. "I'm sorry, Damien."

The instant she walked away, he felt like a knife had been sunk into his chest. *God,* he thought. *If only he could find a way to change her mind.*

* * * *

When everyone left the meeting, Jace and Tessa stayed behind. Scooting his chair closer, he grasped her hand and brought it to his lips. With an intense expression, he pressed a kiss on her soft skin. "If only I'd known about this," he sighed in frustration. "I can't believe I had the power to destroy the demon all this time."

"Jace, it's not your fault. There was no way you could have known."

He nodded. "Yeah, but—"

She put her hand up to stop him before he said one more word. "Let's talk about something else." With the other hand, she squeezed his. "Cheer up, honey. Remember, you're the headliner for Big Star tonight. And afterward, I have something romantic planned back at our room."

Immediately, memories flashed into his head of the last time she'd watched him play. Later that night, they'd made love... and more than once. With a big smile on his face, he winked.

Just as they started to leave, a soft meow came from under the table.

Turning around, Tessa kicked up her chin. "Aren't you forgetting something?"

"Sorry..." Jace shrugged his shoulders. "I almost forgot." Reaching under the table, he picked up the cat. "This is our new cat, Buddy."

Narrowing her eyes, she crossed her arms. "What does Tim think about all this?"

"Now that Natalie's already attached to it, he couldn't just toss it out."

"So, where did he come from?"

"I guess he's a stray." He smoothed his hand over Buddy's soft fur. "Somehow, he found his way inside Mia's apartment."

Arching her brows, she reached for the cat. "I guess this means I need to buy cat food."

Leaning close, he kissed her cheek then said, "Thanks, honey. I'll catch up with you later. I've been summoned by my sister. She mentioned something important she wanted to tell me."

With the cat nestled in her arms, it rubbed against her shoulder. "Okay, I'll be in the kitchen when you get back."

Popping a brow, Jace looked at her suspiciously. "Do you know what it's about?"

She smiled broadly, and without reserve. "Go on." Reaching out, she brushed his face. "Be a good brother, and go talk to your sister."

"Women and secrets," he mumbled. "Not a good combination."

* * * *

Standing outside his sister's door, Jace reached out as it suddenly swung open.

Cassie's eyes widened with surprise. "Oh..." She stepped back, "I was just about to go downstairs to see if you remembered to stop by."

"Nope, I didn't forget." He grinned. "Oh, yeah, before I forget, I want to invite you and Drakon to Big Star tonight. Our band is the headliner."

"That's fantastic, Jace! I'm so proud of you."

"Thanks, sis."

As he stepped inside, she motioned him toward the couch. "Actually, I've got some good news too."

Sitting down beside her, he appeared curious. "You do? What's going on?"

Briefly, she closed her eyes and said a little prayer. Knowing Jace's overprotective nature, he might not be too thrilled after she told him about Drakon's proposal. Even though she was twenty-four, Jace still saw her as his innocent baby sister.

Opening her eyes, she turned in his direction. Without hesitation, she blurted, "Drakon has asked me to marry him."

Chapter Forty-Eight

After a few hours of sleep, Sebastian woke and struggled to sit upright. As he recalled his unfortunate condition, his mouth twisted into a grimace. Sighing in frustration, he abruptly sensed a presence hovering behind him. Maneuvering his head to the side, he caught a glimpse of a shadowed figure.

"Lucas," he called out firmly. "I know you're there."

As the transparent creature drifted across the ceiling, Sebastian watched it ease down the wall. Instantly, the monstrous figure took form.

"Why aren't you with Taliah?" Sebastian asked, motioning him closer. "You know you're not supposed to leave her sight."

With its head cocked to one side, Lucas blinked as if he didn't understand what Sebastian had said.

"Come here, Lucas."

Floating above the floor, he moved next to Sebastian with his head lowered in submission.

Reaching out, Sebastian stroked the top of the creature's head. Soothed by his touch, he closed his eyes and made a soft noise that vibrated like a lion's purr.

Startled, Sebastian tensed when the door swung open. In the blink of an eye, Lucas transformed into a shadow and drifted back to the ceiling.

"It's just me." Taliah stormed in with Eve behind her.

Noticing the shadowed creature, Eve gasped in horror and stumbled back against the door.

Looking up, Taliah snapped her fingers, motioning him down. "Lucas, come down here, *now*."

As always, he obeyed her command. Floating from the ceiling, he landed right in front of Eve and fell into a crouch. Shifting into his natural form, he was so close to her, his breath brushed her hair as he exhaled. Up close, the thing was shockingly massive: Red narrowed eyes, wings like a dragon, and a tail that curled up like scorpion. His jaw was full of razor-sharp teeth, and his enormous hands had claws like daggers that made Freddie Krueger's look childish.

Terrified, Eve reached behind her, fumbling for the door.

Watching Eve's reaction, Sebastian reached out to her. "Lucas is my son."

Dimly, she heard his voice, but kept her eyes locked on the creature.

With his red eyes blinking, Lucas took a deep breath as he inhaled Eve's scent.

Sebastian's voice dropped, "Eve."

His firm tone caught her attention. "What..." Eve mumbled, and whipped her head in his direction.

"I owe you an apology." He searched her eyes for compassion. "I should have told you."

"Did you say he's your—" Eve didn't get the rest of the sentence out. She turned back to the creature and totally lost her train of thought.

With her hands on her hips, Taliah stared at Eve, her lips tight, and her eyes narrowed. "I hate to interrupt," she waved her hand in front of Eve's face trying to get her attention, "but I need to talk to Sebastian in private."

Eve looked at her with a confused expression, and then her eyes focused on Sebastian. Opening her mouth, she struggled to speak. Instead of saying words, she let out a long exhale.

Sebastian nodded in her direction. "We'll talk about this later," he murmured, breaking the odd silence.

As Eve scooted out the door, Sebastian glared at Taliah. "This better be good news."

"You need to make a decision, and make it quick," she insisted. "Your body is becoming progressively worse, and now your legs are paralyzed. You don't have much time."

"Isn't there anything else you can do to keep this body alive?"

In frustration, she rolled her eyes. "There might be a way... but it's very risky."

"I don't care about the risks," he said roughly.

"This body will survive if—," she paused with a wicked grin, "—the original soul is brought back."

"Then do it!"

"Unfortunately, I can't do this alone. I'll need my sister's help to do the spell. Of course, she's not going to willingly volunteer."

"Persuade her," he urged. "Do whatever it takes."

* * * *

With a worried expression, Cassie waited for Jace's reaction. As silence stretched out, she suddenly felt his weighty and warm hand on her shoulder. "Answer me one thing," he said.

After another moment of suspended silence, she muttered, "What?"

"Do you love him?"

"Yes," she replied without haste. "I'm in love with him. And if you try to persuade me by the fact that we haven't known each other long—"

"You have my blessing," he interjected.

Her jaw dropped. "What did you just say?"

"You're my sister, and I trust your decision. I just want you to be happy."

In response, she nearly knocked him off the couch when she wrapped her arms around him.

"Oh, Jace... thank you!"

Holding her in an embrace, he swallowed hard, fighting back tears. "I'm sorry I was such an asshole around your dates growing up."

Shaking her head, she said, "No, you weren't..." She stopped to think, "Okay, you're right. You were an asshole."

"See?" he chuckled. "We can agree on something."

After a moment, he pulled back. "Have you told Mom and Dad?"

She winced. "Actually, they haven't even met Drakon yet."

Without hesitation, he burst into laughter. "I can't wait to see their faces when they meet him. Mom will have a heart attack when she sees all his tats, and not to mention his Mohawk!"

She frowned, and poked him in the side. "They'll love him once they get to know him."

"Before you introduce him, let me talk to them first."

Nodding in silence, she let out a sigh of relief.

"But—," he held up his hand, "I want one thing from you in return."

With a curious expression, she arched a brow. "What?"

"Promise me you'll always come to me when you need someone to talk to. I know I can be an overbearing jerk sometimes, but I'm your big brother and I love you."

She smiled. "I promise, and I love you too."

"Have you told Jem?"

"I'm expecting him any minute. I wanted to tell you first."

Before he stood, he kissed her forehead. "I'll see you tonight. We're playing at ten."

"Wait a minute." She reached beside the couch. "I want to give you something." When she brought her hand back, she was holding an old, worn-out teddy bear.

His eyes widened in surprise. "Teddy!"

After she saw his reaction, tears welled up in her eyes. "I want to give him back to you," she said, placing the bear in his lap. "He certainly served his purpose. I'll never forget that day you gave him to me." She wiped the tears from her cheeks. "You're the best, Jace. I thought he might come in handy in case you have children someday."

As he looked at the little stuffed bear, memories flashed back from his childhood. And then he thought of his real mother, Katlyn. He'd never forget the day she brought home that teddy bear. She told him it would take away all his nightmares. After her death, he bottled up all his anger and masked the pain in his broken heart. Spinning into a downward cycle, he held onto the bear as a life anchor. When he was adopted by a loving family, he finally let go of Teddy when someone else needed it more. That's when he gave it to his adopted little sister, and the very moment he found the courage to accept his new family.

With his eyes filled with tears, he held the bear close to his heart. Reaching out, he hugged his sister again. "Thank you, Cassie."

With her arms wrapped around him, she whispered, "I love you, big brother."

"I love you too, sis."

With the stuffed bear clutched under his arm, he headed for the door. Just as he reached to open it, he heard a soft knock. Pulling it open, Jem stood on the other side.

Looking over his shoulder at Cassie, Jace muttered, "Make sure he knows—," he smirked in triumph, "—I was the first one you told."

Stepping inside, Jem shrugged. "Tell me what?"

Chapter Forty-Nine

Nathan Gage shut his office door and lifted his wrist to check his watch. Noticing the time, he realized it was a few minutes before he was expecting tonight's headliner to show. As the manager of Big Star Lounge, he had decided to present Jace with an offer to play two Saturdays a month. The bar was located near a busy college strip, and so far their band never failed to draw in a full house.

With his feet propped on his desk, he heard a knock at the door. "Come on in, guys!"

When it opened, Jace came in first, followed by the rest of the band. After he closed the door, he leaned back against it. Jem stood by him while Kyle and Casey sat down in chairs facing the desk.

Nathan shot to his feet and extended his hand out to Jace.

As Jace firmly clasped onto his hand, he muttered, "Hey, Gage. What's up?"

After Nathan finished greeting the others, he stood behind his desk with his arms crossed. "Would you be interested in playing two Saturdays a month?"

In surprise, Jace said, "Seriously?"

Nathan nodded. "Hell, yah! You guys never fail to pack in a crowd."

Jace faced Jem and shrugged. "What do you think?"

"Sure, why not."

Jem turned toward Kyle and Casey. "How about you guys?"

"I'm in!" Casey eagerly agreed.

With a big grin on his face, Kyle nodded. "Count me in, bro!"

Nathan smiled. "All right, sounds great. I'll get with you later to work out the schedule."

With only half an hour to set up, they headed for the stage while Kyle lagged behind. As Celina popped into his head, he sagged against the wall and smiled. An odd feeling suddenly swelled in his chest as he thought of her. Sure, they hadn't known each other long, but he knew she was the one.

"What's up with the shit-eating grin?"

At the sound of Casey's voice, Kyle snapped back to reality. Glancing up, he saw the curious expression on Casey's face.

Kyle shrugged one shoulder. "What?"

Shaking his head, Casey chuckled. "You've got that look."

With a bewildered expression, Kyle mumbled, "What look?"

"The same look a dude gets when his head's stuck in the clouds over a female."

"Damn," Kyle swore under his breath. "Is it that obvious?"

Placing his palm on his shoulder, Casey smirked. "Yeah, and I want details on this one."

In the past, Kyle joked with Casey about never settling down, and swore that one woman would never satisfy him. Wasn't that a joke, he thought. He'd changed his way of thinking because all that was on his mind was Celina.

"She's supposed to be here tonight."

Casey cocked a brow. "Then I guess I'll spare you the who-is-she."

"That's a relief," Kyle muttered, rolling his eyes.

With a half-cocked grin, Casey placed his hands on his hips. "I wasn't being serious. Come on, give me details. Who is she?"

"Her name is Celina."

"Are you talking about the redhead staying at the Covenant?"

Thinking about the question, Kyle looked like a deer caught in headlights. Narrowing his eyes, he said, "Yeah, why?"

"You do realize she's a Wicca, right?"

His words hit him hard, and lingered like an echo. But, he thought, Celina didn't use her powers for evil. Besides, it was no one's business. He was an adult male well within his rights to date whomever he wanted.

"Yeah, but she's a white Wicca."

"Any chance she's got a twin?"

With a grave tone, Kyle said, "You don't even wanna go there, dude."

"Why's that?"

"Her twin is a dark Wicca, and supposedly she's helping the demon."

Casey's mouth twisted into a grimace. "Jeez... never mind."

On their way back into the crowded, noisy bar, Kyle glanced around the room to see if Celina had made it yet. When he looked toward the VIP section, he saw Tessa, Mia, Cassie, and Drakon. Weeding through all the people, he finally made it to their table. Leaning close, he raised his voice over the loud music, "Have you guys seen Celina?"

"No." Tessa shook her head. "Before we left, we asked her if she wanted to ride with us, but she said she would meet us here."

He nodded. "Okay, thanks."

Before he headed back to the stage, he decided to step outside for some fresh air. Breathing in through his nostrils, he took in all the smells of the summer night. Watching people enter the bar, he glanced down at his watch. As show time drew near, he couldn't understand why Celina hadn't made it yet.

Looking out into the parking lot, he searched for her car. With no luck, he pulled out his phone and sent her a text. As soon as he shoved it inside his pocket, he felt it vibrate. Pulling it back out, he was relieved to see a message from her, stating she'd just pulled up.

* * * *

After sending Kyle a text, Celina stepped out of her car. Before she could close the door, a dark shadow covered her like a cloak. Completely engulfed with the strange entity, she struggled to get free. Suddenly, a powerful force whipped her head back, knocking her unconscious. As the shadow disappeared, so did Celina.

❧ Chapter Fifty

Clutching onto Celina's limp body, the dark shadow dematerialized outside of Sebastian's estate and took form.

Waiting for Lucas to return, Taliah's memories of the past came to mind. It seemed only yesterday when the Chiang-shih demon promised her an offspring for her loyalty. Within a year of her son's birth, Lucas developed into an adult with the mind of a child. Born with limitless powers, he had the ability to mimic any creature, transform into a shadow, or become completely invisible with the power to travel from one place to another in an instant. Inheriting their genetics, his true form was hideously beautiful, and as deadly as the most venomous snake.

Her attention snapped back when she saw him approach with Celina in his arms. "It's about time," she said firmly.

They stood under the bare branches of a tall, old oak. The mansion beyond rested in a landscaped acreage surrounded by trees rising up around the old stone's structure, anchoring it to a mammoth lawn, stretching as far as the eye could see.

Looking up, Lucas stared at the night sky. The bright moon poured down, making what would have been pitch dark seem like almost dawn.

With her hands on her hips, Taliah narrowed her eyes. "Did anyone see you?"

Lucas went silent for a moment, his expression puzzled by her question. And then with a shake of his head, he answered with a mumble.

Capturing Celina was a challenge for Taliah. It was easy for her to vanish and transport herself from place to place, but having to wield another person was difficult. But for Lucas, it was a piece of cake.

"Come." Taliah motioned him to follow. "Bring her."

Sensing someone nearby, she stopped and held up her hand. "Wait..."

Standing stock-still with Celina in his grasp, Lucas obeyed.

Listening carefully, she heard voices in the distance. With her lips drawn tight, Taliah pointed toward the noise and muttered through gritted teeth, "Go destroy them."

Some of Lucas's killings were messy, but all that blood didn't bother her. She got an adrenaline rush witnessing his victims choking on their last breaths.

Gently, he placed Celina on the ground. When her hair fell away, he saw her face. He reared back his head, surprise flaring in his eyes. He'd never seen Taliah's twin sister, and when he got a glimpse of Celina, he stood in shock from the identical likeness.

"It's okay." She reached out to him. "She's my twin."

Whimpering, he knelt down beside Celina and wiped the blood from her face.

Snapping her finger, Taliah glared at him. "Do what I said."

Standing straight, his enormous stature towered among the trees. In an instant, he disappeared in thin air. Moments later, she heard bloodcurdling screams. When the noise came to a halt, Lucas reappeared covered in blood.

"Good boy," she praised, her lips turning up into a broad smile. "Now, let's get her inside."

* * * *

After Kyle read Celina's text, he waited outside for her. As he waited, and waited, he felt uneasy and checked his watch again. He frowned when he realized it had been at least ten minutes since her text. Getting a weird vibe, he darted toward the parking lot and searched for her car. Parked in the back, he spotted her yellow Volkswagen Beetle. When he came around the driver's side, he noticed the door wide open. Inside, he saw her purse in the front seat. Glancing down, he found a set of car keys and several drops of blood. In panic, he grabbed the keys, locked her car, and rushed toward the bar. Pushing his way through the crowd, he saw the guys on stage getting ready for the show.

When Jace saw him, he rolled his eyes. "Where have you been? We're fixing to play in fifteen minutes."

"Something's happened to Celina!" Kyle said in a strained voice.

Shock registered on all their faces.

Jace frowned. "What?"

Distraught, Kyle held up Celina's car keys. "I found these on the ground," he gasped for air. "I saw blood—"

Jem jumped off the stage, and rushed toward him with Jace and Casey close behind. Placing his palm on his shoulder, Jem gently squeezed. "Take a deep breath, and tell us what happened."

Inhaling through his nose, Kyle opened his mouth and exhaled in one long breath. "When I got a text from her, she said she was in the parking lot. I waited, and—"

Impatient, Jace blurted, "And?"

"When she didn't show, I went to see what was taking her so long. I found her car with the door wide open, and her purse was still in there. Then, I found her keys on the ground." He looked down at them in his palm, and curled his fingers around, squeezing. "And there was blood."

Jem reached into his pocket, and pulled out his phone. "I'll call Tim."

Jace grabbed a chair and slid it next to Kyle. "Have a seat, bro."

Sitting down, he rubbed his hands down his jeans and drummed his thumb over his knee. "I think her sister took her."

Jace blinked, confusion furrowing his brow. "What makes you think that?"

"I don't know," Kyle said, his voice wobbling precariously. "Maybe she figured out Celina was trying to break her binding spell."

Casey knelt down beside Kyle. "Don't worry, buddy. We'll find her."

"I just got off the phone with Tim," Jem confirmed. "He's on his way."

Kyle shot to his feet. "Drakon's already here. I'll go tell him what's going on."

"What about tonight?" Casey asked as got back on his feet. "We go on in ten minutes."

Kyle looked over his shoulder at the crowded bar. "Can you guys handle this without me?"

Jace went silent briefly before finally making a decision. "We're going to cancel."

"Look at all these people." Kyle gestured toward the fans, and shook his head. "You guys have to go on."

Jem lifted one shoulder into a shrug. "Are you sure?"

Kyle stared at him, worry simmering in his eyes. "Yeah, I'll catch up with you after the show."

Watching him disappear through the crowd, Jace swallowed visibly and then ran a hand through his long hair. "Okay, I guess we're playing."

Jem turned toward Casey. "You okay with this?"

He nodded slightly. "Yeah, let's do this."

* * * *

Left alone in a dark room, Celina finally regained consciousness. Unfamiliar with her surroundings, she could barely see her hand as she held it out in front of her face. She gasped in pain when she tried to sit up. Reaching toward her throbbing head, she felt something wet. Looking down at her hand, she tried to focus, thinking it must be blood.

After several failed attempts, she tried to use her power to transport herself back to her car. The only explanation she could come up with was her sister. She wondered how Taliah managed to dematerialize with another person. She'd never had that kind of power before.

When she finally managed to stand, she went over to the only window in the room. Placing her hand close to the glass, she sensed an energy field.

As she waited for her abductor to come back, her thoughts drifted to Kyle. An image of him came to her mind, his blue eyes resonating in her recollection so clearly, she could see the flecks of gold in them. She remembered when they first met. He had looked at her with such awe and wonder, as if she was his bonded mate.

Focusing through the window on the trees below, she thought of the first time they'd touched. His blue eyes had glowed with the trademark of the Breedline male. She'd felt the spark that instantly told her he was the one.

Snapping back to reality, she had to batten down her mental hatches and find a way to escape.

🐾 Chapter Fifty-One

An hour later, when Chaos prepared for the end of the show, the lights drew low with the spotlight on Jace. Drenched in darkness, the crowd roared. Anticipation weighted the audience, building until the strum of guitar strings broke the heavy expectation. Female screams belt out, as lighters flickered to life, filling the area with hundreds of fireflies.

A spotlight hit the stage, revealing Jace sitting on a bar stool, his long, blond hair glistened under the brightness. As he reached toward the microphone, his hard and defined muscles tightened when he lowered it. The women in the crowd screamed his name, including Tessa, who stood up with an earsplitting whistle.

With Casey on keyboards and Jem on percussions, Jace began to sing a song by 3 Doors Down—"She Don't Want the World." His voice was low and soulful, the words seeming to be meant for Tessa. Seductive and mesmerizing, his voice seduced every woman in the bar.

After his sexy ballad ended, the stage went dark. A brief moment passed as the music came to a halt. Then suddenly, the lights sprung back on as Jem pounded the drums. The sound exploded with energy as the crowd went crazy.

When the show was over, all they could think about was Celina. Struggling to maintain their fake smiles, they thanked their fans and packed up their instruments. Loading them in Jem's van, they heard footsteps approaching at a jog.

"Hey, guys! Hold up!"

With the sound of Drakon's deep, baritone voice, they turned around and saw him running in their direction.

"I was hoping I'd catch you before you left," he caught his breath. "We're all meeting first thing in the morning, eight o'clock sharp. If Celina's been taken, we'll find her." His eyes appeared tense but also sincere.

Casey shrugged. "Where's Kyle?"

"He rode back to the Covenant with Tim."

Jem's eyes widened as Helen came into mind. "Did you notify Helen?" he asked hesitantly. "I'm sure she'll be worried about Celina."

Drakon nodded. "Tim called her."

As thoughts of the past kicked in, Jace's mind drifted to the memory of Tessa's abduction. With a noticeable amount of tension on his face, he dragged a hand through his hair. "We'll see you first thing in the morning."

* * * *

Inserting a key, Taliah pushed open the door to Celina's room.

When the lights flickered on, Celina glared at the doorway. "So, it was you." She gave Taliah a look of pure hatred and distaste. "How did you do it?"

Moving closer, Taliah said pointedly, "You're going to help me."

Celina's hands formed into fists as she looked at Taliah. "With what?"

"You're going to help me bring back a soul from purgatory."

Celina's eyes narrowed as she stared back at her, unwilling to give an inch. "I'm not helping you with dark spells!"

Taliah's lips formed into a twisted grin and her chin kicked up. "Is that so?"

"You can just keep me locked up in here forever." Celina turned her back on Taliah, cursing under her breath. "I'd rather rot in this hell hole before I help you."

"Do you believe in love at first sight?"

"What are you talking about?" Celina retorted.

"Hmmm..." Taliah cocked her head to one side. "Didn't you recently bond with your mate?"

In the silence, Celina focused on her anger. If she showed weakness, Taliah could get into her head and read her thoughts.

Celina exploded in rage, "Go to hell!"

There was nothing Taliah wanted more than to pick a fight and cause an emotional uproar when she was in the mood. And now was the perfect opportunity with her sister held captive. With a conceded tone, she asked, "Does the name Kyle ring a bell?"

Refusing to break, Celina kept her focus, feeling a prickle slithering down her spine.

"I'll give you until tomorrow morning to think about it," Taliah smirked as she reached for the door. Glancing over her shoulder, she said, "If you refuse to help me... Kyle dies."

When she left and the lock clicked, Celina exhaled a deep breath, emotions knotting her throat as tears gathered in her vision. Plopping down in a chair near the window, she lifted her legs and tucked her knees against her chest. Staring out into the night sky, reality started to set in. Blocked from using her powers, she knew there was no way out of this. In the morning, she would be forced to turn to the dark side and help her sister.

* * * *

Later that night, Kyle slipped into Celina's room and climbed into her bed. With his head lying against her pillow, he could smell her scent. Noticing a picture setting on the nightstand, he reached out for it and stared at Celina's image. Remembering every detail of the photo, he tucked it against his chest and thought of her.

To keep himself from going crazy, he thought about what Tim had told him on the ride back. A few weeks ago, Tim and Drakon had been asked to find Amaud Saintclare's missing daughter, Kara. Trying to come up with a clue to what might have happened to her, they questioned all Amaud's staff. After receiving a few helpful tips, it led them to believe that Sebastian had something to do with Kara's disappearance.

With their attention drawn to the property next door, they decided to make a visit. Finding Damien Spence residing in the home, they questioned him about Kara and the estate. When he explained Samuel Mercier—a Breedline council member from France—had recently purchased the estate, it made them suspicious. Refusing to let them search the home, Damien gave them the impression he was hiding something. When a woman's scream came from upstairs, it caught their attention. Deciding to take action, they searched the entire place. With no luck, they didn't find Kara.

Tomorrow morning, Tim promised Kyle they would return to the same estate and search again. If they were lucky, they'd find Kara and Celina.

In his heart, Kyle knew Celina's sister had snatched her. It was the only possible explanation. After all, her car was left as if she'd suddenly vanished. Something her sister had the power to do. Besides, there was no way in hell Celina would just take off and disappear on her own.

Lying in the dark, feeling hopeless, he counted the hours until morning. Before he finally drifted off, he swore to bring her back safe and sound.

Chapter Fifty-Two

Waking up from a nightmare, Kyle shot upright and gasped for air. Unfamiliar with his surroundings, he started to panic. In his foggy mind, images of Celina brought him back to reality when he realized he'd fallen asleep in her room. Glancing at the clock, he noticed it was already seven in the morning. All the memories of her disappearance came crashing down on him like it had just happened. When anger blared into his head, he tried to block it out. Meeting Celina had been the best thing that had ever happened to him. Having to live without her would be on the top of the list of his worst nightmares.

Moving like a zombie, he slid his legs off the bed and headed to his room to change. Just as he put on a clean pair of jeans, he heard his phone buzz. Remembering he'd left it inside the pants he'd tossed in the floor, he bent down and fished it out. Glancing at the caller ID, he saw that it was a text from Tim, reminding him about the meeting at eight.

As he stuffed it into his back pocket, his heart beat with desperation. In the closet, he reached for his gun holster and strapped it on. Grabbing his gun, he stepped into the hall and took a deep breath. As he paused, he thought of all the Breedline that would be gathering downstairs.

* * * *

Worried about Kyle, Casey left his room a little before eight to check on him. Standing outside his door, he placed his ear against it and listened. Hearing no movement, he knocked.

After a couple of minutes had passed, he called out, "Kyle, you in there?"

Giving up, he turned to leave and slammed right into Drakon's chest. Feeling like he'd walked into a stone wall, Casey lost his balance as Drakon quickly reached out to steady him.

"Sorry," Casey muttered with a stunned expression. "I was just looking for Kyle."

"He's probably already downstairs in the library. The meeting starts in ten minutes. I was actually looking for you."

"What for?" Casey muttered, his voice sounding curious.

"Tim wants everyone in this meeting."

Casey was silent for a moment before he finally nodded. "Okay, sure."

As Casey hurried down the grand staircase, he heard Drakon following behind.

"Casey, do you have a weapon?"

Coming to a halt, Casey reached inside his boot and pulled out a pocket knife. Showing it to Drakon, he said, "I've got this. Why do you ask?"

Drakon shook his head and sighed. "Here, take this." He offered him a pistol. "You know how to use one of these?"

"Yeah." He grasped the weapon as his brow arched. "Nice piece."

Drakon opened his mouth on the verge of giving Casey a speech about safety, but he just kept it short, "Just be careful."

Instead of making a smart-ass reply, Casey stuffed the gun inside his jacket. "Thanks, man."

Without haste, they made it to the bottom of the staircase and headed to the meeting. Opening the door, they saw familiar faces waiting for them to take their seats. Tessa was at the head of the table with a black cat in her lap. Jace was sitting beside her with Jem next to him. Glancing around the room, Casey saw Kyle sitting beside Helen. He seemed twitchy as his weight shifted back and forth in the chair.

When Casey and Drakon sat down, they noticed Mia and Alexander across the table. Sitting at the far end, Tim scooted his chair back and stood.

Tim noticed the tension in the room was thick, a tangible air that permeated every single person. Clearing his throat, he said, "I think it's evident at this point we can all positively say Celina has been taken. After speaking with Helen, she's agreed with my theory. We believe her twin sister has something to do with her disappearance."

Kyle's reaction was instantaneous, nearly explosive, "Why are we just sitting around wasting time? Shouldn't we be looking for her now?"

"Kyle, we're doing all we can with the little information we have," Tim said pointedly. "At nightfall, we're going to go back to the same property we suspected when Amaud Saintclare's daughter went missing, and search it again."

Now that Kyle had his inner anger temporarily appeased and was able to think properly, he finished listening to Tim.

Turning in Helen's direction, Tim asked, "Is it possible that Celina's sister needs her assistance with Sebastian's death army she informed us about?"

Helen nodded. "It's possible. Taliah may not be able to do that big a spell by herself."

Tim shifted his focus on Kyle. "Do you think you're emotionally stable enough to go with us?"

Kyle firmly planted his palms on top of the table and his jaw tightened with fear and fury waging a war in his mind. "I'll be fine," he replied in a tight voice. "I just want to find her, and bring her back safe."

"I want you to keep a level head," Tim demanded. "Do you understand?"

"Yeah," Kyle grumbled. "I get it."

* * * *

When Sebastian woke the next morning, the first thing he did was try to move his legs. With no luck, his body felt like a cold slab of meat.

With a curse, he struggled underneath the covers. When he finally pushed his body upright, he shoved the blanket off and noticed something black on his hands. As he brought them closer to his face, he saw it had spread down to his wrists. When he smoothed his finger across it, he couldn't feel his own skin. He realized the decay was spreading, and his body was still dying.

"Damn it," he cursed under his breath.

Bracing his hands on the side of the platform, he dropped his head and wondered how much time this body had left.

Startled, he looked up when the door opened.

Taliah stepped inside with Lucas on her heels carrying a female. She was blindfolded with her hands bound together. Noticing the resemblance, Sebastian realized she must be Taliah's twin.

Taliah narrowed her eyes at Celina, and her lips formed a satisfied grin. "My sister has finally come to her senses, and agreed to help. With our powers joined, we'll complete the ritual and bring back Sebastian's soul."

"It needs to be done soon," Sebastian urged, revealing the black wounds spreading throughout his hands. "I'm running out of time."

Taliah turned in his direction with a smile, showing her white orderly teeth. "I'm making all the essential preparations right now."

Chapter Fifty-Three

When Kyle left the meeting, Casey hurried to catch up with him. "Kyle, wait up!"

Focused solely on a destination, Kyle ignored him and kept moving. Trying to grab his arm, Kyle shook him off. Finally, Casey jumped in front of him and blocked his way. Then, he held up his hands, motioning for him to stop. "What the hell are you up too, Kyle?"

"I'm not waiting around until nightfall to search for Celina." Kyle jogged around him and resumed his pursuit. As Casey followed, Drakon fell in step with them when he overheard their conversation. Drakon understood, though. He knew instinctually why Kyle was desperate to find Celina.

Drakon called out, "Hold on, Kyle!"

Just as Kyle's anger was getting away from him, Drakon grabbed him by the shoulder and gave him a shake. "Take a deep breath, son. We're going to find her, and you're not going to do it all alone."

As the confrontation caught Tim's attention, he walked toward them. "Is there a problem, here?"

Kyle glared at Tim. He knew additional support was a smart thing, but the longer they waited, the greater the chance Celina could be harmed. For a split second, he almost tore his uncle's head off, getting ready to spit out "you're-not-my-babysitter" shit. What stopped him was the fact that no amount of arguing was going to help find Celina. Yelling at Tim wasn't going to get them closer either. Besides, he'd be diggin' his own grave.

Tim's voice deepened, "I asked you a question, Kyle."

"Please, Tim," Kyle pleaded. "We need to start searching for her *now*."

"You think we all don't want to find her?"

When he shrugged, Tim pressed his index finger to Kyle's chest. "Get your head on straight, Kyle. We're going to find her, and we're going to do this together. And I'm here to make sure no one gets killed in the process. I get your desperation to find her, I do. But you've got to trust me on this."

With his hands on his hips, Kyle lowered his head. When his temper started to cool, the logical side of him knew his uncle was right. The nightfall would give them better cover. But the damn waiting could wear a guy out. Every dragging minute waiting around was a forever in hell.

"Are you hearing me?"

Glancing up, Kyle saw the hard expression on Tim's face. Offering his palm in agreement, Tim grasped his hand and pulled him into a hard embrace. "Have faith. We'll find her."

Casey came up and clapped Kyle on the shoulder. "Come on, buddy. Let's get something to eat."

After checking his watch, Tim announced, "We'll meet back here at five o'clock. Is everyone clear?"

When everyone in the group agreed, they headed down to the kitchen for breakfast. Before Kyle walked out, he turned toward Casey. "Sorry, man. I didn't mean to snap at you."

"Don't worry about it." He smiled. "We're good."

* * * *

"You'll need to feed before we start the ritual," Taliah urged, her expression growing serious.

"Then, I will need Eve," Sebastian's voice was so weak, she had to strain to hear him.

As soon as Taliah left the room and came back with Eve, Sebastian inhaled her scent. When she moved next to him, his eyes locked on her jugular.

Deep in his belly, his hunger grew stronger, twisting and pounding in his gut. As soon as Eve held her wrist over his lips, it happened so fast. One second, he was inhaling her scent, the next he was drinking from her. The rich blood against his tongue was the stimulant he needed.

When he finally released her vein, he licked her wrist to seal the wound. Sagging back, he reveled in the fact that his hunger was sated, but his body seemed sluggish, which wasn't normal considering he'd just fed.

In her black robe with the hood draped over her head, Taliah stood hovering above the floor. Her voice echoed across the room, "Lucas, release my sister."

Gently, he lowered Celina to the floor and stood in front of her. Before he untied her hands, he leaned in and inhaled her scent. Moving behind her, he removed her blindfold.

As Celina regained her vision, she turned side to side scanning the room. The first thing she saw was her sister draped in a black, hooded robe. Next to her was a man lying on an elevated platform supported by large pedestals. His long, jet black hair matched the color of his eyes. From Tim's description, he had to be the Sebastian they were searching for. The very one that was possessed by the Chiang-shih demon.

Shifting her focus, she saw a tall female that remarkably resembled Jem's bonded mate, Mia. Standing next to Sebastian, the woman trembled in fear as if she was being held against her will.

Over the fireplace mantel, black candles burned red flames. Looking down, she noticed the floor was made of marble. From an angle, the color appeared black, and at another, it looked blood red. Given the source of illumination that was constantly flickering, both colors combined together.

Hearing a noise behind her, Celina gasped when she turned around. Towering above her, she saw an enormous creature with features of a dragon and a man. His skin was covered in shimmering blue scales as if he'd been dusted with glitter. Tucked into his back, close-set wings ran from its shoulder to its hips. With his red eyes steadied on hers, she froze as chills slithered up her spine.

Gliding across the floor, Taliah stopped and stood next to Lucas. "This is my son."

In terror, Celina's jaw dropped as she stared at Lucas in disbelief. "I didn't know you had... a child."

With lack of patience, Taliah snapped her fingers and pointed toward Sebastian. "Let's just get on with the spell."

Keeping her eyes trained on Lucas, Celina stepped back and slowly moved to the opposite side of Sebastian.

"Join me, sister," Taliah said as she offered Celina her hands.

Celina nodded in agreement, feeling nauseous by the idea of helping her sister with a dark spell. What they contemplated now went against the laws of both nature and their species. Reanimation of souls in purgatory was not an appropriate or allowable course of action under any circumstances.

When their hands joined, Taliah gripped tightly and began to chant.

Out of nowhere, a loud roll of thunder crashed from outside. As the candles in the room flickered, a strong current of air whirled around the room, lifting Celina's hair as if she was in the middle of a windstorm.

Ten of the longest minutes of Celina's life passed by her in slow motion as she watched Sebastian's body rise above the platform, hovering in midair.

Tears gathered and burned in Celina's eyes, but she blinked them away, knowing she needed perfect vision and her senses sharp. They might get only one shot at this. If her sister suspected her weakness, the crazy ass bitch would probably kill Kyle just for spite.

With her eyes the color of fire, Taliah raised her voice over the noise, "Return from whence you came!"

Startled, Celina jumped when the room exploded with a crackling sound. She caught her breath when she looked toward the ceiling and saw it split down the middle. Emerging from out of nothingness, a dark entity appeared. With shadowed claws, it dug into the upper surface and pulled itself free. When it spotted Sebastian, it rushed into his body like a bolt of lightning. Stunned by the force, Sebastian's body slammed back down. When he jack-knifed at the waist, he clawed at his chest as if he was trying to tear into the flesh.

In the mix of all the mayhem, Celina started to teeter side to side. She blinked, confusion furrowing her brows. For a moment, her gaze locked with Taliah's, and panic swamped her eyes before her vision blurred. Her unsteady movement swayed until she lost her balance, blacking out before she crumpled to the floor.

Chapter Fifty-Four

An hour after the morning meeting, Tim received a call from Amaud Saintclare's butler, Herbert Stanley. Deeply distraught, he'd told him that Mr. Saintclare and his son Dimitri had been missing since the previous night. Herbert was extremely concerned since Mr. Saintclare never left the estate without notifying him first.

After Tim ended the call, he immediately contacted Drakon. When they met downstairs in the foyer, he told him about the phone call.

"It's probably a good idea to get there using the portal," Drakon suggested. "I'll call Jem."

When Jem arrived, Tim decided that only the three of them would go. They had plenty of time to travel through the portal to the Saintclares' estate and get back before five.

In a flash, they stepped through the portal into the ring of woods that separated the Saintclares' estate and the property next door. In agreement, they decided to search the grounds before speaking with the butler.

With every step and every breath, Drakon had a sudden crushing feeling of dread. "This place feels haunted." He frowned, with his hand close to his weapon.

Jem nodded, swallowing the knot in his throat. "Yeah, I'm getting an eerie feeling too."

As they moved closer to the estate next to the Saintclares', that sense of dread, of being in an evil place, swelled in Tim's chest. Out of nowhere, he was short of breath as sweat beaded off his forehead. He noticed Jem's expression, and had a feeling he was suffering from a similar paroxysm of anxiety.

Coming to a halt, they scanned through the mass of trees. Drakon nervously shifted his weight back and forth, ready to draw his weapon.

The sun was just about to pierce the veil of forest when Tim said, "Do you smell that?"

Instantly, Jem covered his nose. "Damn, it smells like death."

Tim walked forward, picking up the pace that led to a cast-iron gate. Drakon and Jem followed in pursuit, reaching the gate as Tim popped the latch free. "The smell is coming from inside this fence," he said in a strained voice.

Without losing his stride, Tim moved onward, ducking and weaving around the thick forest. Tight on his heels, Drakon and Jem followed closely behind. As they came upon a spring, Tim got a deep lungful of decaying flesh.

Although he braced himself for what he was about to come upon, he cringed and choked when he saw the bloodbath. "Wait!" Tim held up his hand, gesturing them to stay back.

Jem whipped his head away and gagged. "What the hell—"

Moving closer, Drakon hollered, "What is it?"

With a grim expression, Tim turned and shook his head. "I'm pretty sure it's Amaud and Dimitri." He placed his hand on his face, shielding his nose and mouth. "Or what's left of them."

* * * *

Celina awoke screaming. As she glanced around the room, she finally recognized where she was. Slapping a hand over her mouth, she shut herself up. She was back in the room where her sister first brought her, locked up and unable to use her powers. Taliah had placed a binding spell in the estate that kept her from transporting out.

Noticing a bandage around her hand with blood soaked through, she winced in pain. With her other hand, she rubbed her temple and tried to replug into reality. Suddenly, she felt weak and lightheaded. After being threatened into participating in Taliah's dark ritual, she couldn't recall her memory since she'd passed out. Glancing at her palm, she realized her sister used her blood to wake Sebastian's soul.

In the silence, her thoughts drifted to Kyle. She wondered if he was searching for her. Startled, she turned around when a knock on the door broke her thoughts.

She watched as the lock on the door clicked, and slowly creaked open. A low voice whispered in, "Are you okay?"

When Mia's doppelganger came into the room, Celina felt uneasy. "I'm fine. Who are you?"

As she stood in the doorway, her stare was not frightening but tense. Her eyes were the exact same odd shade of crimson, and her skin was just as pale as Mia's. "My name is Eve."

With a nervous stare, Celina stepped back as Eve walked into the room. "What do you want?"

"You and I have something in common," Eve muttered quietly.

At first, Celina prepared to defend herself. And then, she felt a cringing, cold shiver rush through her body. As she looked at Eve's expression, it was clear as day. "You're a prisoner here, aren't you?"

In despair, Eve held a finger over her lips, gesturing Celina to be quiet. "Please," Eve pleaded. "I don't want anyone to know I'm here."

Celina's brows pulled tight. "Look, Eve," she kept her voice low, "I don't know what your situation is here, but if my sister keeps her word and lets me go, I'll bring help for you."

Eve opened her mouth to speak, but halted her words. Instead, she let out a long sigh. The sadness left her feeling nothing but a strange, blank numbness. Eve just shook her head.

With her lips pursed, Celina swore under her breath. "My sister isn't going to let me go, is she?"

"I'm sorry." Eve stepped back. "I've said too much." Scrambling for the door, she rushed out and locked it from behind.

* * * *

The bedrooms at the back of the Breedline Covenant had the benefit not only of a view of the beautiful landscape, but a second-story terrace. It worked wonders if you were anxious, or felt claustrophobic. You could easily step out and grab some fresh air.

Opening the french doors, Kyle stepped into the bright, sunny day. Prepared for war, he sported several weapons of which two were locked and loaded with silver.

Staring out into the vast of trees, he felt antsy. Bracing himself on the railing, he leaned in and inhaled the warm breeze. The sun's golden illumination poured onto the lawn and the patio on the lower level.

In confusion, he tried to comprehend why Celina had bonded with a guy like him. They were on two completely separate paths. She had landed a job as an editor, and he was just an amateur mechanic/bass player in a band that only played on occasion. She was going somewhere with her life, and he was—

When he heard a loud buzzing noise coming from inside, it brought him back to reality. Stepping in, he saw his phone light up. Before he looked at the caller ID, he expected it to be his uncle, but when he saw the number, he noticed it was Jem.

"Hello—"

"Just giving you a heads-up," Jem sounded out of breath. "I'm headed your way. We came upon a situation back at the Saintclares' estate. I'm coming to get you and Jace. We're going to start the search early. I'll explain when I get there."

Kyle stiffened, his entire body vibrating with tension, but he kept in control. In a deep voice, he muttered, "I'm ready."

Chapter Fifty-Five

Four hours earlier...

Standing beside the platform, Taliah leaned over Sebastian's unconscious body. Trailing her fingers over the side of his face, she murmured, "He's beautiful, isn't he?"

Confused, Eve wasn't sure what to say. It was as if Taliah had presented her with a god for the praising.

Looking down, Eve nervously shook all over as Sebastian's limp, white hand fell off to the side. She carefully returned it to the cold, hard platform and looked up at Taliah. "Is Sebastian's soul back?"

Taliah hesitated, which made Eve's insides twist into one huge ball. She could barely breathe from the tension gripping her. "Taliah, please," she pleaded, unable to bear it any longer.

Finally, Taliah nodded and kept her eyes on Sebastian. "I've kept my end of the bargain."

Shifting her eyes on Eve, she pointed toward a wooden case and snapped her fingers. "Quick," she demanded, her nostrils flaring. "Bring me a dagger."

Without hesitation, Eve obeyed her command. Offering her the blade, Eve glanced down at Celina's limp body lying on the floor. She had lost all her color. "Is she... okay?"

"She'll be fine." Taliah's lips formed a wicked smile. "I wouldn't harm a hair on her head since she's going to be my son's bride."

"But she's your twin sister. Why would you—"

"Quiet!" she interjected, and snatched the blade from Eve's grasp.

Kneeling beside Celina with the dagger in one hand, Taliah took Celina's palm with the other. With a swift motion, she sliced deep into her skin. Glancing over her shoulder at Lucas, she ordered, "Take her back to her room."

Gently, he picked her up, cradling her securely and carried her out. As the door clicked shut, Taliah began to chant the same words over and over. With all her strength, she plunged the blood-soaked blade into the center of Sebastian's chest.

Eve's sudden intake of breath was deep. As she stared at the events unfolding in front of her, it brought tears to her eyes.

Turning toward her, Taliah barked, "Fetch me a flame!"

Eve visibly shook off her grief and refocused her attention. Forcing her eyes away from Sebastian, she quickly retrieved a candle and handed it to Taliah.

Placing it over the embedded dagger, the wax dripped into his open wound. When the last drop fell, her voice casted in an echo, "You shall wake with your body and powers restored."

Abruptly, Eve felt an impending reaping of some unseen energy flow around Sebastian. As the vibrations grew louder, the room started to shake. Eve instantly shielded her head when dust fell from the cracked ceiling. The shattering force made her wonder whether the room was going to crash in on them. Managing her footing, dread clutched her by the throat as she moved closer to Sebastian.

A few moments later, Sebastian's eyes flipped open. With uncoordinated limbs, his arms flailed like a puppet on strings.

When the force in the room receded, Sebastian stiffened. "Don't fight this, Sebastian," Taliah said as she grasped his hand, squeezing tightly. "The time for your second birth has arrived."

With wide eyes, he bared his fangs and roared.

* * * *

A circle of light flashed, catching Tim and Drakon's attention as they waited in a stretch of thick, wooded terrain. Just as Jem, Jace, and Kyle stepped through the portal, it vanished. Moving closer to Tim and Drakon, Kyle immediately covered his mouth. "Good God..." He choked. "What's that smell?"

On impulse, Jace bent over and threw up.

Based on the information Tim gave Drakon, he told them the smell was coming from the bodies of Arnaud and Dimitri Saintclare. Someone or something had torn them into pieces.

With his hand still covering his mouth, Kyle swallowed hard. "Who would do this?"

"My guess it's the same person that took Kara," Tim declared.

Kyle lowered his hand. "And who would that be?"

"Sebastian Crow," Jem interjected.

Regaining his composure, Jace wiped his mouth and turned in Drakon's direction. "You think he's hiding out in the estate next door?"

Drakon nodded. "And if we find him, that's where Taliah has Celina."

With his hands on his hips, Jem shook his head. "What are we going to do about the bodies?"

"Our primary mission is to search for Celina," Tim vowed. "I'll notify Herbert, and make sure they're properly taken care of."

Unfortunately, it was still daylight, which didn't provide them cover. Instead of walking up to the estate in front of all those cameras, they had Jem take them to the roof of Samuel's estate using the portal.

Stepping through it, Kyle tripped. With a quick reflex, Drakon grabbed his arm and steadied him before he fell. "Careful, twinkle toes," Drakon lightly chuckled.

When Jace heard Drakon's response, he snickered under his breath. Peering over the rooftop, he watched a black Mercedes pull in the driveway. "Psst!" Jace kept his voice low as he waved at his comrades, trying to get their attention. "Someone just pulled up."

As the guys watched closely, the Mercedes stopped in front of the garage. When the door opened, they saw Damien Spence step out and walk toward the back of the mansion.

"This has to be where Sebastian is," Jace said quietly, remembering how Sebastian was a guy who'd been into material things, and had grown up with designer clothes and expensive shit. Not even the demon in him would be able to take that out, he thought.

They waited a moment as Damien came back around and disappeared inside.

Lifting his chin, Tim looked at Jem. "Can you use the portal to get us in front of the garage?"

* * * *

Sitting by the window, Celina sensed Kyle's presence. Concentrating on his thoughts, she tried to use her powers to focus on his location. He was close by. Tilting her head back, she looked to the ceiling...

Kyle had been on top of the roof, and now he was inside the estate. But something was off. Something just wasn't quite right. Taking a deep breath, she tried to relax her breathing. Although she couldn't use her powers, her ability to sense someone's thoughts was compromised due to her sister's spell, but it was still workable. She knew there was somebody other than Kyle around the house.

In relief, she let out another deep breath. "Thank God," she said out loud. They'd found her. The Breedline had really found her. Even though no one could hear her, she yelled Kyle's name at the top of her lungs in hopes it could reach out beyond Taliah's spell.

* * * *

As Sebastian's awareness came quick, he immediately sat upright and glanced around the room. In the midst of his near panic, Eve reached out and smoothed her hand down his arm. His breathing calmed as her warm palm fell into a soothing rhythm.

Sensing someone on the roof, Taliah looked toward the ceiling. "We've got company," she said in an icy tone. "It's the Breedline, and they're here for Celina."

Sebastian went silent for a moment, curling his fingers into tight fists. "Get rid of them," he demanded, grinding his teeth.

"I'll surround us with an invisible shield," Taliah said in a smug tone. "If they come in, they'll find the place empty." And then with an iron resolve, she pushed her surroundings from her mind, and focused into the dark realm of her powers.

Chapter Fifty-Six

When Jem took Jace, Tim, Kyle, and Drakon through the portal, they stepped out in front of the garage. Inside, they saw Damien in complete oblivion as he went about his business with the door wide open.

This time, Jem thought, he wasn't going to ask questions nicely. Anger simmered and boiled up in his throat. He flexed his fingers, finally balling them into tight fists in an effort to rein himself in. The last thing he wanted to do was kill Damien in the heat of the moment.

As the first one to go inside, he took action and grabbed Damien. Cranking the bastard's arm behind his back, he slammed him face down onto the floor. "Where's the girl?" he seethed, his voice ending in a growl.

Struggling against Jem's hold, Damien groaned, "What—"

Standing beside them, Tim got in Damien's face and held a knife to his throat. "Don't play games with us, Damien. We know you've been lying," he barked. "You have two seconds to tell me where the hell she is, or I'll start carving you up into tiny pieces. And it won't be quick and it won't be painless. I'll make you suffer, but you won't die. You'll only wish you had."

Damien went deathly white, and it was obvious that whatever threat Jem had issued paled in comparison to the one Tim just promised.

Drakon had to admit, Tim in badass mode was pretty damn impressive. Jace just smirked, pride in his gaze as he watched Tim in action. Kyle stood back, a half-smile quirking his lips as he too watched with interest.

"As I told you before," Damien gasped in pain, "I don't know what you're talking about!"

With his free hand, Jem seized Damien's jaw. Twisting it around, Jem glared at him. "We're looking for a different girl this time," he snarled.

"Her name is Celina." He tightened his grip and raised his voice. "Tell us where she is!"

"I swear," Damien grunted in agony as he kept his eyes on the blade held close to his jugular. "I don't know anything!"

In frustration, Kyle burned with the need for revenge. He wanted to punish every person responsible for Celina's disappearance, but finding her was his first and only priority. Revenge had no place in his priorities right now.

Letting out a deep breath, Tim narrowed his eyes and lowered the knife. "He's not gonna talk," he muttered, grinding his teeth. "Just keep him here." Looking over his shoulder at Jace, he ordered, "Stay with him. I'll go with Drakon and Kyle to search inside." Shifting his focus on Jem, he said, "We'll need you too, especially if we run into Sebastian."

Before Jem released Damien, Tim looked at him in disgust. "This is not over," he warned, flashing the knife in front of Damien's face.

Damien started babbling and pleading for his life. "Please don't kill me," he begged.

What a pathetic, ball-less coward, Jem thought. With his hand wound into a tight fist, he reared back and punched Damien right in the face, knocking him unconscious. "That ought to keep 'em quiet for a while," Jem said, his eyes brimming with rage.

Tim pinned him with a glare. "Let's go."

Moving quietly through the house, they entered through the foyer. Pointing toward the staircase, Tim motioned for them to follow.

As they climbed each step, Kyle's instincts screamed the higher they went, sensing Celina's presence. Taking two steps at a time, he rushed past Tim, Drakon, and Jem.

In a flash, Tim caught up with him and grabbed his arm. "I need you to stay calm," he said in a low voice. "If she's here, we'll find her."

Kyle flinched, sucking in his breath, his eyes suddenly glittering with fire. "We've got to find her *now*."

With his brows clenched, Drakon shoved into Kyle's face, going nose to nose with him. "Listen to me, son. You've got to get yourself together."

"He's right, Kyle," Jem said as he came up behind Drakon. "We've got to do this together."

Instead of arguing, Kyle nodded in agreement.

After checking all the bedrooms and finding them empty, Kyle and Drakon came to the last room down the hall. As Kyle moved closer, he felt the hairs on the back of his neck stand. With Drakon's help, they broke through the locked door.

Finding the room empty, Kyle's stomach was in a permanent knot, and even though he refused to consider the worst-case scenario, that Celina was already dead, he couldn't help the surge of grief that threatened to buckle his knees. "She's been here," he said, holding back tears. "I know she's been kept here."

Plopping down on the bed, he reached for a pillow. Bringing it to his nose, he inhaled Celina's scent. As he was consumed with defeat, tears dripped off his chin.

As Celina stood invisible beside Kyle, she watched him sob, shattering her heart into a million pieces. Weakened herself, she sat down next to him, her eyes wet with tears. Staring into his beautiful face, she saw his hopeless state. Reaching her hand out to touch him, she stopped when she heard a voice coming from the doorway.

"Kyle?"

Looking up, he saw Tim standing beside Drakon and Jem. As they stepped in, Tim moved closer and approached the bed. "Kyle, we've searched the entire estate. I'm sorry, but she's not here. I was sure we'd find her." Reaching out, he placed his hand on Kyle's shoulder. "That doesn't mean we've given up."

In desperation, Celina tried to make them hear her, "Please, don't leave me!"

With an expression of defeat, Kyle turned in her direction as if he'd heard her. But no, he was just staring through her to Tim.

When he stood, she panicked. This might be the last time she saw him. Lifting her hand, even though it would do no good, she lay it on the side of his face. Trying to wipe his tears, she imagined she could feel the warmth of his skin and the wetness on his cheeks.

"Kyle, I'm right here," she pleaded.

He frowned, and then with his own hand, he placed it where she was touching him. But it was just to sweep his tears away.

Dropping the pillow, he moved past her. Confused, he could have sworn he felt her presence. With all his strength, he walked toward the door.

As she watched him leave, her heart felt like it was going to stop. "Kyle!" she called out.

He paused, and glanced over his shoulder. The faraway look in his eyes expressed grief.

"I love you," she whispered.

"I love you, Celina," he muttered under his breath. Turning away, he slowly walked to the door and left.

With her arms outstretched, she ran after him. As she hit the confines of her prison, it knocked her back and sent her crumbling to the floor.

* * * *

When Sebastian awoke, he was in precisely the same place he'd been when he'd fallen asleep: flat on his back with his arms crossed over his chest like a corpse in a coffin. As he sat up, the first thing he did was look at his hands. Turning his wrists over and over, he noticed that the decaying flesh was gone. Next, he glanced at his feet and wiggled his toes. "My legs... I can feel my legs," he beamed with excitement. With his mobility back, he pulled his legs in and straightened them again.

Bracing himself, he shifted off the platform and landed on his feet. Feeling off balance, he grabbed the platform and steadied himself. Regaining his strength, he let go and stood on his own.

When he approached the door, he saw the knob turn. He moved aside just as the door swung open.

Surprised, Eve's eyes widened. "Sebastian!" Instantly, she covered her mouth. "Oh, thank God," she mumbled against her hand. "You can walk!"

Without warning, he dropped to his knees in agony. Squeezing his eyes shut, he placed his hands over his head and gasped in pain. Feeling like deflated balloon suddenly filled with air, he sensed another presence take over his body.

Eve knelt down beside him. "Sebastian, what's wrong?"

At the sound of her voice, he calmed and opened his lids. Lifting his chin, he stared at her through a different set of eyes. The dark depths changed into a deep yellow, flecked with gold. Tentatively, he reached out to her. "My darling, Eve," he said in a sincere voice. "It's me."

Noticing the golden hues of his irises, she looked at him, shell-shocked. In his arms, she sagged against him as the past slid back into place. "Sebastian," she let out a contented sigh. "Is it really you?"

* * * *

Amid the silence, Celina paced around and ended up at the window. Without thinking of her sister's spell, she placed her hand against the glass. Instantly, she realized the force field was gone. Somehow, it had been lifted.

Quickly considering her potential exit alternatives, she glanced at the door that was left open.

The last thing she wanted was to get caught. Without knowing her way around the place, she hadn't a clue where to go. The only way out of here was to use her powers. Closing her eyes, she concentrated on her body. Freeing her mind of all her surroundings and focusing on becoming free, she thought of the blue sky, the summer breeze and the green grass. Breathing in deeply and exhaling slowly, she willed her body outside. When she slowly opened her lids, she took form in the sheltered wooded field of the Breedline Covenant.

Chapter Fifty-Seven

After returning back, Kyle dragged himself up the staircase and into his room. With a grim resolve, he sank down on the bed. Rubbing his face, he thought of Celina. He'd swore he'd felt her presence back at Samuel Mercier's estate. Even though they found the place empty, he was sure she'd been there at some point.

When he heard a soft knock coming from the door, he answered with a grunt. As it opened, Casey stepped inside and sat down next to him. The lamp on the table beside Kyle cast a glow in the dark room, illuminating both him and his miserable expression.

As he looked closer, Casey noticed that Kyle's face was pale, his hair appeared darker in contrast, and his breathing deeper.

Turning in Casey's direction, Kyle muttered, "Thanks for coming."

"Wanna talk about it?"

Kyle nodded. "I was so sure we'd find her. Our timing must have been off. I know she'd been there. Somehow, we must have just missed her."

He wanted to support Kyle, but with each passing minute, it didn't look good. "Come on, man. We'll find her."

When another knock came from the door, it caught their attention. This time, it was a knuckle-buster, loud enough to make an echo. The instant Kyle heard it, his voice dropped, "Come in."

As the door opened, Drakon and Tim stood in the doorway, and they were not alone. Jace and Jem came too. There was a reason the group had come. Recognizing Kyle's desperation, they were relieved to have good news.

"Kyle... she's here," Tim said with a smile. "Celina's downstairs in Helen's exam room."

Kyle took a second to internalize the information. Without haste, he shot to his feet. "What—"

Moving aside, Tim pointed toward the open door. "Go to her."

Hurrying past them, he almost knocked everyone down. Hightailing across the hall, he scurried down the stairs with tears of joy.

With a soft knock, he peered around the half-open door and muttered, "Celina?"

Helen's voice echoed inside, "You can come in."

As he pushed past the door, his mouth dropped when he saw Celina sitting on top of the exam table.

Her voice was barely a whisper, "Kyle..."

Holding out his arms, he rushed over and wrapped them around her. "Thank God." He squeezed her tight. "I thought I'd never see you again."

"I was there with you," she whispered in his ear. "I was in that room."

He pulled from their embrace, and looked at her confused. "Where?"

"My sister put some kind of spell inside the estate, making everyone seem invisible," she explained. "I couldn't use any of my powers."

"But... how did you get out?"

Her eyes softened as she shook her head. "She must have weakened after the spell."

"I'm so sorry, Celina," he said in a strained voice. "I'm sorry I couldn't save you."

Scooting to the edge of the table, she sagged against him. "There was nothing you could have done. My sister's powers are stronger than I thought."

In a gentle tone, Helen said, "Celina, you're fine to leave. Just make sure you change the bandage on your hand every day until the wound heals."

Celina nodded, and looked down at her hand. "Thank you, Aunt Helen."

"What happened?" Kyle said, noticing the bandage.

"My sister did this, but I'm okay, Kyle," Celina reassured him.

At the sound of a light tap at the door, Helen looked over her shoulder. "Come in." When Tim peeked inside, she said, "Just the person we need to talk to."

Helen focused on Tim and smiled as he came over. "Celina has some information on the demon."

Tim stood motionless, bracing himself for bad news.

Celina cleared her throat. "I'm not sure why, but my sister has brought Sebastian's soul back from purgatory. That's why she took me. She threatened to kill Kyle if I didn't agree to help her. They're still in that estate you searched. You just couldn't see them. Taliah must have placed an invisibility spell on us."

Tim felt his mouth drop open. "Well, I..." He placed his palm on her shoulder. "I'm sorry, Celina. We're just glad you're back safe."

* * * *

"Yes, my darling," Sebastian's voice sounded different. "It's really me."

Confused, Eve tried to withdraw from him, but his free arm shot out. His palm landed on her shoulder, holding her in place.

"I've missed you, Eve."

She swallowed hard. "You have?"

With his head nuzzled in the crevice of her neck, she felt his warm breath blow across her skin. "There's nothing like your scent," he murmured. "Let me pleasure you, my darling."

Goose bumps trailed down her arms as she felt worshiped. "It's really you," she said, staring into his golden eyes.

Gently, he lowered her flat on her back. As he hovered above her, he used his arms to brace himself. Glancing down her body, his eyes stopped at the buttons on her jeans. "Take them off," he whispered.

After she slid them down her legs, she arched her body, desperate to feel him inside.

Fire blazed in his eyes as he leaned down to claim her mouth. He kissed her with passion, and so very reverently. He lifted his head, his expression filled with so much warmth and compassion. When he undid his pants, he joined her body, fitting perfectly.

His breath came quick and heavy, mingling with hers. She inhaled deeply through her nose, trying to catch up as her body tightened and began the upward climb to the ultimate release. Her eyes flew open as the moment seemed to shatter around her. The tension snapped, releasing the most intense pleasure she'd ever experienced in her life. When her euphoric release receded, she felt him stiffen as if he was in pain. With his lids squeezed shut, his body began to jerk into some kind of seizure as every muscle in his body violently shook.

Reaching up, she smoothed her hand over his cheek. "Sebastian? What's wrong?"

In an instant, his eyes flashed wide. She gasped, and quickly pulled her hand away from his face when she saw the color change. With his brows clenched, the black depths glared in hostility.

She scrambled to get out from underneath him as he forcefully held her down. "Not so fast," he growled. "Did you enjoy yourself?"

"Please, no," she begged. "Let me go!"

With a blank stare, he released her. "Enjoy him while you can," he smirked, fastening his pants. "Sebastian's soul will only be allowed to come out while I'm resting. In the meantime, you belong to me."

Chapter Fifty-Eight

After Tim found out Celina's sister had created an illusion of invisibility to hide Sebastian, he immediately decided to call a meeting.

"Kyle, I'll need you to inform everyone to gather in the library," Tim urged. "We're having a meeting right now."

Kyle went silent for a moment, his expression promising as he gazed into Celina's eyes. "I'll meet you there," he said as a smile quirked the corner of his mouth.

With a broad smile curving her pretty features, she nodded.

Tim turned in Helen's direction. "I'll need you there too."

"Of course," she agreed. Before Tim left the room, Helen asked, "Do you want me to let Alexander know?"

"Yes," he said decisively. "I want him there as well."

When Kyle jogged up the staircase, he saw Drakon and Cassie coming out of their room. "Good, I was going to come find you." Kyle pulled up short as Drakon shut his door. "Tim has called an urgent meeting in the library." He glanced at Cassie. "He wants everyone to attend."

"Okay," Drakon replied. "We'll head that way."

Kyle hurried across the hallway, and stopped at Jace and Tessa's door. After a couple of knocks, Jace finally answered. Standing in the open doorway, Kyle noticed Jace's shirt was partially tucked in—hanging loose in front, and his hair was tousled as if someone had been running their fingers through it. Apparently, he'd interrupted something.

"Sorry to bother you," Kyle uttered. "Tim asked me to gather everyone downstairs. He's called an urgent meeting."

After tucking his shirt in, Jace smoothed his hand through his hair. "Sure, we'll be there."

Rushing to the other end of the hall, Kyle halted when he came up to Jem and Mia's door. Just as he was about to knock, the door swung open.

"Hey, Kyle," Jem greeted, his expression appearing concerned when he saw the anxiety on Kyle's face. "What's going on?"

"Tim just called a meeting. He wants everyone there."

With his brows furrowed, Jem asked, "Mia too?"

"Yeah, he said everyone."

Overhearing their conversation, Mia came up behind Jem. "Thanks, Kyle. We'll be there."

Next, he headed toward Casey's room. Reaching up, he pounded on the door. When there was no answer, he yelled, "Casey, it's me... Kyle!"

When the door opened, he saw Casey with a glass of wine in his hand, wearing a silk robe reminding him of Hugh Hefner. Grinning, he lifted the glass. "What's up?"

Kyle chuckled, looking at his outfit. "Dude, what are you wearing?"

Casey arched a brow. "Hey, don't knock it. This is Ralph Lauren's new sleepwear."

"Seriously, Casey?" Kyle shook his head. "Sometimes, I wonder about you."

"So, how's Celina?" Casey asked, changing the awkwardness. "She's okay, isn't she?"

"Yeah, she's fine."

"So, what are you doing here? Shouldn't you be with her?"

"Everyone is supposed to come downstairs to the library. Tim's called an urgent meeting, and he wants everyone there."

"Really?" Casey asked in a puzzled tone. "It sounds serious."

"Just hurry." Kyle rolled his eyes. "Get dressed. I'll meet you there."

Just as Kyle wheeled around, Casey said, "Hang on. Just give me a couple of minutes to change. I'll go down with you."

As Kyle patiently waited in the hall, Casey finally emerged from his room.

"Damn," Kyle swore. "What took so long?"

With his brows popped, Casey smiled ruefully. "Sorry."

"Whatever," Kyle grimaced. "Let's go!"

* * * *

With a yawn, Taliah opened her eyes and glanced at her watch. In disbelief, she rubbed her eyes thinking the time couldn't be right. She'd been asleep for two hours. After using all her energy creating an invisibility spell, she came downstairs and crashed on the couch.

As she shifted her eyes toward the staircase, her sister's room seemed miles away. She wondered if it was worth the effort to go up and check on her. It took another ten minutes before she could throw off the lethargy and stand. As she took each step, she felt stronger.

When she saw the door half-open, she pushed through it. When she found the room empty, her anger boiled. Hearing a whining noise, she looked over her shoulder and saw Lucas. "Shhh..." she soothed him. "Don't worry." Her eyes softened. "We'll get her back."

* * * *

As Kyle and Casey entered the library, they scanned the room. In silence, everyone was patiently waiting for the meeting to start. Looking toward the head of the table, they saw Tessa. Standing beside her, Tim nervously shifted his weight back and forth from one foot to the other. As she sat next to Helen, Celina's face entered Kyle's line of vision, and in contrast to the pale cast of her skin, her green eyes expressed anxiety.

When he sat down beside her, she opened her mouth, but all that came out was the air in her lungs. She was too nervous to speak. Instead, she swallowed hard and the corner of her mouth lifted into a half grin.

With an expression of compassion, he took her hand and whispered, "It's going to be okay."

As they waited for the meeting to start, thoughts of Celina's past flashed into her head. She saw parts of her life going all the way back to a time she'd tried to forget. Memories of her parents' death were something she consciously didn't want to remember. There were too many crossroads to count where things couldn't be stopped. Destiny was like a passage of time, however, opening old wounds and bringing back the pain all over again. And yet... as her mind churned beneath all her forgotten memories, her path had been set upon one task: to finally put an end to her own sister.

The sound of Tim clearing his throat brought her back to reality.

"Celina has finally confirmed our suspicions," Tim announced. "Indeed, the Chiang-shih demon still exists. Somehow, he has managed to possess Sebastian's body. As of now, he's hiding in Samuel Mercier's estate." He paused, noticing everyone's shocked reaction. "So, that means Samuel Mercier and Damien Spence have betrayed the Covenant, in which they will be dealt with in due time. Our first priority is destroying the demon." His eyes focused on Jace.

Jace nodded, knowing exactly what he had to do. They all depended on him to release his inner Beast and destroy the demon.

With a grim expression, Tim continued. "Before we move on, I must discuss another matter. Unfortunately, we found the bodies of Amaud Saintclare and his son Dimitri during our search for Celina. I've contacted their relatives and the estate's staff. I'm guessing the demon had something to do with their deaths. In conclusion, I've considered the possibility he's also responsible for Kara Saintclare's disappearance."

In the silence that followed, his eyes shifted in Celina's direction. "Celina has some information she'd like to share with the rest of us."

When Kyle gently squeezed her hand, she turned to face him. His smile gave her the courage she desperately needed.

As she glanced around the table, Celina's eyes expressed regret. "I'm sorry, but I helped my sister with a ritual... to bring Sebastian's soul back to his body."

In an explosive response, Jace shot out of his chair with a murderous look on his face. "What—"

Next to him, Jem shook his head in frustration. Suddenly, he felt like a heavy weight had been dropped onto his shoulders. With his eyes locked on Celina's, he said hoarsely, "Why?"

Kyle was at her defense in a flash. "Take it easy on her! She's been through hell!"

Tears sprang to her eyes. "I'm so sorry. I didn't have a choice. She threatened to kill Kyle if I didn't help her."

Sitting back down, Jace held up his hands in defeat. "Jesus," he breathed. "What would Taliah want with Sebastian's soul?"

"The demon cannot survive in a body without the soul," Celina explained. "Eventually, he would have to possess someone else."

Jem sighed, feeling like he was repeating history. "So, after we destroy the demon, we've got to deal with Sebastian all over again."

Tim held up his hand. "Everyone, please... just calm down. Right now, our main concern is destroying the demon. We'll deal with the rest later. I'm going to contact the other council members and set up a meeting."

"There's something else you need to know," Celina warned. "My sister has a child that I wasn't aware of, and it's... some kind of creature."

Tim frowned. "What exactly does that mean?"

Celina took a deep breath. "It looks like a dragon with human male features. That's how Taliah managed to kidnap me. Apparently, he has inherited our powers, except he can dematerialize from any place with another person. I think the demon is the father."

Jace's fury screamed inside of him. "Great!" he exploded. "How in the hell do we deal with that?"

Closing her eyes, all Celina could do was repeat her words. "I'm sorry." Lifting her lids, she shook her head feeling powerless. "I don't know."

"What about the book?" Tessa suggested. "Maybe there's something in it about this particular creature?"

Abruptly, Celina remembered reading about a creature in the book called the Katako. "Wait a minute," she said, rising from her chair.

Everyone watched in silence as she scrambled toward the mythology section and pulled out the book on the Chiang-shih demon. Hurrying back to her seat, she was on a mission as she opened it and flipped through the pages.

Finally, she stopped and pointed to a page. "Here it is!" Scanning through it, she read out loud. "The Katako is the offspring of the Chiang-shih demon and a Wicca. It also says that if the Katako is born of a Breedline species, this lineage makes them incredibly powerful. With its blood, a Wicca can summon the souls from purgatory."

"So, how do we destroy it?" Tessa queried.

"Let me read on, and see what I can find." Celina continued to scan through the page, searching for more information. With wide eyes, she looked at Tessa and whispered, "You..."

Tessa stared back at her in clear confusion. "What?"

Without hesitation, Celina replied, "It says that only a Breedline queen can destroy it."

Chapter Fifty-Nine

After Taliah delivered the disappointing news of her sister's escape, Sebastian knew it wouldn't be long before the Breedline found out he was here. He reached into the pocket of his jacket and took out his phone. Pulling a number from his contacts, he initiated a call and impatiently waited for Samuel Mercier to answer.

When he answered, Sebastian cleared his throat. "I need you here *now*."

"Yes, Master."

"The Breedline Covenant knows I'm here," he grumbled. "It won't be long before they devise a strategy to attack. I want all my council members here. Do you understand?"

"Of course," Samuel agreed without haste. "I will inform everyone immediately."

"Be prepared to do anything that's necessary, even if we have to kill the queen."

"But Master?" Samuel hesitated for a second. "No Breedline can kill the queen."

"You won't be doing the killing." Sebastian's last word lingered, carrying the pronunciation of a curse. "My son will kill her. Do you have any objections with that decision?"

Samuel opened his mouth, but all that came out was a squeak.

"Is that a no?" Sebastian queried in a menacing tone.

"No, Master. I don't object."

When Sebastian finally hung up, he stared into the eyes of his son. Lucas had suddenly appeared in the room and stood beside Taliah. She had an agitated expression with her lips pursed tight.

"We don't have much time," she said bluntly. "I must start the ritual now. If you're going to defeat the Breedline, we must have an army."

"Do it," he demanded. "Bring forth my death army."

With a smug grin, Taliah held up a dagger. "I'll need your blood before I begin the ritual."

* * * *

Before Tim dismissed the meeting, he told everyone not to leave the Covenant, and that he would contact them when the other council members arrived.

As everyone got up to leave, Jace pulled out Tessa's chair. When she stood, he intended to take her back to their room, and finish what they started earlier.

Instead, he met the eyes of Alexander. The instant the connection was made, some combination of neurons went off in his brain, and his equilibrium went haywire. Without warning, he went into a free fall, his weight shifting backward as a seizure took over his body, rendering him into spastic convulsions. *Oh, shit!* He thought. *Here we go again.* He blacked out before he hit the floor...

Shock registered on Tessa's face as she rushed to his side. "Oh my God... Jace!"

When he finally regained consciousness, the first thing he saw was the ceiling. Blinking slowly, he tried to focus his blurred vision. As his eyesight registered, he saw Tessa and a lineup of concerned faces. Dr. Helen Carrington was next to Tessa, and on his other side were Jem and Drakon. Alexander was down at his feet with everyone else.

The moment Alexander's presence registered, the seizure started up again. A second go-around of spasms lifted his torso off the floor.

Helen pulled out something from her coat pocket, and flashed a small light into his eyes. "Jace, can you hear me?"

Focusing on whatever was shining in his pupils, Jace struggled to speak. He couldn't get his mouth to work as he soundlessly moved his lips.

In desperation, Tessa turned in Jem's direction. "I can't understand him. What's he trying to say?"

Jem stared back at her in clear confusion. "I don't know. I can't read his thoughts."

With her hand in his, Tessa gently squeezed. "Just hang in there, Jace."

Looming above her, Alexander's face changed into an agonizing mask as if he could feel Jace's pain.

"The Beast in him wants to kill me," Alexander spoke out.

Jem turned toward him and frowned. "How do you know?"

Looking at Jem with wide eyes, Alexander said, "I can hear his thoughts."

"I don't understand. How can that be?"

"I-I'm not sure," Alexander stammered.

Trying to pull himself from the downward spiral, Jace breathed slowly through his nose.

"Someone please get my medical bag from the exam room," Helen called out.

When Kyle came back with her bag, she took out a stethoscope and pressed it to Jace's chest.

With her hand over her mouth, Tessa's voice trembled, "Is he going to be all right?"

In silence, Helen wrapped a blood pressure cuff around his arm and puffed up its inner tube. There was a long hiss that seemed to go on forever as Tessa waited for Helen to say something.

Jace figured he must have passed out, because he became awake and felt something tight around his arm. And then he heard familiar voices.

"A little on the low side," Helen said, ripping the cuff free with a popping sound as the Velcro came apart. "But it's nothing to be concerned about."

He lost consciousness again. When he came back, he heard Jem's voice. "Jace, can you hear me?"

When Jace's eyes slowly opened, his long eyelashes blinked up and down.

Kneeling beside him, Jem muttered, "Nod your head if you can hear me."

With a slight nod, he looked away from Jem's face and searched for Tessa. A moment later, he groaned when he felt hands gripping under his armpits and latching onto his ankles.

"Easy there, Jace. We're just gonna move you to the exam room," Drakon said.

Jace let himself be carried out of the room and down the hall.

"All right, bro," Jem muttered as he helped Drakon lower him onto a padded table. "Down you go."

Jace felt his head get tilted up and then something soft was placed under his head. Collapsing against a pillow, he was about to pass out again when he heard Helen's voice.

"He'll be all right in an hour or two," she said in a hushed voice. "He should recover quickly with some rest, but I want to do an MRI on him just as a precaution."

"Thanks... Doc," Jace mumbled in a hoarse voice.

She placed her palm on his shoulder. "I'll give you some privacy. Let me know if you need anything."

Tessa hugged her. "Thank you, Helen."

She smiled. "You're welcome."

When everyone left the room, Tessa sat down next to Jace and held his hand. "Do you remember anything before you passed out?"

He frowned as if he were running a check of his memory. "No." He shook his head. "I really can't remember anything."

"You were trying to say something. Can you remember what it was?"

Jace frowned again. "No, I—"

Suddenly, she felt his hand start to tremble. His eyes rolled back, and his body stiffened as the seizure took him over again.

Tessa squeezed his hand. "Stay with me, Jace."

Chapter Sixty

The following evening, Taliah crept through a foggy field in her black, hooded robe with Lucas close behind. Crowded in tight, they were surrounded by a forest of trees. With their leafless branches interlaced, it created the impression of black lace. As she came upon an old graveyard, she reached for the latch of an iron gate that led to a mausoleum.

Once inside the massive vault, she knelt down on the floor with Lucas hovering by her side. Opening a wooden box, she pulled out three red candles. The dark room instantly brightened as she waived her hand to animate the flames. Reaching into the box again, she pulled out a dagger and a small vial of Sebastian's blood.

Extending her palm, she said, "Lucas, give me your hand."

Crouching down, he offered it to her. Startled, his eyes widened as she placed the eight-inch blade close to his palm and sliced across it. With her face half hidden by the hooded robe, she began to chant.

As tears fell down his cheeks, she gently wiped them away. Opening his mouth, he tried to speak, but all that came out was a mumble.

"Yes." She smiled, reading his thoughts. "I love you too."

When she held the vial of Sebastian's blood underneath Lucas's palm, his blood dripped into it. The moment it was combined, it started to bubble and simmer. Lifting it to her lips, she witnessed the future as it unfurled. When it finally settled, she drank the vial down. Swaying on her knees, she caught herself before she crumpled over. Grasping her throat, she started to choke. "I'm going to be—"

As the retching tackled her again and again, she felt herself being tenderly lifted. Lucas supported her through the vomiting, and when it was over, she sagged into him. For a moment, she felt him stroke her hair.

From out of nowhere, crackling thunder rolled in and rain started to pour. With shaky hands, she grabbed the sleeve of her robe and yanked it up. On her forearm, she saw a permanent symbol burnt into her skin.

As she arranged her arm to read the words, her voice echoed inside the dark sinister tomb.

Letting herself go limp, she breathed through her mouth trying to regain her strength. Closing her eyes, she felt all the death in the room. Their evil souls were lost in purgatory, scratching and clawing at their chance to break free.

* * * *

With each step, Sebastian prepared to meet with his council as he headed down a long, spiral staircase. At the bottom, he let out a deep breath and straightened his slim-fitting, black blazer. The souls of his boots clicked as he walked across the marble floor. Entering inside a set of double doors, he passed the formal dining room and cringed at the interior design. The estate was close to the size he had in Paris, big and spacious, except the furnishings were dreadful, all done in military style. The runner on the floor was a plain, well-vacuumed cream, not like the spectacular Oriental he once had. Instead of tasteful swaths of color with fringe and tassels, the windows were covered by thick steel.

Quickly, he stalked past the rest of the grim décor to his destination ahead. Before he opened the doors leading to the conference room, he lifted his chin and sighed. Pushing his way into the room, he prayed that all his council members had arrived.

His prayers were answered as the inner door gave way, and male voices flooded his ears. Around a mahogany table, there were six council members dressed in suits with ties, and cravats at the throat. There was a noticeable dip in the conversation as he made his appearance. Every one of the members fell silent, and instantly stood, bowing to their master.

On a sudden, gripping instinct, Sebastian's head cranked around the room, and his eyes focused at the head of the table.

Without haste, Samuel Mercier quickly shuffled over to Sebastian. "Welcome, Master." He dipped his head. "May I take your coat?"

There was a hesitation as Sebastian stared at him with an evil glare. "No, you may not," he bit out.

"Please forgive me, my lord," Samuel apologized, scurrying back to his seat.

Sebastian stood behind his chair facing the council, and lifted up his hand, motioning for them to take their seat. "Just so we're clear, the Breedline Covenant has knowledge that I'm in this estate. I should also mention that they know of Samuel and Damien's betrayal."

Damien abruptly stood and cursed. Violence replaced the very veins in his body, spreading throughout him to the point where he began to feel his brain boil within the confines of his skull.

In the blink of an eye, Sebastian launched himself at Damien. Grabbing him by the throat, he tossed him back down in his chair. With his hands clutched into fists, Sebastian wanted to rip Damien's head right off his shoulders. But since Eve cared about his pathetic life, he would spare it for now.

As Sebastian sat down, all eyes of the members flipped to him. "As I was saying before being rudely interrupted," his voice was cold, his eyes locked and loaded with deadly intent.

Damien made a noise in the back of his throat, as if, through his regret, he couldn't find the voice to speak. Upon a deep, bracing breath, he spoke clearly, "I can't apologize enough for my abrupt outburst. It was utterly rude and unforgiveable. Please forgive me, Master. I did not mean to disrespect you."

Sebastian focused on him with a glare. "There's a part of me that wants to tell you to go to hell... to take your apology, and your weary eyes, and never, ever show your face anywhere near me again."

A sudden shot of fear jerked Damien upright. After a short pause, he nodded.

"Instead, I'm going to give you a second chance to prove your loyalty to me. As we speak, Taliah's preparing an army to fight against the Breedline. I will need all of you to band together and fight if necessary. If anyone in this room has any objections, say your peace now."

Sebastian just stared at them for the longest time, as if he were giving them a chance to see just how sure and dedicated they were.

Abruptly, Sebastian focused on the sound of someone clearing their throat. At the end of the table, a slender distinguished gentleman with blazing red hair and a goatee raised his hand for permission to speak.

Sebastian narrowed his eyes. "What is it, Harold?"

Harold Crampton was a Breedline council member from North Carolina. He'd despised the Breedline Covenants, and their laws. After his father was sentenced to a life as a rogue wolf, he swore revenge against the Covenant.

"I've been summoned to an urgent meeting tomorrow morning at the Breedline Covenant," he confirmed with a bow.

Sebastian's eyes lit up like a child on Christmas morning. "Were you informed on the reason?"

"No, Master." He shook his head. "I was just told it was urgent, and to be prepared to stay in California until further notice."

Sebastian's upper lip curled up like a bow. "Go to this meeting, and make no haste to enlighten me afterward."

Harold nodded without hesitation. "Yes, Master."

"Does anyone else have anything they would like to discuss?" Sebastian said with a hint of impatience in his voice.

As the room kept its silence, Sebastian rose from his chair. "Everyone will remain in this estate until further notice." He tilted his chin up with an expression of power, and gallantly stalked out of the room.

Chapter Sixty-One

After Jace finally came around an hour later, he was in the back of a Hummer with Tim at the wheel. Beside Tim, he saw Jem in the passenger side. Shifting his focus, he noticed Tessa sitting in the back seat next to him, a faraway look in her eyes as if she were lost in thought. When he jogged back his memory, he'd remembered Helen had insisted on an MRI immediately. Whatever was causing his seizures, they were getting worse.

As Tessa stared out the tinted window, the ride to the hospital seemed to go in slow motion. All she could think about was whether Jace had some kind of embolism, or a tumor. The more she thought about it, she remembered what Alexander had said earlier when Jace went into a seizure. He'd told them he heard the inner thoughts of Jace's Beast.

Abruptly, a soft touch on her shoulder startled her, instantly shifting her mind back. "Sorry," she said as she felt Jace's warm palm.

His brows furrowed. "Are you okay?"

"Of course." She patted his hand, knowing this whole thing with the seizures had to be weighing on his mind as well. "How do you feel?"

"I'm fine," he whispered. "Is my sister riding with Helen to the hospital?"

"Yes." Tessa had to shake her head, her gratitude to Helen and Cassie. "Those two are amazing physicians."

"Yeah," he exhaled in a hard rush. "But this whole being-driven-in thing is ridiculous. I could have driven to the appointment myself."

"It's better to be safe," her voice cracked as if she was going to cry.

"What's wrong, baby?"

She batted away the concern. "Oh, it's just my allergies."

"Really?" he looked at her with a cocked brow. "You've never had any allergies before."

Before she could reply, the vehicle slowed as they entered the hospital's entrance and parked close to the front. As Tim turned off the ignition, Jem said, "I just got a text from Cassie. They're waiting for us at the front desk."

After Jace checked in at the hospital's admitting office, he and the rest of the group followed Helen into the neurology unit. They were all squeezed in a lobby that had high-tech equipment with the massive MRI machine in another room beyond a thick plate-glass window. The neurologist that was on staff was a Breedline physician Helen had known and trusted for years.

She introduced the neurologist, a tall, thin gentleman that looked like Bill Nye the Science Guy. "Jace, I would like to introduce you to the hospital's chief of neurology, Dr. Cletus Remington," Helen stated as she turned toward the physician. "Dr. Remington, this is Jace Chamberlain."

Sitting behind a small desk facing a computer screen, he stood and shook Jace's hand. Motioning toward the chair across his desk, he said, "Please have a seat, Mr. Chamberlain."

Jace nodded, and sat down.

"I just have a few questions before we start your MRI," Dr. Remington confirmed. "How long did your most recent seizure last?"

"About five minutes," Cassie blurted out as Jace glanced over at her.

"Have you been experiencing any numbness or tingling?"

Jace shook his head. "No... nothing."

An hour later, Jace had completed the MRI and changed from his hospital johnny back into his jeans and T-shirt.

The neurologist scrolled through all the images, as Helen and Cassie peered over his shoulder at the X-ray pictures.

"What do you see?" Helen inquired.

"There's nothing abnormal in there that I can see," he reported. "All of the brain structure is normal."

When the neurologist informed Jace on the results, he let out a sigh of relief. Tessa sagged against him with her arm wrapped around his waist.

As Jem watched them, the Bill Nye doppelganger launched into a whole lot of physician language that luckily meant something to Helen and Cassie, given the nodding. But Jace and Tessa ignored all that, and their affection toward one another was actually a beautiful thing to witness.

Helen and the other physician shook hands before the rest of the crew got in line to thank him.

Jace jumped in last, and shook his hand. "Thanks, Doc."

Before heading back to the Covenant, Tim glanced down at his wrist and checked his watch. "The council members won't be here until late tonight. We'll meet with them first thing in the morning after breakfast. I'll expect everyone in the Covenant to be there," he confirmed, stepping into the driver's side.

In agreement, Jace held the car door open for Tessa as she ducked into the back seat. When he got in and sat down beside her, Tim turned on the ignition and followed the lane that led to the hospital's exit.

* * * *

In the bathroom mirror, Mia stared at herself and let out a long sigh. Meeting her own eyes in the reflection, she shifted back in time as she remembered herself before she'd met Jem. She was a different person now, not the selfish, unsympathetic, cold-hearted person she used to be. After falling in love with Jem, she'd changed.

Turning away, she glanced down at her finger to the square black diamond Jem had given her. The breathtaking heirloom that belonged to his mother was set in sturdy white gold. It was the only piece of jewelry she could ever imagine wearing for eternity.

Heading into the bedroom, she opened the closet and pulled out a cream satin gown. Given the fact that she wasn't a material girl, it was the sort of dress that took her breath away, and the only one she'd ever owned. Staring at her wedding gown, she sucked back a wince. She couldn't ignore the fact that inside her chest ached. The idea of Jem facing the demon again made her panic-stricken.

After she pulled the gown out of the plastic, she slipped it on. Positioning herself in front of the mirror above her dresser, she forced herself to calm the jitters.

Abruptly, a soft knock at the door pulled her away from her thoughts. Quickly, she reached up and wiped her wet eyes.

"Mia," Tessa called out from behind the door, "are you in there?"

"Yeah, come on in."

When Tessa opened the door, she hesitated at the threshold. "Oh, Mia." She smiled. "You're dress is absolutely gorgeous."

"Do you think Jem will approve?"

Walking into the room, she nodded. "You'll definitely take his breath away."

"Thank you, Tessa." In a low voice, she asked, "How's Jace?"

"His MRI results didn't show anything abnormal." She let out a sigh. "I was so worried he had something horribly wrong. The thought of him having a brain tumor, or —-"

Mia moved closer, and grasped her hand. "You'll get through this. You're a strong woman, Tessa."

"Thank you, Mia." She squeezed her hand. "So, how are you doing? You seem anxious. Are you worried about them fighting the demon again?"

Mia blinked tears. "I'm terrified."

Tessa pulled her into a hug, hiding the worried expression on her face. "It's going to be okay," she soothed, and then took a step back. "I'm going to help them win this fight. And this time, the demon will be destroyed."

Chapter Sixty-Two

Later in the night, Taliah stood outside the cemetery with Lucas by her side, his enormous wings spread wide. "It is completed." She grinned with satisfaction. "The death army will obey my every command."

* * * *

Sebastian stood in the recessed doorway of the estate as he surveyed the area, impatiently waiting for Taliah's return. Lifting his forearm, he checked his Emporio Armani for the second time. "Damn it!" he cursed under his breath. What the hell is taking so long? He thought. It had been four hours since he'd heard from Taliah. *And where was his damn army?*

As he turned around to walk back in, he heard footsteps coming from behind. Pausing outside the door, he placed his hand inside his blazer to get his weapon—

Wheeling around, he pointed the muzzle in Taliah's direction. "What the hell took you so long?"

She shot him a glare with her lips pursed in a tight line. "To form an army with this magnitude takes time," she scoffed. "Just so we're clear, they will only obey my command."

Sebastian put his gun away. "Prove it to me."

"Fine," she replied with anger sharper than the blade that she had just used. "I will order them to hunt humans."

"Release them now," he ordered.

She nodded, and left without saying another word.

* * * *

Alexander drifted into sleep on the lounge sofa, waiting for Jace to return from the hospital after the MRI Helen insisted on. Slipping into a dream, it was the same nightmare he'd had since he came to live in the Breedline Covenant.

When the dagger sunk deep in his chest, pain hit him like he'd been ripped in half with a lightning bolt. Burning, his skin felt like it had been doused in gasoline and lit on fire.

"Oh, God," he gasped in agony, realizing he was dying. Dropping to his knees, he noticed a shadow hovering above him. When he raised his head, he saw—

Waking up, Alexander shot to his feet like he'd been fired from a rocket launcher. In a panic, he whipped his head side to side trying to focus on his surroundings.

He needed a drink, and soon. Anything in the form of alcohol that was strong and pungent enough to scratch his dry throat would due.

On shaky legs, he went to the bar, grabbed a fresh glass, and poured himself a shot of whiskey. Realizing he wasn't alone, he paused with the drink at his lips.

"Alexander?"

"Jesus!" he breathed, wheeling around. "Helen, you startled me."

"Oh, I'm sorry. I didn't mean to—"

"No, you're fine," he said in a sincere voice. "I was just having a drink. Would you like one?"

She shrugged. "Sure, why not."

When she moved closer, he felt a soothing feeling overcome his tensed shoulders. "What's your poison?"

"I'll have what you're having."

He nodded, and reached for another glass. "Straight up whiskey it is."

After he handed it to her, he lifted his. "Cheers." Tilting the whiskey, he swallowed it like it was water. He wanted more, but didn't pour another, not wanting her to think that he was a lush. "Would you care for another?"

As the liquor went down her throat, she immediately coughed. "No, thanks," she muttered in a hoarse voice. "I think one's enough for me."

"How's Jace?"

She placed her hand over his. "I'm sure you've been on pins and needles with worry. His MRI came back normal."

"That's good news." He glanced down at her hand. The sensation sent a warm flush through his skin, and straight between his thighs.

"Yes, it is." She smiled ruefully. "I just wish I knew what was causing all this."

Alexander felt like he stopped breathing, his chest going bonkers on him as the pace of his heartbeat picked up. "Do you think it has to do with his Beast?" his voice got lower, trying to concentrate on the conversation.

"It could be, but I just don't know for certain."

As she replied to his question, he became dimly aware of a humming in his head, like a train was gathering speed. Opening his mouth to breathe, he blinked in a nervous twitch.

She cocked her head to the side, noticing something in him was off. "Alexander? Are you all right?"

Staring at her in silence, a voice muttered the word *beloved* in his head. On the heels of the word, an all-powerful need to make love to her lit him up. In his mind, he saw it happening. *She was underneath him, lying in his bed skin-to-skin with her arms around him enjoying having his weight covering her.*

"Alexander?" she repeated, and still he did not respond.

As she reached out to him with concern, he sprang into action. He took her by the waist and lifted her on top of the bar, the element of surprise shocking her into surrender. He stripped her white coat off, handling her gently while her body went freely.

Fighting to get air into her lungs, her mouth opened with a gasp.

Trying to stop his instincts, the urge to subdue her took over. Suddenly, he was on top of the bar above her, slowly easing her onto her back. Grasping her wrists in one hand, he stretched her arms over her head, trapping her thighs with his hips.

Watching him wide eyed, her chest rose higher with each excited breath.

Arching into her, he sucked in a breath... only to freeze. Her scent carried the sultry sweetness of a female arousal. *I am in love*, Alexander thought as he looked at her. *I have so fallen in love.*

Silence stretched as Helen stared into his mesmerizing eyes, swallowing hard. He was so beautiful like that, she thought, with the dim light above falling on his hard jaw and his silky blond hair. *God, what was that scent?* She breathed in deep, recognizing the mix of dark spices. Sex came to her mind, the kind that you had when you lost all your inhibitions. The kind you felt for days afterward.

He went still, his entire body vibrating with anxiety as he pulled away. "I can't take you like this," he said pointedly. "I'm sorry, Helen."

In silence, she tried to catch her breath. There was such respect shining in his eyes, and all she could do was nod. "I think I need another drink," she croaked out.

Chapter Sixty-Three

Tessa awoke with a feeling of nausea that was rising quickly. She glanced at the alarm clock on the nightstand and froze. It was two o'clock in the morning. In the blink of an eye, she immediately placed her hand over her mouth and jumped out of bed.

The sound coming from the bathroom woke Jace. At first he wasn't sure what he was hearing. But then, he recognized it as retching.

Sliding out from underneath the covers, he shot to his feet and nearly tripped on the corner of the bedside rug. "Tessa?"

"I'm okay," she called out from inside the bathroom.

Hustling over to the toilet's separate space, he found her kneeling on the floor with one hand holding her hair back, and the other braced on the seat.

Quickly, he grasped a hold of her long hair, and gently held it away from her face. "Can I get you anything?"

"No, I'll be—"Cut off by a series of heaves, she groaned in agony.

Concerned, he smoothed his hand across her back. "Are you going to be okay?"

She finally stopped, and flopped down on the floor, landing on her butt. With an exhausted breath, she said, "I must have a stomach bug."

Letting her hair slip from his fingers, he moved in front of the sink and turned on the faucet. After he soaked a washcloth in cool water, he placed it on her forehead. "This should make you feel better, baby."

She sighed. "That feels good." Bracing her hand against the wall, she tried to stand. "I think the worst is over." As she stood on shaky legs, he quickly grabbed her waist and helped her back to bed.

Just as she thought her nausea was over, two minutes later, she was back in the bathroom on her knees with Jace at her side holding her hair.

After five minutes of heaving up absolutely nothing, she finally eased back in bed. Staring at the ceiling, she let out a deep breath. "I hope you don't catch this."

"Don't worry about it, baby. I'm just concerned for you."

Feeling restless, she turned her head on the pillow and looked in his direction. He was lying on his back, jaw tensed, and his brows furrowed.

"I think you should go see Helen tomorrow."

She yawned. "I'll be fine."

Turning his head in her direction, he raised a brow. "Uh-huh. It sounded like you were throwing up your liver."

"I did not," she said stubbornly.

"Okay... so what organ where you trying to throw up?"

She crossed her arms over her chest and rolled her eyes.

"Just please go see Helen. It wouldn't hurt to get a check-up."

"All right, I'll go if it will make you feel better."

Rolling on his side, he grasped her hand. "Love you, baby."

"I love you too." Moving closer, she cuddled against him. "Let's try to get some sleep."

Sagging against the pillows, Tessa wondered if it was possible that her birth control had failed. She placed her hand on her stomach, trying to imagine a baby inside. She really wanted children, but she wasn't sure if Jace was ready. Pushing the thought out of her mind, she pondered on the idea of marriage. Sure, they'd talked about it, but he still hadn't proposed to her. When she closed her eyes, she smiled as an image came to her. She saw a little blond-headed boy that looked just like Jace.

* * * *

The next morning, Tessa awoke with her kidneys screaming for a release. When she got out of bed, exhaustion crept in as she stiff-walked across the floor to the bathroom. Catching a glimpse of her reflection in the mirror, she paused and took another look. Her skin was radiant and her eyes sparkled even without much sleep, like she went to bed with her makeup on. Even her hair seemed more vibrant and glossy.

With her hand on her lower belly, she wondered... *could I be pregnant?* Her stomach let out a loud growl, and her appetite went into overdrive.

Before she stepped into the shower, Jace staggered into the bathroom, rubbing his tired eyes. Yawning, he muttered, "How are you feeling this morning?"

"Hungry!"

His eyebrows popped. "Really?"

"Yes! Pancakes drenched in a lot of syrup sounds like heaven right now."

He chuckled. "You must be feeling better."

Stepping under the warm spray, Tessa closed her eyes. Startled, her lids flipped open when she heard the shower door squeak.

Batting his brows, Jace smiled. "Care if I join you?"

The instant she wrapped her arms around him, he hardened in all the right places.

After finally emerging from an extended shower, they got dressed and headed downstairs. Standing outside the kitchen, they smelled a wonderful aroma of eggs and bacon.

Opening the door, Jace and Tessa saw Jem, Mia, Casey, Kyle, and Celina sitting at the kitchen table. In the corner of the room, their attention was drawn to sounds of tiny feet, and high-pitched squeals. Instantly, their mouth dropped in disbelief.

Finally, Jace managed to get his mouth to move. "Natalie?"

He couldn't believe his eyes. Natalie was running to the refrigerator where Tim was standing, and back across the kitchen to Angel. With her hands held out, she giggled, balancing her movement. The last time he'd seen her was just yesterday. In one day, she was a crawling, and now... she was walking?

Looking shell-shocked, Tessa's eyes widened. "I don't believe it. Is that really Natalie?"

Tim nodded. "Yep, she's walking now."

Placing his hands on his hips, Jace shook his head. "By tomorrow, she might be full grown."

With her arms out waiting for Natalie to run in her direction, Angel laughed. "Helen said her rapid growth spurt should be over. From now on, she will grow at a normal rate."

Tim sighed. "I hope so. She's a handful already."

When Drakon and Cassie walked into the kitchen, they fell silent when they saw Natalie.

Surprised, Cassie clapped her hand over her mouth. "Is that baby Natalie?"

Jace shrugged. "Can you believe it?" Bending over, he reached for Natalie. "Come here, you little rascal."

Natalie squealed, and ran over to Jace with her hands out. When he scooped her into his arms, she pointed at the kitchen doorway and mumbled, "Woo... ster."

Jace asked, "What is it, baby?"

Pointing in Drakon's direction, she wiggled her little finger. "Woo... ster! Woo... ster!"

When Jace finally caught on to what Natalie was saying, he cracked up. Everyone in the room looked at him puzzled.

"What's she trying to say?" Tim asked.

Moving next to Drakon, Jace blurted, "She's saying, rooster!"

Drakon smirked. "Very funny, Jace."

"Oh my, gosh," Cassie giggled. "It's your Mohawk, Drakon."

When Angel caught on, she immediately placed her hand over her mouth, trying to muffle her laugh. "I'm so sorry, Drakon."

Drakon smiled, and reached for Natalie. "Come here, cutie."

Immediately, she stretched her tiny hands out to him as Jace placed her in Drakon's huge arms. With wide eyes, she reached up and touched his Mohawk. Feeling the softness of his hair, she whispered, "Woo... ster."

With a smug grin, Jace joked, "Well, I guess that's your nickname around here."

Drakon shot him a glare.

"All right, let's eat," Tim announced, changing the subject. "In an hour, we've got a long meeting with the rest of the council."

Everyone's expression grew grim when they were reminded of their task ahead. They had to come up with a plan to stop the demon. Just as they sat down, Helen entered the kitchen with Alexander close behind.

"Has anyone seen the news?"

Everyone turned their attention on Helen.

"No," Tim replied. "Why?"

"It's been broadcasting all morning," she said out of breath. "There are reports of over a hundred thousand deaths in ten different cities."

In shock, Tim's eyes widened. "Jesus, what happened?"

"All of them were found asphyxiated."

Drakon's voice echoed across the room, "How in the world did that happen?"

"I've been on the phone this morning talking to a physician that examined some of the bodies," Helen explained. "The autopsy reports revealed all the victims were internally and externally saturated with mud."

Chapter Sixty-Four

Reclined back in a soft leather chair, Sebastian watched the televised reports on the unexplainable deaths in the San Francisco Bay area. As he glared at the flat screen, his lips formed into a twisted grin. Being the cause of pain fed his inner demon, a meal consumed by his evil side that just left him hungry for more.

In the midst of his thoughts, his mind retreated to the Breedline. He wondered if they cared about the thousands of human lives his death army took. The question he wanted answered was, how far would they go to help save the useless and pathetic lives of humans? And yet he didn't want this work of his to end. Like an addict holding to a fix that never wanted it to end, he planned on killing more.

When his phone went off, he was determined to ignore it until he noticed the number. It was Harold Crampton. With a touch of his long index finger, Sebastian answered. "This better be important," he said impatiently.

After a short pause, Harold finally spoke in a nervous tone, "Master... the Breedline council's meeting has been postponed until this evening."

With a curse, he wanted to reach through the phone and choke Harold out of rage. "Just report back to me as soon as the meeting is over. I want to know what they're planning."

"Yes, of course, Master."

In frustration, Sebastian shot to his feet and headed upstairs. Standing outside the room with Eve on his mind, he reached for the bedroom door. Swinging it open, he saw her standing by the bed wearing only a towel, fresh from a shower. He inhaled a scent that swirled around him and enticed his arousal. Noticing her nervous reaction, he stepped inside.

Eve's eyes flared. "Are you the reason all those humans died?"

"Why does it matter? When did you ever care for them anyway?"

She frowned. "I was just asking."

Crossing his arms, his shoulders appeared larger than usual. "Do human's mean anything to you?"

With a shake of her head, she looked at him without an emotion.

"Answer me something," he said, closing the distance between the door and Eve.

"What?" the tension was thick in her voice.

His eyes roamed over her body. "Would you still desire me, even if Sebastian's soul weren't inside this body?"

"If I answer truthfully, will you hurt me?"

"No, Eve." His face softened. "I gave you my word. I will never hurt you again."

On so many levels, she couldn't imagine having sex with the demon again. There was a side to him that was monstrous, but in truth, he was still in her beloved's body. After a long silence, filled by the pounding of her heart, she swallowed hard and whispered, "Yes."

At that, a familiar scent overtook his body. "I want you, Eve."

She had to sit down before she fell over—and went toward the bed before thinking. Settling in, Eve found herself struggling to stay still. Her internal compass was spinning around so fast, she could barely form a sentence. With a wave of anxiety shooting through her gut, all she could do was stare at him.

As he sat down beside her, she reached up with one hand, keeping the towel from slipping free. Images of his touch hit her like painful blows.

They fell silent for the longest time, and then he whispered, "Let me love you."

With a struggle, she tried to hold back tears. Finally, she gave up as they poured down her cheeks.

Clasping onto her other hand, he gently squeezed. "The feelings I have for you have eaten me up until there's nothing in here." As he pointed to the center of his chest, she realized that he was, in fact, hollow. There was no light in his eyes, and his aura dissipated as if it had never been.

Overcome with sadness, she shook her head. "I love the real Sebastian. I don't know you."

So empty, he was vacant down to his soul. "Please, Eve," he pleaded. "Love me."

* * * *

After Helen informed everyone on the recent deaths in the city, Celina scooted her chair from the kitchen table and stood. With a grim expression, she said, "This is the beginning of the destruction of the death army my sister promised Sebastian. She must have used her son's blood to bring back souls imprisoned in purgatory. She's using them to create Golems."

Confused, Jace shrugged. "What the hell are Golems?"

"They're creatures made from earth," she explained. "They have the ability to consume their victims, leaving them dead, saturated inside and out with mud."

As the frustration set in, Tim rubbed his hand over his short trimmed hair. "How do we stop them?"

"Taliah's the only one that can control them," she confirmed. "Unless..."

With impatience simmering in Jace, he blurted, "Unless what?"

"There's a book on Golems, but I'm not sure where we can find it."

"My cousin might have it," Helen spoke out. "She's a Wicca that practices both white and dark witchcraft. She has everything in her possession written on necromancy. I'm sure she has something on these creatures. But I haven't spoken to her in over twenty years."

"Helen, do you know where we can find her?" Drakon queried.

She nodded. "Yes, but she won't give up the information without a hefty price. Plus, she cannot be trusted."

"We'll bring this to the council meeting this evening," Tim said, swallowing the knot in his throat. "Celina, I need to speak with you in private."

Her brows lifted in surprise. "Okay."

Motioning her to follow, he muttered in a low voice, "We'll talk in my office."

Before she left, she looked at Kyle and mouthed silently, *Wait for me?* With a smile, he nodded.

When Tim held his office door open for Celina, he gestured her inside. "Please, have a seat."

As she sat down in the chair across from his desk, he took a seat and asked, "Before the council meeting this evening, is it possible for you to do a spell that will detect a traitor?"

"Yes, I can." She looked at him curiously. "Do you think one of the council members could be one of Sebastian's spies?"

With his elbows on the desk, he leaned forward. "Judging by Damien and Samuel's betrayal, I don't want to take any chances."

Reaching out, she said, "Give me your right hand."

When he placed it in hers, he looked confused. "How will this spell work?"

Celina's lips formed a sly smile. "If anyone with the intension of betraying the Covenant shakes your hand, you'll instantly know."

Chapter Sixty-Five

Eve was confused by the sound of Sebastian's pleading voice. His tone seemed like a kind of defeat when he asked her to love him. There was an electric moment as their eyes met. Instantly, she felt the connection between them, and knew it was not one-sided anymore.

Squeezing his hand, she nodded in response.

"My Eve... my precious Eve," he murmured. Leaning closer, he gently took her face in his warm hands. Brushing his lips against hers, he captivated her mouth, soothing her while arousing her at the same time. She moved with him as he gently lowered her down on the bed.

Bracing himself above her, he said exactly what he thought: "I need you."

Reaching up, she smoothed her palms across his broad shoulders. Pressing his body against hers, he inhaled her intoxicating scent. She drew a deep, shuddering breath when his warm breath brushed across her skin.

His strong body shook as he lowered his head. With his lips close to her ear, he whispered, "You're so beautiful."

Easing between her thighs, she felt his arousal smooth against her sensitive skin.

With patience, he opened her towel and exposed her breasts. Her nipples tightened to the point of pain, aching for his touch. Slowly, his tongue glided around one, and then the other.

Arching in pleasure, she watched as he touched her with such tenderness. God, he was beautiful. With waist-long hair, his striking features tugged at the strings of her heart. As her heart beat faster, she became breathless. Without hesitation, she begged, "Please."

The words she spoke triggered an immediate response in him. *Mine*, he thought. Unleashing his fangs, he felt an urge to taste her blood. Instead, he took her mouth again, drinking in the feel of her, the taste of her lips.

Slipping his hand down her hip... and lower... he tugged her in against his arousal. Lifting his lips from hers, he moved to the crevice of her throat. As he dragged one fang across her skin, she shivered with anticipation.

When a soft moan escaped her lips, he felt within his black heart a great welling of warmth, and he let the emotion take over. Before he kissed her again, he reached over her head to her long, silky hair. Spreading the dark waves out over the satin bedspread, he ran his fingers through the lengths.

Curling his hips into her core, he pushed and retreated, continuing the same rhythm. Wanting more, his body couldn't wait. With shaky hands, he fumbled with his pants, cracking his belt and sliding down his zipper...

Arching her hips against him, he was all over her, driving her into a desperate climax as she swallowed a cry.

The sound she made almost drove him to his own release. Snaking a hand around the back of his neck, she pulled him close to her throat and whispered, "Take me."

On impulse, his mouth opened with a hiss. The strike was strong and sure, two points going in deep, the sweet pain robbing her of sight and sound. Palming the back of his head, she pushed him down tighter, holding him to her, not caring whether he drank her dry.

When his massive orgasm stilled, he went to pull away, but she was desperate for him to keep going, and tried to force him to stay at her throat. It was no contest, though. He was so strong, it was as if she had put up no protest at all.

As overrun as her nervous system was, she felt the retraction of his fangs from her neck and knew the exact moment he was out of her. Closing her eyes, she felt a soft, lapping stroke move across her skin, as if he were sealing her closed.

When she lifted her lids, she saw him looking down at her with a frown. "I'm sorry." He let out a contented sigh, the soft exhalation blowing over her skin. "Did I take too much?"

Falling into a semi-trance, Eve relaxed as his body heat soaked into her, making her feel warm and contented. "No," she whispered as her eyelids fluttered closed.

Hearing her response, he was relieved. And then he said, "I love you, Eve."

* * * *

As the evening drew near, the Covenant's library started to fill up with council members, shaking Tim's hand after they entered the room.

A tall man with gray hair and a goatee extended his hand. "It's good to see you again, Tim. Unfortunately, I wish it was under better circumstances."

Shaking his hand, Tim nodded. "I agree, Victor. How's the Covenant in Pennsylvania responding to all the televised death reports?"

"Not well, I must say," he said grimly. "Everyone's in lockdown in fear of the worst. We're all hoping this meeting will give us some answers to why this is happening."

"We're doing all we can," Tim replied. "Please, have a seat." He motioned Victor inside.

Watching him closely, Tim didn't notice anything unusual as Victor sat down.

Turning his focus to another council member, Tim extended his hand. "Luther, how are you?"

Luther Proxy was a council member from the Tennessee Covenant. He turned wide eyes on Tim and firmly grasped his hand. "I've been better. I hope the Queen has some good news to report. With all the recent human deaths, our Covenant has been terrified of what will happen next."

Releasing his hand, Tim responded with a reassuring tone, "Have confidence, Luther. We'll figure this out."

"I hope so," he said bluntly, and entered the room. When he sat down beside Victor, Tim didn't notice any changes in Luther.

Celina stood by Kyle, watching in the far corner as everyone shook Tim's hand. So far, no one acted unusual. Patiently, she waited for someone to show signs from her spell. If a traitor shook hands with Tim, they would have an instantaneous reaction.

Most of all, the council members were already seated, chatting with one another as their voices muffled around the table. Tim searched the room and made eye contact with Celina, shrugging his shoulders.

Abruptly, a timorous voice caught Tim's attention. "Thanks for including me."

Turning around, Tim smiled when he saw Malachi O'Conner with his hand extended. With a firm grip, Tim shook his hand. "Glad to have you here, Malachi."

"Is the Queen going to attend the meeting?" Malachi queried with a blushing expression, "I think she's so beautiful. Jace is lucky to have such a prized mate."

Tim chuckled, and patted him on the shoulder. "Of course, she'll be here shortly."

Malachi's face lit up with a sizable grin. "Should I go ahead and take a seat?"

Tim nodded, pointing to the chair beside Drakon. "It looks like there's a vacant seat next to Drakon."

Just as Malachi walked away, a tall slender man with blazing, long, red hair strode past Tim. He was the last council member that was expected to show.

"Excuse me," Tim called out. "Harold Crampton... is that you?"

Catching his attention, Harold stopped in his tracks and slowly wheeled around. "I'm sorry." He faked a smile, and moved closer to Tim. "I didn't mean to ignore you. I'm just shocked about the human deaths. It's such a devastating blow to us all."

Tim narrowed his eyes. "Yes, it is." He extended his hand. "I'm glad you could make it here all the way from North Carolina."

"Thank you." When Harold grasped Tim's hand, he violently started to choke.

Tim shot another glance at Celina, and motioned her over.

As she rushed toward Tim with Kyle close behind, she saw Harold drop to his knees with his hands clutching his throat.

When Harold's face turned purple, Celina looked at Tim with a worried expression. "The spell completely closes the throat of anyone that has betrayed the Covenant."

Leaning closer, Tim glared into his panic-stricken eyes. "Did you hear that, Harold? We know you've betrayed the Covenant."

With a pleading gesture, Harold reached for Tim, gasping for air.

"Do you admit betraying your own Covenant to help the demon?"

Continuing to choke, he managed a desperate nod.

"Go ahead, Celina," Tim urged. "Release him."

Finally, Harold choked out a breath and crumpled to the floor.

After waiting for Tim's approval, Helen knelt down beside Harold and checked his vitals. "He'll be fine," she confirmed. "He's just passed out."

With his nostrils flared, Tim looked at Drakon. "Lock him up. When he's conscious, I want answers."

Chapter Sixty-Six

Sebastian smiled when he woke with Eve beside him, nestled in the curve of his arm, her hair spread out over it and the pillow. He could lie this way for hours, simply watching and enjoying the sight of her in bed with him. Looking at the clock, he realized they'd been asleep for hours. "Damn it," he cursed in a low voice, trying not to wake her. When he sat up, he quietly slipped out of bed and grabbed his clothes.

Eve's stare shifted over just as Sebastian finished zipping his pants. The irises that met hers were completely black. And beneath his cold composure... the hatred in those dark depths was different when he looked at her now. She could feel it in her very bones, a link between them, giving her insight beyond what her eyes saw: On the surface, he was her beloved with a lost soul trapped within. Inside his skin, however, he was an empty vessel, hollow... seeking for love he'd once felt long ago.

"Where are you going?"

His mouth twitched like he was going to smile. Instead, he leaned down and pressed a kiss to her forehead. "Get some rest. I'll be back later," he said haltingly.

Moving toward the door, he reached for the knob and paused. Turning his head, he stared at Eve. As her eyes closed, his heart ached to be with her. Deep inside his skin, at his very core, his inner string started to vibrate. He hadn't had this sensation since he'd fell in love with Katlyn, and its return was... an utter shock.

Shifting back around, he reached for the door once more, opening it, and stepped out. Slipping his hand inside his slim fitted blazer, he took out his phone. After he checked all his calls, he still hadn't heard from Harold. With his brows clenched tight, he ascended the stairs wondering what was taking him so long to report back. The Breedline council meeting should have been over hours ago.

Searching for Taliah, he pushed through a set of double doors and found her lounging in a plush sofa with a joint in her hand. With one long inhale, she offered him a smoke. Waving it away, he glanced toward the window, noticing Lucas standing outside alone.

Shifting his eyes back on Taliah, he asked, "What's wrong with him?"

"He's depressed," she replied, exhaling smoke at the same time. "He favors my sister, Celina."

"What do you mean he favors her?"

"He's in love with her."

"Don't you think that's a little twisted since Celina's your twin sister?"

She rolled her eyes. "He has the mind of a child. He doesn't comprehend all that."

Sebastian frowned. "I have bigger problems. Harold hasn't got back to me after the Covenant's council meeting."

"Oh?" she raised a brow. "Maybe they figured it out. You have to admit, Harold has just enough intelligence to open his mouth when he wants to eat, but certainly no more. I was shocked when you let him go."

Blowing out a frustrated sigh, he crossed his arms over his chest. "Release my army again," he ordered. "This time, send them to the homes of humans and... Breedline."

Confused by his demand, she stood up and glared at him. "Are you sure you want to kill Breedline?"

"Don't question my decision," he snapped. "Just do it."

* * * *

In frustration, Tim sat in front of his computer with a migraine spreading from the top of his head to the base of his skull. Planting his elbows on each side of the laptop, he rubbed the back of his neck, trying to soothe the pain. When he'd questioned Harold Crampton, he never denied betraying his own Covenant, but he swore he didn't know anything about what caused the recent human fatalities, or Sebastian's plans. The only question he refused to answer was the names of the rest of the traitors. He told Tim he would take that to his grave. And maybe he would... and soon.

Other than the illumination coming from the laptop, Tim was sitting in the dark. Staring at the screen, he thought of all the innocent people that had lost their lives for nothing. After they'd gotten rid of Alexander's demon, he'd hoped things would calm down. And now, things had taken an unforeseen turn. The demon had possessed their worst nightmare... Sebastian Crow.

God, there had been so much death, he thought. And knowing how evil the Chiang-shih demon was, he wasn't finished releasing his wrath.

Catching his attention, he shifted his eyes toward the door when he heard a light knock. "Come in."

As the door slowly opened, his headache instantly vanished when he saw Angel step inside. She was wearing a white silk robe that was tied at the waist. When she closed the door, her robe fell open, exposing her cleavage. With his arousal kicking in, he watched her move in his direction. Inhaling a deep breath, he caught the scent of her sweet fragrance.

Leaning against his desk, she tilted her head and smiled. "I hope I'm not bothering you. I just wanted to check to make sure you're okay."

With his hand extended, he motioned her closer. "Come here, honey." His eyes sparkled with excitement. "I'm glad to see you."

Just as she reached her hand out, ready to join his, an e-mail came through, and the laptop let out a beep.

"If you're busy, I can go—"

"No, honey," he muttered. Gently, he clasped her hand and pulled her into his lap. "Where's Natalie?"

Resting her head on his shoulder, she let a contented sigh. "She's with Jace and Tessa."

"Good." He smiled. "You deserve a break, plus they need practice being around little ones."

Quickly, she lifted her head off his shoulder. "Why? Do you know something I don't know?"

"No, sweetheart," he said with a chuckle. "I just meant in case they decide to have children of their own someday."

She nodded. "Oh, okay."

"It's amazing," he murmured, brushing a strand of her hair back. "When I'm around you like this, nothing else seems to matter. You make all my problems drift away."

With her lips slightly parted, her eyes traveled down his chest, knowing exactly what she wanted. Reaching underneath his shirt, she smoothed her hand over his warm skin. Shifting her eyes, she stared into his with a pleading expression. "Take me like you used to," she whispered.

Without hesitation, he carefully grasped her waist and lifted her on top of the desk. When she parted her legs, her robe fell open, showing him everything. Gliding his fingers around the silk fabric that was tied around her waist, he pulled it free.

"Give me your hands," he said quietly.

When she offered them freely, he wrapped the fabric around her wrists. "Lie back with your hands above your head," he said in a deep, assertive tone.

She shuddered at his demand.

Holding them with possession, he slowly eased her back until she was lying on the desk.

She swallowed in anticipation when his palm ran down the back of one of her legs, and extended her foot so it rested on his shoulder. He peppered light kisses at her calf and followed the path, going higher and higher. Her head was turned to the side, watching him with huge crimson eyes as she opened her mouth and let out a sigh.

"I've missed this," he muttered against her soft skin.

When he placed his lips to her belly, she relaxed, letting her legs fall open. Sweeping his hand down to her hip, he slipped his tongue lower, and kept going and going...

He let out a soft growl. "Mine..."

With a tight grip on her thighs, he continued in a circular rhythm, feeling her warm skin against his tongue. Arching her hips, she nearly sobbed, so aroused her legs started to shake. In a hoarse voice, she whispered, "Please—"

Arching off the desk, her body stiffened as the need to release caged her.

"Come for me," he demanded against her core.

With the sound of his voice, a wave of energy crashed down all over her, sweeping her up and away as her body surged. When all her tension snapped free, the release brought tears to her eyes. It felt wonderful to the millionth power.

When it was over, he lifted his head, and pressed a soft kiss to the inside of her thigh.

She opened her mouth and tried to speak, but all that came out was a heavy breath.

Gathering her up, he tenderly pulled the fabric from her wrists and held her in his arms. "I love you, Angel."

"I love you too."

🐾 Chapter Sixty-Seven

Early the following morning, Tessa quietly slipped out of bed. Before she left the room, she looked over her shoulder and saw Jace stretching his arms. "You're awake," she muttered.

Rubbing his eyes, he yawned. "Where are you going?"

"I'll be right back. I'm going to check on Natalie."

As he focused his eyes on her, he felt himself harden. "What... no kiss good-bye?"

Sweeping her hair back, she laughed.

"Come over here, Tessa," he murmured, puckering his lips.

"You're an incorrigible flirt, you know that?"

He winked. "You make me that way."

She smiled, and moved toward the bed. When she leaned down to kiss him, he tugged her back in bed.

"Jace," she giggled. "I've got to go check on Natalie. We can finish this when I get back."

With a sulky expression, his lips pouted. "Promise?"

"Yes, I promise," she replied with a quick kiss.

When the door clicked shut, Jace stretched again and shifted his feet off the bed. Slowly standing up, he groaned as he moved toward the bathroom. His legs felt like they were cemented to the floor. Before he turned on the light, he stumbled back when he caught his reflection in mirror. In the darkness, his eyes were glowing.

He panicked and fumbled for the light switch. Flipping it on, he stared at his image and froze. Hell, he looked as if he was going to change. Watching closely, his face twitched along the scar on his temple. Opening his mouth, his canines suddenly elongated. Gasping for air, his chest expanded as he sucked in a deep breath. With wide eyes, he saw his face pull and twist out of shape. Pain ripped through him, slicing him until he wouldn't have been surprised to find his body bleeding.

Feeling dizzy, he quickly gripped the sink and closed his eyes. Lowering his head, he sagged against it, trying to steady himself. He felt his heart race as if the Beast was trying to break free.

Why? He thought with heavy anxiety. *Why is this happening now?*

And then there was another reason to be worried. Tessa would be back any minute. Concerned for her safety, it sent his heart on a sprint which made the situation worse. In desperation, he tried to relax. Concentrating on his breathing, he inhaled through his nose and exhaled a long breath through his mouth.

When he'd finally calmed down, he opened his lids and looked in the mirror. In relief, he blew out a heavy sigh when he saw a normal reflection. Ever since he'd found out about his curse, raging anger had been the reason to set the Beast off. But now, it was trying to break free at random.

He put the toilet lid down and sat on it, resting his hands on his knees. He took another deep breath and finally got to his feet. When he stepped out of the bathroom, he braced himself. He was worried when Tessa came back, the change would return again.

As he sat down on the bed, he heard the door open. Turning his head, he saw Tessa. When she looked in his direction, her face tensed and her eyes grew leery.

He frowned. "What's wrong?"

Sitting down on the bed next to him, her chest constricted and her lids squeezed shut. With a long sigh, she opened her eyes. "I just talked to Tim." Her shoulders tensed up. "He said there were more deaths last night."

Jace stiffened with his jaw going rigid. "Where?"

"Here in Berkeley. And this time, it included Breedline families."

His eyes popped wide. "Shit, are you serious?"

She nodded. "The Bates Hospital was also attacked."

"Oh God," he gasped. "My parents!"

"Don't worry." She reached out for him. "They're safe. Cassie called them early this morning. They were home during the attacks."

"Thank God," he said relieved.

When she looked at him with her brows clenched, Jace blinked tears. "Oh, Jace... it's going to be okay. They're safe at home."

He gathered her close and tucked her head into his neck. "I'm bringing my parents here," he firmly stated. "I would never forgive myself if anything happened to them."

Tessa inhaled a deep breath. "I'm just ready for all this to be over," she sighed. "I'm tired of everyone looking over their shoulder, fearing for the worst."

God, he felt the same. It was if he'd been waiting forever for things to settle down, for the demon to finally die, for the Covenant to be able to take a deep breath and start living in peace.

Jace went over to his closet, and as he opened it, the full length mirror on the back side caught Tessa's reflection. As their eyes met, she smiled a little. "I'm sorry, Jace," she said, because she had no idea what else to say.

In the long pause that followed, he nodded. "Me too."

After he quickly got dressed, he held her in a brief embrace. "I love you, Tessa."

As he turned around and headed for the door, she swallowed back tears. "I love you too."

Before Jace and Jem left to pick up their parents, they asked Drakon to go. For precaution, they might need extra backup, and it was time Drakon was officially introduced to their parents since he'd proposed to their sister Cassie.

* * * *

"Okay... we're here," Drakon muttered in a tense voice.

Jace chuckled from the backseat. "You're not nervous, are you?"

Drakon shrugged. "Are you kidding me? I'm petrified." He looked out the window at the Chamberlain's estate. "What if they don't like me?"

"I'm sure they'll be thrilled when they meet you." Jace rolled his eyes, and grinned. "I mean... with all your tattoos, and that Mohawk of yours."

"Yeah, and you're like a giant," Jem chimed in with a chuckle.

Even though they joked and poked fun with Drakon, he had their unwavering loyalty. In their eyes, he was already considered part of the family.

"Thanks." Drakon smirked. "That makes me feel much better."

Jem opened the passenger door, and stepped out. "Come on, Drakon. We're just giving you a hard time."

Jace shut his door and laughed. "Yeah, they'll learn to love you just like we do."

Drakon got out of the driver's seat and glanced at the house again.

The three of them went to the front door, and for the first time in his life, Jace knocked and waited for an answer. Normally, he'd just barge in, but since they were introducing Drakon, he didn't want to appear rude. Plus, barging in with Drakon would probably scare the hell out of them.

Mrs. Chamberlain answered the door, looking exactly as she always did, with her hair pulled up in a bun and reading glasses on the tip of her nose. Sarah was a lovely woman in her early fifties who had a warm smile and a charming voice. Drakon realized, as he stared at her, that she was exactly like Cassie had described.

With Jace standing in front, she threw her arms around him. "You know you don't have to knock—" She looked up at Drakon, then at the tattoo on his neck. As she stepped back, her eyes widened. "Oh, I didn't know you brought a guest."

Jem quickly moved next to Drakon. "Mom, this is Drakon Hexus." He faced Drakon and said, "Drakon, this is our mother, Sarah."

With his hand extended, Drakon bowed his head. "It's a pleasure to meet you, Mrs. Chamberlain."

"Oh, my." Her eyes lit up with excitement. "You're Cassie's Drakon."

Drakon stood in silence with his nerves on pins and needles, not knowing if she was happy or disappointed. "Yes ma'am," he replied in a deep tone. "I am."

Without hesitation, she reached for his hand that was three times the size of hers, and pulled him into an unexpected embrace. "I'm so excited to meet you, dear." She patted his back. "We've heard all about you." She stood back from their embrace, gesturing them inside. "Please, come in. John's going to be thrilled to meet you."

Drakon smiled and sagged in relief.

As she stepped back to let them in, she grasped Jem's arm, pulling him into a hug. "I'm so glad you brought him here, honey," she whispered in his ear. "We've been dying to meet him." In a louder voice, she said, "John... they're here, honey!"

When John appeared at the bottom of the stairs, he extended his arms. "Come here, you two. It's been too long since you last visited us." He wrapped his arms around their shoulders, and glanced behind them at Drakon.

"It's good to see you, Dad." Jace sighed in relief. "Thank God you two are safe. When Tessa told me about the attacks at the hospital this morning, I almost went into a panic attack."

"We're fine, son." John patted his shoulder, eyeballing Drakon. "And I see you brought a friend."

Turning around, Jem introduced them. "Dad, this is Drakon Hexus. Drakon, this is our father, John."

John placed his hands on his hips. "Are you our Cassie's Drakon?"

Drakon stiffened. "Yes, sir." He quickly extended his hand. "It's a pleasure to meet you."

With a firm grip, John grasped Drakon's hand. "It's about time we met you."

Drakon nodded. "I agree, sir."

"Please, call me John."

Sarah went over to the refrigerator, and opened it. "Okay, I've cleaned out the fridge, and there's nothing perishable in the pantry. As she closed it, she glanced at all the suitcases next to the door. "I hope we packed enough clothes."

"Are you sure it's okay for us to stay with you?" John asked, looking back and forth between Jace and Jem.

"We don't want to impose on anyone, especially at such a short notice," Sarah added.

"No, you're not," Jem said, grabbing a leather duffle bag. "There's plenty of room."

Jace nodded and reached for a suitcase. "He's right. The estate has more than enough space. We want to make sure you stay safe until all this stuff dies down."

Sarah smiled. "Thank you. I just can't believe someone would do such a horrible thing. We lost almost everyone on staff last night. To think if we were..."

John moved next to her, and wrapped his arm around her waist. "It's all right, honey." He comforted her by pulling her close. "We're safe."

Changing the subject, Drakon quickly jumped in, "Could I help you with your suitcases, Mr. Chamberlain?"

"Oh, thank you Drakon. And please, it's John."

Lifting the duffle bag, Jem placed the strap around his shoulder. "All right, let's get your stuff loaded in the car," he said, clapping his hands, rubbing them together in anticipation.

"Oh, I forgot my purse upstairs," Sarah said. "I'll be right back."

Seconds later, a high-pitched scream came from the top of the staircase.

Jace dropped the suitcase, and yelled, "Mom!"

The four of them were out of the kitchen like a bomb had gone off, shot up the staircase and rushed toward the master bedroom. As Jace sprung the door open, they all stood in shock when they saw their worst nightmare had come home.

Chapter Sixty-Eight

In the far corner of the bedroom, Sebastian Crow had Sarah with a knife held to her throat.

"Let her go!" Jem threatened, his nostrils flaring. He felt sucker-punched as he stared at the events unfolding in front of him. He was numb, utterly numb.

Jace's reaction was instantaneous, nearly explosive. Jem caught his arm right before he surged forward. "Hold on, Jace!" he exclaimed. "He's got a knife!"

Sarah stumbled as Sebastian dragged her back.

Behind Drakon, John's eyes widened. "Sarah!"

She opened her mouth to scream, but found herself incapable of saying anything with a knife pressed against her throat.

It all took but a few seconds, but time had yawned for Sarah and everything was moving in slow motion, terror and helplessness filling her as she realized she was being kidnapped. But where was this strange man taking her? And *why?*

John and her children flashed through her hazy consciousness. There's a possibility that she'd never see them again. Tears slipped from her eyes as a bright light appeared, and Sebastian vanished through the portal, taking her with him.

"Mom!" Jace shouted, stretching out his arm as if he was trying to reach her. When Jem let him go, he crumpled to his knees. "No... not her!" He said furiously, pounding his fist into the floor in front of him.

* * * *

After Jace left, Tessa suddenly felt nauseous. As she went downstairs to the exam room to see if Helen could give her a routine physical, she got worse. Reaching up to knock, her stomach churned.

As the door swung open, Helen paused in the doorway. "Tessa, are you okay? You look don't look so well."

"Bathroom," Tessa muttered, with her hand over her mouth.

Helen quickly moved aside, and pointed to the bathroom. After five minutes of wrenching up her breakfast, Tessa finally stepped out. "I'm so sorry, Helen. I don't know what's wrong with me. I've been feeling sick to my stomach on and off for the last two days."

"Well, let's take a look." Helen gestured her to the exam table.

Tessa went over to the padded table and glanced at the stirrups at the end. When she sat down, the paper on top crinkled. "Helen, can we keep this between us?"

She nodded. "Of course."

There was a long moment, and then Tessa said, "I think I might be pregnant."

Helen pulled a chair next to Tessa and sat down. "Have you taken an over-the-counter test?"

Tessa shook her head and sighed.

"I can do a blood test here if you want," Helen offered. "If the test comes back positive, it's perfectly normal to get morning sickness that sometimes comes and goes during the first trimester."

Tessa dropped her head as if she was utterly exhausted. "I can't believe I might be pregnant. I just don't know how Jace will react if I am."

Helen reached out, and put her hand over Tessa's. "Jace really loves you, Tessa. I can't imagine him not wanting to have children with you."

Tessa's jaw tensed. "I just don't want him to feel trapped."

"Stop worrying." Helen shifted in her chair, reaching into a cabinet. Glancing over her shoulder, she said, "Everything's going to be fine."

"I hope so," she said, her nose wrinkling skeptically.

Five minutes later, Helen filled three vials of Tessa's blood.

"Will the results take long?"

"After I drop them off at the lab, I should get them back within a couple of days," Helen explained. "Actually, we could do an ultrasound right now. If you're pregnant, we'll know how far along you are. And you can hear the baby's heartbeat."

For a split second, Tessa didn't know what to say. In a voice that cracked, she replied, "Um... okay."

* * * *

Jem knew what was about to happen next, and there was nothing he could do to stop it. Like the strike of dual matches, Jace's pupils flashed white. His shoulders thickened as he bore down on his hands and knees, bracing himself.

Jem dropped to one knee, getting face-to-face with Jace. "You've got to calm down, Jace."

When a snarl twisted over Jace's face, Jem got to his feet and stepped back. Within seconds, a brilliant flash of light blasted through Jace's body like a nuke had gone off. As the brilliance receded, the Beast took form. With a deafening roar, it rose on two feet, towering above Jem. Narrowing his eyes, it sunk into a crouch looking for something to kill.

Jem knew Jace was in there... somewhere. Using his telepathic powers, he tried to communicate with him. *"It's me, Jace,"* he pleaded. *"It's your brother, Jem."*

"What the hell happened to my son?" John gasped, moving forward.

Drakon stepped in John's path, motioning him to stay put. "John, don't move," Drakon said in a low voice.

"Please, Jace." Jem slowly eased his palm toward the Beast. *"Listen to me, brother. You've got to calm down before you hurt someone."*

The Beast cocked its head, glowing eyes blinking and focused on Jem's thoughts.

"That's it," Jem encouraged. *"You can remember."*

Leaning toward Jem's hand, it inhaled his scent. Abruptly, it snorted and shook its massive head. With a light whimper, it dropped to its knees. There was another flash of light, and then Jace reappeared, lying motionless on the floor.

As Jem knelt down next to him, Jace's lips quivered, and he could positively see the pain in his eyes. When he opened his mouth to speak, his voice was so faint, Jem had to move closer to hear him.

"Hurt... anyone?"

"No," Jem reassured him. "Everyone's fine."

Relieved, Jace seemed to relax. "Thank God," he gasped.

Drakon grabbed a blanket off the bed and covered Jace.

Pulling the blanket higher on his shoulders, Jem said, "Hang tight, brother. We'll get you home."

John stared at Jace, not at all sure what to say. Moving closer, he looked back at Jem and said, "Is he okay?"

Jem took a deep breath. "He'll be fine, Dad. He just needs to rest."

With a confused expression, John asked, "Can you please explain what just happened?"

"Let's get him home, and I'll explain on the way," Jem said quietly, putting a hand on his father's shoulder. "We have a lot to talk about. And I swear on my life... we'll get Mom back safe."

Chapter Sixty-Nine

Leaning back onto the exam table, Tessa exposed her stomach so Helen could do the ultrasound.

With a plastic tube in her hand, Helen said, "This is just ultrasound gel. It's a type of conductive medium that enables a tight bond between the skin and the transmitter unit. It helps create images of the baby." She warned, "It will feel a little cold when I put it on."

When Helen squeezed the tube, Tessa flinched as the gel squirted on her belly. Moving the transmitter unit around, an image appeared on the ultrasound screen.

Feeling anxious, Tessa asked, "Do you see anything?"

Before Helen could answer, a tiny beating rhythm sounded out. "Is that?" Tessa paused with her brows clenched.

Helen smiled. "Yep, it's a heartbeat."

"Oh, my God," Tessa uttered gripping the table. "I'm really—"

"Wait a minute," Helen interjected, listening carefully. "There are two heartbeats."

Tessa quickly lifted her head off the table. "What?"

"Look, Tessa." Helen pointed at the screen. "You're having twins!"

Tessa's mouth flapped open and her eyes widened as she stared between the image on the screen and Helen as if trying to decide if it was good news or bad news. When she finally managed to speak, she blurted, "Twins?"

"Yes, you're pregnant with twins. The heartbeats are nice and strong," Helen confirmed. "You're about four months along."

Tessa looked down at her belly, the small place that would soon expand to accommodate the two tiny lives nestled there below her heart.

"Can you see what they are?" She asked, her voice as watery as her eyes were. "I mean... are they girls, or boys?"

Helen faced her and grinned. "Congratulations, Tessa. You're having boys."

* * * *

After Tim received a call from Drakon, he paced around the foyer's tile floor, acutely aware of three things: One, Sebastian had kidnapped Jace and Jem's mother. Two, Jace turned into his Beast again. And three, he had to prepare Tessa and Cassie before they got back.

Trying to focus, he looked at Angel with his hands crossed over his chest.

Holding onto Natalie, Angel shifted her to the other hip. "Do you want me to tell Tessa and Cassie what's happened? You should be here when they get back."

He nodded. "Thank you, honey. I'd appreciate it. I think it would be better if they heard it from you."

As John held the door open, Drakon and Jem came through practically carrying Jace.

Tim rushed over. "Do you need any help?"

Jem groaned, helping Drakon get Jace in a chair. "No, I think we got it."

Leaning back in the chair, Jace shook underneath the blanket.

"Jace," Tim said concerned. "Are you okay?"

"Yeah." He took a deep breath, and slowly exhaled. "Sorry about all this. I just need some time to recover."

"It's okay." Tim patted his shoulder, and turned toward John. "I promise, Mr. Chamberlain, we'll do all we can to get your wife back."

John was swept over with a combination of despair and disbelief. He was having a hard time comprehending everything that had happened in the last few hours: His wife had been kidnapped by some madman that was possessed by a demon and taken to God knows where, his son had turned into a creature, Jem had told him they were born entirely another species including his daughter Cassie, and their real father was living under this roof. He shook his head, thinking he was losing his mind.

"I don't understand." John sighed. "What does this Sebastian want with Sarah?"

Jem rubbed his jaw. "Dad, I—"

Damn it, what exactly could he tell his father that wasn't going to make things harder for him. Long-term solutions evaded him at the moment, but he would find them. His parents had become his responsibility when the Breedline got them mixed up in their world, and he wasn't going to leave them undefended.

Instantly, Jem wrapped his arms around his father and held him in a tight embrace. When he pulled back, he saw the look in his father's eyes. "Dad, listen to me." He kept his focus, trying not to fall apart as his father's tears tore him into pieces. "We're going to bring Mom back."

The one thing John knew about his son was that he had faith in him. Jem was too honest to lie to him. When John looked into Jem's eyes, he smiled a little. "Just bring her back, son."

Jace slowly stood, and shuffled behind his father. With the blanket draped around him, he placed his palm on John's shoulder.

John flinched and glanced behind him. "Jace..."

Jace took a deep breath, and then everything went silent. "I swear, Dad. I'll get her back."

He wheeled around and hugged Jace. As John looked up, he saw Tessa coming down the stairway with Cassie close behind. When they got closer, Jace felt the floor underneath him shift.

"I think he's going to pass out!" John shouted while reaching forward. "Jace!"

Strong arms came around his waist as Jace's knees buckled. The last thing he heard before blacking out was Jem saying, "Let's get him upstairs."

With Drakon's help, they muscled him up the stairs with Tessa following behind.

As Drakon and Jem laid him out on his bed, Tessa sat down beside him.

When Jace stirred and opened his eyes, he said, "Sorry about going over like I did. I'm not usually a fainter."

"It's perfectly understandable." Jem nodded. "Look, I'm going back downstairs to be with Dad and Cassie. You stay here with Tessa and get some rest."

When they stepped out of the room, Tessa brushed Jace's hair back, tucking it behind both his ears. She wanted to kiss him, but instead she got to her feet.

As she looked down at him nestled in the mountain of pillows, all she could think about was what Helen had told her. It was shocking enough to find out she was pregnant, by Helen's approximation, at least four months along, but when she'd done the ultrasound, she'd found two heartbeats. *She was having twins.*

Keeping that secret to herself, she bent down and stroked his cheek with her forefinger. "Get some rest, honey. And don't worry, we'll figure all this out."

When she shut the door behind her, she saw Alexander waiting outside in the hallway. He looked grim, his eyebrows clenched together, and his lips drawn in a tight line.

"Tim sent me," he kept his voice low. "There's been another attack. He just got a call from Kyle and Celina. They're with Casey. His mother and stepfather were killed, and everyone that lived in the same housing addition."

❧ Chapter Seventy

When Tim and Drakon arrived at Casey's mom and stepfather's housing addition, they saw a TV van parked in the street with several Berkeley Police Department cruisers. As a reporter stood addressing a camera, men in uniform walked around within circles of yellow tape surveying the crime scenes.

The gust of wind blowing around them carried the smell of death as well as the stench of mud.

Tim exhaled. *Jesus.* He hadn't expected the situation to hit this close to home. As he searched for Kyle and Celina, his anger rolled out into the humid, night air. He worked his molars, grinding, biting. He calmed himself down by rubbing his jaw and focusing on his breathing. When he lifted his wrist to check his watch, his cell phone buzzed. Reaching inside his jacket, he pulled it out and saw it was Helen calling.

As he answered the phone, he glanced over his shoulder as Kyle and Celina walked up.

"Tim, I found out my cousin has the book on those creatures," Helen said on the other end. "And I'm going to get it."

He hesitated. "Wait until we get back. We're going with you."

When he ended the call, Kyle came forward. "Bad news," Kyle dropped his voice, but not his eyes. "Casey just left with his Dad. He's really broken up over his mother and stepfather's death. He told me to tell you he's going to stay with his Dad until the funeral arrangements."

Tim fell silent. "Head back to the Covenant, and stay put. I'm putting everyone on lockdown. As soon as Drakon returns, we'll head that way."

* * * *

Moving close to the edge of the yellow tape, Drakon stood by a parked police cruiser. Surveying the scene, he noticed a coroner he recognized waiting to examine the bodies. Fortunately, as Drakon walked up to him, the police weren't paying attention.

"Alberto?" Drakon's voice was low, insistent. "Alberto Battista?"

The coroner wheeled around in Drakon's direction. "Drakon Hexus." He smiled, and extended his hand. "It's been years since I last saw you. How are you doing, buddy?"

Alberto Battista was a Breedline military buddy Drakon had known for years. They'd grown up in the same neighborhood since they were young children. Alberto's family was originally from Spain until his father moved his family to America for an opportunity in medicine.

Without hesitation, Drakon shook his hand. "I'm doing fine, except for all this." He glanced at the crime scene.

"Yeah, I know what you mean. It's all a mystery." Alberto shook his head. "I've never seen anything like it. It's like right out of that old black and white TV series, The Twilight Zone. So, what are you doing here?"

Crossing his hands over his chest, his face hardened. "A family of a friend I know lives here."

"Sorry to hear that. So far, there are no survivors that have been reported."

"Do you know if there are any suspects yet?"

"As far as I know there's nothing except a call to nine-one-one from a family member after the bodies were found."

Reaching into his leather vest, Drakon pulled out his card. "I'm working with the Covenant here in Berkeley. We're trying to figure out what is causing all the deaths. We may have a good lead. Please don't hesitate to give me a call if you find anything out that could help us."

Reaching for the card, Alberto nodded. "Sure thing. And it's good to see you again, Drakon."

"Thanks, Alberto. You too."

As Drakon headed back to report to Tim, he knew it was going to be a long night. When he heard a well-modulated voice, it caught his attention.

"This is Rosa Hernandez of Channel Fourteen News team reporting live from the scene of another downtown unexplainable massacre. According to police, the victims were suffocated internally with a substance resembling mud—"

Moving past the reporters, Drakon stopped when he stood in front of Tim. "There were no survivors, and no eyewitnesses reported."

Tim's face tightened and his voice grew flat, "We need to get back. We're going with Helen to get that book, and I've put everyone in lockdown until further notice."

* * * *

Hours later, Tessa went back upstairs to check on Jace. With his head propped against the pillows, the lamp beside the bed amplified the anxiety in his face.

"Hey," she said in a soft voice. "Are you okay?"

"Yeah." He yawned. "How long have I been out?"

"You've been asleep for nearly four hours."

Jace cursed, "What?" He jerked the covers off, and shot out of bed. "I didn't realize I'd been out that long."

"Are you sure you're okay?"

He took a deep breath and let it out. The exhale did nothing to ease the set of his tense shoulders. And then he remembered. Sebastian had taken his mother. "Oh God," he gasped. "My mother!"

"Calm down, Jace." She wrapped her arms around him, feeling the fast pace of his heart. "Trust me on this. We're going to bring her back."

Feeling his trembling body against hers, she wondered whether it was possible for miracles, and not as in the really-good-luck kind, but the incomprehensible variety.

When he pulled from their embrace, he took a deep breath and flopped down on the bed. Ever since he'd been cursed, his brother had been the only person that could bring him back from the Beast. He took another deep breath. In and out, he tried to control his breathing. The only saving grace that he could get himself back under wraps quickly was concentrating on his breathing. Otherwise, his anger would intensify and his Beast would be unleashed.

Sitting beside him, Tessa placed her hand over his.

He faced her and smiled. "My mother is a good Christian. She has faith in God and salvation and eternal life," his voice cracked. "She always told me I was special. She was convinced I had an important purpose in the world. When I was little, she used to say that every time someone called out for me, or wrote my name, or thought about me, it brought them good luck."

Tessa's breath caught, and then she smiled. "I think she's right. You're my good luck charm."

When she leaned down to kiss him, he stopped her. "There's just one other thing."

"What?"

"Well, you're stuck with the Beast. Do you think I'm still your good luck charm?"

She stared at him, and smiled again. "I told you, he doesn't scare me. I love you no matter what you are." She kissed him.

"Even if it means you're going to have to live with it forever?"

"Yes, I love you, Jace."

"I love you too, Tessa." His mouth was tight, his eyes intense. "I'm going to always take care of you. You know that, right?" As she nodded, he smiled a little. "I'll love you, forever."

❧ *Chapter Seventy-One*

As time went by, it seemed like hours since Sarah Chamberlain had been taken against her will and locked in a room that was almost entirely pitch-black. Trying to focus, she recalled getting ready to leave earlier with Jace and Jem, and then going upstairs to get her purse. When she opened her bedroom door, a hand closed on her shoulder. As she turned around, she looked up into a stranger's face. He had dark, long hair with black eyes. Quickly putting her into a choke hold with a knife held to her throat, she screamed. Then, the last thing she remembered was the terrified look on her family's face.

Abruptly, the door opened, catching her attention. And then a sharp, sinister voice came from across the room, "Good evening, Mrs. Chamberlain."

Frantically searching the dark room, she stopped and focused on a shadowed figure. "Who are you? What do you want with me?"

Just as her feet hit the floor, a light flickered on. One look into his black eyes and she knew now was not the time to push her luck. His long, black hair was pulled back away from his pale face, and his body illustrated a presence of pure evil.

He narrowed his eyes, the dark depths appeared hollow. "My true name is Ramael, but in everyone else's eyes, I'm called Sebastian."

Swallowing hard, her tongue was so dry it felt like sandpaper. "What name should I call you?"

"Sebastian is fine," he said with the lingering *s*'s. Stepping back, he gestured with his hand and motioned someone in the room. "Lucas, bring Mrs. Chamberlain something to drink."

Her eyes rounded in terror when she saw the creature that came into the room. "Oh, God—" she clapped her hand over her mouth to keep from screaming.

"Don't be rude." He scowled at her. "This is my son, Lucas. He'll be looking after you, making sure you don't try anything stupid."

Crouched on all fours like an animal, Lucas moved closer with the bottle of water. Stumbling back, Sarah stared up into Lucas's glowing eyes. The hair on the nape of her neck stood as she feared of what her fate may bring.

Leaving them alone, Sebastian stepped out and locked the door from behind. After Lucas set the water on the floor, he mumbled something to Sarah.

"I can't understand you." She dropped her head in fear, and squeezed her lids tight.

When she opened her eyes, Lucas's face was right in front of hers.

She jerked back, banging against the wall, and screamed.

Confused, he cocked his head to the side, took two long breaths and dematerialized.

Feeling herself beginning to hyperventilate, she tried to keep it together. In all her years as a physician working in the ER, she'd seen plenty of blood, dead bodies, some of which had been hard-core gruesome. But she'd never witnessed something like this. She felt as if she were watching the sci-fi channel with the sound on mute. From out of nowhere, anger lit off a firestorm in her chest. She had to find a way out of here, and soon.

* * * *

Startled, Jace jumped when his cell went off. When he picked it up and answered, Tim's voice was urgent, "In ten minutes, we're meeting in the library. Are you going to be up to it?"

"Yeah, I'll be there," he replied without hesitation. "See you in ten." When he ended the call, he looked at Tessa. She knew it was serious, judging by his expression.

Without delay, everyone gathered into the Covenant's library, and took a seat around the table. Jem and Mia were sitting together, and Kyle and Celina sat across from them. Drakon and Cassie sat down next to Helen and Alexander. Tim sat at the far end of the table with Angel beside him. When Jace and Tessa walked in, everyone stood and bowed. Moving past Tessa, Jace pulled out a chair for her at the head of the table. John came in last, shutting the door, and took a seat on the other side of Tim. Sitting down, Tessa motioned for everyone to take a seat. When everyone settled in, she glanced over at Tim and nodded.

"Here's what we got," Tim uttered an exasperated sigh with a book in his hand. "The death toll from all around the world has risen to the thousands, and now Sebastian has taken Sarah Chamberlain as hostage. The heads of five Breedline council members are dead, and most of all, the Covenants have issued a lockdown. Although there's been a massacre or two throughout our history, this is a hit of unprecedented gravity."

Drakon took a deep breath and swallowed his anxiety. "We should have predicted something like this a lot sooner."

"True, but we didn't expect Sebastian to have this kind of power," Tim replied. "This is what we know so far. Sebastian has an army of demon souls that were supposed to be permanently stuck in purgatory. Celina's sister has given them the power to use the earth to become physically alive. That's why all the victims were left saturated internally with mud. These creatures are called Golems... and we now have the knowledge to destroy them."

Jem leaned forward clearing his throat. "So how do we kill them?"

"With a spell," Celina spoke out, snapping everyone's attention on her. "A dark spell... and I'm the only one that can do this."

Tessa frowned. "I thought you couldn't do dark magic without your sister."

"No, it's not like that. I choose not to do dark magic," Celina explained. "If a Wicca practices dark spells, evil can consume them, making them turn toward the dark side."

Kyle's face hardened. "So if you do this spell, you could become like your sister?"

Everyone's expression grew grim, waiting for her response.

She calmed herself down by inhaling a deep breath. As she exhaled, she said, "Yes."

Kyle shook his head. "It's too risky."

"It's the only way," Tim ground out. "We don't have any other option."

Jace felt a growl condense in his chest and he just couldn't suck it back. The sound filtered through the room like an odor. "My mother is in danger. I won't allow her to be killed over this."

Tim dropped the book on top of the table, getting everyone's attention. "I've assembled a little over a hundred ex-rogues to fight with us. They're on their way as we speak." His tone was insistent. "So, this is what we know. Celina has the spell to stop Sebastian's army. Jace's beast is the only one that can destroy the Chiang-shih demon. Tessa can destroy the Katako, and Jem can use the portal to get us there. And his powers can be used as a weapon," he added. "We have no choice but to go in and fight."

Alexander shifted in his chair, and inhaled sharply. "I would gladly like to offer my assistance. There's no way I'm staying behind while everyone else risks their life."

Tim nodded in agreement. "Thank you, Alexander. We'll need all the help we can get."

"I'm going too," Kyle insisted. "The idea of staying behind is simply not an option."

Tim fell silent for a moment, and rose from his chair. "We leave as soon as the others get here."

Chapter Seventy-Two

That night, with doubts weighing heavy on his mind, Jace finally fell asleep. Naked under the soft, silk sheets, he slept nestled against the back of Tessa's warm body. Floating into a dream state, his eyes began to move under his lids.

It was in a thick, wooded forest where he and Tessa walked alone in his dream amid the foggy night. The blood moon was bright, reaching over the tree tops in soft colors of orange and reds. With their arms wrapped around each other, it was if they were as one.

From a distance, they saw a clearing by a nearby spring and stopped. When a cool breeze blew Tessa's hair away from her shoulders, he caught a hint of her intoxicating scent. Sitting near the water, with their arms around each other, Jace held onto her close. In the dream, the dark forest belonged only to them, and nothing else mattered. Taking off their clothes, they felt free, their bodies wondrously naked. As Tessa lay beneath him, her emerald-green eyes looked up and stared into his blue. With her long strands fanned out against the soft earth, he bent down to kiss her. There was a wealth of emotion in the light brush, like a butterfly's wing against his mouth, soft and delicate, just like her. With her body pressed against his, he felt the warmth of her breasts and the fast beat of her heart.

"I love you, Tessa," he whispered in her ear.

Her eyes pleaded. "Make love to me."

Kissing her neck, he positioned himself between her thighs and felt the warm dampness as he pushed inside of her. Arching into him, her lips parted with a blissful sigh.

Holding onto his shoulders with a tight grip, Tessa's pulse ratcheted up several beats as Jace began to move into a slow, steady rhythm. Moving with him, she gave herself completely to him, feeling like she was floating. With her eyes closed, she came apart as he watched from above. When she came back down from the intense pleasure, her heavy-lidded eyes opened.

He flinched, sucking in his breath when he saw the color of her eyes. Staring into the black depths, he quickly pulled free. "Tessa—"

Lying under him, her breath came out in a hiss. When her eyes rolled back, pain contorted her features.

Without warning, Jace's entire body vibrated with an electrical shock as it sent him into the air. Pain ripped inside him as he hit the ground. Closing his eyes, he was dazed and disoriented, but he forced his head forward and opened his eyes.

When he saw Tessa, she was reaching for him with her mouth soundlessly screaming. With tears streaming down her face, she gasped in silence and coughed blood. It all happened fast, but time had paused for Jace and everything was moving in slow motion, panic and powerlessness filling him as he realized Tessa was dying.

Struggling to get to her, visions swam in his head. Oh, God... he felt like he had done this before. He put his head down and screamed her name. Screamed until the blood rushed into his head and stung.

On his hands and knees, he tried to move forward, but no matter how much he dug and clawed at the ground, his body wouldn't move.

When something warm touched his arm, he heard a firm voice calling out his name, "Jace... wake up."

He roared in horror, thrashing wildly in the tangled sheets. Opening his eyes, he blinked hard, frantically searching for Tessa.

"Jace... it's okay." She smoothed her hand over his face. "I'm right here."

Reality snapped back into place as he struggled to sit up.

Tessa's instincts knocked around in her chest, sending all kinds of tread-carefully signals. "Easy, honey." She halted his movement, and guided him back down. "You're okay."

Locking his eyes with hers, his heart slammed against his rib cage. He had tears in his eyes as he drew in a breath and blew it back out. He tried to say something, but he couldn't quite get it out. Flashes of his dream returned: the blood moon, the smell of the forest, Tessa's eyes, her tears, *and the blood.*

Abruptly, a loud knock came from outside the door. "Jace? Tessa? Is everything all right?"

Grasping Jace's hand, Tessa turned toward the door. "It's open!"

Jace's pasty-white face entered Jem's line of vision when he rushed inside. "Jace, what's wrong?"

When he didn't answer, Jem moved closer. Jace's eyes were wide and colorless like they'd rolled back in his head. He'd seen that look in him before, and knew he was about to change.

Opening his mouth again, Jace tried to speak, but all that came out was the air in his lungs. Hanging by a thread, he fought the urge to release the Beast within him.

Tears clogged Tessa's eyes as she looked at Jem. "I think he was having a nightmare."

Sitting on the edge of the bed, Jem placed his hand on Jace's shoulder. "It's all right, brother. You're going to be just fine."

Against the tide of fear that overtook him, Jace realized that his brother's words were exactly what he needed to hear. Squeezing Tessa's hand, he closed his eyes and nodded.

He must have passed out, because when he woke up, Helen was looking down at him.

As she swept a washcloth down his face, his eyes searched for Tessa. When he made a noise that sounded like her name, Tessa moved next to Helen and grabbed his hand.

"You're okay, Jace," Tessa muttered in a soothing voice. "You just passed out."

Maneuvering his head to the other side, he saw Jem with his brow's clenched tight. "How are you feeling?"

Jace cleared his throat, feeling like hell as he tried to speak. "Like crap."

Jem stopped tensing and laughed a little. "Sounds like you're gonna live."

With his legs and arms hanging like heavy weights off his torso, not exactly useless, but damn close, he slowly lifted his other hand and formed a fist. "Thanks, bro."

"No problem," Jem muttered as he tapped his knuckles against Jace's.

As he walked toward the door, he stopped and looked over his shoulder. Relieved to see Jace was back to normal, he shifted his focus on Tessa. "Let me know if you need anything."

She nodded. "Thank you, Jem."

After Helen finished examining Jace, she placed her palm over his shoulder. "Get some rest. I'll be back in the morning to check on you."

"Thanks, Doc," Jace said hoarsely.

As Jace watched Helen leave, his stare dropped to Tessa's hand. With a gentle squeeze, he brought it to his lips. "I'm sorry I scared you," he murmured against her warm skin.

When her head eased to one side, her long strands fell down her shoulder. Her hair reminded him of a warm summer day, glowing with highlights mixed with the deep browns. God, she was beautiful, he thought.

Looking down at him, her eyes watered a little. "It's okay," she whispered sliding in bed next to him. "Try to get some sleep. I'll be right here."

Closing his eyes, fears consumed his inner thoughts. He was afraid that if he fell asleep, he'd dream the same nightmare. But as tired as he was, he gradually drifted off.

Lying next to him, Tessa watched him sleep. Even in his slumber, she noticed how his brows tensed, and his lips seemed taut. Closing her eyes, she wished she could hold him until all the pain washed away, and all the old wounds he held onto finally healed.

Chapter Seventy-Three

Late into the night, Cassie quietly crept out of her room, trying not to wake Drakon. With all the recent disasters and her mother being kidnapped, she couldn't rest. Finally coming to the conclusion that sleep would not come, she decided to go downstairs for a warm cup of milk.

As she descended the stairs, she heard the wind howl and the rain pound against the stained-glass windows. Stepping into the kitchen, she saw her father sitting at the table with his hair sticking out on one side like he'd been tossing and turning all through the night. Twisting his wedding band around his finger, his features reminded her of a dark-skinned Renaissance prince.

Clearing her throat, she said, "Dad, what are you doing up?"

Startled, he whipped his head around. "Cassie... you startled me."

"Sorry," she said quietly.

His lips formed a tight line. "I'm too worried about your mother to sleep."

Moving beside him, she pulled out a chair and sat down. Reaching out, she grasped his hand. "I can't stop thinking about her either."

"Drakon and I had a conversation earlier," he said, changing the subject.

"Oh?" she raised a brow. "May I ask what it was about?"

John smiled a little. "I believe his exact words were, Mr. Chamberlain, may I have your permission for your daughter's hand in marriage."

With wide eyes, Cassie suddenly placed her hand over her mouth. When she removed it, her lips formed a big grin, revealing the dimples on each side of her cheeks. "Oh, Daddy," she gasped. "I love him so much."

"And he loves you too." He kissed her forehead. "Very much."

"What did you say?"

"I told him it would be an honor to have him as a son-in-law."

Cassie wrapped her arms around him. "Thank you, Daddy."

When they pulled from their embrace, John asked, "Cassie, can I ask you a question?"

"Of course you can."

With some hesitation, he finally said, "How long have you known about..."

"The Breedline?" she finished his sentence.

Clearing his throat, he shifted nervously in his chair. "Yes."

"Not long," she replied. "Jace and Jem didn't even know I was Breedline. It was only when Drakon and I bonded that they figured it out."

Confused, John shook his head. "Bonded?"

"Oh, you don't know about the Breedline bonding thing, do you?"

"No, but please explain."

"Okay... I'll do my best. When a Breedline comes in contact with their bonded mate, they feel an instant connection. The connection is so strong, it's almost as if they've known each other for their entire life."

"So, you felt that with Drakon?"

"Yes, I did. I couldn't imagine my life without him."

John lowered his head and stared at his ring. "I don't think you have to be born a Breedline to feel that connection with someone." Lifting his chin, he turned toward Cassie. "I've felt that way about your mother since the first time I saw her. I don't know what I'll do without her."

Placing her head on his shoulder, she said, "You won't have to. They'll bring her back. I just know they will."

"Will you pray with me, Cassie?"

"Yes, Daddy."

After they prayed for Sarah's safe return, Cassie made two cups of warm milk. Listening to the rain, they sat in silence, and watched out the window as the storm finally calmed.

Stretching her arms over her head, Cassie yawned. "I think I'll go try and get some rest."

"Actually, I was just thinking the same thing."

Before they left the kitchen, John hugged her. "Thank you, honey."

She shrugged one shoulder. "For what?"

"For always making me proud," he whispered. "I love you."

"I love you too, Daddy."

* * * *

Early the next morning, Angel, Tessa, and Mia met downstairs to make breakfast. They were gathered all around the kitchen busy cooking a big breakfast before the guys woke up. In the far corner, Natalie was sitting in her highchair eating a bowl of cereal with most of it smeared all over her face. Just as Tessa popped a pan of biscuits in the oven, the doorbell rang.

"I'll get it!" Tessa called out. "It's probably Jace and Jem's uncle Jackson. His flight was supposed to arrive early this morning."

When Tessa opened the door, Jackson stood in the doorway with a mournful expression on his face.

Moving aside, Tessa gestured him in. "I'm glad you could make it."

As he stepped inside, he dropped his bags and hugged Tessa. "I'm so sorry," he said in a low voice. "Tim called me about Sarah last night. I got here as soon as I could."

Pulling from their embrace, she said, "We're just about to eat breakfast. Please, join us."

"Thanks." He followed close behind as he glanced up at the vaulted ceilings and toward the enormous staircase. "Whoa." He stopped and stared. "I almost forgot how huge this place is."

Tessa looked over her shoulder at him. "Yes, it's definitely spacious." She smiled and motioned him toward the kitchen. "While you wait for the guys to come down, I'll introduce you to our new family member."

"I've been looking forward to meeting Natalie." The corner of his mouth lifted into a half-grin. "It's seems like an eternity since the last time I held a newborn baby," he declared. "As I recall, it's been since Jace and Jem were that size."

Before entering the kitchen, he heard little giggling noises coming from inside. When he walked in, he saw a child around the age of two sitting in a highchair with food all over her face.

Bewildered, Jackson shrugged his shoulders. "Whose little one is this?"

"This is Natalie," Angel said wiping the cereal off her face.

"What?" he asked with a baffled look on his face. "But... how can that be?"

"I know," Angel laughed. "I had that same look on my face when I first found out. I had no idea that she would grow this fast. But since she was born with my genetics, this is what happens," she explained.

Jackson shook his head. "Unbelievable."

"Would you like to hold her?"

His eyes gleamed with excitement. "I would love to."

When Angel lifted Natalie from the highchair, she stretched out her little chubby hands toward Jackson. As he took her from Angel, she began to talk gibberish. The only word he understood was kitty.

Jackson smiled. "Do you have a kitty cat?"

Natalie giggled, pointing toward the door. Turning around, Jackson saw a black cat in the floor licking its paws.

"What's your kitty's name?"

"Ki... tee!" she kicked her feet, wanting to go down.

Jackson lowered her onto the floor. "Okay, sweetheart... there you go."

Wobbling on two feet, she maneuvered toward to the door. As she plopped down beside the cat, it rubbed against her, waving its tail.

With his hands crossed, Jackson cocked a brow. "Tessa, when are you and Jace going to give me some nieces and nephews?"

She froze and muttered, "Uh?"

Abruptly, the kitchen door swung open and Jace walked in. "Uncle Jacks!"

Chapter Seventy-Four

After everyone entered the kitchen and welcomed Jackson to the Covenant, they gathered around the table. When the food was placed out, the delicious aroma silenced the room.

When Jackson saw an enormous man with long, pale, blond hair enter the kitchen with Helen, he suddenly recognized his face. It was Alexander Crest, the same man that kidnapped and murdered his sister and put him in a coma years ago.

Jackson stiffened in his chair. "What's he doing here?"

Jem shot to his feet and placed his hands firmly over Jackson's shoulders, halting him from lunging at Alexander. "It's okay, Uncle Jacks." He loosened his grip. "Remember what I told you? Alexander isn't possessed by the demon anymore. He doesn't even remember what happened to Mom."

At first, Jackson glared at Alexander, and then he finally relaxed. He was so used to feeling anger toward the guy, it was a shock to have nothing of the sort light him up. And then, he felt a crushing sadness. "I'm sorry." He let out a deep breath. "It's just going to take time to absorb all this."

Alexander cleared his throat. "I'm so sorry. I can leave if it makes you uncomfortable."

Jackson shook his head. "No. Please, sit down."

"Thank you," Alexander said as he pulled out a chair for Helen and sat down beside her.

"Would you say grace, Tim?" Angel asked with Natalie in her lap.

When Tim gave grace, and amen was whispered amongst the group, Tessa uncovered the basket of fresh, hot biscuits and passed them around. Jace devoured two before even touching the rest of his plate.

After wiping his mouth, Jackson said, "Good job, ladies. Everything tastes wonderful."

286

"Mmmm..." Jace rubbed his stomach and smiled with a mouth full.

Jem leaned close to Mia and kissed her cheek. "Thanks. You girls outdid yourselves."

Mia nodded. "You're welcome."

"We're glad everyone enjoyed our cooking," Tessa added, and Angel smiled without saying a word.

When Jackson reached for his cup of coffee, he held it to his lips. "The police don't have a clue what's going on, do they?"

"Not the human police," Tim responded. "The Covenant has informed all Breedline in the department, but there's nothing they can do. This is way over their head."

"What about Sarah?" John jumped in. "Are they doing anything to find her?"

Hearing his father caught Jace's attention. Images, more than thoughts, came rushing through his mind, jumbled and jarring images of his worst nightmare. The horrific immolation of humans and Breedline, and of the bastard who'd kidnapped his mother. A blast of heat rushed through his veins of what he was going to do to Sebastian when he got his hands on him. Then, his mind went blank as he looked down at his plate, trying to focus on keeping his thoughts in control.

Tim shook his head. "There's nothing they can do, John. We're the only ones that can get her back. Don't worry, we have a plan."

After Jace had been hit with a bomb of energy, he forced his head on straight and managed to take a deep, calming breath. Lifting his chin, he looked at John. "Dad, I swear on my life I won't stop until Mom is home safe."

John was simply staring at Jace, his thin face depicted a placid and agreeable expression. He nodded his head and took a sip of his coffee. "I hope so," he said under his breath.

Jackson reached into the basket and took out a biscuit. Placing it on his plate, he smoothed butter on top. Before he took a bite, he cleared his throat. "I want to thank you all for letting me come here. I wish there was something I could do to help."

John shifted in his direction. "I'm glad you came. Sarah would want you here with us."

"Thank you, John."

Before everyone finished breakfast, they felt a sudden change in the room, a faint draft that blew around the kitchen. Drakon straightened in his chair and looked sharply toward the far end of the table. Tim sat back heavily in his chair with his eyes glued in the same direction.

Jace blinked as if he'd seen someone, or something sitting in an empty chair. "Does everyone see what I'm seeing?" he pointed at the far end of the table.

Jem shifted in his chair and looked in the direction Jace was pointing. "Yeah, I see it," he said in a low voice.

Out of the blue, something indistinct took shape. It was if a shadow itself managed to develop. And a figure gradually appeared—resembling first a faint image and then brightening, and rapidly changing into a man.

His stature appeared tall, and the bones of his face were fine and delicate. His skin was pale, white as porcelain, and he had large, almond-shaped, green eyes. His irises glowed from his pasty face, giving him a slightly deranged look, heightened by his pointed ears, and the sly smile on his large, thin lips. He had a high forehead from which red hair erupted in long, curly ringlets.

He was wearing a pale green-colored outfit that resembled leather. The belt he wore was wide and had a large gold buckle in the shape of a shamrock. He had large hands with long, thin fingers.

There was no identifying him as a species in Tim's mind. He'd never seen anything like it. He looked like something right out of a child's book of fairy tales.

The man looked at Tim with a smile and made a little bow. Then, he looked at each of the others in the same way, and his face dramatically brightened when his eyes settled on Natalie.

Jace shot out of his chair. "What the hell—"

Tim scooted his chair back and stood. "Who are you, and why are you here?"

The man's eyes fixed back on Tim's. Quickly, he rose from his chair and came around the table toward Natalie. "She's beautiful," he said in clear unaccented English. He dropped down on one knee as Natalie reached her arms out to him.

Angel held onto Natalie firmly as she struggled to get closer to the stranger.

"Please," the man grinned, reaching for Natalie. "May I hold her?"

Everyone in the room sat in disbelief. No one seemed to feel danger coming from the stranger that suddenly appeared in the room. There was nothing even faintly frightening or horrible about him. It was if they were dreaming this imaginary person.

In a swift motion, Tim moved beside Angel with his hand shielding Natalie. Looking at the stranger, he frowned. "I asked you a question."

"Forgive me," the man stammered. The scent rising from the figure was the smell of the outdoors, of leaves, but also a clean, fresh scent. "The child is just so mesmerizing. Let me introduce myself." He rose to his feet and bowed again. "I'm called Chester Ewan." He offered his hand to Tim. "I mean no harm. I'm here to destroy the Golems."

With hesitation, Tim slowly extended his hand and shook Chester's. "Is that right? And how do you plan to do that?"

Chester acknowledged his question with a low, rolling laugh, as his intense eyes glowed beautifully. Then, he looked intently at Tim. "Often, we assist someone who is in need, and who is not fully prepared for battle, you understand. We pride ourselves with being subtle."

Jace interrupted, "What do you mean, we? Is there more of you?"

"Yes," he said without haste. "Our population is in the thousands, but just ten of us live here."

Jace eased back into his chair. "What do you mean by that? Are you saying you live here in this Covenant?"

"Indeed, and it's thrilling for us to live in the shadows among such beautiful creatures," his voice was lively and youthful. "We simply adore your Queen and all Breedline species." He turned toward Tessa, and bowed gracefully. When he stood straight, he looked at Jem and said, "Especially you." His eyes shifted back to Jace. "You two are gifted, and we didn't realize how gifted until recently."

The green, glowing eyes on his pale, white face were the most startling trait of this man, and even if they'd been small they would have been mesmerizing.

Jace shrugged. "What gifts are you talking about?"

"You have the gift of the Beast," his voice was enthusiastic. "Its venom has the strength to destroy any demon. In four more years, you will stop aging and nothing can kill you... not even silver to the brain. And your offspring will carry the same genetics," he explained, glancing in Tessa's direction.

She immediately froze.

With his eyes narrowed, Jem gripped the arms of his chair. "How do you know all this?"

"We know all things." Chester smiled at Jem. "You are the chosen one. You have the ability to heal all creatures, and will soon have the power to create an energy that can destroy cities with one strike. And you will also live forever. There's no amount of silver that can kill you."

Helen's mouth dropped. "But... I thought silver would kill them?"

"No." Chester shook his head. "Not them. Silver can slow them down, but it's not fatal."

"So, what kind of species are you?" Jace queried.

"We're called Guardians, or spirits of the forest!" he praised. "We originated during the Middle Ages. We have the ability to move through any barrier, through any wall, and over any distance instantly. And we can take visible form, a form as solid as yours. We were here before you ever came into existence. Our purpose is to protect all creatures from dark magic."

Tim glanced over at Celina. "Have you ever heard of them?"

Almost in a state of shock, she quickly shook her head. "Does this mean I won't have to use dark magic to destroy the Golems?"

"Precisely!" Chester expressed a wicked grin. "That's one of the reasons why I'm here. We don't want you to use dark magic."

"Good God," Jace blurted. "I can't believe they've been walking around amongst us this whole time."

Kyle brought his hands together on top of the table as if in prayer. "It doesn't matter where they stay, as long as they can destroy those creatures and keep Celina from having to use dark magic."

In excitement, Chester clapped his hands together a couple of times. "No, she won't. In fact, we've already taken care of the Golems."

"You mean... they're all dead?" Celina insinuated.

"Yes!" Chester chuckled. "Every last one."

Tim smiled, and placed his palm on Chester's shoulder. "Chester... welcome to our Covenant."

Chester's eyes quivered as though he was about to cry. But he looked steadily at Tim in spite of his emotions and asked, "May I hold the baby now?"

Chapter Seventy-Five

Later that morning, Taliah groaned when she awoke with a sick feeling deep down in her gut. Instantly, she felt pressure building in her skull like her head was about to pop off. In response to the pain, she wrapped her arms around her head and pulled her knees against her chest. Feeling the dampness in her hair, she looked down at her drenched nightgown and cursed.

In a junkie-fueled rage, she ripped open her bedside drawer and frantically dug inside. Ripping the drawer completely out, she slung it onto the floor and screamed, "Where the hell is it!"

Feeling panic-stricken, she jumped out of bed and grabbed her jacket off the floor. Reaching into breast pocket, she took out the near-empty stash inside. There was barely enough for a thin one, which meant she'd better hightail it to the nearest dealer before she ran completely out.

After she slid a pair of jeans over her thin, pale legs, she pulled a T-shirt over her head. Before she hauled out of the room, she grabbed an oversized purse so that she'd have someplace to hide a full bag when she came back. Hurrying down the staircase with Lucas right behind, she hit the foyer and felt a stinging sensation on her arm. Looking down, she noticed the permanent symbol that gave her the ability to control the death army had mysteriously vanished.

"No," she muttered in a low voice. Smoothing her hand over the place where the symbol had been, she cursed through her teeth. "No... no... no!"

Rage ate at her. It was acid in her blood, eating a hole in her very soul. The only explanation was, the death army she'd created... had been destroyed.

* * * *

After Sebastian's computer booted up, he went to the Berkeley's Courier Journal site and went to the front page. The latest attack from his death army was covered in a number of articles—the bodies were found completely saturated with mud internally and externally. Reporters also interviewed the police who'd been there at the crime scenes. The mayor—who was evidently calling upon the fine men and women of the Berkeley PD—promised to solve this horrific massacre against the Berkeley community.

With a satisfied grin, he reached up to shut down the computer just as his office door swung open. The exerting physical force behind it created a loud bang when the door slammed into the wall.

Seethed in anger, Taliah stormed into the room. "All my army has been destroyed!"

Sebastian growled under his breath. "What?"

"You heard me!"

His empty, black eyes narrowed. "How?"

With her upper lip lifted into a snarl, she glared at him. "How the hell would I know?"

Rising from his chair, his hands formed fists at his side. "It doesn't matter. They served their purpose."

In frustration, Taliah wheeled around heading toward the open door.

"Where are you going?" Sebastian's voice amplified loud, and she froze with her hands wound into fists.

"Taliah," he said in irritation, "I asked you a question."

She thought about turning around and flipping him the middle finger, but instead she muttered, "Out." With the car keys in her hand, she flashed them over her shoulder.

At this point, the lie didn't bother her in the slightest. All she cared about at the moment was scoring drugs. When she got high, her head would calm, no longer pounding like a time bomb ready to go off, and she could return to feeling normal again.

"You're not going anywhere," he demanded. "I need you here in case the Breedline decide to attack."

With her back facing him, she said mockingly, "I'm leaving."

"The hell you are!" he fumed.

With her eyes full of fury, she spun around and tossed the keys at him. "I won't be long. Lucas can stay here until I return." With a smug grin, she waved good-bye and vanished. As she dematerialized downtown, she didn't give a shit what happened while she was gone.

Her hunger for drugs weighed over anything else. Besides, he knew where she was going anyway. And there was no reason to delay the trip to PulseZero by taking the car just to live up to a falsity they were both well aware of.

* * * *

After breakfast, everyone in the Covenant went directly to the library to discuss their next plan of action. Twenty of the ex-rogues as well as other council members were jammed into the room—and almost everyone, including the cat, was milling around.

When Tessa walked in, her eyes sought out and held onto Jace, but short of a nod in her general direction, he stared straight ahead, looking only at those people who wandered through his field of vision. By his side, Jem was standing tall and confident, and she got the sense their strong connection meant they were mentally preparing to take down the demon.

In the far corner of the room, two figures instantly appeared from out of nowhere. It was Chester and a petite, slender female. Her hair was white as snow, pulled back into a long, thick braid. It was so long, she had it wrapped around her arm to keep it from dragging the floor. Her skin was the same pale, white porcelain as Chester's. Her tiny pointed ears supported a pair of sparkling red, jeweled earrings, and her bright, green eyes were friendly and attentive.

Tessa was the first one to greet them. "Hello, I'm Tessa." She held her hand out to the female.

She looked down at Tessa's hand and smiled. Noticing her ring, she recognized it as the Queen's. "Greetings, your Highness." She bowed her head. "My name is Amelia Ewan," she said in a soft voice, and gently shook Tessa's hand.

"It's a pleasure to meet you, Amelia." Tessa shifted her eyes on Chester. "Are the rest of the Guardians going to be attending the council meeting?"

"They're here," he replied with a raised brow. "But they are very shy around large crowds. They prefer to stay invisible, if that doesn't offend you."

"Oh, no," Tessa said, shaking her head. "I understand. But I do hope to get the chance to meet them someday."

"Indeed you will." He smiled. "Just give them time."

When Jace walked over, Amelia lifted her eyes up, way up... at the most beautiful Breedline she had ever seen. And indeed, with that long, blond hair and his captivating blue eyes, she knew exactly who he was.

Turning toward Chester, she asked, "Is he the one?"

"Yes," he eagerly replied. "He's the one."

Jace's brows popped. "Chester, aren't you going to introduce me to your—?"

"Wife." Chester blushed. "This is my lovely wife, Amelia."

Jace offered her his hand. "It's nice to meet you, Amelia."

With a slight nod, she clasped onto his hand. "It's an honor to meet you. I've always wanted to officially meet the white beast."

Confused, he shook his head and muttered, "White beast?"

"Oh, yes." Chester's eyes widened. "This is what we call you. It's a true honor to be under the same roof as you."

Jace chuckled, placing his hand on Chester's shoulder. "Come, I'll introduce you to the others."

Just as Jace finished introducing Chester and Amelia to the rest of the group, he turned his attention toward the voice coming from the other end of the room.

Clearing his throat, Tim raised his voice over the crowd, "Can I have everyone's attention?"

Instantly, silence filled the room as their attention turned in his direction. Before Tim opened his mouth to speak, someone's cell phone went off.

Looking across the room, Tim saw Jace's expression when he looked at his phone. Without hesitation, he yelled, "It's my mother!"

🐾 *Chapter Seventy-Six*

Switching his phone to speaker, the entire room went dead silent.

"Mom?" Jace answered, his lips barely moving.

On the other end, her voice cracked, but not because the connection was bad. "Jace... I'm—"

John rushed over. "Sarah!"

Listening carefully, Jace heard sounds of another woman in the background, then silence.

"Mom, are you there?"

"Yes, I'm here," her voice trembled.

Jace stammered, "W-where are you?"

"I'm okay, Jace. I'm here at the house."

John sighed in relief. "Thank God."

"Stay there, Mom!" Jace urged. "We're coming to get you." When he ended the call, he looked at Jem, his expression one of utter seriousness.

Suddenly, a bright ball of light flashed. When everyone turned toward it, they saw what looked like a fireball coming out of Jem's palm. Within seconds, it grew wider and extended over the entire wall.

With his free hand extended out to Jace, he said, "Let's go get her."

It all happened so fast. As Jace grabbed his hand, they quickly vanished through the portal.

* * * *

Refusing Sebastian's orders, Taliah left in a hurry, leaving to score drugs to satisfy her addiction. Feeling infuriated, he marched upstairs to check on his new prisoner. He stopped in his tracks when he saw the door wide open. Rushing over, he looked inside and found the room empty. Sarah was gone.

The room was quiet and Lucas was nowhere in sight. With his upper lip curled back, he growled, smashing his fist through the wall.

* * * *

When Jem and Jace stepped through the portal, they instantly ended up at their adopted parent's estate. As Jace opened the door, he almost jerked it off the hinges.

Rushing inside, he called out, "Mom, where are you?"

"I'm in here, honey," Sarah's voice carried down the hall. "I'm in the living room!"

Bolting down the hall with Jem close behind, Jace skidded to a halt when he saw Eve sitting on the couch next to her. "What the hell is she doing here?"

Too disoriented and shocked to speak, Jem's knees almost buckled at the sight of Eve so close to his mother.

Immediately, Eve's eyes widened in terror when she saw the murderous look on Jace's face. It was a pretty good bet that she was going to die if she didn't take cover. Quickly, she shot to her feet and moved away from Sarah.

Without hesitation, Jace lunged at Eve. It was about saving his mom, not revenge. Because when it came down to it... his mother was the only thing that mattered to him at the moment.

With a powerful grip, Jace's hand curled around her nape and he all but shoved her down. The contact threw her off balance, and she stumbled forward, crashing into a wall.

Sarah screamed, "No, Jace!"

Eve gasped in pain, crumpling to the floor as her life flashed before her eyes. She was probably not going to survive this, she thought. But at least Sarah was going to be safe.

Ignoring Sarah, Jace focused on Eve. With a firm grip, he locked onto her throat with incredible strength. Her feet dangled as he lifted her effortlessly.

With her eyes squeezed tight, she choked, frantically fighting his hold.

When a low growl rumbled deep in his throat, it brought back memories of what she'd done to his beloved. For her past sins, she was going to pay a hefty price.

Jem's throat tightened as he sensed Jace's emotions. The hatred toward Eve was clearly evident, with his anger overriding all his common sense. And the end result wasn't looking good.

Standing behind him, Jem pleaded, "Jace, think about what you're doing. She's not worth it."

In desperation, Sarah rushed over, trying to defuse his temper. "Jace, she's the one that helped me escape!"

Snapping back to reality, Jace looked at Sarah with a confused expression.

"Please, honey," she pleaded with him. "She didn't hurt me. Please, let her go. She's pregnant."

Focusing back on Eve as if the words Sarah had said didn't register in his brain, he threw his head back with a roar. Jace's fury screamed inside of him. Embracing the change, he unleashed the Beast.

In his peripheral vision, he saw Jem scream soundlessly. *Nooo*—

In what seemed like slow motion, Sarah saw a bright flash explode out of Jace. The force threw her against the wall crashing into a mirror. With the sounds of shattering glass, real time snapped back into place as she fell to the floor, dimly aware of a huge presence taking the place of her son. Dragging herself, she hid behind the couch and covered her face with her hands, too terrified to watch.

Jem calmly stood back, trying to telepathically communicate with Jace before he killed Eve. *"Jace... please listen to me,"* he begged. *"Please stop. Don't do this."*

White rage tore through the Beast when his eyes locked on Jem. Dropping Eve from his grip, she fell to the floor in a heap, gasping for air.

Jem's heart pounded, his mouth falling open when he saw the glare in the Beast's eyes.

Sarah crawled out from behind the couch reaching toward the Beast. "Jace, please," she said, her voice filled with tears. "Please stop."

In the midst of all his anger, the Beast felt the echo of a voice from long, long ago. As his eyes shifted to Sarah's, there were tears falling down her cheeks. All the pain she'd borne in her heart was exposed before him, and all the burdens she'd lifted from him as a child. And then he drew in a deep breath, and blew it back out.

Looming over her, the Beast lowered its head as if it were seeking her touch. Inhaling her scent, he stiffened, his eyes popping wide.

The creature standing before her was beautiful, Sarah thought. Beautiful in the way a bear or a lion was, his monstrous appearance overshadowed by graceful, shifting movements and the intellect of predatory skills.

"I love you, Jace," she muttered in a soft tone as if she was speaking to a child.

Startled by her voice, he stumbled back. Moments later, she felt her body being nudged. The Beast was sniffing her again.

"Mom," Jem called out in a whisper. "Don't move."

"It's okay," her voice was shaky, but her determination remained strong. "I know he won't hurt me."

Against the tide of sadness that overtook him, he dropped to the floor with a whimper. Surrounded by a brilliant flash of light, the Beast disappeared and Jace's form took place. Naked and slick with sweat, he shivered with his knees tucked against his chest.

As he struggled, her heart sank. And then she heard him say hoarsely, "Mom..."

Moving fast, she grabbed a quilt off the couch and covered him. "I'm right here, sweetheart." Smoothing his wet hair out of his face, she whispered, "Don't worry. Everything's going to be all right."

"I'm sorry," he said blinking tears. "Are you okay? I didn't hurt—"

"Shhh... I'm just fine."

Jem wouldn't have believed it if he hadn't seen it himself. His mother had calmed Jace's Beast, like turning a pit bull into a lap dog.

With her hands occupied, she turned toward Jem. "Would you please go check on Eve?"

When her words drifted over to him, he turned around and saw Eve huddled in the corner with her arms wrapped around herself. *Oh, hell no,* he thought.

Noticing his hesitation, Sarah said, "Please, Jem. If it wasn't for her, I don't know what would have happened to me."

Shifting his eyes back on Sarah, he looked at the face of the woman who had been his savior... the closest thing to a mother after his birth mother died. As their stares locked, Jem had the sense that she wasn't going to take no for an answer. He swallowed hard and nodded. "Okay, Mom."

Chapter Seventy-Seven

When Taliah returned, Sebastian was waiting by the door. As she walked in, he grabbed her by the sleeve of her leather jacket and jerked her back, getting mouth-to-mouth tight. "Where's Lucas?"

"What are you talking about?" she said mockingly, trying to wrench herself free from his grasp. "He was supposed to stay here with you."

Her attitude jacked his rage so high, he became his own blazing inferno. The air around his body grew magnetically charged and heated like a volcano getting ready to erupt.

"He was supposed to watch over the woman!" he growled in her face. "She's gone and Lucas is nowhere to be found!"

"Are you sure?"

Tightening his grip, he hissed, "He's not here!"

She stared up at him, wide-eyed and stiffened in anger. "He wouldn't just let her go. Did you ask Eve if she's seen him?"

"No, I haven't!" he fired back. "I thought he went off with you even though I ordered him to stay here."

She positively itched to knee him in the balls and then kick his ass on the spot, but she managed to control those urges and instead glared up at him.

"Lucas needs to learn to obey," his voice was stern. "You coddle him like a child. I don't know how much more of this I can take."

On a lot of levels, it didn't make sense why the civilian woman mattered to him, Taliah thought. Then again, he would stop at nothing to seek revenge, even if it meant using an innocent bystander.

"I'm going upstairs to find Eve," he grumbled, releasing her arm.

He turned around with his chin held high. Before he walked away, he looked over his shoulder and gave her a look that told her without words that his patience was running thin. And then he said, "Don't ever disobey me again."

* * * *

Considering his alternatives, Jem decided to call Tim and explain the situation. With the phone in his hand, he dialed his number and wondered what the hell he was going to say as the line rang. Without a lot of options, he had to bring Eve back with them to the Covenant.

When Tim answered, there was a brief silence before Jem spoke. "Tim... we have Eve. She helped my mother escape. I'm bringing her back with us."

As Jem waited for his response, he slid his eyes to Eve's. With her instincts screaming, she wrapped her arms over her stomach, fearing for the worst.

The whole lot of non-negotiable Jem sensed coming from the other end must have been right because Tim cursed, which made sense. Going by Eve's past and the terrible things she'd done to Tessa and Mia, it was obvious that Tim wasn't pleased with the news.

Refocusing, Tim changed the subject. "Is Sarah okay?"

"Yeah, she's just a little shook up."

"What happened?" Tim asked, even though he had a good idea. On an instinctual level, he knew Jace must have unleashed the Beast when he encountered Eve. "Did Jace turn?"

Nodding against the phone, Jem muttered, "Yeah, but everyone's all right."

Although it wasn't possible to see Tim through the phone, the sounds of his breathing gave him a good indication of the expression on his face.

"Oh, and there's one more thing," Jem added. "Eve's pregnant."

Instantly, Jem heard Tim's breath halt, and then exhale in one long sigh. "All right, we'll be waiting for your return."

There was silence as the call went dead. Without a doubt, Jem knew Eve would be put on trial for her crimes against Tessa and the Breedline. At the moment, Eve's current condition was the only thing keeping her safe and under the protection of the Covenant.

* * * *

Instead of following Sebastian's orders, Lucas had other plans. Anger made his powers stronger, and he was tired of being chained to his mother's beck and call. Standing outside, he looked across the thick forest of trees and thought of Celina. She belonged to him, and he was going to have her. Dematerializing under her bedroom window, he sensed her inside.

Upstairs in her room, Celina's nerves were shot as she paced back and forth. After Jem brought Eve back with Sarah and Jace, everyone in the estate was on pins and needles.

Changing into a pair of jeans and an oversized sweatshirt, she looked out the window and sensed someone watching her. For a split second, she froze. Acknowledging she was in danger, she rushed toward the door.

Someone was behind her—she could sense a shadow in the air as it spread wide until it fell to the floor like a cloak. With a quick sweep, the shadow covered her body, making her disappear though in fact she was still in the room. When it scooped her off her feet, she struggled, but a blunt force to the head and she went lax, making Lucas's exodus so much easier.

When Lucas returned to Sebastian's estate, he carried Celina down into the basement where he'd prepared to keep her hidden. Carefully lying her face down onto a pallet in the corner of the dark room, she was conscious, but incapable of movement. *What's happening to me?* She thought. *And why can't I move my body?* She had a vague thought that something was dripping into her eyes... probably her own blood.

Her scope of vision swung around as she was turned over. When she looked into her abductor's face, she screamed in horror.

* * * *

Now that Jace had his inner Beast caged and was able to think properly, he still disagreed with Jem's decision to bring Eve back to the Covenant. With his nerves shot to hell, and needing to burn off some steam, he headed downstairs to the gym. Using his bare hands, he beat the holy hell out of a punching bag that was hanging from the ceiling. Breaking through the skin, blood covered his knuckles and the bag. He didn't stop until Jem peeled him off and shoved him back.

"What the hell!" Jace bit out, stumbling back in anger. With Jem blocking the bag, Jace had half a mind to go at him.

"Come on, Jace," Jem pleaded. "Talk to me. What's going on in your head?"

As Jace gritted his teeth, he let out a soundless snarl. "I want to kill—"

Jace's jaw clenched so hard, he was surprised when he finally opened his mouth, he didn't spit out his teeth in pieces. He was losing it as memories came crashing down on him all at once. "What Eve and Sebastian did to Tessa..." he choked off, emotion knotting his throat as tears gathered in his vision, "...makes me want to kill someone."

Moving closer, Jem planted his palm on Jace's shoulder and squeezed lightly. "I get it. Just take a breath."

Jace slumped and dropped his head. He lost the battle, and broken sobs welled in his throat. Inhaling in two breaths, he exhaled in one.

Waiting for Jace to calm down, he asked, "We cool?"

Jace lifted his chin and nodded. "Yah."

Abruptly, their attention was drawn toward the door when it swung open and slammed into the wall. Standing in the doorway, Kyle eye's looked panic-stricken. "Has anyone seen Celina?"

Chapter Seventy-Eight

Without bothering to knock, Sebastian opened the door to his and Eve's bedroom. Stepping inside, he called out to her.

When there was no answer, he went into the bathroom and searched, but she was nowhere in sight. Running his hand down the top of a dresser, he stopped and pulled out a drawer. It was empty. Pulling out another drawer and another, he found them all empty. Eve's things were gone. Rushing over to the closet, he looked inside finding nothing but empty hangers left in place of her clothes. With a curse, he sagged against the wall and dropped his head.

Scrubbing his face, his brain played tricks on him, flashing images of her betrayal. A deep and feral growl rose up from his throat as he thought of Eve escaping with Sarah. He only had two questions: why would she do this and where did she go?

Closing his eyes, he imagined his hands around her neck, squeezing until he choked the life from her. His nasty mood made his head feel like he had a bomb inside ready to explode. With gritted teeth, he punched the wall. Before he opened his mouth to call for Taliah, his voice was halted when he felt a sharp object jab into his back. And then a warm breath whispered next to his ear, "Where's my son?"

Realizing it was Taliah, his body stiffened. "I don't know. I just found out Eve is missing."

With that said, she lowered her hand and stepped back. Turning in her direction, he saw the blade in her grasp and the expression on her face. Her lips curled back and she gave him a look of pure hatred and distaste. He'd never seen Taliah this angry. Evidently, she also had balls.

"I can kill you," she said bluntly. "Anytime I want. And I don't need a weapon to do it either. Your powers are stronger, yes—I give you that. But there are things I am capable of that you can't imagine."

With a scowl on his face, he grumbled, "Then, why don't you do it."

She went silent a long moment, her expression boiling. "I need you alive... not in a grave."

Sebastian's hands tightened into fists until his knuckles cracked. "We can go around in circles arguing and it still wouldn't get us anywhere. We need to find Lucas. Isn't there a way for you to summon him?"

"Do you honestly think I haven't already tried that?" she ground out. "I don't know why he hasn't come to me. He's never defied me before."

"I'm surprised to hear that," he smirked. "He's full grown and you continue to treat him like a child. Maybe if you started treating him like an adult, he would act like one."

Taliah took a bracing breath, and seemed surprised. Out of nowhere, she sensed her sister's presence. Her brows popped. "Lucas has my sister. I can feel them somewhere near."

* * * *

With the help of everyone in the Covenant, Kyle frantically searched the entire estate for Celina. Fury rose within him, such that it choked his throat and made his hands shake. After all that had happened, she wouldn't have left without telling someone. When his thoughts drifted toward her sister Taliah, it made him anxious, not knowing if Celina was hurt, or even alive.

"Kyle?"

The sound of a deep voice whipped his head around. He saw Drakon standing a few feet away, his massive form dominating the hallway, waving his hand, motioning him over. Without a word, Kyle moved in his direction, gathering speed that quickly led into a jog.

When Kyle approached Drakon, his shallow voice drifted off and then returned, "Did you... find her?"

Drakon's response was long in coming, "I'm sorry, Kyle. There's no sight of Celina in the estate."

Kyle bared his teeth, wanting to punch his fist through a wall. "Damn it. I just know her sister has something to do with this."

As Drakon opened the door to the security room, he said, "Let's check the cameras." He gestured Kyle to follow. "Maybe it will give us a lead."

Following Drakon, they came to another door. As he accessed the security, Kyle heard a series of clicks and then the door unlocked. Moving inside, Kyle prayed the cameras had footage that would give them clues to what happened to Celina. Punching in codes and typing numbers,

Drakon brought up the camera that showed the upstairs bedrooms. On the computer screen, they watched Celina enter her room. As the footage kept rolling, the last thing they saw on the camera was Kyle knocking on her bedroom door. After that, he'd stepped inside to find the room empty.

Anger crawled around Kyle's chest on all fours until he was panting from the ugly, familiar feeling. Except... damn, the whole thing didn't make sense. There were no signs of a struggle in her room.

Out of the corner of his eye, he saw Drakon shake his head. "Taliah could have used her powers to dematerialize in Celina's room and take her the same way she did last time."

Man, he regretted hearing that. "But why would her sister want her now?"

"I don't know." Drakon shrugged. "Before, Taliah needed Celina's help recovering Sebastian's soul. Now that the Guardians destroyed all the Golems, maybe Taliah needs her powers to help her create more."

From behind them, the door opened with a creaking noise. When they turned around, Tim was standing in the doorway. "We're going to raid Sebastian's estate. I have enough ex-rogues to help us. Be ready." He nodded once. "We leave tomorrow."

* * * *

Confused, Lucas didn't understand why Celina wasn't able to move her body. He'd hit her hard, but not hard enough to have done permanent damage. Hovering above the ground to the pallet he'd left her on, he clicked on a flashlight and trained the beam on her face. Her eyes squinted and her brows scrunched as the blinding light blared at her. Noticing her discomfort, he quickly pulled it away.

His enormous wings tucked into the small of his back with a flapping noise as he knelt down beside her. Anxious to feel her skin against his, he wanted to touch her, but instead he opened his mouth to speak. Trying to form words, all that came out was a jumbled mess. Out of frustration, he gave up and stared into her eyes with a soft expression.

When Celina focused her eyes on him, she fought the urge to scream. Without the ability to move, she had to stay calm and figure some way to escape. Thinking fast, she tried to communicate with him. "What's your name?"

Opening his mouth to speak, she saw several rows of sharp teeth as he forced his voice like a baby saying its first word.

"Luuu... caass."

She faked a smile. "Hi, Lucas." Her voice was shaky and weak, "You're Taliah's son, aren't you?"

Hearing his mother's name instantly hardened his face.

When she saw his response, she immediately changed the subject. "My name is Celina. Can you say... Celina?"

There was a long wait as he struggled to pronounce her name. As he finally sounded it out, the voice that came to her was more of a mumble. In a tone of approval, she felt like she was praising a pet—good doggy!

An hour later, he dematerialized from the room, leaving her alone. On impulse, she struggled to move, and felt her fingers wiggle. *Thank God*, she thought. Maybe there wasn't any permanent damage after all. Her breathing picked up as she concentrated on moving her toes. She let out a sigh of relief when they moved. Now, all she had to do was get the rest of her body motivated to get up so she could use her powers to dematerialize the hell out of here.

Chapter Seventy-Nine

At the top of the stairs of the Breedline Covenant, Jace had to open the door to his and Tessa's room with two fingers and a prayer that he didn't dump the tray of food onto the floor.

"You need help?" Tessa said, as she stepped out of the bathroom.

"Nope," he said kicking the door shut. "I got it, babe."

Fresh from a relaxing shower, Tessa slipped into a robe and went over to him. "Mmmm, it smells good."

After he set the tray on the nightstand, he looked over his shoulder. "I hope you're hungry."

"I'm famished."

With that familiar look he always had when he was aroused, he winked at her. "I thought we'd eat and then work it off later." He batted his brows and grinned. "If you know what I mean."

She winked back. "Sounds like a good plan."

"Wait till you try the hot chocolate," he said, handing her a mug. "Look, I even added marshmallows."

Tessa stared down into the mug as she held it under her nose. Inhaling the combination of chocolate and the sweet scent of sugar, her stomach growled.

She ducked her head and he heard her sip. The "ahhh" that followed was what he was hoping to hear. "It's perfect."

Going around the edge of the bed, he reached for a plate and sat down. Placing it on his lap, he inhaled the delicious aroma of warm bread. There were croissants, sweet jams, and an assortment of fruit and berries. With his hand, he patted the empty space beside him, motioning her over. "Come here, honey. I'll feed you."

Moving toward him, she settled in beside him on top of the silk duvet. As she took another sip of her hot chocolate, she looked into his eyes and thought about the secret she was keeping from him. In an awful mental snapshot, she imagined his face if he found out she was carrying his twin sons, and risking her life. If he knew she was pregnant, there would be no way he would let her go fight with them tomorrow. Not being there to help her family was out of the question, pregnant or not. She was their only hope in destroying the Katako.

He picked out a deep, red strawberry and held it close to her lips. "Here, try this."

Glancing up over the rim of her mug, she snapped back to reality. Opening her mouth, she took a bite, tasting the sweetness of the berry.

With half a berry in his hand, he watched her lick her lips. "Want another?"

Eagerly nodding, she parted her lips as he feed her the rest.

Staring into his eyes, she felt a warm feeling flush through her body. She loved him so deeply, and wanted to tell him she was going to have his babies.

Reaching for one of the croissants, he pulled it apart and spread jam on each half. Offering her a piece, he popped the other half into his mouth and chewed in silence. When they finished eating, he leaned over and placed the plate back on the nightstand.

The mattress dipped as he pulled her close and gathered her in his arms. He felt warm, even hot, from her flesh against his. Closing her eyes, she rested her head on his chest and wished she could hold onto this moment forever. She was worried about what would happen when they traveled through the portal to take down Sebastian.

With his head against the pillows, he cuddled her close and whispered into her hair, "Tessa... is something wrong? You seem different."

Unsure what she should say, she shook her head. As a sudden headache cut off her thoughts, she rubbed her temple.

"Talk to me, Tessa." He smoothed his fingers through her hair. "What's going on?"

She took a deep breath, and let out a long sigh. "I guess my mind is lost in thought about what's going to happen tomorrow."

Something about the sound of her voice brought his head toward her. He noticed the worried look on her face as her brows clenched tight. Jace looked out over their two bare feet, and then to the window on the far side of the room. The moon was barely visible through the lace curtains, nothing but a soft glow on the dark horizon. Reaching down, he took her hand, giving it a squeeze. "Listen... there's something I want to talk to you about."

He felt her stiffen—which made two of them. He was suddenly bracing himself as well.

Jace cleared his throat in the thick silence. "I don't want you to go with us tomorrow."

There was a tense pause—at least on his part. "What?" she asked, sitting up.

With an intense expression in his eyes, he shook his head. For some reason, he sensed something off about the plan tomorrow. Remembering his reoccurring nightmares of Tessa, he felt like they were visions and somehow they'd come true. He couldn't risk losing her. In all his adult life, he'd been through the full gamut of emotions, and he'd never once felt like this until he'd met Tessa. Now, he was whole... complete, and at peace.

"It's too risky." He brushed her cheek. "I can't bear the thought of something..."

As those lovely eyes of hers grew watery, she said, "Nothing is going to happen. Trust me... everything's going to be okay."

He croaked out, "But?"

She quickly put her mouth to his and kissed him. "I love you, Jace," she murmured against his lips. Pulling back, she kept eye contact with him. "As the Queen, it's my responsibility. You have no choice but to honor that."

With a sigh, he nodded in agreement even though it made his stomach feel like he'd chugged spoiled milk. In a soft whisper, he said, "I love you more."

No matter what, he thought, he wasn't going to let anything happen to her. And he was going to take care of her the right way, just as she deserved for... well, forever had a nice ring to it, didn't it? When this was over, he was going to marry her.

Tessa gently grasped his face and embraced him with a passionate kiss. Pulling away from his lips, she whispered, "Make love to me."

Taking his time, he touched every inch of her body, caressing it with his hands and mouth. As their bodies joined together, the fit was so perfect, the moment so right, he just fell still. Life had brought him here to this time with her, with them together...

An hour later, Tessa placed her ear against Jace's chest and listened to the beat of his heart and the sound of his breathing. Before drifting off to sleep, she said a silent prayer and closed her eyes.

Chapter Eighty

It was well past midnight when Tim woke to the sound of his phone vibrating. Reaching over toward the nightstand, he grabbed it and saw a text from Helen.

WE NEED TO TALK ASAP. MEET ME DOWNSTAIRS.

As he slid out of bed, Angel rolled over. Glancing at the clock, she rubbed her eyes. "It's one o'clock in the morning." She yawned. "Where are you going?"

"I got a text from Helen," he muttered in a whisper. "She asked me to meet her downstairs. It sounds important."

"I hope everything's okay."

He ran his hand over his military cut, and let out an exhausted sigh. "Me too. Go back to sleep, sweetheart. I'll check on Natalie before I head downstairs."

"Thank you, honey."

After getting dressed, he peeped in the next room to check on Natalie and headed downstairs to meet with Helen. At this hour, the estate was silent as a tomb. Halfway down, he came to a quick halt when he heard a high-pitched crying noise.

"Meeeooowww..."

"What the—"

Looking down, he saw the cat at his feet. In a quick response, he jumped over it. In aggravation, he waved his hand, motioning it away. "Shoo!"

Following him all the way down, the cat weaved in and out between his feet, nearly tripping him. At the bottom of the stairs, he looked down and glared. Normally, Tim didn't like animals in the house—and he definitely wasn't a cat person. But since his daughter loved it so much, he agreed to let it stay inside. With his eyes trained on the cat, he grumbled, "This is not a good time, cat."

Suddenly, it lifted up on its hind legs and then...

Next thing he knew, it leaped into his arms. Startled, he quickly balanced it in his grasp to keep from dropping it onto the floor. In his arms, the cat purred and licked his hand.

With a curse, he narrowed his eyes. "You're lucky Natalie loves you."

Pawing at his shirt, the cat meowed until Tim finally gave in and petted him. Looking down into those wide, green, contented eyes, he rubbed under its chin and behind its ear.

Feeling a slight headache trying to emerge from his frontal lope, Tim craved hydration, sugar, and a lot of caffeine. As soon as he finished speaking with Helen, he would definitely make a trip to the kitchen.

"Okay, that's enough." As he went to put the cat down, it somehow managed to claw its way onto his shirt, hanging off the front like a tie.

Tim groaned, "Buddy, you're pushing your luck."

The cat meowed, hanging on for dear life.

"You need some help?"

Tim bit out another curse and looked over at Helen in desperation. "Yes, please."

Reaching out, Helen gently peeled the cat off, prying both of its front claws from his shirt. "There you go," she said, lowering the cat toward the floor. "I think he likes you."

"The feeling is not mutual."

With its tail held high, the cat gingerly sauntered off.

Tim blew out a long sigh. "Thanks, Helen."

"You're welcome," she chuckled softly.

Wiping the cat hair off his shirt, he asked, "What was it you wanted to talk about?"

"I'm sorry to get you up at this hour." The expression on her face was all he needed to suggest something was wrong. Motioning him to follow, she kept her voice low, "Let's talk in private."

Following her inside the exam room, she offered him a chair next to her desk. "Please, have a seat."

After he sat down, he looked at her perplexed. "What's going on?"

"What I'm about to tell you goes against my physicians protocol, and I'm also betraying the Queen's trust." She sighed removing her glasses. "But I feel like I should tell someone before it's too late."

"Helen, please," he urged. "Whatever it is, I won't hold you responsible for anything."

"It's Tessa." With a frown, Helen paused briefly. "She's pregnant."

He stiffened in shock, his mouth falling open. "What—"

"That's not all," she said in a calm, measured voice. "She's going to have twins."

"I take it Jace doesn't know anything about this," he said, crossing his arms over his chest.

"No, he doesn't. Tessa didn't want me to say anything because she knew he would insist she stay behind while the rest of you go fight. She was waiting until all this was over to tell him. I promised I would keep it a secret, but I'm worried she's taking a risk. I had to say something before it was too late."

"Thank you, Helen. You did the right thing coming to me."

"Are you going to tell Jace?"

"Not yet. I'm going to talk to Tessa first."

With a slight nod, she rose from her chair. "Good luck."

When he stood, he reached for her hand. "Thanks. I'm going to need it."

Chapter Eighty-One

When Jace opened his eyes, he was in a different position when he'd fallen asleep: flat on his back instead of curled up next to Tessa.

As he sat up, the first thing he did was look at the clock. Christ, he thought, it was just two in the morning. *What the hell?* He thought. Wide awake, he reached for Tessa in the dark. Finding the bed empty, he called out to her in a whisper.

For a moment, he thought about the full day ahead—which meant they needed plenty of rest. As the hours passed, the clock paid no attention to the changing destinies they were faced with. It all felt like a fucked-up nightmare.

Shifting his legs off the bed, he pushed his butt off the mattress and shot to his feet. Staggering toward the bathroom, he called out a little louder, "Tessa..."

Expecting her to answer, he got nothing but silence. Getting closer, he heard someone throwing up. Which meant Tessa was sick again.

As another wave of morning sickness tore through Tessa's body, sweat burst from her pores. With a death grip around the top of the porcelain bowl, she heaved inside. Motherhood was like a pair of fists winding her gut into a tight knot.

Popping his head inside, he found Tessa on her knees in front of the toilet, one hand holding back her hair, the other braced on the seat.

"Tessa, are you all right?"

"I'm fine," she said reaching up to flush.

"I'm calling Helen," he muttered reaching for his phone.

Tessa slowly rose to her feet. "Jace stop. Don't bother her at this hour. I'm perfectly fine."

"Then, why are you throwing up again?"

"Nothing's wrong. It's just my nerves." She wiped the sweat off her forehead. "I promise."

Exhaling a curse, he wondered if she could be pregnant. Oh, God, now he felt like throwing up. Either she was or it was just nerves, in which case she wasn't going with them to fight the Katako in this condition.

With one hand propped against the door frame and the other on his hip, he frowned. "Tessa... is there something you need to talk to me about?"

"Jace, I'm going to be just fine..." Quickly placing her hand over her mouth, she dropped back to her knees with her head back over the toilet.

Calmly, Jace followed her inside and held her hair back. "I'm going to call Helen," he said before she could protest further. "That's final. And I'm coming with you."

"I had a feeling you were," she groaned, rolling her eyes.

It was a waste of time arguing with Jace when he had his mind made up. But in truth, she didn't mind him being pushy at all. He was going to be an excellent father—and that made her heart beam with joy—even though he didn't know yet.

After Jace phoned Helen, he helped Tessa get dressed.

"Let's go," he urged as he slipped on a T-shirt. "Helen's already downstairs."

Tessa crossed her arms. "This is really not necessary."

Ten minutes and a couple arguments later, they were standing outside the exam room as Jace knocked on the door.

"Come in," Helen's voice echoed from inside.

Opening the door, Jace held it open for Tessa.

"Hey, you two," Helen said, as they entered. Glancing in Tessa's direction, Helen appeared nervous. "So, I hear you're sick again."

"It's nothing serious. I'll be fine," she said, peeking at Jace from the corner of her eye.

He shook his head forcefully. "No, she's not."

"It's just my nerves."

Jace threw up his hands in defeat and groaned.

Helen motioned Tessa to take a seat on the examination table. As Tessa eased on top, Helen cleared her throat. "Well, tell me what's going on."

Tessa shrugged her shoulders. "I just threw up."

"Yeah, like a dozen times," Jace interjected.

"Oh, you're exaggerating," Tessa said stubbornly.

In frustration, his face bloomed with heat. "Remember... I was the one standing over you holding your hair back." He leaned in closer, and murmured in Tessa's ear, "I'm not exaggerating."

Helen put up both of her hands and looked back and forth. "Calm down." Focusing on Jace, she smiled. "If it's okay with you, I'd like to talk with Tessa alone for a minute. I'm not kicking you out. I just think maybe things will be much easier if I talk to her one-on-one."

Jace frowned clenching his jaw. "Fine, but don't let her leave without being checked out." He shifted his eyes toward Tessa, looking at her suspiciously.

"All right, I promise." Helen nodded.

Jace muttered under his breath as he moved toward the door. Before he left, he looked over his shoulder and narrowed his eyes. "I'll be back."

Helen watched for the door to close before she muttered a word. When it clicked shut, she said, "Tessa, you need to tell Jace you're pregnant."

Tessa felt her mouth drop open. "Helen, I..."

In a calm voice, Helen came clean. "I've already told Tim."

Tessa dropped her head, and placed her hands on her stomach. "I wish you wouldn't have done that." She sighed, feeling exhausted.

"Tessa... where's your head at?" Helen sat down in a chair next to her. "It's too dangerous for you to put yourself at such risk in your condition."

Tessa lifted her chin and stared at her. "That's exactly what I was thinking. And yet... I don't know—I have to defend my family. It's my responsibility, Helen."

She shook her head. "Not at the risk of your unborn children."

Just as Tessa was about to reply, Jace burst through the door. "I'm back," he announced. "Well... what's wrong with her?"

Tessa looked up at the ceiling and rolled her eyes again.

Helen forced a smile as she got to her feet. "She's good to go right now. I couldn't find anything wrong, but she's promised to notify me if she's sick again—and I have the feeling, if she doesn't, you will."

Jace frowned. "Damn straight I will."

* * * *

Tim was on autopilot as he poured himself a cup of coffee. As the kitchen door creaked, it alerted his attention. Looking over his shoulder, he saw Jace and Tessa walk in.

Taking a sip of his coffee, Tim arched a brow. "I guess I'm not the only one up early."

Rubbing his eyes, Jace yawned. "Yeah, Tessa's wasn't feeling well this morning."

"Sorry to hear that." Tim frowned in her direction. "Are you all right?"

"Um... I'll be fine."

Looking over the rim of his cup, Tim asked, "Are you sure?"

She nodded and quickly looked away. Meanwhile, she was withering with worry that Tim would reveal to Jace her secret. Knowing Tim, he wasn't going ignore the situation.

"Jace, I need to speak with Tessa in private. Do you mind?"

"Why? Is something wrong?"

"No." Tim smiled, pouring another cup of coffee. "Just give us a few minutes, please."

When Jace stepped out, Tessa sat down at the table waiting for Tim's lecture.

As he didn't want to let the conversation get out of hand, he took a seat next to Tessa and placed the cup in front of her. "Helen told me this morning. What were you thinking, Tessa?"

Briefly closing her eyes, she let out a deep breath. "Are you going to tell Jace?"

Tim shook his head. "No, but I think you should. If something happens—" He placed his palm over hers. "Jace will never be the same."

She faked a smile. "Everything's going to be fine."

"Tessa, you don't know that for sure."

"As your Queen... I order you to keep this between us."

Chapter Eighty-Two

As the bright moon filtered through the window, Kyle set on the edge of the bed, rubbing his eyes. Running out of time and the not-knowing what had happened to Celina was killing him. He had to find her before it was too late.

Closing his eyes, he thought about the first time she'd touched him. Her fingers had been soft and elegant, with pretty, pink, polished nails. As the urge to find her took over, his desperation grew deep down into his core.

Opening his lids, he shot to his bare feet with a curse. Kyle was a Breedline male who protected his bonded mate—and he would do everything in his power to get her back. It was pretty obvious that there would be no reasoning when it came to risking his life to save her. Clearly, his personal safety meant nothing to him, his objective overriding all his common sense and patience. He would be all animal as he faced off with the enemy. Bottom line... he didn't care what happened to him as long as Celina was safe.

* * * *

Inhaling a deep breath, Celina smelled the dampness in the basement that Lucas kept her in. She felt helpless in the darkness as she tried to sit up, but her body wouldn't obey what her brain commanded. God, if only she could move her legs. Opening her mouth, she gasped for breath as the panic set in.

Sensing something above her, she looked up. As a light flicked on, she heard her name mumbled in soft purr, "Cee... li... naa."

In gentle hands, she was lifted off the mattress and cradled in a set of massive arms. As she looked at Lucas in terror, his eyes softened with tears. The instant they fell down his face, she blew out a sigh of relief, realizing he wasn't going to harm her.

Carefully, he caressed her hair with his claws, pushing it away from her face. With one hand, he reached over and picked up a bundle of clothes. As he tucked them under his arm, she wondered if they belonged to Taliah.

Still in his grasp, he floated above the ground toward an open door. Moving inside, sounds of water pouring brought her head around. In the corner of the room, she saw a bathtub. It was so full, it looked as if it was about to overflow. Sitting down on the edge, his eyes glittered with excitement as she met his stare. Powerless, she squeezed her eyes tight while he carefully undressed her. With the sounds of sloshing water, he slowly eased her inside.

* * * *

After Kyle finished getting dressed, he jogged downstairs toward the kitchen. As he moved closer, he halted his movement when he saw Jace. He was standing outside with his ear pressed to the door as if he was eavesdropping on a conversation from the inside. As Jace stepped back, Kyle noticed his hands were shaking. It was obvious whatever he'd overheard had upset him. Shifting his body toward the wall, Jace slumped back against it and dropped his head. With his hands covering his face, he cursed under his breath.

Watching in the shadows as Jace fell apart, it was difficult for Kyle to draw an even breath. Struggling for the right thing to do, he froze, and for a whole lot of reasons. Just as he was about to offer him comfort, he decided against it when Jace shot upright. Unfortunately, however, regardless of what had pissed him off, the expression on his face could not be undone. Instead of taking the chance of being ripped into little pieces, he waited until Jace stormed off before he went into the kitchen to find out what was going on.

Without knocking, he pushed open the door. Inside, he saw Tim and Tessa sitting at the kitchen table. "I think you should know—" Kyle paused with his arms crossed. "Whatever you were talking about... Jace overheard."

Tessa covered her face and groaned, "Oh, God... he knows. What am I going to do?"

Tim sighed. "Go talk to him, Tessa."

Confused, Kyle shrugged. "What's going on?"

Holding up his hand motioning for Kyle to wait, Tim gently helped Tessa to her feet. "Are you going to be all right?"

Forcing a smile on her face, she fought back tears. Through it all alone, she made it across the kitchen floor and toward the door. By the time she closed it behind her, she was choked of breath—

Instantly, her stomach felt nauseous. Easing back against the wall, she braced herself for the next wave, preparing for yet another round of morning sickness. When it didn't immediately come, she thought of what she was going to say to Jace.

* * * *

Jem was coming down the staircase when he saw Jace storm past him. Sensing his brother's emotions, he didn't even need to turn around to see the anger stewing inside him: the temperature in the air had changed—and not in a good way.

Pivoting around, he followed Jace up the stairs. "Jace... wait!"

Ignoring Jem, he continued, moving into a faster pace.

In a dead run, Jem caught up to him at the top of the stairs, grabbed him by the arm, and spun him around. "Talk to me, damn it! What's going on?"

Jace leaned into the iron grip, baring his teeth. "Fuck you, Jem. Leave me alone!"

"What the hell is wrong with you?" Jem growled.

"Don't push me—"

"I'm trying to talk to you, asshole!"

As the pair of them escalated toward an explosion, Tessa walked over and spoke evenly.

"I'm sorry..."

When she didn't finish, Jem frowned. "What's wrong, Tessa?"

"I'm... pregnant," her voice trembled.

Jem stilled. "What?"

"I'm sorry, Jace. I wanted to tell you, but—"

Staring into the painful look in his eyes, her agony twisted inside her chest. "But I knew you wouldn't understand."

"Understand what?" he said roughly. "Risking the life of my unborn child?"

In the silence that followed, there were no sounds from downstairs as everyone in the Covenant gathered to witness Tessa's confession.

Tessa opened her mouth to answer, but only a croak came out.

Jace stiffened, the muscles in his neck strained and his body shook in anger. "Well, answer me!"

As her voice cracked again, she cleared her throat. "I'm sorry," she mumbled. "Oh, God... I'm so sorry."

Jace shook his head. "I can't believe you would keep this from me."

"But I—"

There was no time for her to reply. Abruptly, Jace's temper geared up once again, that uncontrollable tide rising, the heat uncoiling inside him and ripping through his heart. Keeping his eyes locked onto hers, he took two steps back, turned around, and walked away.

"Please, Jace," she pleaded. "Don't walk away."

Jem seemed surprised as Jace stopped and looked over his shoulder in his direction. The two of them just looked at each other as if they were communicating without words spoken a loud.

"We'll keep her safe, brother," Jem said telepathically.

Shifting his eyes on Tessa, Jace muttered through gritted teeth, "She's not going..."

As Jace turned around, Jem shouted, "Jace!"

When he didn't reply, Jem watched him leave, cursing long and low. Yeah, he wanted to kick his brother's ass—but he absolutely understood why Jace was reacting this way.

Chapter Eighty-Three

Before the morning sunrise, and after bathing Celina, Lucas finally dematerialized in his mother's room. "Maa... maa," he murmured.

Recognizing his voice, she spun around placing her hands on her hips. "Lucas, where in the hell have you been?"

With tears in his eyes, he hung his head in shame.

Acknowledging his remorse, she sighed. "It's all right, baby. I know about Celina. You don't have to hide her anymore."

Lifting his head, his eyes widened with surprise. As his lips cracked a smile, it was if she promised to let him keep a pet.

"Come." She reached out to him. "Mommy will help. Let's go tell your father what you've been up to. He's very upset with you."

* * * *

As Sebastian stalked over to the closet, he leaned inside and inhaled deeply. He was still furious to the core, but as he caught Eve's lingering scent, it eased his aching heart.

With vengeance throbbing in his veins, he went over to the bed and sat down. Moving slowly, he leaned back, placing his head on her pillow. Just as he closed his eyes, a knock snapped them back open.

He cursed under his breath as he stirred. "Who is it?"

"It's Taliah... and your son, Lucas."

Sebastian glared at the door. "It's open."

As Taliah walked in with Lucas close behind, Sebastian's eyes went back and forth—training his dark depths on Lucas, and then at her. "Where the hell has he been?"

"He told me," she cut in. "Everything. He has my sister, and she's unable to use her powers."

Taliah looked at Lucas at the same time Sebastian did. As the pair of them stared at him, Lucas did the unheard of—-and stepped forward into a defensive position, waiting to attack.

Sebastian got to his feet and pointed at Lucas. "Tell me something son, you planning on keeping Celina locked up forever—pretending she loves you?"

With his body fisted in anger, Lucas slashed his hand through the air and growled.

Moving in front of Lucas, Taliah held out her arms, preventing him from lunging toward Sebastian. "He's just protecting her." She braced herself for Lucas to move her aside with one push, but instead, he stepped back.

Sebastian held Lucas's stare without wavering. "I'm not sure it's going to work out the way you've planned. The Breedline will be coming for her."

It was a while before Taliah spoke, and when she did, she forced a smile. "That's what we're counting on."

As she stared across the short distance between them, she thought about all things she'd done, starting when she was just a child. She'd begun experimenting with black magic, and advanced in just a short period. Then, at age twelve, her parents discovered her secret and demanded her to stop. When that had proved difficult, she'd put her powers to use and killed them both. And whatever scars might have formed on the inside of her, they never freed her from the dark side. Her heart was hollow, always had been—and she had done what she had without a conscience, sucking in her emotions and physical sensations, and doing what was necessary.

Desperation made her wonder, was she still useful to the demon at this point? After spending all her time trying to prove her worth, she had realized that, to him, she was just another tool in his determination to gain power. The question now was, would she keep her side of the bargain? Regardless of any 'agreement' she'd had with him, if he disrespected her son again, he'd pay a hefty price.

Striding over, Sebastian bared his fangs. "If he ever disobeys another order, there will be consequences—and nothing you say will stop me."

Taliah threw her head back and laughed.

Sebastian's eyes flared like the promise of violence. "Then, maybe I should punish you instead."

Abruptly, she went inanimately still. Leaning in, the air of her breath was like a dragon breathing fire. "Let me make myself perfectly clear. You touch Lucas and I will release a wrath upon you that nothing can fix. Your last breath will be mine, and your heart will still be warm when I rip it out of your chest and feed it to Lucas."

"You know, it's a wonder we don't get along better," he said, a clear smirk in his voice.

Taliah tilted her head, wondering if he was serious or not. "If the Breedline come for my sister, they won't have a fighting chance up against Lucas. That is... if they make it past me in the first place." She extended her hand. "Have we come to terms?"

Sebastian clasped the palm that was offered briefly. And then Taliah and Lucas were gone, like a nightmare banished upon waking.

* * * *

As Jem started to go after Jace, Tessa caught his arm. "Let him go."

Jem stopped and looked over his shoulder.

Tessa kicked her chin up. "I'll talk to him. I'm the one that's caused all this."

"I just... I don't know." Jem shook his head, and gave her a look that seemed regretful. "I guess I didn't expect him to talk to you that way."

"Don't blame him for being angry. It's my fault. I made a mistake. I thought I was doing the right thing."

"So, you lied."

"Yeah, I did." Wiping her wet eyes, she thought of Jace—and felt a lance of pain through her chest. If she could take it all back, she wouldn't have kept this from him. In truth, she wasn't sure how he'd react. The end result may have still been the same. "Now, it's my responsibility to make it right."

Jem found himself nodding. "Go to him."

When she went to leave, Jem reached for her hand and gently squeezed. "He loves you, Tessa. Don't worry, he'll come around."

She smiled a little, releasing his hand. Moving down the hall, she prayed silently. Bonding with Jace had been like touching the sun and not getting incinerated. And now, she was carrying a part of him inside of her. Living without him would be like an eternity in the darkness.

Standing outside the bedroom, she noticed the door was half open. Before she pushed through, she took a deep breath. As she entered the room, she froze. Facing the wall, Jace was on his knees with his hands pressed together as if he was praying. There was blood dripping on the floor, though she couldn't see where it was coming from.

Ordinarily, she would have rushed to him, but this was not the time. Instead, she slumped back against the wall. "Jace?"

Chapter Eighty-Four

Dropping his hands, Jace turned around. "Tessa..." His voice was deep, warped. Not Jace's.

She looked down and two glowing pupils stared up at her. There was a hypnotic quality to them, an animalistic appearance she couldn't deny, even though she knew it wasn't just Jace she was with. His Beast was inside, clawing to get out.

"Jace, are you okay?"

"Come here," as he spoke, his voice deepened.

She moved toward him slowly, stopping at arm's length.

"Closer, Tessa." Even the way he said her name was not the same.

Moving closer, she ended up on her knees with her face mere inches from his. She'd sensed the Beast and knew it was nothing she needed to be frightened of. And as she met his eyes, it was if a separate presence was looking at her, but Jace was just the same.

Looking down, she noticed one of his hands was covered in blood. "Jace," she gasped. "What happened to your hand?"

As she reached for him, his body responded in a sudden protest. At the same time, his eyelids peeled back, and a bright light pierced the room. On impulse, Tessa quickly covered her eyes.

"Tessa," his voice sank down and disappeared into a growl. "Run!"

"Jace... please."

"You need to leave! Now... before I—" Pushing her out of the room, he dragged her when she resisted.

With a tight grip, she grabbed his arm. "I love you, Jace!"

And then a low-level electrical shock flowed through his body and charged the air. Every light in the room popped, leaving them in the darkness. She gasped and glanced around, and in a flash, the lights came back on. She looked at Jace. His eyes were normal again, the light blue color shining.

"Tessa?" he said in a dazed, indistinct voice.

With tears running down her cheeks, she covered her mouth. "Oh, Jace... I'm so sorry."

In a panic, he reached out to her. "Are you okay? Did I hurt you?"

Sobbing, she shook her head. "No, I'm fine."

In relief, he sunk back onto the floor dropping his head. "Thank, God."

Looking down, she saw the blood on his knuckles. Reaching out, she grasped his hand. "What happened?"

Jace lifted his chin. "I'm not sure." He peered around her body, looking at the wall. "But I think it has something to do with that hole."

Turning her head, she saw where it appeared he'd punched his fist through. She hadn't meant for all this to happen, she thought. All this had been her fault. If only she'd been honest with him from the beginning.

Tessa grabbed his face, planted a passionate kiss on his lips, and looked him straight in the eye. "I love you with all my heart. I'm sorry for lying to you."

Without hesitation, he wrapped his arms around her and buried his head in the curve of her neck. "I don't deserve you, Tessa."

She pulled back and shook her head. "Jace... you're the best thing that's ever happened to me."

He looked at her worried. "Even though—" he shrugged his shoulders, "I'm a monster?"

"Of course," she whispered, urging him back into her arms. "I love every part of you." She kissed the top of his blond head and felt a warm hand smooth over her belly.

"I love you, Tessa," he murmured, caressing the place that held his child. "And I love him or her too."

Lowering her head, she smiled as she watched his palm gently move around. "It's a boy... two of them."

Pulling from their embrace, his jaw dropped. "What—"

Tessa would never forget what Jace looked like after she'd told him she was having twins. His face grew pale, his eyes widened, and he was absolutely speechless.

In response, Jace shot to his feet, and swept her off the floor. Holding her in his arms, he pulled her body close to his.

Startled, their attention was drawn toward the sound of a light tap at the door. With it half open, they heard a deep voice coming from outside, "It's Alexander. May I come in?"

Jace slowly lowered her back down to the floor. In the silence that followed Tessa's big announcement, Jace couldn't get his brain to work. A combination of shock and joy took the breath right out of him until he found himself sitting on the bed. "I can't believe it. We're having twins?"

"Yeah," she choked out. "Twins."

As soon as another knock came from the door, it instantly caught Tessa's attention. "I'm sorry, Alexander." Moving toward the door, she pulled it all the way open. "Please, come in."

Stepping inside, Alexander noticed the expression on Jace's face. He looked as if he'd just seen a ghost. "I hope I'm not interrupting."

"I'm going to have twins," Tessa blurted.

Alexander threw a hand out to steady himself. He couldn't have heard that right. "What? Did you say you're having twins?"

"—-having boys," Jace mumbled.

All of a sudden, Alexander felt the widest, happiest grin hit his face, stretching his cheeks until they hurt, and making his eyes water. "That's wonderful news," he boasted. "Congratulations."

"Helen said they're healthy," Tessa sniffled. "And I heard their heartbeats."

Before he knew what he was doing, Jace burst to his feet and wrapped his arms around Tessa. And as he held her, he stared out over her head in Alexander's direction.

"You're going to be a grandfather," Jace said firmly.

"Yes, he is," Tessa said as she wiped under her eyes and looked back at Alexander.

Yes, Alexander thought. He was going to be a grandfather. "I don't know what to say." He wiped his eyes. "I'm honored."

Shaking her head, Tessa took a deep breath and decided to go with the moment. There was still a long haul in front of them as time ticked by until they were faced with the Chiang-shih demon once again—which, she was still going with them to fight. With so many hurdles ahead, and so many unknowns, it was making her nauseous thinking about it.

But for the next hour, she just wanted to enjoy this miracle with Jace. She'd been so worried he wouldn't accept her pregnancy. She was relieved and elated that he was ecstatic, and even acknowledged Alexander as a grandfather. Life sometimes took you in the opposite way in which you expected it to.

As Alexander's emotions of joy took over, he'd almost forgotten the reason he was here in the first place. There was something he had to share with them. It was difficult to explain, he thought, even to himself.

"There's something—" Alexander cleared his throat. "I wanted to tell you."

As Jace and Tessa looked at him, the admiration he felt for them was so strong, he would drag the moon down to earth if they needed it.

"Before your mother, Katlyn... passed on to the other side, she shared a vision with me," Alexander explained. "The vision was of our grandchildren... your children."

Abruptly, a cold rush hit Jace. When he took a deep breath, that terror he'd dreamed about involving Tessa's death came crashing back. He exhaled and shook his head. "Please don't say there's something wrong?"

"Of course not," Alexander quickly replied. "I saw them, Jace. Your sons were running outside in the gardens, and they were laughing." His lips formed a proud smile as he kept his eyes on Jace. "You were laughing and chasing after them. I watched you scoop them into your arms. You were happy."

Immediately, Tessa turned and looked up at Jace. Tears were rolling down his face. And then he looked down at her with a smile. Reaching around her, he found her lower belly with his hand. Lifting his chin, his face expressed forgiveness as he looked at Alexander. "Thank you."

🐾 Chapter Eighty-Five

As the day pressed on and darkness fell, everyone in the Covenant prepared to face their worst nightmare. Taking the stairs to meet with the others, Jace thought back, shifting the weeks and then the months. There had been a night, about four months ago, when Tessa had awoken him in the middle of the night to make love—and it had been a blood moon. Afterward... come to think of it, they'd changed into their wolves and went for a run. All this time, she'd been pregnant with his twins.

After Alexander had shared a vision of the future, all his fears from the dreams of Tessa's death were a thing of the past. Now, he felt in control of the universe, an old, familiar part of him waking up once again.

With his hand in Tessa's, he guided her down to the last step. Waiting at the bottom, with a fresh military trim, they saw Tim. The lights above streamed down across his square jaw and wide shoulders.

Keeping his hand entwined with Tessa's, Jace nodded in his direction. "We ready to go?"

When there was no immediate response, Jace braced himself, preparing for bad news.

Tim clasped his hands behind his back. "Jace, can we talk for a sec?"

Tessa squeezed his hand. "I'll be in the kitchen." Lifting up on her tip-toes, she kissed Jace once, twice, three times before she walked away, giving them privacy.

Before Tim managed to open his mouth to speak, Jace cut him off, "I know what you're going to say." He held up one hand in ward-off mode. "I've already had this conversation with Tessa. She's going with us."

"I'm not disagreeing to piss you off," Tim said calmly. "That's the last thing I want to do—for reasons I'm sure you get."

Jace's brows pulled tight. "This is her decision, Tim."

"Look Jace, I don't like people getting into my personal business and I'm the last person who wants to tell you how to handle your relationship with Tessa. But this is too risky."

In the brief silence and with a heavy heart, Jace knew Tim was right. The sadness that crushed him took his words away, leaving him with a strange, blank stare. All he could do was nod. And then he said, "You're not going to change her mind. Besides, she's the Queen." He shrugged. "Are you going to disrespect her decision?"

Unfortunately, Tim had no other choice but to give up. Feeling the tension building in the back of his neck, he shifted his head to the side sharply and a crack sounded out. Tim finally nodded. "No, I guess not," he muttered, massaging the nape of his neck. "But I still think it's a bad idea."

There was a tight, awkward silence, as if neither of them knew how to get back to normal. Then Jace stuck out his fist. "Let's do this."

Briefly tapping Jace's knuckles with his own, Tim cursed under his breath. "All right," he said, feeling defeated. "There's one more thing."

Jace crossed his arms. "Which is?"

"I want Jem and Drakon to stay with Tessa the entire time," Tim said firmly. "No matter what, they don't leave her sight."

Jace's head tilted slightly to the side, his mind clearly working. "I'm not leaving her side either."

Suddenly, the tension in his neck came back. "You might get separated, especially since you're dealing with the demon and she's going up against the Katako."

Tim waited, clearly expecting him to argue.

Jace's trembling hand brushed back his long hair. For some reason, he thought about Alexander's vision. Pegging Tim with a hard stare, he didn't have the energy to disagree. "Yeah," he sighed, and dropped his head. "I guess that could happen."

Jesus Christ, he felt like Doomsday was breathing down his neck, stalking him—and even though he'd felt in control just minutes ago, he was starting to get worked up all over again, like Tessa's expiration date was around the next corner. It didn't mean he was going to survive her, he thought, but quite the contrary. If things ended up going south, his unborn sons could end up without a father.

It took a moment for things to sink in, and then Jace realized that this was a moment in life when the path that was presented had only two forks—and in his mind, neither was a good one.

His attention snapped back to reality when he felt a warm hand on his shoulder. Looking up, Tim came into his vision. "Jace, I promise... we'll do everything in our power to keep her safe."

Jace closed his eyes briefly. Instead of a response, he nodded—and in the tight quiet that followed, he said a silent prayer. *Dear God, please keep Tessa and my sons safe.*

Tim followed alongside Jace as they walked to the door that would take them into a room where everyone was waiting. When Jace looked down, he saw Natalie's pink bib stuffed into Tim's back pocket. Life goes on, he thought. No matter what the world did to you, you have to find a purpose to fight to survive.

As they approached the kitchen door, Jem was leaning back against it. "Jace, can we talk?"

"Yeah, sure," Jace muttered, shifting his eyes in Tim's direction. "We'll be right there."

Reaching for the door, Tim pushed it half open. "Don't be long. We need to go over some things before we leave."

Standing beside Jem, Jace felt an odd sense of intuition. But when it came to his twin brother, he'd always had them.

Jem's eyes softened. "Are you going to be able to handle this? I mean, now that Tessa's pregnant?"

Jace felt his brows lift as he looked at his brother, thinking of all the times Jem had to clean up after all the messes he'd made. It had to be an exhausting task all these years. He felt like a total ass.

In the silence, Jem breathed out a curse, "Listen, Jace. You can't do anything more for Mom. She's gone. She's in a better place. But the living... you can take care of the living. I know what kind of hell you've been through—she was my mother too. I can't go through losing you over all this. Stop worrying about Tessa. She's going to be fine. Everyone's going to protect her."

When his brother's words faded, Jace felt like he'd been sucker punched—and yet he wasn't angry. Because he knew Jem was the kind of brother that always had his back. Christ, for all the crap they'd been through, it was a miracle they were still sane. But they were all coming to realization... shit just happens. Nonetheless, you had to keep going. Keep your friends, family, and your mate as safe as you were capable of. And keep fighting even after you were knocked down.

Never one to hesitate in stating his opinion, Jace nonetheless cleared his throat. "Let's do this... together."

The two of them embraced, chest to chest. And when they pulled apart, they went inside as a team just like it always had been.

Pivoting around, Jem faced him. "Oh, I almost forgot. Congratulations."

Jace smiled. "Thanks, bro."

"Have a seat," Tim muttered as he drummed his fingers on the table, his brain overwhelmed by the grim task ahead—as well as the silence. "Tessa, will you please lead the group?"

With a sound of a chair getting pushed back on the tile floor, Tessa stood. "As I'm sure you've already heard—" She paused and took a deep breath. "I've decided to go with you."

"Are you sure that's a good idea?" Drakon queried.

Her eyes shifted to his. "As your Queen, it's my responsibility to protect this Covenant." She ducked her eyes briefly. "I have no other choice. I'm the only one that can destroy the Katako." And as Tessa said her peace, without apology or backing down, the words she had kept hidden finally set her free.

In that moment, Drakon could see the weight bearing down on her, sensing the tension on her face. Tessa was the leader of the Breedline race... something you didn't sign up for, but instead, was born into. He knew all too well what it was like to be forced into a mold you didn't fit—and yet she'd taken on the responsibility.

"Any questions?" she asked—scanning the room, searching their eyes for disappointment.

"We've got your back," Drakon said in a deep voice.

Hearing his words of approval brought back memories of when she'd first acknowledged she was their Queen. At first, taking on the magnitude of responsibility was something she was not prepared for. Funny... right now? All that stuff didn't seem like a burden anymore.

Seconds later, there was some shuffling and suddenly, everyone dropped to one knee and bowed their head. She'd never known such... respect? Was that what it was? It definitely brought forth deep emotions from within her. That was for sure.

Tessa wiped her eyes as tears fell down her cheeks. Before she could say anything, though, a stream of humble words fell from everyone's mouth, "Hail to the Queen."

"I am honored," she said modestly, gesturing them to rise. "I'll do my best to keep this Covenant safe."

❦ Chapter Eighty-Six

Splitting everyone up into teams, Tim placed Jem and Drakon with Tessa. It was their responsibility to protect her as she went up against the Katako. Including himself, Tim teamed up Jace and Alexander. All three of them would take care of Taliah and the demon. Kyle and the ex-rogue wolves mission were to retrieve Celina, and act as backup.

In no time at all, the group was loaded with weapons and ready to go. As they gathered up, Jace moved next to Alexander.

"I want to thank you," he said with a genuine tone in his voice. "What you said to me meant a lot."

"You're welcome, Jace."

"I also want to apologize—"

Alexander held up his hand before he could finish. "You don't have to apologize. I understand."

Without saying a word, Jace smiled.

Extending his hand, Jem conjured the portal, and one by one they disappeared, ready for battle.

As they stepped through the portal, they took form in a stand of pines and bushes outside Sebastian's estate. The huge stone structure had high security fencing with rod iron on every window.

"Charming place," Jace smirked. "That is, if you're into the prison look."

In moments like this, Kyle didn't know why he suddenly sensed Celina nearby. The urge just came upon him—so strong, it was undeniable.

Yeah... he could feel her presence... she was here. And the certainty reminded him of what he'd felt when he'd been in the bedroom where Taliah held her captive before. He had sensed her then, but was blocked by an invisibility spell.

"She's here," he said in a low voice. "Celina's in there somewhere. I just know it."

Instantly, all their attention was drawn toward Tim as he whistled quietly, "We'll, let's not waste time. Let's go in from the back."

Everyone followed, hoofing it around the back while Kyle took off in a more intensive approach, running across the lawn holding his gun down at his thigh. Up ahead, there were rows after rows of security cameras mounted in each corner. Passing by them, they kept their focus on getting to the back without being seen. Even though there were cameras everywhere, fortunately there was no security personal or guard dogs on the outside of the property.

Tessa bounced on the balls of her feet as she ran with them and fell into a quick rhythm that carried them to the back relatively quiet. Other than that, the rest of the estate was nothing but more stone, covered in ivy all the way to the roof.

Coming to a halt, Tim searched the scene before him, focusing on the several steps that led to a set of glass doors with iron bars over them. Stepping behind Jem, he clapped his palm over his shoulder and muttered quietly, "Can you get us inside?"

With a nod, Jem stretched his palm forward. But there was nothing. For some reason, he couldn't conjure the portal. His jaw tightened and his brows furrowed as he concentrated... but still nothing.

Jem cursed under his breath, "I don't understand? Something's blocking me."

"It's Taliah," Kyle raised his voice a little. "She's probably put some kind of spell on this place."

Jace frowned. Something is off with all this, he thought. When there was an odd sound from behind, Jace looked back. And from out of nowhere, he felt a cold chill slither down his spine. Turning back around, he saw Kyle, Alexander, and Jem looking through the glass doors. Drakon and Tim were facing each other, whispering something. And then he turned toward Tessa. She was staring at him.

She shook her head. "What is it, Jace?"

"That chill... I sense him near," he uttered.

Blindly turning on his heel, he headed off walking, and then breaking into a run. A second later, he heard Tessa call out to him, but there was no stopping to explain... or stopping him.

Tessa took off after him the instant he left. She didn't like the independent thinking, or his direction—he was heading toward the front of the estate alone.

When Tim saw Tessa running after Jace, he turned toward Kyle. "Call for backup, *now!*"

Jem jogged in Tessa's pursuit, and as he followed her, Drakon, Alexander, and Tim fell in step with him. Kyle and the ex-rogue wolves were closing in as well, roaring across the estate's grounds like a herd of bulls. Dirt flew in all directions as their claws dug in the earth beneath them.

Before Tessa could catch up to Jace, she called out to him once more. It was pretty obvious that there would be no reasoning with him—even if she screamed into his ear, she knew there was no derailing him. She stopped and felt the breath go out of her. Watching his transformation begin, she saw a bright flash engulf his body. With a deep rolling roar, Jace disappeared and the Beast stood in his place. He was all animal rushing forward like a predator stalking its prey.

As Tessa watched Jace disappear in the distance, she heard a noise coming from above. Looking up, she saw a large creature with enormous wings heading in her direction. Dropping from the sky, it landed right in front of her. When the creature focused solely on her, Tessa recognized what it was. From Celina's description, it had to be the Katako.

Jem froze a few feet away, his face going blank. Beside him, Drakon stood motionless as he watched the creature tower over Tessa. With a scorpion shaped tail, it moved back and forth like a rattle snake preparing to strike.

Standing her ground, Tessa's senses told her this would end in a violent frenzy in which she could be killed if she didn't act now. With no time to spare, she brought forth her wolf. Instantly, her skin itched with a rippling sensation as black hair descended from her shoulders and trailed down her arms. Looking down at her hands, claws pushed from the tips of her fingers. Kicking off her shoes, she dropped to the ground and tore off her clothes. Rising on all fours, a deep gargling roar rose from Tessa's monstrous, Breedline wolf.

When the Katako saw her transformation, his eyes widened. In the blink of an eye, his half-human and half-dragon form changed into something different. With a savage snarl, he stalked around Tessa with an image mimicking hers. It was like a standoff. Two huge black wolves with teeth the size of daggers slowly circled each other... waiting for the other to make the first move.

Chapter Eighty-Seven

With an ugly, patronizing facial expression, Taliah stood outside the estate's front entrance above several stone steps. With her lips pursed, she turned to the left, as though she heard a noise.

Something immense and heavy thundered in the near distance as she waited for it to appear. It was the Beast, emerging from around the back as if from nothingness, a great seven-foot creature in white wolf-fur with blazing yellow eyes, and a deep seething roar rumbling from its throat.

Taliah merely watched unaffected. Even though fury ran rampant inside her, her skin was like an icy armor containing her.

Looking ahead, the Beast stared wildly at her. With bright red hair, she was the spitting image of Celina.

When there was a loud noise coming from behind, the Beast whipped his head around. Across the way, he saw hundreds of rogue wolves enter into view. As they surrounded the Beast, they circled back and forth ready to fight with him in battle.

From overhead, the sound of shrill laughter refocused the Beast. Shifting his head forward, he locked his eyes back on Taliah and growled. She was grinning widely, the wickedness of her face pulled into a demonic smile.

Rage tore through the Beast, the curse in him screaming as he positioned himself into an attack stance.

With only seconds to spare, Taliah created a diversion. Bringing forth her dark magic, the wolves collapsed onto the ground, howling in agony.

As they writhed in pain, Tim arrived with Kyle and Alexander, all their guns pointed in Taliah's direction.

Tim watched utterly helpless as the wolves reacted to her spell. Snapping back into real time, he looked over his shoulder at Kyle. His eyes were glued to the grim scene before them.

Waving his arms, he tried to draw Kyle's attention. Turning in his direction, he heard Tim shout, "Go!" Then he added, "Find Celina!"

* * * *

In a split second, Tessa rushed the Katako, her powerful body sending it crashing to the ground. Struggling beneath her, it thrashed against her weight. Moving fast, it lunged forward, sinking its teeth into her neck nearly hitting a main artery. She felt the hot breath on her face and the burning stab of its sharp canines ripping into her flesh. As it clamped down, she roared in pain.

Gripping his weapon, Drakon uttered a desperate tone, "Do something, Jem," he said, the words rolling out forcefully. "Use your powers!"

Watching in horror, Jem shook his head. "I can't..." The tension was unbearable. "I can't tell them apart."

Instantly, a mass of Guardians materialized, seeming to multiple out of nowhere. As they crowded around the two wolves, Jem appeared dazed and Drakon stood stock-still. Sliding between the two, Chester Ewan stepped in front of them and said, "Help her, Jem! Hurry, before it's too late!"

When a great howl came from one of the wolves, Jem dropped to his knees. "But which one is... Tessa?"

Within seconds, the Katako overtook Tessa, pinning her down with its massive body. Its jaws opened instinctively, tearing into her flesh.

Chester knelt beside Jem and whispered firmly in his ear.

Jem rose to his feet, keeping his eyes locked on the target, and extended his palm. As he aimed toward the Katako, Chester, Drakon, and the Guardians backed away like melting shadows. Hurling a blazing ball of energy, Jem watched as the surge hit the Katako. With its jaws gapped wide, his howl of pain echoed sharply in Tessa's ears.

Ready for round two, Jem blasted another strike. The second blaze caused a round of twitching, which wasn't going to be any trouble as he waited for Tessa to come at the Katako and finish it off.

Springing to her feet, Tessa lunged on top. Going face-to-face, she looked into its eyes, meeting its shocked stare. The Katako scrambled as it tried to disengage her jaws from its torso—which suggested his fear of her venom. With a seething growl, she bit deep into the Katako's throat, tearing through his windpipe, air escaping in a long hiss as it went limp.

Stepping over its lifeless body, she licked the blood from her fur even as it was shrinking, and vanishing into her skin. Suddenly, she felt her paws shape into fingers. When her human form emerged, she reached up to touch the wound on her neck. She was so weak from the loss of blood, she could barely stand. Looking over her shoulder at Jem, the respect she paid him hit harder than anything he'd ever felt. As Tessa went down, Jem rushed over with Drakon close behind.

Peeling off his shirt, Jem pressed it against her wound to stop the flow of blood. "Tessa... are you okay?"

Looking up at him, she felt like she should be dead, considering the pain all over her body. With all her strength, she lifted her hand and gave a thumbs up.

Drifting in and out of consciousness, she felt her body being covered and carefully enfolded in a strong pair of arms. And when she cracked her lids, Jem's face came into her field of vision, his long, blond hair slipping free of his shoulders and falling forward.

"I've got you," Jem whispered, his voice choked. It sounded like he had tears, but she was nearly unconscious now.

"Blood... all over you," she managed to whisper.

"Don't worry about it," he said softly. "I'm going to get you out of here."

He twisted around in search of Chester, but the only person standing behind him was Drakon. Chester and all the Guardians were gone. "We need to get her back *now*," Jem said with urgency. "She's lost a lot of blood."

Tessa shook her head, and struggled in his arms, trying to grasp Jem's neck to gain his attention. But she was so weak. She had to remain conscious, and find out if Jace was okay. With all her strength, she mumbled, "No—" She dragged in a breath, "Take me to Jace."

No affirmative answer came back to her, but nor did a denial. There was only silence as Jem looked down at her. "Tessa, think about your babies—"

"Take me... *now*." As a wave of exhaustion rolled in, her lids flickered shut.

* * * *

Taliah gasped, "Lucas—" There was silence and then her voice was barely louder than a whisper. "No..."

Realizing Lucas was gone forever, she directed her anger toward the Beast to such an extent, the tear that fell from her eye landed on the concrete as fire.

"No, no, no," Taliah muttered through gritted teeth. With her brows clenched, she moved forward in a silent rage. Quickly pulling her hand back, she slugged the Beast right in the face as her voice cast down the steps in an echo, "That bitch killed my son!"

As Alexander watched Taliah hit the Beast, he felt the blood drain from his face. He knew all too well what was coming next.

Dropping her hand, Taliah fisted it at her side. "I'm going to rip your Queen's heart out with my bare hands!"

Instantaneously, the Beast's huge wolf-hand reached out and snatched her by the throat, lifting her off the ground.

"I demand..." she gasped for air. "...let go of me!" Squirming in his grip, her feet thrashed, struggling to get loose.

Opening his jaws, the Beast roared like a lion. Without hesitation, he sunk his razor sharp teeth into her throat. Blood gushed from her body, covering the Beast's white fur.

At the same time, the door sprung open and shots rang out, hitting the Beast.

Undeterred, the Beast clamped down on Taliah's neck, ripping her head loose from her body. With her head in his jaws, he swung it back and forth, sending it flying to the top of the steps.

The instant Taliah was sent to her death, the wolves were released from the spell.

Stunned, Damien stumbled back and tripped over Taliah's head, dropping his gun. As it skidded from his grasp, he struggled on his hands and knees to reach it, slipping in the blood.

As Damien looked up, he saw the Beast moving toward him, glowing eyes staring forward, effortlessly dragging Taliah's headless body with his claws.

Watching from below, Alexander noticed the way the Beast moved on the balls of its feet as it stalked closer toward Damien and dropped the body.

After the Beast reached down and ripped Damien's head off as though pulling apart a piece of rotten fruit, Tim cringed and turned his head. With one powerful toss, the Beast vaulted the head where it burst through glass doors. As it shattered, Sebastian appeared.

As he met the Beast's stare, hatred glared out of his dark depths. Looking down, Sebastian saw Damien's severed head. Stepping through the broken glass, he saw another head with bright red hair. It was lying on its side, staring blankly at nothing.

Lifting his chin, Sebastian looked at the Beast with a murderous intent. "After I kill you—" he growled, "I'm going to rip your beloved into little pieces."

Exploding with an uncontrollable rage, Sebastian lifted high in the air, moving with his mind, not his legs. Hovering above the Beast, he extended his palm. As he aimed at his target, the Beast leaped off the steps and tackled him around the waist at the very moment he started to throw a blazing inferno. The collision knocked Sebastian flat on his back. The shock of the impact snapped his head, slamming it against the concrete. With the Beast's massive weight pinning him down, Sebastian's ears rang like they had fire alarms going off in them.

Rage got the better of the Beast. Instead of killing him outright, he grabbed Sebastian around the neck with an iron grip and squeezed the air out of his throat.

Somehow, his voice emanated up even with the lock the Beast had on his larynx. "Your beloved's fate has already been sealed," he gasped. "Soon, she'll met her—"

The Beast tightened his grip so hard, Sebastian's eyes rolled back in his head.

With that, Sebastian disappeared, dissolving into nothing—but that didn't last. Seconds later, the Beast was hit from behind, knocked to his knees with a burning blast.

After the Beast was hit, he was dazed and disoriented, but he forced his head forward and managed to brace himself upright, shaking off whatever surge of electricity had knocked him down. He couldn't feel some portion of his body, and the other half screamed in pain, but neither mattered. Struggling to stand, a blade suddenly appeared from behind. The bright silver flashed right next to his eye—so close, if he moved it would pierce through.

"Did you think you could actually destroy me?" Sebastian's voice was distorted. "You and your brother had your chance to join me. Now... both of you will die at my hands."

The point of the weapon dipped out of his visual field, and then he felt the tip go into his cheekbone and drag slowly downward toward his throat until a line of blood appeared.

"No!" Alexander yelled, limping up the steps. He'd taken one of Damien's stray bullets. "Take me instead!"

Without looking behind him, Sebastian raised his voice. "Oh, I will," he said pointedly, his voice sounding cold. "I'll make sure you're next."

Using all his strength, a deadly purpose took over the Beast, replacing the beat of his heart as the driver of his physical form. Blinking hard, he felt something inside of him—a vision. It was boiling up from somewhere deep in his mind, playing images of Tessa's death. Releasing a growl, he quickly returned to the present. The Beast's fury screamed inside of him. As his hands twitched and his shoulders tightened, he quickly knocked the blade from Sebastian's grasp, sending it clattering to the ground.

In full force, he pounded into Sebastian like the weight of a train in full speed. Sinking his teeth into his throat as swiftly as any animal of the wild moving to slay, the venom sent spasms running rampant inside the demon.

As his black eyes rolled back again, his body stiffened. Sebastian was cold as ice, lying motionless and stock-still.

Towering over his body, the Beast breathed down into his face. Suddenly, Sebastian's eyes popped wide. The color of his irises shifted from the soulless black into a golden yellow. At the same time, a smirk formed on his lips and a flash of light blasted from his body. When the light faded, Sebastian instantly vanished, leaving behind a sinister laugh that echoed in the distance.

❧ Chapter Eighty-Eight

When the Beast turned around, his eyes focused on Alexander. With his jaws gapped wide, he stalked in his direction searching for something to slay.

For a moment, Alexander felt a prickle of tension filter through the nape of his neck realizing he was the Beast's next target. It was pretty obvious that there would be no reasoning with him—Jace was all animal as he faced off with what he thought was the enemy.

It was a good bet he was going to die, and he was ready to accept whatever punishment was given. Bottom line, Alexander knew he wasn't going to survive this time.

"Go ahead son," Alexander said firmly. "It's okay... I understand. I'll gladly give my life to render your suffering."

Confused by Alexander's words, the Beast stopped and cocked his head to one side.

"No, Jace!" Tim shouted. "Please don't do this," he pleaded, trying to reason with the Beast. "What was done to your mother is not his fault."

Shifting his focus, the Beast turned in Tim's direction and curled back his upper lip, releasing a deep growl. Locking his eyes back on Alexander, flashes of memories came crashing into his head. In a soft whisper, he heard his mother's voice, *"The demon that possessed Alexander is the one responsible for my death, not the man."*

In a quick twist, reality warped and distorted on him, his sight momentarily blurring and then becoming clearer. Suddenly, something flashed before his eyes—another vision. Surfacing from somewhere deep in his mind, he saw it in his head like pages being turned in a picture book.

It was in a field outside the Breedline Covenant. On a sunny day... he saw two little boys with blond hair running and laughing. As he caught up with them, he scooped them into his arms and heard their little voices call him Daddy.

And then he focused back to the present, looking into Alexander's terrified but compassionate eyes.

Abruptly, a seizure took over his body. Scrambling his neurons, his head started to spin. Feeling like he was on a carousel, the Beast swayed back and forth. Usually, he ended up on his ass, but the rage in him kept him upright, giving him a kind of power that came from inside.

Without warning, a bright light completely engulfed his body like a bolt of lightning. Losing his balance, he dropped to his knees. Bracing himself on all fours, the Beast slowly transformed until Jace's body resurfaced. When his arms gave out, he collapsed against the steps.

As Alexander rushed over with Tim right behind, they saw Jace shivering with his knees tucked into his chest.

When Alexander knelt down, Jace's eyes locked onto his as a midst of recollections came, echoing through him. Images of Sebastian's cruel, twisted grin came crashing into his head. The demon was a representation of all the evil in the world, and all the pain he'd caused. Alexander wasn't to blame for all the sinister deeds. But at the moment, Jace felt like the repercussions had lasted a lifetime.

With tears in his eyes, Jace reached for Alexander. He tried to say something, but he couldn't quite get it out.

"Shhh..." Alexander soothed, placing his palm on Jace's shoulder. "It's okay," he whispered. "It's okay, son."

With every passing second, Jace sensed Tessa slipping further and further away. He prayed silently as he hadn't since he was a little boy. *Please God, keep her safe.*

After losing his mother, his adoptive family had pulled him and his brother into the fold just like they were their biological sons. That love had later extended to his little sister Cassie. His life had been fine before. He wouldn't consider his life perfect, but neither could he have said he was unhappy. *But now?* He couldn't imagine his life without Tessa. She was going to be the mother of his children.

Shrugging out of his jacket, Tim draped it over Jace. "Stay here with him," he told Alexander. "I'm going to check on the others."

As he turned to leave, Kyle appeared above the steps, standing amongst the broken glass holding Celina in his arms.

Tim gave him a concerned glance. "Is she okay?"

Celina lifted her head sluggishly, and looked in Tim's direction. "My legs don't want to work right now, but I'll be okay."

"Jesus..." Kyle winced at all the blood. And then he saw a head by the door, and stepped back. Feeling a cold shiver, unease crept up his neck. "What the hell happened?"

"The Beast, that's what happened," Tim said sharply. "He destroyed the demon and a few others that tried to stop him."

Tim's words settled over him, relieving his anxiety, but he cringed when he saw two headless bodies.

"I'm sorry, Celina," Tim said remorsefully. "One of them was your sister."

As if sensing her sudden turmoil, Kyle lowered his head and buried his face in her sweet-smelling hair, such a contrast to the scent of blood that hung obscenely in the air.

She nodded, her eyes filled with tears. "She brought on her own death." Her lips quivered and tears crowded the corners of her lids, glistening on her eyelashes. "Justice was served," her voice trembled. Tears slipped openly down her cheeks as she swallowed back a raw sob. Kyle tenderly kissed each drop of moisture away and tightened his hold, anchoring her through the storm.

"You two stay here with Alexander and Jace," Tim stated firmly. "I'm going to check on—"

Tim went silent when he saw Drakon just a few feet away. Following close behind him, Jem had Tessa in his arms. And then to his utter shock, Tim's jaw dropped when he saw Tessa covered in blood. Immediately, the dread in his gut intensified and the blood in his veins froze. "Oh, God," he gasped. "What happened?"

"She fought the Katako... and won," Jem replied as worry clutched him by the throat. "But we need to get her back, she need's medical attention."

"Jace!" Tessa bellowed. "Where's Jace? Is he okay?"

"He's fine, Tessa," Tim reassured. "Jace did it. He destroyed the demon, and took out Taliah as well."

"Finally, thank God." Drakon sagged in relief.

"I want to see Jace," Tessa insisted. "Please, take me to him."

As they approached the steps, Tessa looked down from Jem's arms and saw Taliah's head lying on the concrete, eyes glassy with death. Quickly looking away, she spotted Jace on the opposite side. She went silent and stared long and hard at him as tears flowed, mixing with the blood on her face.

When Jace saw her, he blinked, worry furrowing his brows. For a moment, his gaze locked with hers and relief swamped his eyes before going glossy with tears. It ripped his heart right out of his chest to see her hurt.

"Tessa," he muttered in a hoarse voice.

Jem gently lowered her down as Jace caught her in his arms, cradling her securely. "Tessa, talk to me, please," he said with panic in his eyes. "Are you okay?"

"Yes," her voice was so faint he had to strain to hear her. He kissed her hair, just wanting to touch her, reassure himself that she was alive and in his arms. "I'll never leave you," he vowed.

There was an ache to his words that touched the deepest part of her soul. With tears flowing from her eyes, she'd never felt so helpless in her life. All she could do was nod so he knew she heard him.

Closing his eyes, Jace buried his face in Tessa's soft hair. Even though there was a possibility that Sebastian Crow was still alive somewhere, the worst part was over. The demon was dead.

"I love you," she said brokenly. With all her strength she had left, she lifted her head and smiled at him. "I love you, Jace." Her smile broadened and she slipped her hand in his, squeezing.

Against all the odds, he realized that those three little words were exactly what he needed to hear. They actually meant more to him than anything else in the world. And now he was going to have a family. He whispered a thanks to God for seeing her safely back to him, where she belonged. He pressed his lips to her forehead, uncaring of the blood that smeared his own face. "I love you too, baby."

Lifting her hand to his lips, he pressed a kiss on her soft skin and said with pride, "Marry me, Tessa."

Take a sneak peek at the first chapter of Unleashed Chaos, a Novel of the Breedline Series coming soon, plus a bonus feature. With the author's artwork, she has portrayed her version of the main character, Jace Chamberlain.

Enjoy...

Chapter One

Death was messy, painful and without rules... especially when you were faced with decisions to risk your life, and the life of the ones you love.

An hour later, as Tessa opened her eyes, she realized she was back at the Breedline Covenant... safe and sound, lying on top of an uncomfortable, thinly padded exam table. The same one Helen gave her the exciting but scary news that she was pregnant with twins.

"I think she's awake," Cassie said, looking down at Tessa with a cheerful grin on her face. "Welcome back, Tessa."

She felt like hell, and her entire body was stiff, but she was alive.

Jace suddenly entered her vision as he leaned over and stared at her with a worried expression in his icy blue eyes.

She opened her mouth to speak, but all that came out was a low whisper, "Are the babies—"

He smiled. Nodding his head, he took her hand and caressed it. "They're fine," he said softly. "Don't worry, baby. Everyone is just fine."

Exhausted, Tessa closed her eyes, the faint sounds of voices carrying her off into a drifting sleep. In her dreams, her mind sensed that everything had worked out as it was supposed to. That path she had been set upon to help the Breedline fight in battle against the Chiang-shih demon had taken her precisely where she was supposed to end up... safe back in Jace's arms.

* * * *

On the other side of the room, Celina blinked as tears sprang to her eyes when she heard her aunt Helen say, "I'm sorry, Celina, but the break in your spine is beyond my expertise. You'll need an orthopedic surgeon."

Celina swallowed, trying to clear her dry throat. "I thought I was going to be okay," her voice croaked. "I mean... I thought it was just a head injury. I wiggled my toes and—" She took a deep breath, "Will I ever walk again?"

Trying to soothe her, Helen put her hand on Celina's shoulder. "I have faith that you will," her voice suggested hope.

"We'll find you the damn best," Kyle promised, his eyes locked on Celina's. "Find her the best, Doc... no matter what it takes."

Staring at him, Helen's concerned expression soothed Kyle's anxiety. "I'll find her an excellent surgeon. You have my word."

Kyle's shoulder sagged a bit as if all the air escaped him at once. When he nodded, Helen checked the IV in Celina's arm. Plugged into a bag, it hung off the medical monitoring headboard. Before she left the room to give them privacy, she looked over her shoulder at Kyle. "She needs to get some rest."

When the door clicked shut, Celina felt a warm hand over hers. It was Kyle's hand against her own, and the connection between them eased her in ways she couldn't explain.

In truth, she'd lost her parents when she was just a child to the hands of her own sister—and now she was dead. If she wasn't ever to walk again, she still had her aunt Helen, her new family here at the Covenant, and Kyle, her Breedline bonded mate.

Leaning close, Kyle captured Celina's mouth in a quick, tender kiss. "I'm so glad to have you back safe."

"Me too," she whispered just as her consciousness slipped from her grasp, and she drifted asleep. In her heart she believed she would come back to him whole. One way or the other, she was going to walk again.

* * * *

Tessa woke with Jace right by her side, sitting in a chair holding onto her hand. "How are you feeling?"

Staring up at him, she saw him for all he was: A fierce fighter, compassionate lover, the lost soul, the Beast, and the bonded mate who was now her family.

"Forgive me," she murmured.

Confused, he shrugged his shoulders. "Forgive you for what, honey?"

As she thought about all their ups and downs, he'd always put her first. Covering her face with her hands, she unleashed all her emotions and fell apart.

Grabbing a box of Kleenex, he placed it in her lap. "Please, baby. Don't cry."

Snapping a tissue out, she sniffled wiping her eyes.

"Why would I need to forgive you?" Jace asked her again.

Clearing her throat, she muttered, "For being so hardheaded and risking the lives of our unborn children." She snatched out another tissue. "Can you forgive me?"

"There's nothing to forgive." He stared at her with compassion. "You did what you had to do in order to save the lives of others. But part of its true," he chuckled. "You're definitely hardheaded."

She laughed, and he loved the sound. "I love you." Her wet eyes stared into his. "I love you, and I'm sorry." She laughed again, scooting higher onto the pillows. "You've always done the right thing by me... always putting me first before anyone else."

Jace grasped her hand, and brought it to his lips. After he pressed a kiss on her soft skin, he put it over his heart. As she kept it there, he cleared his throat. "You never gave me an answer," he said in a raspy, tear-laced voice. In another attempt to repair his completely botched effort of proposing, he muttered, "Tessa, will you marry me?" *Oh, God, he thought, please say—*

She smiled up at him, so much love in her eyes that it took his breath away. God, she loved this man. "Of course I'll marry you," she said, sincerity ringing clear in her voice.

Smiling at her response, his dimples beamed on each cheek.

"You knew I would say yes, right?"

He leaned over and gently kissed her lips. "I was praying you would."

"Good." She placed her hand to his face. "Then it's settled."

Tenderly, he gathered her close and held her. Pulling from their embrace, he smoothed a strand of her hair behind her ear. Reaching into his pocket, he pulled out a small, black velvet box. When he opened it, her eyes widened with excitement. Inside, she saw a beautiful princess cut, ruby ring.

"Oh, Jace." She smiled down at him with a sheen of tears obscuring her vision. "It's absolutely breathtaking!"

Taking it out of the box, he gently slid it on her finger. "Alexander passed this down to me, to give to you. It was my great grandmother's wedding ring," he said, putting his palm over her stomach to the warm and loving place that held his sons. "We're going to be a happy family now."

"I love you, Jace Chamberlain."

With his fingertips, he traced over her belly and whispered, "I love you more."

🐾 About the Author

Following a career in health and fitness, Shana Congrove has always had a passion for the arts, and her idea of heaven is a whole day of nothing but creating new adventures for her Breedline characters. She's an avid reader of fantasy, romance, and action, and loves to entertain readers with her Breedline series. She very much enjoys interacting with new readers on Facebook as well as in her Yahoo. Visit her website at shanacongrove.com.